CAMPBELL OF DUISK

Also by Robert Craig:

Lucy Flockhart (1931)
O People! (1932)
Traitor's Gate (1934).

Campbell of Duisk

Robert Craig

*with an introduction
by
Brian D. Osborne*

Kennedy & Boyd

Kennedy & Boyd
an imprint of
Zeticula
57 St Vincent Crescent
Glasgow
G3 8NQ
Scotland.

http://www.kennedyandboyd.co.uk
admin@kennedyandboyd.co.uk

First published in 1933 by John Murray
Copyright © Estate of Robert Craig 2009.
Introduction Copyright © Estate of Brian D. Osborne 2009

Cover photograph Copyright © Ronald W. Renton 2009.

ISBN-13 978-1-904999-35 5 Paperback
ISBN-10   1-904999-35 2 Paperback

To My Mother

Robert Craig 1900-1955

Robert Craig published four substantial novels: *Lucy Flockhart* (1931), *O People!* (1932), *Campbell of Duisk* (1933) and *Traitor's Gate* (1934). The first three were issued by the prestigious publishing house of John Murray and the last by the idealistic Porpoise Press. All four were well reviewed in the *Times Literary Supplement* with a decent mixture of praise and reasoned criticism – and yet the name of Robert Craig is all but unknown to scholars of modern Scottish literature.

Light was shed on Craig's identity and perhaps reasons for his neglect by literary historians when in 2004 the author of this introduction discovered a suitcase containing his papers in Glasgow's Mitchell Library. This had been deposited there some years earlier by his nephew Mr James Craig. Among other things it contained typescripts of several unpublished works, poetry, a long biographical sketch of his mother and a series of hardback notebooks entitled "Days and Hours" which proved to be autobiographical notes started in 1947. From these it was possible to assemble a picture of Robert Craig's rather unhappy life.

On top of all the papers was a manuscript note dated 10th July 1950 asking for somebody to take care of his papers after his death. This note is worth quoting at some length because it does give a certain flavour of the man:

> I hope they will be treated with care, as I believe they are of value ... There is a good deal of dishonesty in the literary world ... so it would be necessary that a careful note and record be kept of any MS before it be trusted to the hands of strangers. I prefer that I, and no one else, receive the credit or discredit for what I have written, and that no loophole be left for literary theft.

He went on to suggest that if his relatives could not manage the papers they should be given to Glasgow University Library.

Robert Craig was born in 1900 in Glasgow. His father James was a coachman, working for Professor James Robertson, who had the Chair of Oriental Languages at Glasgow University. His mother Isabella Leitch was a native of Lochgair, Argyllshire, and her mother was one of the Glenshira Munros.

James Craig died in 1908 leaving his widow Isabella to bring up six children. Isabella lived to the ripe old age of 94 and died in 1950. Robert and his mother lived together (at 57 West End Park St, Glasgow W) and were evidently very close – his biographical account of her life is more than a routine work of filial piety.

Young Robert went to Garnetbank School and left aged 14 with a School Certificate that noted he had reached Very Good standard in all subjects (except manual instruction - where he only rated Good!) and his Character was described as excellent.

Craig grew up as the youngest child in the family and without many friends outside his family circle. He developed bookish habits from an early age. His family home was well furnished with books of all sorts.

This being so it might be thought that he had struck lucky when he left school, because he found a job as an office boy on the *Evening Citizen*. This in normal circumstances could surely have led on to a career in journalism but Craig does not seem to have found working on the *Citizen* congenial. He writes in one of his notebooks "journalism is a bad background for a creative writer" – an interesting, if hardly well substantiated, viewpoint and perhaps not one that Neil Munro, George Blake and half a hundred others would agree with.

He left the *Citizen* and had a series of office jobs before being called up for the Army in 1918.

Craig seems always to have been conscious of the fact that he was not like other people and seems to attribute this to hereditary factors. He writes:

> What fusion gave me, at the age fifteen, when I ought normally to have been frequenting the Italian ice-cream shops, the urge to write verse? What fusion made Ann, my eldest sister, dress herself when a schoolgirl in her mother's clothes and feign the role of tragedienne?

He goes on to say that Ann wanted to go on the stage but their parents, despite themselves being theatre-goers, disapproved of the stage as a profession for their daughter.

What appears to be his first appearance in print is a series of letters to the *Weekly Scotsman* in 1915 and 1916: the first on The Foreign Scot, the next on the Craig family and the third – and these were all written before his 16th birthday – on Scottish Nationalism.

In due course Craig was called up and joined the Highland Light Infantry – Glasgow's own regiment. He was too late to see active service but his battalion was sent to Germany after the war as part of the occupying force. It might be expected that a solitary bookish and introspective youth like Craig would not have much enjoyed his military service but he does seem to have made some friends in the barrack room and the interest and excitement of being abroad presumably made up for much. He describes himself at this time as "Tall, slender and self-centred. A dreaming youth but not unsociable."

His time in Germany did not mean a cessation of literary activity – while in the Army of Occupation he completed

Chronicles of Cosmo which he describes, somewhat off-puttingly, as a 2000 line melodramatic novel in verse. Perhaps not too surprisingly *Chronicles of Cosmo* was never published.

Demobilised in March 1920 he started on a series of what he saw as soul-destroying clerical jobs. His real life was as a writer. He claimed later that his real love was poetry, but he was working on novels from the mid 20s.

His interest in Argyll and in family history and architecture – all of which found fulfilment in *Campbell of Duisk* – continued throughout this period. A revealing episode from 1927 tells us much about the man and his outlook. He had written an article about the Craig family and had received a letter from an Edinburgh solicitor of that name who was anxious to correspond and meet and exchange notes on family history. Robert Craig declined to meet the Edinburgh solicitor, convinced that the lawyer would be disappointed to meet, not a fellow professional man, but a 27 year old office worker.

Craig's breakthrough came when the London publishing house of John Murray accepted his novel *Lucy Flockhart* and published it in 1931. It owes something to Craig's father's family roots in Portencross, Ayrshire, and tells the story of an Ayrshire girl who comes to Glasgow to seek fame and fortune. It was reviewed in the Scottish and UK press and must have done well enough because Murray published a second novel called *O People!* in 1932.

This is a slightly weird and at times amusing novel which tells of John Grant, a World War I veteran, who has a vision in which Sir William Wallace instructs him to secure Scotland a seat in the League of Nations. Grant becomes involved in an election campaign in the fictional Glasgow constituency of Nether Overton and some leading figures of the period appear in remarkably thin disguise. The "Red Clydesider"

David Kirkwood pops up as David Birkwood, Winston Churchill contributes a cameo appearance as Mr Winshill and Sir Harry Lauder is somewhat unsympathetically portrayed as Sir Dougal McGugan. The *Times Literary Supplement* felt that there was a problem with the credibility of the story but concluded that:

> … laughter and sentiment go hand in hand in these pages, a refreshing if at times not entirely harmonious combination.

About this time Craig gave up his day job and resolved to live by his pen. 1933 saw the publication of what is certainly his best novel, *Campbell of Duisk*. Craig, with this book, had arrived.

In 1935 the Scottish Daily Express identified Craig and James Barke as the most gifted of the younger Scottish writers, and suggested that *Campbell of Duisk* was one of the finest Scottish novels produced in the last decade – quite a large claim when one thinks that Gunn and Linklater were also in the picture.

In February 1934 Craig signed up with James B. Pinker, the London literary agents, and in May 1934 decided to leave John Murray for the recently established Scottish publishing house, The Porpoise Press. This decision was driven by the need for money. Murray was an old-fashioned house and would not pay an advance against royalties. The Porpoise Press offered a contract for his new book and an option on another two titles and proposed to pay £50 advance on publication. Craig was living with his mother, and basically on her old age pension and the small sums that came from his first three novels. He was desperate for money and so left a major London publisher to sign up with a small Scottish publisher. Undoubtedly his Nationalist aspirations also played a part in this decision – which was sadly fatal to his hopes of a career as a novelist.

In the interests of a quick publication he went back to his bottom drawer, took out a 200,000 word manuscript, *Conspiracy*, he had written in 1926/27 and, in two weeks' work in 1934, cut it down to the 78,000 word *Traitor's Gait*. Perhaps a somewhat dubious literary process!

Perhaps as a result *Traitor's Gait* is a somewhat uneven book – but not entirely without merit. It is set at the time of the Radical troubles at the end of the 18th century and the *Glasgow Herald* thought:

> … Mr Craig's deft handling of detail makes this seem a highly original as well as an exciting story

while the *Times Literary Supplement*, though praising the dialogue "in half a dozen different intonations of Scots and Scots English" felt that it was an "unequal piece of work".

In a comment that must have infuriated Craig the reviewer criticised the court scenes where he detected "carelessness that mixes English forms of process with Scots". In fact Craig's description of the trial is perfectly accurate and does credit to his research – after the scandals of Lord Braxfield's conduct of the trials of Muir and his co-accused English treason law was introduced into Scotland and special courts established to remove the control of these cases from the High Court of Justiciary and specifically from the Lord Justice Clerk.

So with four books published, and with a certain degree of critical success – even if financial success escaped him – Craig's career seemed to be moving forward.

However the Porpoise Press rejected his next book and Craig noted that "he accepted the refusal as the end to my novel-writing career". There is no suggestion in his papers that he ever seriously thought of re-submitting work to Murray – rather he simply accepted that fiction was a thing of the past and he would now concentrate on writing poetry.

He noted in his journal:

> I have felt for some time that my incursion into story-telling, 1924 to 1934 or thereabouts, wasted years that I might have devoted to the perfecting of whatsoever poetic talent I possess.

A few articles for periodicals are all that Craig published after *Traitor's Gait* together with a few letters to the *Oban Times* on family history matters.

His papers suggest a continuing production of poetry but without any very serious attempt to market it.

There is an evident bitterness in Craig's papers – he clearly feels that somebody should have helped him. He was unemployed, had very small returns from writing and the only income for the household was his mother's pension.

> That period left in me a lasting bitterness, not for my own sake, a bitterness that she should have to want, and that I could not support her as I should. It was a time of severe unemployment. I had written books that had gained some notice. My financial plight was known in literary circles.

Again he writes:

> I succeeded in making myself better-known to the reading Scottish public and those further afield, than some

of my fellow Scots novelists who were free of financial embarrassment and who received ample publicity from certain cliques and critics.

In 1936 he got a job working as a cashier in the Locarno dance-hall in Glasgow. In 1938 he found work in the office of the Scotstoun ship-builder Charles Connell & Coy Ltd. – he continued to work there until his death from cancer in 1955.

Craig, who had always seen himself as an outsider, became even more isolated and convinced that the world was wrong. He wrote:

> Glasgow is no city for a creative writer. It has great vitality and surface life, but it lacks cultural depth and background. One is a prisoner in Glasgow, never a resident.

and

> There is no real Scottish reading public: there is not a cultured inquisitive class in Scotland to make such a book profitable in fact of money.

Craig wrote in 1947 that he would have welcomed

> … and still would welcome, a fellow-writer with whom to discuss matters of mutual artistic interest. I am alone.

Whether he would have actually admitted another writer into his confidence is fairly unlikely. The only literary figure that Craig felt had helped him was R D MacLeod – of W & R Holmes and editor of *The Library Review*. MacLeod published a few articles in the 30s and 40s by

Craig who wrote of MacLeod's "kindest encouragement". However, and with Craig there is always a however, even this relationship did not prosper.

> Two years ago [i.e. around 1946] I made an appointment to lunch with him. He altered the arrangement to a foursome, telling me on the phone that the two strangers "would be of vital interest to my future". By one of those very brutal ironies that have wrecked almost everything I have attempted, an ugly temporary eruption appeared on my skin, caused by nervous or physical overwork (it was July 1946 and most of my spare time during the previous six months had been devoted to "The Voices of the Standing Stones") and made me so shrink from meeting strangers that I excused myself from keeping the appointment. I have made no attempt since then to meet MacLeod. Why should I? – some mischance would intervene.

There are some people whom it seems very hard to help. Craig's (presumably psychosomatic) skin eruption was unfortunate, but his pessimistic conclusion that another meeting with MacLeod was pointless because "some mischance would intervene" simply causes us to feel sorry for his lack of confidence in himself and others.

A hard man to help and probably a hard man to relate to. After the Second World War Craig joined the Glasgow Film Society. He wrote that he enjoyed foreign films,

> But after two seasons I resigned my membership as I do not like an interest to become a habit.

Perhaps these character traits go some way to explain why Robert Craig's work is not better known.

Campbell of Duisk

Campbell of Duisk was first published in January 1933 and then reprinted in a cheap edition in 1935. It tells the story of the rise and fall of a mid-Argyll landowning family from the 18th century through to the 20th century. It is both the best of Craig's novels and the one he was happiest with – probably because in it he told a story about an area which he knew well and was emotionally connected to.

The picture on the cover of this book shows the south end of Loch Awe near the village of Ford and is taken from Arichamish. The location of the imaginary Duisk estate is on the far shore, probably corresponding roughly to the modern Finchairn farm. A stream near the northern boundary of the property named in Gaelic Dubh Uisge (Black Water) and pronounced Duisk is clearly the inspiration for the name of the estate and title of the novel.

The story opens with Colin Buie Campbell and his wife celebrating their acquisition of the 15,000 acres of the Duisk estate from its traditional owners the MacLachlans who had come out in the '45 on the Jacobite side. Colin, as befitted a Campbell lawyer and resident of Inveraray, had followed the Duke of Argyll in supporting the government. Colin had been the law agent for Dugald MacLachlan of Duisk and, when he was killed at Culloden, seized the opportunity to take over the debt-burdened and confused estate, thus supplanting the clan who had had ownership there and in other parts of neighbouring Argyll for generations.

Colin Buie himself has three sons – one, young Colin, is simple, the oldest, Neil who farms Uillian is dull and unimaginative, and the middle son, Captain Archy, a soldier, is the pick of the crop.

However Colin Buie's plans go astray almost immediately

– Neil Campbell has an illegitimate child by Peggy MacLachlan but refuses to marry her and plans to marry a Lily Munro. It is when he goes to tell Peggy this and offer her money that a fight breaks out in which he and Archy are killed by followers of the dispossessed MacLachlans. The shock of her sons' murder kills Mor Campbell, Colin Buie's wife, and the old man's hopes are transferred to Archy's three boys.

These three are truly memorable characters. The oldest, Scipio Campbell (perhaps appropriately with that name), joins the Army and rises to the rank of General. His next brother Archibald becomes an advocate and rises to the Court of Session bench as Lord Drumgesk and is depicted in terms reminiscent of the famous "hanging judge", Lord Braxfield. The third, Colin Ban, becomes an Admiral in the navy. All three are powerful and ambitious – and all gradually grow too grand for their own folk and away from their Highland roots. Peggy MacLachlan who has become housekeeper at Duisk tells us that:

> strange English-speaking people had arrived as servants… And they all touched their hats when they spoke to Scipio Campbell, and called him Sir. … And what had happened to those three brothers who had once used good Gaelic among themselves and now did not choose to speak it? They were none of them old men, and yet they all looked so old; old, proud and domineering. (pps 107-8)

When Scipio inherits Duisk he uses the wealth he had gained through service in India to build a new Duisk house – more fitted to his ideas of a Laird's dwelling – and Craig's lifelong interest in architecture shines through here. An Edinburgh architect builds Scipio the neo-classical mansion

on the site of the MacLachlans' old modest dwelling which
is to become so important in the story:

> The country people walked from twenty miles distant
> to see this wonderful house. There were twenty six rooms in
> it, they said with hushed voices. It was finer than Lochgair,
> finer than Barbreck. Surely there was not another house
> in the county like it, save the Duke's [Inveraray Castle].
> (p88)

The plot of the novel is fairly complex - a family saga
with murders, duels, elopements, betrayals, even a very vivid
drowning in the notorious whirlpool of Corryvreckan. But
one major thread which runs through it is the growing
division of the house of Duisk between the increasingly
alienated and anglicised grandsons of Colin Buie and their
descendants and the Leitches and Fletchers, descendants
of the daughters of Colin Buie who retain a much closer
affinity with the spirit of the country.

The three grandsons rise up the social hierarchy and they
and their offspring marry such exotic creatures as the Creole
heiress Cydalise Coeur de Roi and the Prince of Zelle.
They become foreigners in their own land. The final breach
comes during the proprietorship of Harriet, granddaughter
of Scipio, whose draconian measures in dealing with the
tenantry in order to convert Duisk into a sporting estate
ensure the permanent unpopularity of herself and future
Campbell landlords. Whilst we have sympathy with the
penultimate laird Colin Otway Campbell who fought
bravely in First World War and had the good of the estate
at heart, the irresponsible actions of his spendthrift wife seal
the fate of the impoverished estate and make its sale by the
last laird inevitable.

Justice, however, is done in the end. Duisk is bought by the Fletchers, who are descended from Colin Buie through his daughter Eilidh – a family much more sympathetic and acceptable to the people and the area. And, significantly, Kirsty MacLachlan, a direct descendant of the MacLachlans who were supplanted by the land hungry Campbells, remains a tenant at the home farm.

Craig's account of Argyll in the 18th and 19th century is informed by a serious and sustained study of the local history of the area. The history of the Duisk Campbells may at times seem to be a little improbable but time and again one is brought to realise that Craig's research is thorough and the background to the story well founded.

Craig writes of the period at the start of his novel before the Jacobite Rebellion of 1745:

> In those days there was no distinction of birth, where all the population were of ancient stock, and bore mostly, as they still do, a few honoured surnames. A ladder of social standing led down by imperceptible rungs from the greater lairds to the smaller proprietors, and thence to the tacksmen, the farmers, the co-farmers, the crofters, the fishermen. There was no claim to nor admission of superiority in birth, for there was none in actuality. (p72)

However much one might think that Craig exaggerates this essential democratic unity of the clan system there is undoubtedly a germ of truth in it. The novel then goes on to demonstrate the consequences of the breakdown of the clan system in Argyll.

Campbell of Duisk is also a novel about the Highland Clearances. Indeed it is one of the earliest such novels. While the Argyll clearances may not have had the reputation for dramatic brutality of the kind that happened in Sutherland, which we read about in the more or less contemporary works of Neil Gunn or in Iain Crichton Smith's novel *Consider the Lilies* (1968), it was nevertheless a significant clearance of small tenants and crofters and the clearance of traditions and values. The second Campbell laird of Duisk tells his cousin:

> You'll mind, Jock, how the farms used to be worked by anything from four to eight families. It was a bad enough system, except it kept them all employed ... But now its one farm one tenant. ... At Errachan Mor, where there were six families of local folk, I've got one man now for a tenant. He's a Border fellow. Of course, some of the native folk are hard pressed ... but, as I said, the younger lads could take the king's shilling. (p136)

Greater hardship comes in Argyll with the conversion of Duisk into a sporting estate when Harriet, the grand-daughter of Scipio and great-great-grand-daughter of Colin Buie was laird. Scipio had reduced the communal farms but had left the cottar houses alone:

> Little disturbed these peaceful cottages save the late appearance of the shooting tenant and his dogs; they felt secure and happy, they lived in the place where they had been born and bred. (p340)

However the grouse moors had brought a new interest in deer-stalking and Harriet, now the Duchesse de Sarge and living in Paris, was advised by her factor that deer would do well on the upland part of the estate if it were not for the presence of sheep and of men and she orders the clearance of the cottars – and this time they are burned out of their houses and forced to seek shelter with charitable kinsfolk.

This is followed inevitably by emigration for some. Harriet's aunt, Emmeline, who had retained more of the traditional spirit and lived on LochFyneside, near Ardrishaig is shocked by Harriet's action. In a moving scene she goes to Crinan to see the cottars taking ship for America. She goes among the emigrants but, despite the fact that she is sympathetic to them, she is suddenly afraid of them:

> She stopped as though an invisible wall had stayed her movement. For a minute the Duisk tenants and the Duisk lady stared at each other in mute surmise, and Emmeline understood that they had ceased to regard her as a friend. Her heart failed her and she turned timidly away, and returned trembling to the carriage. (p343)

As Craig takes us through his vivid saga of the Campbells of Duisk he skilfully relates the events of rural Argyll to the world of Scotland and beyond. He has his characters take part, for example, in the American War of Independence, become affected by the French Revolution, fight at Waterloo, meet Sir Walter Scott at Abbotsford or participate in the First World War. By doing this he skilfully contextualises his novel in the wider world and protects it from any charge of provincialism.

Campbell of Duisk is a sophisticated, significant, and very readable Scottish novel. It is also an important piece of the history and literary history of Argyll. For all these reasons it is well worth reading.

Robert Craig, too, is unfairly neglected. Perhaps he was his own worst enemy, but he had talent, ideas, and an agenda and his name and work undoubtedly deserve to be included in histories of Scottish literature.

This introduction is an edited version of the talk "Robert Craig, Author of *Campbell of Duisk*" given by the late Brian D. Osborne in Inveraray on 15th May, 2004 to The Neil Munro Society of which he was Secretary. Brian was an outstanding biographer, historian and literary scholar with a special interest in Argyll. His sudden death on 30th May, 2008 deprived Scotland of one of its most accomplished academic researchers. One of Brian's cherished ambitions was to see *Campbell of Duisk* brought back into print. We are, therefore, greatly indebted to Mr James Craig, Robert Craig's literary executor, and to Kennedy and Boyd for making this possible.

Ronald W. Renton
Chairman of The Neil Munro Society
February, 2009

GLOSSARY OF GAELIC WORDS

Ban : fair.

Bean-an-tighe : lady of the house.

Bean-shìth : fairy-woman.

Bheag : little.

Buidhe : yellow.

Cailleach : old woman.

Céilidh : friendly visiting.

Cléirich : clerk.

Crubach : lame.

Deoch-an-doruis: door or parting drink.

Do'l Mór Mac-a-Mhaighstir (pr. machk-a-vyastir) : Big Donald, son of the Master ; master = master of arts, a minister.

Duin'-uasal : gentleman.,

Eas : hill torrent.

Gaidhealtachd : the Gaelic-speaking lands.

Gealach bhuidhe nam broc : the badgers' yellow moon— the harvest moon.

Gillespic Saighdear : Soldier Archibald.

Mo ghaol : my darling.

Mo laochain: my little hero.

Òg : young.

Sgadan : herring.

CONTENTS

CAMPBELL OF DUISK

COLIN "Buie" CAMPBELL = Mor Campbell of Uillian
b. 1676

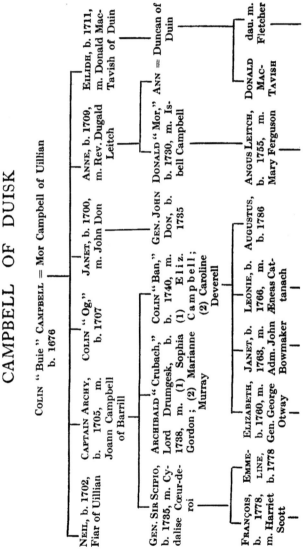

NEIL, b. 1702, Fiar of Uillian

CAPTAIN ARCHY, b. 1705, m. Joann Campbell of Barrill

COLIN "Og," b. 1707

JANET, b. 1700, m. John Don

ANNE, b. 1709, m. Rev. Dugald Leitch

EILIDH, b. 1711, m. Donald Mac-Tavish of Duin

GEN. SIR SCIPIO, b. 1735, m. Cy-dalise Cœur-de-roi

ARCHIBALD "Crubach," b. 1735, m. Lord Drumgesk, m. (1) Sophia 1738, m. (1) Sophia Gordon; (2) Marianne Murray

COLIN "Ban," b. 1740, m. (1) Eliz. Campbell; (2) Caroline Deverell

GEN. JOHN DON, b. 1735

DONALD "Mor," b. 1730, m. Is-bell Campbell

ANN = Duncan of Duin

ANGUS LEITCH, b. 1755, m. Mary Ferguson

DONALD MAC-TAVISH

dau. m. F'letcher

FRANÇOIS, b. 1778, m. Harriet Scott

EMME-LINE, b. 1778

ELIZABETH, b. 1760, m. Gen. George Otway

JANET, b. 1763, m. Adm. John Bowmaker

LEONIE, b. 1766, m. Æneas Cat-tanach

AUGUSTUS, b. 1786

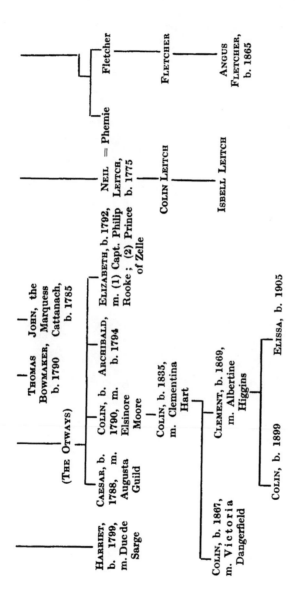

BOOK ONE

DAWN

ONE

I

"DUISK," said the old man.

He repeated the word, sibilantly, and was silent. It was evening, in autumn. The low-ceiled room absorbed the word expectantly, quivering with dusky curiosity.

The waters of Loch Shira were dark and restless ; over them Duniquoich rose to its bush-fringed summit; beyond, the dusky hills were cleft for the passage of the Shira—all seen framed in the window, like a picture.

"Duisk," said the old man. Without moving from his chair he called loudly for lights. They were brought, and he turned then to the other occupant of the room, a woman of his own age, red-haired, with a high proud look.

"Was it hard ? " she asked.

The old fat man smiled with a confession of complacent superiority, bringing the tips of his fingers together across his waistcoat. He was handsome, with finely shaped lips and a beautifully predatory nose. The stamp of determination and command was expressed in that hawk beak ; a youth of surpassing fascination was commemorated there in spite of the pendulous cheeks and mottled skin. Age, care, and intemperance had brought his eyes to see the world through mere slits of puffy flesh ; and they

15

were cunning eyes, with a sleekness grotesquely at contrast with his vast and heavy body.

" It was and it wasna," he said, and licked his lips, a voluptuous movement again at variance with his lineaments and reminiscent of the savage satisfaction of the jungle cat. " I'm the pleased man," he said abruptly. " And I ken you're the pleased woman.

" Duisk," he repeated, regardless of her answer. " Fifteen thousand acres if an acre. And a bonnie place. I was glad of Uillian," he added quickly. " I was glad to get Uillian, Mor. And Duisk is yours now forbye being mine. It's interest on the principal, Mor . . . at ten hundred per cent. ! "

" I'm glad for Neil's sake, and for Archy's," she replied composedly. " It's not long that we'll enjoy it."

" We'll see," he said, smiling secretively. " We'll find better ways of using it than the MacLachlans, I'm thinking."

" Where are they now, Colin ? "

" The MacLachlans ? Tach ! poor landless loons," he said contemptuously, " they've taken to the hills like their friends."

" Watch them, Colin."

" Tach ! " said the man easily. " They daurna breathe a wheesh. With old Lachie Stra'lachlan slauchtered, and Lachie Innischonnell slauchtered, and the haill clan in a fleg ower the heid o't ! . . . there are no more MacLachlans of Duisk, Mor."

" There's Lachie Beg at Kames, and the smith at Durran, and——"

" Aye, there's a wheen of them," said the old man derisively. " And I fancy their opinion of Charles

Stuart this day is not unlike yours and mine."
Breathing heavily, he pulled himself from his chair
and crossed to the window. He watched the fishing
boats riding at anchor and the swooping gulls with
indescribable satisfaction. Every landmark around,
every hill and *eas*, every tree, had been familiar to
him since boyhood. His heart sang with exultation,
and the world seemed lovelier to him than usual.
"It's a fine night," he said. "It's a fine night,
Mor," he said reverently.

"Mor." He turned round to her, leaning on the
table so close to the candles that his face was an
impressive mask of purple and black. "We'll make
nothing of Colin, so you needna fash wi' him, poor
soul. But Duisk! When Neil comes after me,
woman . . . he can leave his farming. There are
bigger blockheads than him in Parliament or govern-
ing the King's colonies. Duisk will do that for him.
Archy'll no' cool his heels in his old age with a half-pay
captaincy. We'll no' live to see the day," he ended
regretfully.

"Land," he said, coughing excitedly. "It's land
that does it. Uillian wasna big enough, Mor. It is
big enough for you and me, but not for what we want
for the lads. Archy's a smart lad. It's a blessing
he has the boys." He sank into a chair, drumming
with his fingers on the table. "I had a struggle to
get it," he said abruptly, "but I've got it, and we'll
keep a haud o't. Dugald MacLachlan was the thow-
less fool. To gang awa' and—tach! poor deevils,
they'll be finding there's nae thatch above the
moors."

"It is cold, Colin," she said, and shivered, thinking

B

of the fugitive family. She rose, and the old man, with greater grace than could have been expected, opened the door and held out his arm to assist her descent of the stair. It was a commodious house, for Colin Campbell, Writer to the Signet, lived in much comfort in the new and still building town of Inveraray that was replacing the old burgh by the Aray's mouth.

A man shrewd and wise, the younger son of a petty gentleman in Lorn, Colin Campbell—called Colin Buidhe or Buie because of yellow hair that had long since whitened—possessed much say and no great influence in the affairs of the county. He was familiar with the numberless Campbell lairds of Argyllshire, by whom he was treated as an equal, as he had every right to be, but early he had realized that property means influence, and the acquisition of land had been his lifelong passion. He had not grudged the pragmaticism of those landed clansmen whose impecuniosity had hindered his own ambitions in his professional dealings with them ; he had not stooped to take advantage of those puzzled men with their muddled lawsuits whose lands came so temptingly within his grasp, for he regarded the race he sprung from with peculiar loyalty and reverence.

He had accepted the supremacy of lairdship as inevitable and desirable, and had married the proud-faced, red-haired Mor, daughter of Campbell of Uillian, and she had brought him that small property, too small for the ambitions of Colin, but there had been no other heiress in sight. The capable woman had won an influence over him that none others had ever achieved ; they grew to love each other.

Colin Buie had reached his seventies, an important man in the ducal capital, a welcome presence in the bien society of lairds, sheriff, fiscal, officers, when in 1745 Prince Charles Edward landed in the north and raised his standard. From the districts influenced by the Duke of Argyll detachments were sent to join the Government forces. No alarm was felt in the small town where the thoughts of every Highland chief, the moods of every Highland clan, were known and assessed. In northern Argyllshire the Jacobites —Stewarts, MacInneses, Camerons—moved quickly enough to the Prince's standard. But in Argyll itself and the surrounding lands the Whig influence of the Campbells kept the peace.

Some neighbouring lairds, actuated by ancient loyalty or ancient wrongs, sped north to join the insurgent clans. MacLachlan of Castle Lachlan, an old man, with a Lochfyneside domain hemmed in on all sides by Campbells, hurried his dependants through a scowling countryside to meet with a graceless welcome in the Jacobite camp, and to meet in the long run with his gallant death at Culloden. His namesake, the Captain of Innischonnell, on Lochawe-side, chose the same course and met a similar fate. Among others of the same clan who had gone was Dugald MacLachlan of Duisk, a man of middle age, of a quiet disposition, hopelessly in debt, who had once been a student of divinity at Glasgow College; a gentle, quiet man, seeing in the arrival of the Prince a rash opportunity for rebuilding his fortunes. In the odd scraps of information that were now coming into Inveraray it was learned that the gentle, quiet man had slain ten men before he fell, and that eight wounds and a horse's hooves had been necessary to kill him.

These men had gone from districts violently hostile to the Prince, and they deserved greater credit than their much-lauded northern confederates who lived in an atmosphere wholly Jacobite.

MacLachlan of Duisk left a widow and four young children, now frightened travellers to relatives in Morvern. His tangled affairs and estate had been in the care of Colin Buie, who had now possessed himself of it.

The acquisition of Duisk coincided with the arrival in Inveraray of Captain Archibald Campbell, home on furlough after the suppression of the rising, and the presence of this his second son completed the reunion of Colin's family for the moment and, the old man thought, gave a divine approval to the completion of his fortunes. At supper, gazing on his wife and six children, the writer's heart swelled with a satisfaction that was supremely unselfish. He thought of Duisk, and what it meant for them.

Beside him sat Neil, his eldest, the fiar of Uillian, the physical replica of his father ; a big, heavy man, slow-thinking, with bold eyes and an ingratiating smile. He was contemptuous of book learning, both the legal lore of his father and his brother's classical loves, and had farmed his mother's lands of Uillian in Arisceótnish for twenty-four years, since he was twenty ; a man unmarried and reputedly fond of gaiety, although his approaching marriage had lately been announced. He wore carelessly and well the tartan and homespun of a rural gentleman, and had fastened his red hair loosely behind with a narrow piece of ribbon. He ate and drank heartily, paying much attention to his mother, to whom he was devoted and who loved him passionately.

Facing the fiar was a brilliantly clad officer. His sparkling glance roved around the table, good humoured and playful ; his head never relaxed the calm erectness of one used to command. It was not the head that might be expected to bend, but it inclined now, with its hair neatly arranged in military fashion in a queue and powdered, in deferential regard to a parent. Captain Archy Campbell had seen forty-one years and several campaigns, and was an ardent student of the classics. He was looking forward to belated promotion, and, more immediately, to the arrival of his darling Joann and their three young sons, summoned from her father's home at Clachan Dysart to rejoin him.

The youngest son of the family had features so beautiful as to dazzle at first sight with a sense of awe. His haughty nose and jutting chin were relieved of their severity by lips of surpassing sweetness and appeal. His inherited fair hair grew back from a high forehead and clustered carelessly about the bow that tethered it. Like Neil, he wore the native garb, and it graced well his stalwart limbs. He sat now silent, turning his eyes full upon each person who spoke, and regarding that person thereafter for a fraction of time with a curiously speculative gaze. And at times he laughed.

Of the writer's three daughters, the eldest, Janet, sat near the mother she resembled so closely. She was a silent determined woman who had chosen as her husband John Don, the lawyer son of a Lothian laird. Her own ambitions had ended with the lawyer's premature death from hard drinking coupled with a fall down a precipitous descent to the Cowgate in Edinburgh called the Parliament Stairs. She had one son, a lad of eleven, and she brought him for long and frequent visits to her parents for reasons of economy.

Her sisters were handsome matronly women with the paternal face : Anne, the wife of the Reverend Dugald Leitch, to whom she had borne two sons and a daughter ; and Eilidh, married to MacTavish of Duin, a small proprietor in Glassary. They were near neighbours at home, and had journeyed up Lochfyneside with their brother Neil expressly to meet the soldier.

Many-branched candelabra were on the table, casting warm light upon the diners and making moving shadows in the dark corners of the room. The appointments of the table, of the whole apartment, spoke of comfort and the many refinements of life. A peat fire glowed upon the hearth.

They were merry, heavily jocular, with the satisfaction of seeing their officer safe from the fighting and the joy of their new possession. Neil said little, feeling shy in the glory of swollen heirship, but his father, inflamed by claret, could not keep Duisk off his tongue. Abruptly he would cease, as half ashamed, and turn to Archy and demand some information about the fighting. But the pleasure of his acquisition could not be hidden.

" Well," he said, and licked his lips, " the heritage fits the descent, and the pedigree is a good one."

The captain rose. With a movement of the hand

he signed his brothers to do likewise. " Your health,
Duisk," he said, bowing to his father, and the brothers
drained their glasses. Colin Buie smiled and nodded
like a pleased boy.

"Your health, madam mother," said the captain,
and bowed to her. She acknowledged the toast with
grave affection.

"And I drink," said the captain courteously, " to
the younger of Duisk—to you, Neil. May your rule
be long, and may it be long before you rule."

Neil grinned and nodded happily.

"You're good callants," said the old man, with
emotion that he could not conceal. " No man has
better sons, no sons have better brothers." His
glance flickered momentarily on the beautiful
questioning face of his youngest. " Here's my toast,
then. No—no," he said peremptorily, as they would
have assisted the heavy old man to rise. " It would
be ill luck, I'm thinking, to oxter my wishes in this
business." He filled his glass with a shaking hand.
His face grew composed and majestic, losing all trace
of his potations in his moment's impulse. " To the
Campbells of Duisk, to you and yours and all who may
come after—I drink." He threw the glass over his
shoulder ; it shattered. Bending his head, he raised
one arm in benediction.

"Almighty Father," he said, " it hath pleased Thee
to call Thy servant to unexpected fortune. We are
thankful to Thee for Thy gracious mercy. Guide our
steps, Gracious Father in Heaven, and assist us in
our outgoings and incomings. If it please Thee,
help us to attain those things we desire for Thy glory,
aid us in our assistance of our friends of the name of

Campbell, preserve us from the trickery of our enemies. Let the days of Thy servant's wife and children be long upon the land, preserve them from calamity, and suffer them to enjoy comfort. And let Thine be the power, the honour and the glory. Amen."

He seated himself amid the murmured responses of his family, regarding them all with a serene and challenging glance. " And now," he added briskly, " I've a wheen things to vizzy about the Lephinmore business. If you lads desire a turn before you bed yourselves . . . the women here have a heap of clash in hidlins," and he laughed buoyantly. " Colin," he said to the beautiful man, " take a light to my study, like a good lad."

The younger Colin suddenly burst into a peal of laughter, shrill and unrestrained, and looked at his father with mingled rebuke and gaiety.

" What is't, Colin ? " asked the old man gently.

" My birthday ! " exclaimed the son. " It is my birthday ! You never knew that it was my birthday ! "

" So it is, Colin," the father observed, while the family maintained the affected gravity usual in such circumstances. " I was forgetting."

" It was my mother there who told me," Colin explained in a cheerful manner. " I am—what is it I am, mother ? "

" You are thirty-nine, *mo ghaol*," she answered softly.

" Yes, I am thirty-nine," Colin assured everyone. " That is what I am. Thirty-nine."

Neil wished him many birthdays to come, and the others did likewise.

" Thank you, thank you," he responded effusively.

" Surely you've brought us luck, Colin," said
the captain. " Duisk ! This is a lucky day for us
all."

Colin beamed on them all. " Yes, I have brought
my father and my mother luck. I will go and get
the candle, father." They heard him in the passage
repeating the words ' thirty-nine '. His departure
was followed by a moment's absolute silence in the
room. Then the elder Colin took a pinch of snuff.
" You lads will mind to bar the door when you come
in," he cautioned them, and, bidding them all good
night, followed his son. Neil and Archy placed chairs
for the four women around the fire, and after a little
general conversation passed from the house on to
the front street of Inveraray.

II

As they closed the outer door they heard the glucking of the waves and smelt the keen night saltness
of the sea, for the house of Colin Buie directly faced
Loch Shira, where that child of Loch Fyne merges
with its parent. A full moon appeared and reappeared amid a mass of scurrying clouds. Against
the darkened sky the darker mass of Duniquoich,
its watch-tower apeak, rose darkly forbidding.

Passing the end of the main street, where lights
splayed the night and there were sounds of revelry,
the brothers took to the shore road, walking in step,
and silently. There were yet people abroad, going
to and from the burgh, and to them Neil bade a
courteous good night, whether he knew them or not,
as was the custom. But Captain Campbell had

learned other things in the army than the recognition
of countrymen.

On the bridge of Aray they stopped, listening to the
roar of the river and glancing back to the frontage
of the town, with its graceful arches, ghostly in the
light of the moon. The captain regarded the burgh
wishfully. " Could we not go back to Achnaba's ? "
he suggested. " He could surely provide a bottle
and a pack of cards."

" I am going to Kilblaan."

The captain echoed him incredulously.

" I have business there," said Neil. " But if you
are not caring for the walk it does not matter, Archy
laochain."

" Oh, I can walk to Hades with you," the captain
said agreeably, " but you choose queer times and
queer places for your business. If it is to Kilblaan,
we had better be moving."

" You will remember," Neil said, as they resumed
their way, " the woman, Peggy Bheag MacLachlan,
at Uillian. She had a daughter. That was sixteen
years ago." Archy did not answer, and the brothers
listened to each other's breathing. But as they
neared Kilmalieu, the graveyard, the elder man
resumed speech hurriedly, as though to banish superstitious fears. " The woman brought up the child at
Uillian. But she is not at Uillian now. She is at
Kilblaan. Archy," the fiar added, speaking quickly,
" Peggy is a friend of the MacLachlans Duisk. She
was not pleased to learn of their misfortune, for she
was Duisk's foster-sister ; and that, and the passing
of Duisk to my father, and the news of my coming
marriage to Lily Munro, have angered her."

" Poor Peggy," the captain exclaimed involuntarily. " She was a pretty creature, Neil. And she is over the forties now."

" It is for that I am sorry," replied his brother shamedly. " She left Uillian in an anger, and she came to Kilblaan, to a cousin's, and it is doubly awkward for me, who has to pass Kilblaan every time I go to Lily Munro's. And old Stucguie would not like to know that I see my own daughter every time I go to visit his. But Archy ! " said the big heavy man, " Lily Munro is a very fine woman." He stopped, and to sense some sympathy in the darkness placed a hand on his brother's sleeve.

" That is more than liking," said the officer, and they proceeded.

They had passed from the highway to the avenue that stretches to the Dubh Loch, the sheet of water at the entrance to Glenshira. Shortly they saw the glitter of the moon upon its surface.

The captain inquired the purpose of their present visit.

" I shall offer Peggy Bheag a little present of money——"

" And that is madness, Neil."

" A little present of money," said the fiar stubbornly. " But there may be difficulties to arrange," he ended with the composure of one certain of meeting trouble, " and I do not want everyone passing up and down Glenshira in the daylight to know of them."

The captain could not forbear pity for the blundering stupidity of his brother, for his ignorance of human nature, and for the crudeness of his choice of time and argument. But he said nothing. He recollected instead the plump, brown-eyed girl who was, and wondered what time had done to her in the years since he had been last at Uillian.

They passed the loch and Maam, beyond which the shadowy masses of hill rose from the broad pasture land through which the Shira penetrated. The glen at that time held many people ; their houses, in straggling hamlets or standing solitary on convenient knowes, detracted from the awesome silence of the night.

The fiar left the main track and picked his way carefully over broken ground to a lone house standing in the shadow of a massive rock. It was a small mean erection, so low that the roof thatch was in line with the visitors' shoulders. Beside it rose the sombre hill-side, clothed in shaggy timber.

Neil pushed at the door, and finding that it was barred he knocked loudly. " It is Neil Uillian," he said in answer to a question from within. " Open the door."

It was opened partly, and a woman's face peered out at them. She then threw the door wide, but blocked the threshold with her person. " It is you," she said, ". . . and Gillespic Saighdear. What is it that you are wanting ? "

" I have something to say," replied the fiar, and the woman stood back as he squeezed his bending frame through the doorway, followed by the captain.

They were in a dishevelled apartment in which a cruisie lamp suspended from the wall threw a feeble light. In the centre of the floor burned a fire of peat, the smoke of which seemed reluctant to depart through the hole in the roof above. It suffused the room instead, giving a dim unreality to the occupants. The earthen floor was littered with an untidy assortment of blankets, stools, and rude farming implements, and the pleasant smell of the peat was mingled with a much more pungent odour, explained by the whiteish mass at one end of the room, which on inspection proved to be a recumbent cow.

"I want to speak to you, Peggy," said the portly man abruptly, "and I have an offer to make. It will be good for you and good for me."

She stood before him, resentfully; a grave, dark-eyed woman with a natural dignity. "Is it an offer of marriage?" she inquired. "And have you brought your brother here to witness it?"

"It is not that," said Neil awkwardly. "It is not an offer of marriage." He hesitated and added blunderingly: "It is an offer of money."

"Oh, Neil Campbell," she cried fiercely, "sorrow on the day that first I saw you! Money!—and is my family not as good as yours, yours with your clerk of a father, that you should make me this offer? And you would now shame me further for the sake of Stucguie's daughter. And you will be leading Lily Mac-an-Rothaich to Uillian, past this house, past the dwelling of your child! Oh man," she cried, trembling violently, "your race is black with greed and cruelty; hungry Campbells, savage Campbells, eating up clans and countries and crying for more."

The fiar regarded her stupidly, angry and remorseful, and finding himself empty of words. And the officer, inwardly admitting that the woman's family was doubtless as good as his own, regretted that Neil had not married her at the proper time. But

Archy's alert eyes were becoming accustomed to the haze and gloom, and as Peggy Bheag, shaken by passion, was silent, he cried : " What is that ? " pointing to a black shape on a shakedown by the wall. " It is moving."

" It is the *cailleach*—the old woman MacNicol," said Neil. " She is bed-ridden and deaf. Never heed her."

" You keep company, Peggy," said the captain.

" It is her house," replied Peggy Bheag indifferently.

" And what are those ? " the captain demanded, pointing to where the cow was solemnly regarding them.

" It is the shadows," she answered.

" Come out, my friends, and let us vizzy you," cried the captain gaily. " You have been having *ceilidh* and a friendly time before we knocked, Peggy ! "

Three figures rose from the darkness behind the cow and moved slowly into the light ; a reddish-bearded little man with cunning eyes and abnormally long and sinewy arms, dressed in stained and tattered tartans ; a lithe sullen young savage with a thick fell of hair falling forward to his eyes, clad only in a shirt and a ragged kilt ; and a lean-boned youth attired in breeches and a laced coat much the worse for wear.

" All here ? " said the captain ironically.

" Who are these men ? " the fiar demanded.

" They are my kin," she said evasively.

" All of them ? " exclaimed the captain in feigned surprise. " This lad "—he pointed to the youth in the laced coat—" might be one of my lord Pitsligo's levies whose compass had gone agee. Has he the Gaelic, Peggy ? for he seems to understand little of our conversation." The captain lapsed into English. " Where do you come from, my brave callant ? "

" I'm frae Edinburry," answered the youth hopefully, while his companions exchanged suspicious glances.

The captain laughed. " You're as widely connected as the Duke, Peggy. But the Duke doesn't harbour rebels."

" As these two Highland gentlemen know our names I think we are as well to know theirs," said the fiar in Gaelic.

" Quite true, brother, and we will listen courteously. Are they as deaf as the *cailleach* ? " he remarked, as the two strangers kept silence.

" They are my kin," she said composedly. " They were not last to leave their homes when they were called, and now they have not a home to go to."

" I would not call Inveraray the best place for a Jacobite," the fiar remarked, and studied the wretched fugitives with interest.

" The nearer to danger the less is the danger," she said tranquilly. " But they must leave now, now that they are discovered."

" Tach ! they can bide," said Neil easily. " Poor fools, let them bide in peace."

The captain nodded and dismissed the ragged trio to their places. They either misunderstood, or chose to discuss the discovery of their hiding-place elsewhere, for the clansmen slipped unobtrusively into the open air, and after a moment's hesitation the Edinburgh man joined them.

" Well, Peggy," said the fiar heavily, " is there to be an arrangement ? "

"There is to be no arrangement," she answered simply.

"It is a fair offer I will make," said Neil. "All my feelings——"

"Your feelings," the woman interrupted contemptuously. "And what feelings have I that you can bring Gillespic Saighdear here, and have him by while you bargain with your money!"

The brothers' glances met. "I can cool my heels outside if it suits you, Peggy," said the captain. "And maybe I'll get a taste of something when you please to call me in. But be wise, Peggy."

Archy strolled from the house, humming an air. The clouds had passed from the face of the moon, which now rode serenely above the glen's girdling heights. Captain Campbell breathed the cold air thankfully, and breaking off a branch from a young tree seated himself on a bank some distance from the house, where he proceeded to make a switch as a means of passing the time. He heard the murmur of voices not distant, and recollected that the friends of Peggy Bheag MacLachlan, like himself, were out in the cold. Following the course of the sound with his eyes Captain Campbell could distinguish them sitting some distance away, the two Highlanders conversing animatedly together and the youth in the laced coat silent.

The captain fell into a reverie after a little, counting the time since he had last seen his darling wife Joann, and wondering affectionately what increase of stature would show in his sons. He was smiling with the satisfaction of his thoughts, thinking how soon would be their reunion, when a man rose from the near group and advanced towards him. Archy looked at him sharply. It was the red-bearded clansman. "Well, you rogue ? "

" The gentleman will be having a long wait," the man said ingratiatingly.

" Yes," said the captain shortly, and turned his head away to indicate his disinclination for further speech.

In reply the man squatted on the ground near the captain's feet and looked at him with a smile which showed his teeth like a milky gash in the moonlight. "But it is a fine enough night to be here in the open," he observed, glancing skywards. " *Gealach bhuidhe nam broc*—the badgers' yellow moon."

" Yes, you rebellious dog, and I'll swear that you've spent a good few nights like that of late ; and serve you right, bydam."

The man smiled deprecatingly. " The gentleman knows very well how the business ended. But it will all blow over in time," he concluded philosophically.

" There were bigger fools than you who had sense enough to stay at home," said the officer disdainfully, now finding that the talk relieved his boredom. "What is your name, you rogue ? "

" Is it my name ? It is Ainus MacLachlan," said the man humbly.

" Who brought you out ? " asked the captain curiously, and completing his switch.

MacLachlan seemed in deep thought. " I followed Duisk himself," he said.

" Dugald MacLachlan—he is dead."

" Yes. He is dead."

" At Culloden."

" Yes."

" Well, Ainus," the captain observed cruelly, " your legs were better legs than Dugald's."

MacLachlan's eyes were raised to the officer's, and Archy felt uneasy under the green glaring orbs. But MacLachlan pulled open his shirt, saying simply : " See ! " A hideous scar, as yet unhealed, was visible to Campbell's gaze.

" Ah," he exclaimed.   " You could not do much after that, my friend."

" I was beside Duisk," explained the man calmly enough, and relapsing into his earlier posture, " and my brother's son Callum, the sturdy whelp there, carried me off.   It was Duisk he would have carried, but Duisk was dead.   Stra'lachlan was dead.   Innis- chonnell was dead.   And so we came back to our own country," he concluded evenly.

" It was a daft business," the captain said in- voluntarily.

" It is not my affair to question," MacLachlan replied in a tone of rebuke.   " I obeyed Duisk, as I shall obey the Duisk that has followed him."

" Ah yes," said the captain with a more friendly manner.   " Well, friend Ainus, we may get you a remission for your sins.   If that's the way the wind blows I'll speak a word to my father."

MacLachlan smiled with contempt.   " Is it Colin Uillian ?—Colin Cleirich ? " he asked ironically, " that you will be speaking to ? "

" To my father Colin Campbell of Duisk, you rebel dog," said the captain sharply.   "Petitioners for their lives are not so insolent, MacLachlan."

" Duisk ! " MacLachlan cried, grinning up at him

savagely. "*My* Duisk is the young MacLachlan who is this moment tramping the rough bounds from you and your savage soldiers." He drew closer to the captain, pressing his body up with the aid of hand and foot until his head was above the captain's knees, and scowled venomously at him. "Duisk ?—the fat writing body in Inveraray ! "

The captain's nostrils quivered. "Be careful," he shouted angrily. "Shall I have you hanged ? "

"Colin Cleirich—the thief of Duisk ; Neil Uillian —the thief of my kinswoman ; Gillespic Saighdear— the burner and slayer. Oh, Campbell," cried the man savagely, "the women and children whose houses you have given to the flame bear curses against you," —the captain drew back haughtily from the outthrust malignant face—" bloody son of the crafty boar, of the fat Campbell."

"Then take that from a Campbell," cried the incensed captain, and struck MacLachlan across the face with the switch.

"And here's my thanks," whispered the man, and drove a knife into the captain's breast.

A sob broke from Archy's lips. He half rose, fell forward upon his hands and knees, and then rolled over. He lay with his face to the moon, and a red foam came to his lips.

MacLachlan's companions ran forward and regarded the dying man, the Lowlander with panic and the young rebel with indifference. Some words passed between the relatives, whereupon Ainus seized the youth in the laced coat by the throat and in broken English threatened him with instant death if his heart should fail him.

The young Edinburgh man, who had seen some warfare and had now viewed murder, was placating Ainus with frightened assurances when the door of the house was opened and the voice of Neil shouted for his brother. "Archy *laochain*, come for your *deoch-an-doruis*," the fiar cried gaily.

To the silence Neil repeated his words, and then proceeded to where he saw the fugitives. " Is it here you are, Archy, among the Jacobites ? " he shouted cheerfully as he approached. " Man, I heard a glisk of argument, but if it ended as well as my own—God ! " he burst out, " what's this ? "

They came to him, spreading out, and Neil, seeing the dark shape on the ground, backed before them with the fury of a defenceless brave man. He backed towards the house, which he could have reached easily by running but for his bulk. He disregarded the Lowlander, making estimate of his spirit, and was ready when the younger MacLachlan, running low, came forward and sprang at him like a wild-cat.

Neil felt a burning in his shoulder. " Ha ! " he cried, and catching the spitting and struggling Callum in his mighty arms, lifted him above his head and dashed him against Ainus. He turned then and ran with Callum's shrill scream of agony in his ears, but as he neared the house, as he saw the woman he had once loved rush forward to his assistance, a fierce pain entered his body, clogging his breath, and he stopped, surprised because he wanted to run and could not. His knees trembled, and he fell, gently for such a portly man, and he clutched lightheadedly at the grass, with the blade of Ainus sticking between his shoulder blades and the blood of his brother mingling with his own.

Finding himself entwined by arms he wondered if his mother held him, and he opened his eyes unsteadily. " It is Peggy, then," he stammered. Infinite weariness overcame him. " Where is the young one ? " he whispered. " Poor lassie ! " He closed his eyes once more, and in a little time the woman covered him with her plaid, sitting by him and speaking.

TWO

I

SOME weeks later Colin Buie travelled up Glenaray, and boarding a pinnace at Sonachan on Loch Awe sailed down to Duisk. With him were his daughter Janet Don, her eleven-year-old son Jock, and some servants. Of the other members of his family, Anne Leitch and her brother Colin had gone before to prepare for their father's arrival. Neil and Archibald would remain at Kilmalieu, where they had been buried on the same day and in the same grave as their mother, Mor Campbell of Uillian.

The day was sullen and threatening; Cruachan Ben was streaked with snow and the islands sat glumly on the water. As the shore receded, Colin Buie wrapped his cloak tightly around his massive frame and turned a steady gaze towards the southern stretches of the loch, to where the boat was heading.

His daughter sat near him, with an oddly familiar look of someone else. Young John moved restlessly at the bow, delighted with this novel jaunt. The boatmen sang a Gaelic song.

In time they saw the distant termination of the loch, mountain blocked.

" Grandfather," exclaimed the lad resentfully, " we will be stopped in our course. It would have been better if we had never started on this course."

The vessel drew to port. They approached a shore

that rose rapidly to heights of a thousand feet or more. A light spatter of rain had fallen in mid loch, and the gloaming had set in with a threatening sky. As they moored at a little jetty the rain burst suddenly upon them, and the wind moaned past them to the mountain corries.

Leaning upon a sailor's arm, Colin stepped ashore. The younger Colin was there to greet him, with Anne's husband, Master Dugald, and Eilidh's husband MacTavish of Duin.

Duin gripped his father-in-law's hand and murmured some words of sympathy.

" It was a cold and a bitter day," was the reply The old man paced slowly to the roadway, supporting himself on Duin and a silver-mounted cane. He paused there, and looked around him. Checking whatever remark he had been about to utter, he proceeded deliberately to the house, his little train of relatives and dependants following silently.

The house of Duisk stood on a knoll at the foot of a hill, backed by trees and near a burn, and its elevated position gave it a commanding view. It was a long, single-story building of stone, with small windows, and thatched. Behind it clustered the offices or farm buildings, consisting mainly of low, dry-stone erections, grass growing liberally upon their rotting thatch and some of them ruinous. These were silent and deserted now, but from the mansion house came sounds of preparation, and light splayed from the windows.

Inside, the old man permitted to be disrobed of his cloak, and handing his pistols to Leitch he sank heavily into a chair. " Is there brandy ? " The

minister poured him out a draught, and he drank
it at a gulp. Colin Buie then inquired after their
healths and the healths of his grandchildren. To
the replies he listened with interest. "Are any of
the MacLachlans left hereabouts?" he demanded to
know suddenly, and at the assurance that there were
he evinced some satisfaction.

"Well, Colin lad, Colin Og," he said to his son
with a grimly amiable smile. "Have you been keeping out of mischief, *mo laochain*?"

"Yes, indeed, and I have been keeping out of
mischief," he was assured. "Welcome to Duisk,
father. It is a very fine place that you have gained.
For Dugald says so."

"Does he, Colin?"

"Yes, indeed, he says so." Colin the younger
smiled radiantly, feeling for words. "A happy home-
coming to you, father," he added inconsequently,
". . . but where are all the others?"

His father gave him a look like the stroke of a
sword.

"It was a wearying sail, Duisk," Dugald Leitch
interposed gently. "Get you to your bed, man."

"It would be a poor thing to do, that," responded
the old man slowly, "on the first day of possession.
There was to have been a family gathering, Dugald,
a good fire, a good crack, and a good glass." He
smiled a ghastly smile to the minister. "We'll postpone it *sine die*. But Colin's congratulations hearten
me. Thank God, I've one son left . . . what there
is of him." His glance softened as it met the questioning stare of Colin Og. "Aye, Duisk," he said
half to himself. "Anne," he called to his daughter,

"Anne, my girl, there are hungry men here, and myself to sit at the head of the table."

The unimposing appearance of the house of Duisk was not exceptional in the Highlands at that period, and a heavy acreage compensated for the inadequate house. From its frontage on Loch Awe the estate carved deeply into the parish of Kilmichael-Glassary : a tangle of mountainous upland, peat moss, lochs and burns, with a fertile stretch in the Arisceótnish valley. East of Duisk the Glassary uplands continued beyond the valley of the Add, finally dropping down to Loch Fyne ; and south-west of them the beautiful district of Arisceótnish interposed between Loch Craignish—the outlet to Jura and the open sea. This district is celebrated as having been the centre of the ancient kingdom of Dalriada.

The new laird sat by a window, his glance roving from the littoral of his domain to the people in the room, to the bleak-faced Janet Don, the uxorious MacTavish, the austere aloof clergyman. His thoughts were tumultuous. Outside, in the seeping rain, Colin Og was rambling about, like a restless schoolboy. He entered the house latterly, shaking his garments, and smiling. His father asked him without much curiosity what he had been doing.

"It was for my mother I was looking," Colin Og explained obligingly.

His father regarded him dully. "Why do you search outside ? "

"Because she is no longer in the house," said Colin Og.

At this simple statement the old man turned on him a full and penetrating glance. The half-witted

man had expressed unconsciously the full poignancy
of what his father was suffering but trying to deny.
His triumph was tasteless, his confidences uninvited,
his hopes unvoiced, even the trivial moments of
laughter and joy would gain no reflection from kindred
eyes. Mor Campbell of Uillian was no longer in the
house.

II

Captain Archy's widow, his darling Joann, appeared suddenly at Duisk with her three sons, Scipio
—whose name, chosen by the dead Archy in honour
of the Roman, had greatly incensed the grandfather
—Archy, and Colin Ban ; sturdy lads of eleven,
eight, and six years, three shoots of the dead sap-
ling, who would be lusty callants and stout men,
who would preserve Duisk from the fatuous Colin
Og. Joann left them there, flitting across the loch
to Barrill, to keep house for old Malcolm Campbell
her uncle, of whom she had expectations.

"And what do you think you're going to be when
you grow up, my man ? " Colin Buie asked the young
Archy jocularly.

"A soldier," said the boy promptly.

The grandfather frowned. "Bullets stop careers."

"Aunt Janet says it's all we're fit for," said the
boy, daunted a little by the change in tone.

The old man laughed, but forcedly. He liked to
concentrate on planting trees and leave the house
to the care of that hard capable woman. But she
had not the soothing influence of his dead wife. She
domineered relentlessly, she kept the household in a
condition of precise expectancy. She was indulgent

only to her son, believing that providence had treated
her shabbily, and reflecting sourly on the lad's meagre
prospects.   There were four lives between the young
Don and the inheritance of Duisk, and Janet admitted that MacLachlans did not grow on every bush.

She knew her duty.   The years might pass, and
the years did pass, but the dependants at Duisk
scrubbed and scoured and spun and carded to the
calm instructions of the laird's daughter.   Her father,
her brother, the four boys and herself—they abode
in Duisk, and she managed them, being fond of
power, and fully conscious that the Campbell boys
detested her.

Aware of her faults, her father relied upon her.
She was a capable hard woman, and he admired
her type.   But he was relieved when the three elder
boys went to university, Don to Edinburgh and the
Campbells to Glasgow.   Things went more sweetly
after that, and he was ageing ; he was in the mood
for tranquillity.

He had not broken under the pain of longing, for
the moment of agony that slew his wife had been
but a trumpet call to the heavy old man, summon-
ing all his resolution and manhood.   To-day for revenge and to-morrow for grief.   He could have borne
the deaths of Neil and Archy under the old support
of pride, comforting and being comforted by his wife.
But Mor Campbell, with the last entry of her sons
to the house, had chosen the softer part.   And the
death of his wife had struck him as the deaths of
his sons could never.   But it could not break him.

He found consolation of a kind in improving his
dearly bought property, in visiting the MacTavishes

at Duin, and in going occasionally to Dugald Leitch,
who had demitted his parochial charge and taken
a tack of Uillian for his son Donald.

In the summer of 1754 the cousins were home
on vacation, and the house was full of stir. The
Leitches and MacTavishes were invited to Duisk,
but the latter family could not come. The laird
was seventy-eight now, as active-minded as he had
ever been, but mellowed more and seized at times
by melancholy. He scrutinized his growing grandsons with pride. Scipio and Archibald were tall big-
boned lads with their grandfather's hooked nose and
determined chin. Scipio bore a bold and candid
stamp on his features, and his eyes, at once fearless
and ruthless, were such as to inspire confidence. In
the younger's the contours were heavier and the
lips tight and thin.

"Man," said the old man with emotion, "but
you're real Campbells."

John Don reached Duisk on the following day.
He had acquired a stock of Edinburgh mannerisms,
and considered himself a gentleman of elegant and
carnal tastes. These conceits did not assort with
his heavy bully features, nor was his assumed patronage to his cousins met with the expected gratitude.
They had never liked him, nor did they choose to
disguise the dislike.

"John has got the Don face," his mother asserted
during a banal discussion on physiognomy. "He
has not got the Campbell face."

"Aye," said Archy, "and that's his loss."

But the three cousins found a common bond of
dislike when the Leitches arrived. There came the

minister and his wife, their daughter Ann, a soft-
voiced girl who was nineteen and as timid as a
fawn, and their son and daughter-in-law, Do'l Mor
Mac-a-Mhaighstir and his pretty Isbell Campbell from
Knapdale. Do'l Mor, in spite of never having been
further away from home than Inveraray, was not
impressed by their worldly outlooks, was openly contemptuous of them. The young tacksman of Uillian
was a rural Hercules, tall, serious, and rugged. He
was now twenty-four, and looked thirty; and was
the pride of his grandfather's heart.

The old man was gladdened by the sight of so
many descendants, and sat at the long table with
more visible happiness than he had shown for long.
His glance, as it roved from face to face, grew be-
nign; he forgot the past in the pleasure of the
moment. Males, plenty of them; plenty of Campbells to inherit and transmit Duisk—Scipio, Archy
Og, the youngest Colin . . . he smiled.

"Dugald," he said, "we are getting on."

"We pass," said the minister, his gaze resting
momentarily on his own son, "but we do not die."

"There's one loss," said the old man reflectively,
"we cannot see what comes after us."

"Perhaps we do," said Leitch, smiling.

"Man," said the laird banteringly, "I thought
you were a clergyman."

"I am a Highlandman."

Leitch's gaze wandered idly back to his son, and
he wondered what had brought that look of rage
to Do'l Mor's face. The young tacksman sat without speech to his neighbours, eating and drinking
mechanically, and in marked contrast to the younger

Campbells and Don, who had drunk too much and were now making a butt of their Uncle Colin.

" Uncle Dugald," said Don loudly, becoming bored with his harmless relative, " I've wagered Uncle Colin a guinea that you could race him to Errachan Wood and back." He guffawed at his own wit. " What do you say, Skip ? "

" Aye," said Scipio, " and Aunt Janet could try forbye."

Don laughed stupidly under his mother's resentful glance, and feeling in a false position he flared out at the minister's stare of rebuke. " You'll ken me again, won't you ? " he stuttered with an oath.

" Now, lads," said the laird's deep voice warningly, " take your drams like gentlemen." John muttered into silence.

" What is it that you learn in Edinburgh ? " Do'l Leitch asked him sibilantly.

" A heap of things," said Don sourly.

" We will be teaching you other things in Glassary," the tacksman told him with a smile, and there was silence for a moment.

" They are daft young callants," said the laird to the minister, indulgently. " We cannot restrain them ower much, for brawling lads make brave men."

" But brawling men ! . . . are they not men ? "

" The Campbells are all touchy," said Colin Buie with finality.

At the conclusion of the meal Do'l said to Scipio : " I want to speak to you, alone."

They proceeded in silence to a remote part of the garden. The tacksman turned to his cousin, his voice trembling with rage, his features white.

"I did not come to my grandfather's house to be insulted by his grandson. What do you mean by saying that I and my people have the hold of Duisk in our teeth?"

"Did I say that?" said Scipio coolly.

"You said it. And you said it in a voice that none but your brothers and John Don could hear. You dare not say that to the face of Colin Buie, for you are a coward."

"A coward!" cried Scipio violently. "Everyone is clawing about my grandfather for what they can get, while the heir is lost in Glasgow. I'm not a fool, Do'l Leitch, and I see through Janet Don's game and the game of your prayer-peddling father."

"You foul whelp," said the tacksman, taking a step forward, and felled him with a blow.

Without a further glance at the unconscious man Do'l walked back to the house. He was in time to see the younger Campbells and John Don capering where the knoll on which it stood dropped sharply to lower ground in an outcrop of rock. The youths were scuffling; Archy and Don were interlocked. And then Don stood alone. The tacksman ran forward.

Archy was lying still. It was a twelve foot drop. They all scrambled down to him.

Do'l turned to his grandfather, who had come out, alarmed by the commotion. "Your grandson Scipio is lying like that in the garden, where I left him," he said steadily. "He is over quick with his tongue."

III

Mrs. Captain Archy, whose arrival had been delayed by her exacting old relative at Barrill, came

now with much lament. A slender blonde woman
with a sweet manner and a determined temper, she
entrenched herself in her injured son's room, from
where she issued orders, injunctions, and warnings
in a high-pitched complaining voice. A doctor was
summoned to the detriment of the one in attendance. Mrs. Captain Archy suspected the first doctor ;
had no faith in him. He was not to be trusted.

Her hysteria impressed the old man deeply, and
his concern was transmuted into an alarm with which
Janet was made acquainted. Archy, he explained
to Mrs. Don, might have had his neck broken. It
was a piece of fortune that his thigh alone was injured, although that was bad enough.

The bleak-faced woman listened, silent save for a
suggestion that John's neck also might have met
with injury. He was not impressed.

" It's all very well, Janet. But there are only
five male Campbells of Duisk, and we must be careful. Poor Archy."

The angry woman returned to her duties and
listened to the heart that throbbed so violently
within her. She and Mrs. Captain Archy had already
met in conflict.

" Jock," she said to her son, who was sulking in
isolation, " those Campbells . . ."

He reflected that she was one herself, and said
so. But her thoughts were far away.

" I was the bigger fool," she said.

Loch Awe was glassy in the early evening calm,
and the sky and hills displayed the serene brilliant
tints of a southern clime. From the white walls of
Barrill on the opposite shore a lazy spire of smoke

pulsed against the backscene of timber. Beneath it a rowing boat clove the water, propelled by deliberate strokes and leaving a dark streak in its wake.

From the window of his room Colin Buie—vexed by the abrupt interruption to the festivities he had planned—watched the movements of his dependants and relatives with the passionate interest of the patriarch. He saw the sturdy Do'l Mor stride swiftly to the shore and then pass as swiftly by its brink, walking as a man does when he is angry. He saw another of his grandsons pass later in his wake; and a third still later, slowly. Hearing a tap on the door he turned, and saw his daughter Janet.

They had many private discussions on various matters, and in Janet he reposed the confidence merited by a sagacious and tried servant. She was keen, masterful, and economical—an ideal mistress over a numerous staff—and these qualities appealed to her father.

She sat facing him erectly, fingers interlocked in her lap, and without preliminaries of any kind she said : " There is trouble in this house."

The old man smiled indulgently, taking snuff. " I would not just call it trouble, Janet. But there is a kind of strain, certainly. I've noticed it." He laughed complacently that she should imagine him failing in shrewdness or insight. " Archy's tummle has given us all a sore fright, poor laddie. And that's true enough."

" Archy," she echoed ironically. " We will get over that, I hope."

For a moment her eyes turned to the windows and the tops of the familiar hills. " Father," she

D

said sharply, " I have kept this house for eight years. What is my place in it ? "

He was surprised by the question. She continued, speaking with rapid toneless words : " I have done what I thought was my duty. There is not a house on Lochaweside kept like Duisk. Your grandsons —Archy's sons—they come here. They flout me. The very first words of Scipio Campbell were an insult to my arrangements. Your son's widow, Joann Campbell—the daughter of a Glenorchy cattle thief —what other mother has neglected her sons as she has ? She left them here to go and be close with old Barrill. She left them here like a cuckoo. Now she comes from Barrill and countermands my orders to your servants. She despatched John MacDougall that I had brought for Archy Campbell's accident and brings this Kilchrenan quack in his place, and for that I am the jest of the countryside. Before her own son she said that she was the mother of the younger of Duisk and that I was the house-keeper. And what woman can manage a house after that ? My very son, who has as much of your blood in his veins as any Campbell, is shunned and scorned like a leper . . . father," she said with the same dispassionate manner but on a higher note, " is it that I have to go ? "

Under the intense stare of his daughter the old man sat motionless, with incredulous surprise, and then uneasiness. " Is that the way the wind blows ? " he said quietly.

" I am your eldest daughter, Colin Campbell, and I will not remain in Duisk as a handmaiden to Joann Campbell or as a housemaid to her thrawn whelps.

The very dogs in the kennels get more kindness from them."

" May be, Janet," he said sadly, " you never asked for kindness. We're a dour crowd." He stretched out his hand reassuringly, lest she should think herself rebuked. It trembled slightly. " I didna think things were like this. But what does it matter, woman ? The lads will be away again before you can wink. And Joann will gang back to Barrill, and that's my promise. No, no, Janet, you'll not think hard of the foolish notions of thoughtless callants, nor of Joann, who is a good woman and a woman I respect, but not so much as I respect my own daughter. You'll bide at Duisk. If there is any trouble here I shall give the begetter of it a stravalyan that he or she will not forget lightly." He raised his head proudly, the firm lines of his jaw showing beneath their heavy folds of flesh. " I've been ower easy with them all, maybe ; and maybe they think a man of seventy-eight can be taken lightly. Seventy-eight !—by God, though I was ninety-eight I could rule my own house." He patted the responseless folded hands. " Let the lave go by. You'll bide at Duisk."

The hard woman quivered at the touch of her father's hand. For a fraction of a second she was for grasping and kissing it, and was stunned at the thought of such a resolve. She rose instead and from the window looked to the darkening loch and the hills of Lorn which she might soon have been leaving for ever. When she turned, her face showed no trace of her thoughts. She sat down near her father and commenced to speak of the requirements for the coming weeks : the supply of lemons, the killing of a sheep and an ox . . . their talk moved to the old days. Of Mor Campbell of Uillian they spoke, familiarly, as people do of the loved dead ; of the busy times in Inveraray and the house on the shore front there, of the people there with whom they were acquaint, and of the places around and the folk that dwelt therein. The proud cold Janet softened in the relief and reaction of the hour. She lighted the candles and sat there with her father, talking, and her heart sang within her.

And then a woman's shriek banished the quiet, long, piercing, and terrible, and as it wailed away the clamour of many voices froze them with affright.

IV

In the parlour the body of a man was laid upon the floor, and Anne Leitch who had given birth to it knelt by its side.

The lord of the house, hastening, saw from the doorway the dark shapes of his kindred and the two shapes on the floor. He entered, leaning pantingly on the table, and stared with dreadful eyes on the body of Do'l Mor Mac-a-Mhaighstir.

Again the young widow's cry of anguish rang in the room, horrible to the hearing. Anne Leitch turned to her daughter, telling her to take the girl away. " Where is my man ? " she said.

Colin knelt clumsily and took the young man's hand. Do'l Leitch was cold. On his shirt, over the heart, was a spread stain that looked black in the candle light. His camlet kilt was stained and dusty ; a burr was sticking to it.

The minister came, fearful at the summons, and his wife clung to him, sobbing.

"Go, all of you," said the old man, and they left Do'l Mor with his parents and his grandsire.

The calmness of the summer night rested on the lands of Duisk; not a ripple scarred the surface of Loch Awe. Velvet-like, the woods clung to the dim hills, and the hills leant their crests against the dusky sky. The air was cool and pleasant, sighing a little in the corries; and there was a silence that only the plaintive cry of a bird would scatter as it winged close to the shadowing loch.

But in the house of Duisk Do'l Mor lay dead. To-night the knowledge was within the long low house like a spell of evil prisoned in a casket; to-morrow a hundred tongues would swell the tale, through the district, and the county, and the land —and an affrighted world would cry out : " Murder ! "

In the rooms of Duisk there was whispering, words of horror that drew further horror from the moving shadows ; whispering, and fear, and grief. Of a sudden, destiny seemed centred in that house, because that destiny had seized a life.

Destiny seemed centred in the house of Duisk, and from the rebellious minds of man therein a great question, full of despair and sorrow, rose against the Maker of Man. The sun came, coming delicately from distant Cowal, and flung his golden ordnance on the water. A world of wonder quivered at the dawn of day. The bird awoke and shook his wings, the flower opened in the dewy grass and the horse in his stall stamped restlessly. In the cots by the loch side the gathering peat was briskened, and the smoke curled lazily in the caller air. The crofter came to his door, gazed skyward with appraising eyes and tramped tranquilly to his little field. High above Sith Mor a menacing speck floated, questing for a morning prey. The world had wakened. But young Do'l Mor would never.

Do'l Mor, who had loved the earth, was one with earth. He had loved the sights and sounds of the earth, and would know them never more. On the hills he had gazed, as he had been their son, and in their shadow he would remain. Glassary had poured its spirit into him, the sound of its waters, the fragrance of its myrtle, the peace of its comely hills. Glassary had enriched him, and would be enriched by him.

To the master of the house came his son-in-law, aged in the night, with a fey glitter in his eyes. And holding him by the coat, he said : " I know the murderer."

Colin faced him with a look of terror.

" I know the murderer of my Donald," cried the minister, babbling in his face. " My eldest son, I know his murderer.

" Colin Campbell, I know the murderer of my son." His blazing eyes bored into the other man's with the intensity of madness. " Cursed be his mother that she bore him.

" My Donald, my little Do'l who ran by his mother's skirts. My eldest son, the flower of my flock." Leitch sank shaking into a chair. " My son, with his child unborn in its mother's womb. Oh, Colin Campbell, what have you done that your family reeks of blood ? Blood—blood—blood. Your oe is

dead and your oe has slaughtered him," he cried
in a hiss of words. "May my God forgive me, for
my faith is broken."

Colin did not speak. He did not dare. He was
afraid, and trembled violently.

"Aye, murder," cried the minister harshly.
"Murder. But an eye for an eye and a tooth for
a tooth. Murder, of my Do'l, and of his wife, and
mine."

Colin saw blood lust on the clergyman's face—
saw, indeed, no clergyman, but a man of relentless
race with wrongs.

"The spirit of my son cries out for vengeance,"
cried Leitch, and spat the words at him. "It will
not rest till the seed of your seed swings in the tow."
His head sank on his hands and he wept.

"O my God!" cried the old man in an agony,
"what wrong have I done Thee for all those sorrows ?"
His voice sank to a note of fear. "Surely the Mac-
Lachlans have cursed me," he said. He braced himself with a supreme effort. "Which of them struck
the blow ?" he whispered falteringly.

The minister did not seem to hear him. He kept
muttering his dead son's name. At length he looked
up, vacantly, with the old man's words echoing in
his consciousness. "We'll go to Uillian," he said
half audibly. "Who struck the blow ? Oh, the
God who made us could tell us that."

Colin started. His eyes devoured the other man,
full of a horrid mingling of calculation and grief.
"Dugald," he said. "Dugald." He moistened his lips
and touched the minister's sleeve, drawing his hand
down it like a caress. "Has nobody an inkling ?"

"No one," said the other with a groan.

"No one," said the laird. "Is it no' a spite! Dugald. Dugald," he said urgently. "It was Jock found the body. It was Jock found the body."

"The man who says he found my Do'l must be the man who stabbed him," cried Leitch, grinding his teeth. "And who but a fiend would slay a defenceless man for a sharp word at the table? A thousand men and women are crying for his blood," he said savagely, ". . . the dead from whom we come. Oh, Duisk, were it not for the cloth I wear John Don would die beneath your roof."

"You'll not be thinking it could be anyone else, Dugald?" the old man asked feverishly. "You're not thinking that, are you?" His eyes, full of imbecile questioning, sank before the minister's fierce gaze. "It's a mercy it's not a Campbell did it," he said, and groaned. "Poor Do'l."

"He shall hang."

Colin's head sank forward, pressing the pendulous fat of his cheeks over his cravat in pallid folds; his eyes were scarcely visible and his mouth drooped at the corners. "Take him then," he muttered with an effort, "and hang him. I am by with you all." A gradual roaring sounded in his ears, and all things turned darkly crimson. He gripped his chair with an accession of terror. "God have mercy on me," he exclaimed.

"No mercy for my Do'l."

"Dugald. Dugald. He did not do it. He is my kin. He is your kin——"

"And Do'l's kin." Leitch stared fixedly at him. "There was no one else in Errachan Wood. If John

Don did not slay my son, who else has done it ?
He says he found the body. He is lying. He slew
my son. He must have done it. I shall bring all
the justice in Scotland to track the murderer of my
son, though it should break the hearts of all his
kindred."

" The shame, man——"

" Who else could do it ? "

The old man did not answer. He thought momentarily of Mor Campbell of Uillian, and felt very tired.

" Dugald," he said desperately. " Dugald, you are
a clergyman. For Janet's sake, for the sake of your
vows . . . for the sake of my soul. There is no
proof, Dugald. .There will never be proof. You cannot shame your wife's family. Man, will you murder
the grandfather ? "

" He should do that."

" Dugald—if he is *innocent*! Oh, man, for the
sake of my dead wife." He caught the clergyman's
hands, gabbling frantically. Leitch was forced to
see the creased shaking flesh, feel the hot breath on
his cheeks. He drew back with a movement of re-
pugnance, recovering his own sanity as the older
man lost his. " Dugald. Dugald. For Janet's sake,
for mine . . ."

The recollection of the dead Do'l Mor came back
to Leitch. His son was dead ; for ever dead. No
power, no plea, no vengeance could regain him. With
surprise he saw the sun shining brightly on the hills
of Lorn and the cloud shadows sweeping over their
flanks. It was incredible that the day was bright
and fair, with Do'l Mor dead, Do'l Mor murdered.
He shivered a little, and turned his gaze on the

old man, who was sprawled across his desk and weeping.

He thought of the murdered and the murderer; manly beauty struck treacherously by a thing of evil, by an inferior power that could not be proved of guilt, by murder masquerading as innocence. Who other could have done it? A desire came to him at once, to leave the house and its inmates for ever, to go and be with his own and never see the members of this race again.

"I can prove nothing," he said. "But the Lord promises vengeance, and repayment. I shall never look on you or yours again."

v

"Janet," said her father, "I am going to close this house."

Mrs. Don was not surprised. "It has been a terrible grief to us all," she said simply.

"The house will be closed. The house will be closed, and no smoke will rise from its chimneys while I live."

Tears came into the woman's eyes. "Poor Do'l," she said. "But yourself, father?"

"I'll go to Inveraray, Janet, with my son. We were a good fleet at one time, and I was the flagship. I still am, but my sole support is disabled." He smiled a ghastly smile at his daughter. "But Colin Og, at least, is harmless. Make your preparations, and tell the others. I have no heart for it."

"Father," she said solicitously, gazing at the old man's stricken face, "Inveraray is no place now for you. It is a place of memories——"

" Yes, pleasant memories." His glance faltered. " I have a wife and two sons there."

" Father, they are dead."

" Aye, Janet, they'll not harm me."

In alarm at his strange manner she crossed to his side. " If it must be Baile Ionaraora—if we must go there—if you and Colin Og and I——"

" No," said the old man sharply. With an effort he said : " Colin Og and myself."

Mrs. Don was silent, grieved. She laid a soothing hand on his sleeve, with an effort.

" Janet," he said rigidly, " you have been a great help to me, woman. If you are in need, let me know. I'll make an arrangement for your benefit. If you need help write me from Edinburgh."

When, hurt and surprised, she left him, the old man crossed to the open window. The day was oppressively warm. Loch Awe shone like a shield of burning metal, deepest blue, and the hills quivered in the heat. The old man stared thoughtfully at the brilliant prospect. His features had changed dreadfully—one more descent from the descent at his last great tragedy ; the pendant flesh was lifeless, his mouth loose and fretful. His clothes were neat, his stockings as spotless, his wig as neatly powdered, as at any time. The man had never been slovenly in his life.

Beneath the window grew a briar bush. Its blossoms were white and innocent. The sheep— his sheep—were bleating plaintively on the hillside. From near hand sounded the domineering crowing of a cock. All around him trembled with beauty and with life.

For the first time in his life Colin Buie had evaded
the demands of kinship. He was conscious of his
duplicity, thinking of the pathetic little procession
in the dawn when Do'l Mor's body was taken from
the house to the house of Uillian, from whence it
would go for the long repose to Kilmichael. Part
of the old man's heart had gone with it, and he
reflected that now there was little of that heart left.
The slow insistence of the pipe lament seemed still
to hang upon the air. He turned away.

That the Leitches should return to Uillian without revenge was an insult, and that the murderer
should walk his ways in safety was an outrage. And
that all his kin should be in ignorance of the per-
petrator of death was to leave them to extend clean
hands to the hand of blood. Dugald Leitch ?—
Dugald Leitch knew nothing. There was nothing
save frenzied grief behind that wild and baseless
charge. But he, Colin Campbell, knew more. And
for the sake of the new-founded line of Campbell
of Duisk, he was allied with guilt.

He thought of Janet, whom he was banishing to
give foundation to a groundless suspicion, and he
thought of Anne. He thought of them with self-
nausea. He was degraded in his own sight. He
had found his beloved grandson, that beautiful mas-
culine creature, done to death, and he was shielding
another grandson, the possible murderer. He had
abetted suspicion on a third grandson . . . for the
sake of the name of Campbell. The old man thought
of his own father, the fierce old *duin'-uasail* of Glen-
feochanside ; of his wife Mor Campbell ; of his sons,
dead Archy and dead Neil ; of the scarce cold Do'l

Mor—and wondered what they would be thinking of him beyond the grave. Thought of them goaded him, but he could not act. He had grasped Duisk, and now Duisk had grasped him, sweeping him on to sins against his very flesh and blood.'

Six days after Do'l Mor's death he was alone with Colin Og. That morning Scipio and Colin Ban had taken the injured Archy across to Barrill in a boat. With relief the laird saw the last of his guests depart, and knew a profound melancholy at once. It was like the closing of a history.

He had despatched a report of the murder to justice at Inveraray, but he felt certain that nothing would come of it.

The presence of his fatuous smiling son became unbearable to him ; he donned his cloak and hat and paced down to the shore road, walking with the aid of a stick. The sun was drooping down to Lorn, and the hills of Duisk were intimate, the scrub wood on their flanks bright with the purple of the foxglove and frilled with patch of bracken. Like all his race, he was touched by the beauty of creation, and the golden evening soothed him. He was absorbed in it for a time, his eyes fixed where Crua-chan showed her peaks in the far distance, and it was with an additional spasm of anguish that his mind reverted to his recent grief. It was then that he observed two women walking in his direction. They were bare-headed, bare-footed, and with plaids around their shoulders. As they neared him one stopped, leaving her companion to go on a little, and said : " It is Colin Campbell."

He eyed her indifferently, thinking she might be

some tinker woman who had known him in Inveraray. But her dark features, her dark steady eyes, were familiar, and he exclaimed with a start: " I know you. You are the woman MacLachlan."

She assented gravely. " Well," he said with a frown, " what do you want here ? "

" I am a dying woman," she said. " And I have come back to die in my own country."

" Is it a healthy country for you ? " he asked menacingly.

" It has not been healthy for some," she said. " And Anne Leitch has lost her son. So they told me at Sonachan." A look of sadness came to her face. " There will be sorrow in Uillian. Uillian. I was born there."

" Aye," said the old man with an effort. " Changed days."

" You are not the same man who was at Inveraray," she said simply. " You have not known happiness, Colin Buie."

The laird regarded her ponderingly, remembering her link with his son. " I have had setbacks," he said heavily, " since yon time. My grandson, my wife, my son Archy, my son Neil."

" Mor Campbell was a good woman. Yon knife cut deep."

" Yes," he said bitterly, " and you drove the blow."

" Oh, Colin Buie," she cried, " it was no fault of mine. Yon Lowland lad who brought Ainus and Callum to the gallows told you that. I have been in Morvern these eight years, and the face of Neil Campbell was never from my mind. He was a man.

And he would have left me for Stucguie's milk-faced daughter. Well, he is dead, and God give him rest, and blessings on him. I am going back to Kilmichael, to my kin."

"Are you not well ? " he asked, softened.

"I am dying."

"And who is the girl ? " he asked, but without curiosity, and thinking to offer a piece of money.

"Go back," she said, "and look well at her."

Impressed by the woman's manner he did so, and the girl and he scrutinized each other without words. He was astonished. His expression changed. He returned to Peggy Bheag.

"I did not know," he said.

"Mor Campbell knew."

"Ah," he exclaimed. After a little he said : "If you had told me——"

"Yes," she said with an ironical smile. "You w ould have been pleased."

The thought occurred to the old man that he had lost a grandchild, to find another. He connected the expulsion of the MacLachlans with the deaths of his sons and wife. Perhaps if these two women were to remain at Duisk the heavy burden of guilt would lift for ever. It was a superstitious reasoning, and more convincing because of that.

"I am leaving Duisk," he said, "but you can bide here, and she can work on the farm." The woman assented. "It is justice," the old man said. "She can bide at Duisk."

"Had things been rightly done," said the woman, "Duisk would be her inheritance."

Scipio and Colin Ban crossed from Barrill on the

day of their grandsire's departure for Inveraray. The farewells were cold and brief, but Colin Buie laid instructions on his heir as a sacred duty that Peggy Bheag MacLachlan and her daughter were always to have board at Duisk. He did not explain his reason, and Scipio did not venture to ask. Instead he inquired if he could do his grandfather any service on his return to Edinburgh.

" You have done enough for me," said Colin Buie.

In a small house in a land in the main street of Inveraray he found peace for a week, and thereafter misery. Memories returned with scalding intensity. Colin Og became a butt for the children of the town. The old house on the front was occupied by a stranger.

The old man spent much time in Kilmalieu, by the grave of his wife and sons. He was very near them then, he thought, and would often smile happily there, which he seldom did elsewhere. He had erected a classical stone with a pedimented top and Ionic pilasters to their memory, which read :

Sacred
To The Memory
of
SARAH CAMPBELL
dau. of JOHN CAMPBELL of Uillian
and Spouse of COLIN CAMPBELL of Duisk
ob. 25th Sept. 1746.
Her Sons
NEIL CAMPBELL, Fiar of Uillian
Capt. ARCHD. CAMPBELL —nd Regt.
ob. 24th Sept. 1746.

and there was space left for his own name, and perhaps for Colin Og's. No others of his family would lie there.

By the graveside Colin would stand for an hour at a time, his eyes fixed vacantly on Loch Shira and his thoughts still further. From the grave at Kilmalieu to that at Kilmichael which he had not seen his thoughts swung like a pendulum. He had no other thoughts.

And near that other graveyard, at Uillian, the young Angus, Do'l Mor's posthumous son, had been born. And from Uillian Do'l Mor's sister, the gentle Ann, had gone as the wife of another grandson of Colin Buie, Duncan MacTavish, who had made poems about her. And at Uillian they learned one day that the old man had purchased the neighbouring property of Strone ; why, no one knew. A year passed ; two years. The grief for the dead Do'l had lost its sharpest edge. And then one evening Anne Leitch ran into the house crying on her man. Her father and Colin Og were coming.

The old man and his son approached slowly on horseback, Colin Og with his customary amiable smile. When they drew up before the house the laird's face frightened them. He had to be lifted from his horse, a difficult and harassing operation with a man of his weight, and carried into the house. His will alone had kept him in the saddle.

"I came back," he explained shakily, "to see Do'l's grave."

He looked ghastly. The determined and tortured old man had ridden the thirty miles from Inveraray since morning.

"My father is jaunting about too much for my liking," said Colin Og. "He is just like a tinker. He is far too fond of jaunting about."

E

" I came back," the old man whispered to the minister and his daughter, " to see Do'l's grave. I did my courting here."

But he was not to see the grave of the grandson whose murderer he had shielded. There was no time to await the return of the Dons and the Campbells, and only the Leitches and the MacTavishes returned with the old man to Inveraray, over the road he had traversed a few days earlier, where they laid him by the side of Mor Campbell of Uillian. He was in his eightieth year.

Although his dead wife had been for ever in his thoughts he had seldom cared to speak of her to outsiders, and had been considered eminently cold-hearted. But after death his relatives found a thin gold chain with a locket round his neck, and in the locket, which they buried with him, was a lock of red hair turning grey.

BOOK TWO
DAY

ONE

SCIPIO CAMPBELL at once proceeded to Duisk, where he was shortly joined by his mother, but Mrs. Captain Archibald soon returned to Barrill, which property was too considerable to be lost for the sake of a premature exhibition of mother love. Mrs. Captain Campbell was well pleased. She had no desires from her son other than impressing him strongly with the need to keep the Dons, mother and son, but especially the mother, away from Duisk.

Sitting behind the white harled walls of Barrill, she gazed daily eastward to the grey low shape that betokened Duisk, and felt that providence had given her her deserts.

In his will Colin Buie left his estate of Duisk to his grandson Scipio and his heirs male and female ; thereafter to his grandsons Archibald and Colin and their heirs male and female ; thereafter to his son Colin. Failing them, the estate was to devolve on his daughters' families successively, provisional to the adoption of the name of Campbell.

To Dugald Leitch he bequeathed his lands of Strone, to be held in trust for Angus Leitch, son of the deceased Donald Leitch, tacksman of Uillian, and in any case to descend to the heirs of the aforesaid Reverend Dugald Leitch.

The Campbell brothers were savage when they learned of the Strone bequest. None of them had

nourished animus against the Leitches, although they
considered the minister a sour and whiggish man, but
that a part of the Campbell property had been left
away from them at once raised a barrier of dislike
against the family at Uillian. Scipio voiced this feeling to the lawyer.

"Your grandfather bought Strone specially for the
child Leitch," that gentleman explained.

"Oh!" said Scipio surlily, "and why was that?"

"I think it was a kindly thought because the baby's
father was murdered while at Duisk."

Archibald, the heir-presumptive, was louder in
protest than his brother. "Their tack expires soon.
Raise the rent of Uillian, Skip."

"Let them be," said Scipio, gnawing his lip.

"Archy is quite right," Mrs. Captain Campbell
urged. "Make them pay for Strone through Uillian."

But the Leitches did not choose to renew the tack
of Uillian. They flitted to Strone, and Scipio had
to seek another tenant.

Scipio was now a personable young man, strong and
handsome, and good-humoured. He had become
liable to fits of despondency which his inheritance did
not altogether banish, and which his mother, who
viewed this melancholy with alarm, declared did not
derive from her side of the family. His brother
Archibald had followed him from Glasgow, but would
shortly return to the College there with the young
Colin, now sixteen years of age.

But Colin was not going to be a lawyer. He had
set his heart on the sea. Colin had not ventured to
assert his aims during the lifetime of his grandfather,
whom he secretly had feared greatly. Now there was

only Scipio and his mother to contend with. Scipio
was indifferent, and laughed at the whole business ;
and Colin was heartened, and pled his cause successfully with his mother, overcoming that woman's tearful expostulations and harrowing imaginary details
of shipwreck. Old Malcolm Campbell of Barrill
entered the fray. He had not greatly relished the
youthful Campbells' stay at Barrill, and gladly used his
influence to thrust Colin into the navy. The main
obstacle was his age—he was some years behind the
time—but that was successfully dealt with, and
everyone was quite happy save Colin's mother.

" So I've got to go back to yon place alone," said
Archy.

" Well, Archy," his brother said placably, " you've
your career to carve."

Archy had no stomach either for law. He laughed
with a concentration of rage that surprised his brother.
" A career ! What do I want with their instruments of
sasine, and infeftments, and precepts of clare constat !
Yon Edinburgh blackguard ! He tried it, Skip, as
sure as life. He did it on purpose. And I'm lost
for the army because of a Canongate muck-rake."
He walked the floor quickly, and his haste accentuated
the limp that was the conjoined work of John Don
and of Mrs. Captain Archy's choice of physicians.
To the countryside he was known now as Archibald
Crubach, or the Lame.

" He has thrown up the law, Skip. Jock Carruthers
in Glasgow told me. He has got a commission
through his peddling old uncle of the Fifteen. And
him the son of a snivelling little writer-body to the
Signet——"

" So was our grandfather."

" Our grandfather was a man, Skip. He was a Campbell. He wasn't a dried lemon. To think that John Don, who ought to be a lawyer, lames me, who ought to be a soldier . . . Skip, if I can do it, I'll clip his wings."

" Well," said his brother coolly, " that's reasonable enough, and if you can think of a ploy I'll help you. It's an awful loss, a lame leg. But mind you, I'm not bringing Don to Duisk. No foul play here."

After his brothers' departure Scipio grew lonely. He paid a few visits to neighbours, but they bored him quickly, particularly the old relative at Barrill, where he did not go so frequently as he might. He visited Duin, and met all the MacTavishes. But either they had outpaced him or he had them, for the old cousinly feeling had changed to hospitable civility. He did not know what he wanted.

In those days there was no distinction of birth, where all the population were of ancient stock and bore mostly, as they still do, a few honoured surnames. A ladder of social standing led down by imperceptible rungs from the greater lairds to the smaller proprietors, and thence to the tacksmen, the farmers, the co-farmers, the crofters and fishermen. There was no claim to nor admission of superiority in birth, for there was none in actuality. The poorest people had a knowledge of the stocks from whence they came. They were proud of them, and gained dignity from the knowledge ; and with dignity were the natural adjuncts of courage, courtesy, and hospitality.

The luxuries of civilization came quickly to this district through Loch Fyne, so accessible from the

Lowlands. The younger offshoots of the local families
sought prosperity in Glasgow and Greenock, and in
their visits home, which could be frequent, brought
with them a taste for the softer amenities of life.
They infected the friends at home. And so the lairds,
who had been content with homespun, fancied broad-
cloth, and preferred a cocked hat to a flat bonnet ;
and their wives discarded their own weaving for
paduasoy. The women cultivated a taste for dainty
bedquilts and elaborate furniture ; the menfolk's taste
was for French brandies and clarets. They had little
money. Their brothers in the Lowlands might be
making it, but they had none. Their wealth consisted
in their herds of cattle and the produce they extracted
from their paternal lands. These possessions were
wealth enough, but in a period of change they were
not reliable. Too much trust could be placed in
Falkirk Tryst. When hard pressed they got loans,
they mortgaged their properties, and thought they
had saved themselves. A further bad season, an
additional extravagance, and they saw their lairdships
slip from their fingers.

This period had now begun. It was not confined
to the district, being general throughout the Highlands, and at the time it seemed gradual, or trivial.
In effect it was tremendous, socially revolutionary ;
for with the passing of so many small properties and
their absorption in greater and more solid estates,
the rungs in the social ladder were snapped, the
remaining proprietors, influenced by the feudal code
mentality that was soon to penetrate from the south,
were to set up a barrier of distinction of birth that
was in actuality ridiculous and in the course of

another hundred years a prescriptive right to good birth would be formulated by the landowning class, and tacitly ratified by the remnant of the depleted poor, that was absurd and false.

Scipio discovered that some of his grandfather's old neighbours and their families had vanished. He learned the cause. It was one not likely to affect him, for he inherited a good deal of the family thrift, and Duisk was too ample a possession to be easily squandered. But in time he found the place monotonous. The first flush of pride in his possession had passed, and he wondered what he wanted.

During these months at Duisk he had been served at meals and generally waited on by a young woman little older than himself. She knew no English, and that fact had been the means of causing Scipio to freshen his neglected Gaelic. He had accepted her service casually at first. Gradually he paid her more attention. She was a slender girl, dark-eyed and sunburned, with comely features : shapely lips, defined eyebrows, and an aquiline nose. Her hair was black. She was bare-footed, and wore a red flannel skirt and a plain purple-coloured bodice. After the departure of his mother and brothers he dined alone, and it was then that he began to take notice of her.

"What is your name ? " he asked her once.

"Peggy MacLachlan," she said, and waited, but as he said nothing further she hastened noiselessly away with his soiled plate.

She was always very quick and silent in her movements. Her face, naturally grave in expression, was very lively when she smiled, and it was then that she showed her white gleaming teeth. Scipio made inquiries about her.

"It is your mother who lives at the farm?" he said once. She replied yes; Peggy Bheag. He remarked idly: "I hear you're a rebel."

She smiled mischievously. "That is all over and by with," she said.

"Ah," said Scipio, "you ought to be hanged."

"My word," cried the girl, laughing, "if there were no rebels in this world there would be no luck for some people!"

Scipio grinned, and could find no retort. "Where were you before you came here?" he asked.

"We were in Morvern."

"But they were all Jacobites there. Were you not chased by the troops?"

"Yes," she said seriously, "but at least it was friends we were among."

"And what brought your mother back here?"

"She is a Glassary woman. She was born at Uillian."

"Uillian!" said Scipio. "That's mine. Your mother must know my own people well."

The girl's presence became very pleasant to him. At meals he kept her talking, and she was always ready to laugh and joke, showing her pretty teeth. He found that she was attending exclusively to the house and cooking as well, and after that he would penetrate to the kitchen at odd times and while away an hour in conversation. Peggy did not allow these talks to interfere with her domestic duties, but would glance over her shoulder smilingly, and the young man thought she was enchanting.

In time she filled a larger portion of Scipio's thoughts than he would willingly have admitted. He met her frequently outside—he thought by accident. And once he encountered her going with a stoup to the burn for water.

The burn was fringed with bushes, briar rose, and honeysuckle, where it parted company with the hill. Peggy stepped on to a convenient stone and tipped the bucket into the burn's brown water. "It is good for men and horses," she said. Scipio stretched out his hand for the bucket. "Now!" he said, and caught her arm with his free hand. His gallantry was unnecessary; she was so near the bank that he was in her way, and she almost fell back. In his anxiety he dropped the stoup and trod on her bare foot, and Peggy gave a cry of pain.

Scipio was vexed. He caught her and apologized profusely. The girl smiled wryly, and he found himself pressing his lips to hers.

Then, he was standing alone, but for the stoup.

She appeared shyly at the next meal, but Scipio immediately reverted to the subject, and demanded to see her foot. She held it out for his inspection. It was sun-browned and perfectly shapely, for it had never known a shoe. Scipio saw the red abrasion made by his boot, and was full of remorse.

"It is all right—it is nothing," she said, and looked at him kindly. "But you are very bold."

He was inflamed by her presence, and lived in a state of tingling pleasure. He would go out on horseback, and cut short his exercise for the sake of seeing her again. And once, late in the evening, he spoke pleadingly to her.

Peggy listened at first with rapt gladness, submitting her hands to the pressure of his hands and lips. As he continued speaking her expression changed ; a look, at first incredulous, came to her face. She rose hastily, with tears in her eyes. " Oh," she cried, " is this your way of getting rid of us ? You promised Colin Buie that we could live here, my mother and I, and is this your way of getting rid of us ? "

He said awkwardly : " You will never leave here in my time."

" Oh," she cried, and her face flushed crimson, " you would want to make a shame of me, then."

Scipio regarded her, confused.

" Do you know what I am, Scipio Campbell ? " she asked. " I am your servant, maybe. Well, I am your cousin."

Scipio did not sleep soon that night. On the morning he rowed to Barrill and questioned his mother. She told him the detailed story of Neil his uncle, with embellishments. But Scipio believed with reservations. He was very deeply in love.

For days he wondered if he should make Peggy Bheag's daughter his wife. The girl attended to his wants as usual, quickly and silently, but she did not glance at him save when he spoke, and she never lingered now. He watched her dignity of mien with a sense of tragedy, feeling the extent of her wounded pride and desperately anxious to banish it. Moodily he reflected that she was a Campbell of Duisk, like himself, and would be so acknowledged but for an accident. He weighed his mother's anger and the opinions of his other relations carelessly, certain that their right feeling would make them befriend her in the end. He could not banish Peggy from his thoughts. He lay awake at nights thinking of her; of her sunburned skin and shining teeth, and of her fine distinguished features.

One evening she had served him and was returning finally to the kitchen.

"Peggy," he called desperately.

She stopped and took a pace towards him, but misunderstanding his expression, a look of repulsion showed in her eyes, and she ran out, closing the door behind her.

Scipio was hurt, but decided to speak to her later and explain his wish to marry her. He had his horse saddled and rode out on the Innischonnell road. It was an August day, calm and tranquil, and bright yet with the late soft sunshine. He spurred his horse and galloped for a time, enjoying the easy motion in the saddle. His thoughts were pleasant to him, for since his love for Peggy had grown the former moods of melancholy had vanished.

He went far, further than he had intended, and at last turned, vexed that he had delayed the moment of proposing. A new felicity seemed to shape before him. He saw himself and Peggy MacLachlan in the house of Duisk, noise and laughter, and the years ahead.

As he returned he observed the track that led from the public road and ran level through the adjacent wood, and as it was soft turf there he could shorten his return by putting his horse to the gallop, for the rough roadway was tiring it. He twitched the rein, and the beast turned up to the track between the dark and silent firs.

Some time later the horse arrived at Duisk, wild-eyed and covered with foam. Scipio slipped from its back and stumbled into the house. He called to the girl to bring him spirits, and sank into a chair, trembling. She was alarmed by his pale, haggard looks, and questioned him, but he waved her away.

Peggy then left the room, but went no further than the door, where she listened, wondering what had wrought the blank terror on his face. She heard the continual clatter of the glass, the clink as it was filled, and ultimate quiet. Full of anxiety she went to him. He was now maudlin, and the girl simply assisted him to his room and helped him to undress. But his drunkenness had not dispelled the horror from his eyes.

He could not bear that she should leave him. She placed the blankets over him, and would have gone, but he cried on her pleadingly, and shed tears of deep self-pity. Then she approached him, and he placed one arm confidingly around her neck and babbled like a child. He talked, wonderingly and whimperingly, and at times with a whine of anguish that pierced her very heart. He lay back at last, his breath rank with the liquor he had taken, his eyes wide-open and terrible. And drunkenly sane.

" Peggy," he moaned. " Peggy."

She placed her hand on his brow and tried to comfort him.

" But . . . but . . . but you'll marry me, Peggy," he stammered thickly.

" Not now," she said.

TWO

IN Glassary the years pass with a soft and mellow leisure. In the winter there are days of white hills and black water. They pass, and the bright clean weeks of vivid greenery come, to melt into those of burning sunshine when there is a whirring and a quivering on the bracken hill slopes and when the dragon-flies dart upon the margins of the lochs. And from that the days droop to ardent weeks of russet and crimson, and the roads are soft and leafy. And all the year round there is the soft, fine rain.

In Duisk the years passed slowly. Nothing changed in Duisk, save man. And that change was symbolized by the midwife and the betherel. There was no change in Duisk; only that Colin Buie's plantings were growing high and forming into wood land. And the news from the outer world came very slow.

There was activity on the home farm. The crops were sown and garnered; the cattle were on the moors, soft-eyed and wondering at the intrusion of sheep. And in the summer time the workers went to the sheiling on the hills and watched their patient charges; and the air was full of the scent of myrtle and the sound of singing. At nights there were happy gatherings for *ceilidh* there, when old songs were sung and old tales told both gay and grim, and when the people went to the door they saw the hills roll softly

DAY   81

about them and saw the moon lying white on the
bosom of some little lochan.

When it was time to return to the low land they
went with laughter and song by the old worn tracks,
seeing Loch Awe stretch smiling beneath them and
the far peaks of Cruachan Ben strike snow-capped at
the sky.

The old days were growing indistinct and the old
feuds were growing dim. There was family feeling
in some hearts, but it had ceased to be connected with
the original cause, for the original cause was being
forgotten. There was a reminiscence of it when the
woman Peggy Bheag MacLachlan died, and surmise
for a time over her part in the deaths of the two Campbells in Glenshira, and conjecture for the retention
of her daughter at Duisk. But the blood connection
was known, and people ceased to wonder.

Peggy Bheag MacLachlan, worn out by hardship
and exposure, died one year after Colin Buie. She
was a comparatively young woman, and should have
lived much longer, but as her thoughts were thirled
to the past she was not loth to go. Near the end she
requested that Dugald Leitch would read the burial
service over her. "He is a good man," she said,
"and a man with kindness in his heart." When
Leitch knew of her condition he broke his vow and
went to Duisk and sat by her bedside, and they talked
together for a long time of Uillian and the old days.
He officiated at her graveside in Kilneuair, near by,
and his wife and he put up a small headstone. "Neil
would have been pleased," said Anne.

Of the four remaining members of Colin Buie's
family, Colin Og remained with his sister at Strone,

F

and he and the Leitches saw frequently their relatives
at Duin. With them the years passed placidly.
Thanks to his great-grandfather's strategem, Do'l
Mor's son Angus would be a farmer and remain at
Strone. The pretty Isbell had become a serene
matronly woman. Young Ann and her cousin husband the poet Duncan were at Duin with his parents,
and children came to them, more scions of Colin Buie,
with a double share of his blood. The babies were
a profound amusement for Colin Og, who tended them
gently, never quite understanding how they had
appeared. The grandchildren formed an additional
link with the sisters Anne and Eilidh, and as they
drew still closer to each other with the years the bond
of sympathy with their sister Janet seemed to lessen.

There was no ostensible reason for that in the
women's eyes, but it was so. Janet was in Edinburgh, a distant place ; she had married a Lothian
man and had now no link with Argyll beyond that
of birth. She corresponded but slightly with them,
and after her son's change to the army a note of
querulousness had crept into her letters, unintentional,
but there. She was a lonely woman, sitting in her
eyrie in the High Street and watching the passage of
the years with dull hope. At times she thought of
returning to Inveraray, which she loved passionately
with the all-giving love of a hard-souled woman, but
there had been changes there, she learned, and
hesitated. From the cliff height of Craig's Close she
sat and stared down at the roof of St. Giles' and at
the Luckenbooths and the Krames, not seeing them ;
seeing instead the mists rise up from Cowal or the surf
spreading like white gull's wings by the Boshang Gate.

She was grieved that her son had forsaken his father's trade for the grim uncertainty of soldiering. But his progress pleased her ; he had gained a rapid promotion, with a hare-brained courage and his mastiff Session-lord uncle as his sponsors. She wrote often to him, and he wrote to her as frequently.

'You will be surprised, I doubt not,' he said in one letter from India, 'that Scipio Campbell is in the —nd Regt., and in Bengal. James Fullerton, who had writ me from Calcutta, and knew of our connection, tells that Scipio Campbell was under Hector Munro at Buxar, where the Nawáb left £3,000,000 behind him in his hurry. Scipio Campbell, according to rumour, was not blate at the pickings. He is chief with some of the powers in the Calcutta Council, I believe, and in close touch with a few of the Native Courts. He is said to have been privy to Sir Robert Fletcher's Mutiny, but was Very Dexterous in getting out of it, and I believe the whole treasury of Moorshidabad could not satisfy his Greed.' Don, in spite of speedy promotion, had been chiefly in Madras, and the pickings there had not been so frequent or so lucrative.

The course of events that had aroused the envy of Colonel John Don were a source of heartfelt pleasure to Mrs. Captain Archy Campbell. Mrs. Campbell, on the death of her relative, had inherited the estate of Barrill, and Barrill on her demise was to descend to her second son Archibald and his heirs, and thereafter to whomsoever Archibald might devise. This was satisfactory to Archibald, and Scipio, who might least have been pleased with the arrangement, wrote to congratulate his lame brother.

Captain Archy's dear Joann was now a person of importance, and the slender, blonde woman took the reins of government in her long slim hands. She was queen of Barrill and vicereine of Duisk, and the position suited admirably her habits of rule. She did not care for the house of Duisk, which with the influence of new ideas seemed mean and antiquated, and preferred her own home across the loch, a two-storied gabled building standing white against its lambrequin of firs. To Peggy MacLachlan she committed the care of Duisk House.

Mrs. Captain Archy knew as much as was ever likely to be known about the events of that night at Kilblaan when her husband and the fiar of Uillian were murdered. As a Campbell born and wed she hated the MacLachlans, and as a properly married woman she had hated Peggy Bheag MacLachlan.

In Joann's mind Peggy Bheag was an enemy to Clan Campbell and a traitress to her sex. But with the years Captain Archy had become a pleasant memory reincarnated in the stalwart figures of his sons, and the accession to estate had softened the intolerance of her outlook if it had not quite eradicated it, for she realized that the fiar of Uillian's marriage to Peggy Bheag might have jeopardized the prospects of her own sons. Certainly Colin Buie had left Duisk with a preference for heirs male, but there was no guarantee that he would have done that had his eldest son had a daughter only, and a marriage between Neil and Peggy Bheag at any time would have legitimated the daughter, who in any case would have inherited Uillian, which would have passed to Neil on his mother's death. Mrs. Captain Archy had placed no great credence on the report of the fiar's courtship of Stucguie's daughter, for Neil, in spite of his burly exterior, was a sentimentalist, and tender hearted.

She could regard Peggy Bheag's daughter, therefore, with benignness, sure that events had prevented the young woman from an inheritance to the benefit of her own sons. This feeling was nourished by the unassuming demeanour of young Peggy, and Mrs. Campbell was not displeased to note the undoubted lineaments of the dead Neil in the young woman's face. Never once did she discuss the parentage, either with Peggy or anyone else, but the exceptional favour she showed spoke equal to words and had its repercussion on everyone in the neighbourhood, for an increase of respect was accorded to both women.

Sometimes as an afterthought, Mrs. Campbell would speak of her sons to Peggy. She was eminently proud of them and the manner in which they were ratifying the ambitious tenets of their clan. Archibald Crubach had married first. His wife, Sophia Gordon, had brought her husband the Aberdeenshire property of Drumgesk, and with her powerful kin backing him, his prospects were assured.

Colin Ban, whose naval career commenced with the frustrated attack on St. Malo and the victory of Quiberon Bay, had since seen considerable service on the Spanish coast, in the West Indies and North America. He had married at the age of nineteen, his wife, Elizabeth Campbell, of a Cantire stock, being ten years older than himself. The first outburst of surprise and anger following this match was assuaged by the later knowledge of the considerable influence the lady exerted through her mother's people, friendly with Lord Bute.   Colin Ban had justified his ancestry.

Three children had been born of this union, Elizabeth, Janet, and Leonie.   The first two had been named after Campbell spinsters of whom much was expected, and the youngest had received her name in honour of a peeress powerful at court, and for these facts Mrs. Captain Archy willingly surrendered her own wish for a little Joann.

These worldly successes were incense to the ageing mother, and her sole regret was that Archibald Crubach had no children to inherit Barrill and Drumgesk—particularly the latter, which must otherwise pass from the Campbells—and that Scipio had not chosen to marry.   Mrs. Captain Archy could be magnanimous on this last point, as she had a better house of her own.   Yet she would read extracts of Scipio's letters to Peggy, translating them into Gaelic as she went along, and Peggy, listening raptly to accounts of battles and functions and foreign courts, would ask herself if this Scipio Campbell was the Scipio Campbell that she had known.

She thought : " What would Joann Campbell of Barrill there, turning old, with her gold hair whitening and her cheeks falling in, think if she were to know that I might have been Scipio's wife ?   What would she think ? "   Peggy's thoughts would revert often to his return in that wild ride, and his dreadful speech all night, his shuddering speech ; to the deep melancholia of the weeks thereafter and his abstracted talk and manner ; and to his quick resolve to leave Duisk, the relief in his last backward glance.   He was seldom far from her thoughts. She would tremble, thinking of the dangers he would be encountering. To his letters she looked forward as much as his mother did, and would have been affronted had that woman not revealed their contents to her.

Yet, Peggy reflected, she had refused his offer, and might refuse it again. And might not. In the last weeks of his stay she had been a nurse to him more than anything else; a comforter, strong in pity and consolation. She might refuse him again. And she might not. She could not dismiss the handsome Scipio from her thoughts.

He, after service in the Seven Years' War, had been in India long enough to amass a fortune. Thereafter he had been stationed in the West Indies, and finally, in the war in America distinguished himself at Bunker's Hill, New York, and Ticonderoga. And from America came instructions for the demolition of Duisk House and the erection of a mansion suitable for the rank and affluence of its owner.

Scipio's arrangements were completed through an agent in London working in association with an Edinburgh architect and the Duisk lawyer. Workmen appeared at Duisk; the old home of the attainted MacLachlans was removed stone by stone. A new house, stone by stone, rose in its place.

It was a grey, three-story, smooth-stone building with wings. Above the pilastered frontage of the main block was a pediment containing a carved achievement of the arms of Campbell of Duisk, and along the roof ran a balustrade. The stone-work of the ground floor was rusticated.

Two broad drives were constructed that led from

gate lodges on the main road and converged in a gentle sweep before the door.   A high wall was raised that separated the private grounds from the road and continued partly up the hill.   An extension to the old garden was made ; gazebos and arbours and a doric temple were erected in it, and the whole walled off.

Plaster workers appeared in the mansion and left beautiful ceilings behind them.   Mantelpieces of marble arrived, and cart-loads of rare and beautiful furniture.

An artist came from Edinburgh and made a full-length painting of Mrs. Captain Campbell, dressed in a white satin dress, her hand resting on a classic urn, a spaniel at her feet and a landscape in the rear that clearly showed the new Duisk House.

The country people walked from twenty miles distant to see this wonderful house.   There were twenty-six rooms in it, they said with hushed voices. It was finer than Lochgair, finer than Barbreck. Surely there was not another house in the county like it, save the Duke's.

Peggy was vexed.   She regretted the passing of the old house of the MacLachlans.   As a relative of that family, she had felt a proprietary interest in it.   But more than that, she knew that the man who proposed to occupy this large house could not be the Scipio Campbell she had known.

Contemplating this solid proof of her family's prosperity Mrs. Captain Archy sometimes shed tears of joy.   She wrote to all her friends about it, and when it was finished Archibald Crubach took the opportunity of some business in Glasgow to make a hasty visit to it.   He was not over-impressed.   His own house of Drumgesk was almost as fine, and he could have named twenty others offhand that were better. But he was glad that the head of the family should be well housed.

Scipio then wrote announcing the fact of his marriage.

The lady's name was Cydalise Cœur-de-roi. She was of French West Indian family, of Martinique, and had been living temporarily in Philadelphia when he met her in 1777, immediately after the capture of that town by Generals Howe and Cornwallis. She was, he informed his mother, a young lady of elegant manners and attractions, amiable and accomplished, and he had no dearer hope than the felicity of presenting her to her mother-in-law. Mrs. Scipio Campbell, he added, was of an ancient French family, of the Armagnac, and a near relative of the Vicomte Cœur-de-roi de Montauban, the Duc de Rocamadour, and the Marquis de Ferney des Ilettes.

Mrs. Captain Archy's pride and pleasure knew no bounds.

When Peggy was advised of the letter's contents a stound of anguish pierced her like a dagger. Although she had refused Scipio she had never imagined that he would marry anyone else, and she thought of this strange woman with a jealous dislike. She knew little about France except that Prince Tearlach had gone back to live there and that the English Government was constantly at war with it, but someone had once told her that Frenchwomen were very beautiful. Although she bore the news impassively she felt fit to weep, and at the first opportunity stole up to the drawing-room of the new

mansion, in which she was installed as housekeeper.
Long mirrors stretched from floor to ceiling.

She saw a dark-skinned, grave-eyed woman with
black hair drawn back from the forehead ; a woman
plainly, neatly dressed in black ; plainly shod ; grey
hair streaking a little at the temples and lines showing
under the eyes.

For a long time she watched her reflection dumbly,
and then turned away with an exclamation of dismay
and resignation. As she descended the stair to her
proper quarters—the kitchen quarters—she counted
the years since Scipio Campbell had clasped her at
the burn, and remembered with hopeless acquiescence
that it was twenty years gone.

THREE

I

IN the summer of 1782 a light, strongly-built calash drawn by two black horses dashed out from the West Port of Edinburgh and was soon passing swiftly over the road that led through Hollowtown to Glasgow and the west.

A low-swung chaise was at that moment rumbling out of Glasgow, with four bay horses harnessed thereto, and was making for the road to Dumbarton.

And a large spacious coach at the same time left London by the great north road. Four white horses were harnessed to it, frolicsome beasts; this coach was preceded by an outrider armed to the teeth, and on the box beside the driver was a footman, also armed. These horses went like the wind.

There was one similarity in these three vehicles. On the door panels were blazoned the same coat of arms: a shield with gold and black gyrons, and the crest of a boar's head.

In the light calash sat Archibald Crubach Campbell, a senator of the College of Justice by the style of Lord Drumgesk. The Crubach was a judge of Session at the age of forty-four, a post to which his extensively cultivated connections and the brilliant parts that he had inherited from his grandfather largely contributed. He had the handsome large features of his race, but his mouth was thin and cruel, his eyes maliciously appraising, his usual expression coarse and derisive. He had sent many men to the gallows in his short judicial time. Sophia Gordon, his wife, a stout imposing woman of plain features, sat by his side.

They spoke but slightly, and in time the lady began to doze from the motion of the vehicle. She would waken occasionally with a start, prodding out her elbows, to the annoyance of her husband. He grinned irritably.

"What's wrang wi' you?" he asked. "You're aye hotching."

The chaise jogging out of Glasgow held a stout, contemptuous-faced man with a skin ruddy from exposure to the elements and hard drinking. He was elegantly dressed, with a touch of conscious dandyism, and his periwig was a small and confidential creation with rolled side-curls and carefully powdered. There was some powder on his face as well, critically applied to conceal the confession of bloatedness, and also rouge, and the effect was purple and negative. By his side was a thin and hook-nosed woman who talked interminably in a high-pitched, complaining voice, sometimes addressing the man by her side, and occasionally throwing a sentence to a plainly-dressed female servant sitting opposite. The lady was adorned with a quantity of jewellery and wore fine silks. Her gestures had a manner of breeding. She was ten years older than the man by her side, and none would have credited it now, for the man looked sixty-two rather than forty-two. She was Elizabeth Campbell, and he was her husband, Colin Campbell, admiral of the blue.

Meantime, the four fiery white horses were bearing their coach through English country.

Mrs. Captain Archy had crossed over from Barrill House to supervise the preparations for the return of her eldest son and the reunion of the family consequent on it. Under her critical eye girls had been engaged to form a household staff under Peggy MacLachlan, shy silent bare-footed creatures who had never known a word of English. Mrs. Captain Archy thought of them with some misgivings. " But in the West Indies I suppose the black slaves will not wear shoes," she reflected.

With profound disappointment she learned that Scipio's arrival would be delayed by a fortnight; he had been detained in London because of some arrangements connected with the change of ministry. The reason was flattering to her maternal feelings, but she recollected that her other sons were bound to arrive first, and that seemed a bad omen as well as giving the host the ridiculous experience of being received by his guests. But it was now too late to do anything. Archibald Crubach could doubtless have been notified in time, but Colin was coming from London and might be anywhere on the road.

The proud old woman's heart beat high. The public advancement of her sons had been phenomenal. They had explored every avenue of influence for promotion and had deserved it by their own talents. Old Mrs. Campbell was no fool. She knew that there were many admirals and generals, and a good number of Session lords. They were probably of no great account in capital cities, nor in the ante-rooms of peers and ministers of State. But the cumulative

effect of those three personages passing within brief
time through Inveraray, through the capital of her
clan and county, and the rapidity with which the
news would travel into Lorn, and Cowal, and Knapdale, and Glenorchy, made her giddy with joy.

And she had taken care that Poltalloch, and
Inverliever, and Asknish, and all the other neighbours should know of the high races with which
her daughter-in-law was connected—" equal," she
said, " in descent and importance to the Campbells,"
for she would not belittle her own stock in dilating
on that of others.

Colin and his wife were first. A few hours later
Drumgesk and his wife arrived. " Whaur's Skip ? "
he demanded easily, while his mother fussed about
him in the entrance hall. " He'll hae taen a fleg
ower his French madame." He smiled and nodded
in the direction of his wife. " She's fattening, is
she no' ? But she comes of a fat stock."

The mother had seen the judge and his spouse
frequently, and had visited them in Edinburgh, but
Mrs. Colin and she were less acquaint. There was
much mutual satisfaction in reunion. All these
people were pleased with themselves and pleased with
one another. Their careers and interests did not
conflict. The brothers Campbell had always maintained an affectionate interest in each other's progress, and in their family dealings they dropped the
cruelty and inhumanity that had made them detested
in their respective professions. Their mother and
their wives belonged to one class ; women of landed
race, proud and sure of themselves, with an old-
fashioned standard of conduct and outlook. The

minds of Mrs. Captain Campbell, Mrs. Admiral Campbell, and Lady Drumgesk (whose titular appellation came from her estate and not from her husband) however much they might deviate in individualism and however dissimilar they looked, ran in the one groove of tradition.

On the first day the new house was inspected from cellar to attic, and full reports of the admiral's grown daughters who had been left in London were obtained. On the second day a tour of the policies was made, and it was agreed that the late laird's planting was giving them a very mature appearance. On the third day Scipio and his wife arrived.

The roll of wheels, the jingle of harness . . . Mrs. Captain Archy hurried down the stairs, careless of her sixty-seven years. Peggy opened the door. A great scraping of hoofs on the gravel, and a great yellow face at the coach window . . . the door of the coach was opened and the yellow-faced man stepped out.

He assisted a lady to descend, and turned then to kiss his mother's hand, but the old lady threw her arms around him and sobbed her joy. He then introduced his wife to his mother ; the younger lady curtsied low. Two children of about four years were standing wide-eyed in the rear, in the care of a negress.

Peggy stood in the shadow of the door and watched them all.

Major-General Scipio Campbell ascended the steps, supporting his mother on one side, his wife doing the same on the other. The stamp of identity bequeathed by the founder of the family was on his

face : the big nose and jutting chin, the high arched
eyebrows. And, like his kin, his lips had shaped
into a hard and narrow line, but his glance was clear
and challenging. His skin was dry and parchment-
coloured, and the yellow tinge was emphasised by his
powdered hair. Major-General Campbell was wearing the uniform of his rank, richly decorated and
adorned.

As the remaining members of the family appeared
and surrounded the travellers with words of welcome
and congratulation the entrance hall was a stage of
curtsey and bow, and there was loud guffaw and
smiles and runs of laughter. A strange fragrance
permeated the hall; it was the delicate aroma of
perfume, the first that Peggy MacLachlan had ever
sensed, for the Campbell ladies never used it. She
closed the door after admitting the black woman
and her young charges and a fair slender girl who
addressed some words to her which she did not
understand. There were a dozen people in the hall,
nine of them talking. Peggy gazed her fill of the
general's wife.

Mrs. Scipio Campbell had loosened her travelling
pelisse of ermine and grey silk, revealing the grey
silk dress beneath it. She was a girl in her early
twenties, of moderate height and slender figure, and
she did not fulfil the accepted convention of the
creole. She was dark-haired, and had small full lips
and a small delicately shaped nose. Her skin was
of a peculiarly golden transparent hue, as though
illuminated from within, and its strange charm was
marred by the rouge she had applied near her cheek
bones. At once the deep cleft in her pointed chin

and her eyes attracted attention to Cydalise ; the eyes were grey and specked with amber ; in repose they had a fixed attentive stare, as though observing an object some hundreds of yards in front, and it was then that the pupils seemed to contract to pin points.

She was richly and fashionably dressed, and now, as she moved from one to another in a mood of excitement, she appeared scarce to touch the floor.

" And, madame ! " she exclaimed, and presented the little children to their grandmother.

" Well, Skip," said Drumgesk, " you were late in starting, but you got the better of me. When we kenned it was twins ! There's many a good tune played on an auld fiddle."

Mrs. Captain Archy bent down to kiss the children on the forehead, and they returned her caress affectionately. " Nice nice lady," said the boy.

The admiral burst into a sudden roar of laughter, and the others followed his amused glance to the figure of the meek and portly negress.

" That's Juno," Scipio's harsh-timbred voice explained. " The children could not bear to part with her. She is a Virginian, and I called her Juno after my old pointer bitch that died the week before I bought her. She's always a reminder of it."

Cydalise was being escorted to her room, and her husband, following, turned with pride to survey the proportions of the hall and its classic columns. His glance then fell on Peggy. He stood still, in indecision, and then he shook her hand. " Are you keeping well, Peggy ? " he said kindly. " We have lost some youth and gained some years." But observing that she did not understand, he said,

surprised : " *Ciamar a tha sibh, Peggy* ? " [1] and asked
if she had no English.

" *Cha'n eil*," [2] she said, with a new sense of inferiority, and stared at him full of bewildered resentment. She had no English ! But why should she
need English at Duisk, and why should its lack give
her this feeling before those people who had always
spoken the Gaelic to her ?

Colin was calling on him from the landing. The
general spoke a few words more in the native tongue
and then followed in the wake of the others. Dumbly
she watched the big resplendent figure ascend the
stair. Could that be Scipio Campbell ?

II

" Scipio was gey dull after the lang journey,"
Drumgesk remarked to his wife that night.

" What do you think of her ? " she asked him.

" She's gey Frenchified," he said, after a thought.
He chuckled deeply. " Gin Colin runs short he can
aye fa' back on her cosmetics. Losh, woman !—a
sailor o' the King's rouged like an auld duchess ! "

" She's a handsome woman," said the lady.

" Tach ! " said his lordship. " Gie me a woman
wi' a Scots face and a Scots tongue . . . and yin o'
the clan Gordon at that. Colin's easy wark for a
pouthered face."

" You'll mind to wear thick hose the morn, Archy,"
said his wife with anxious affection.

" Hout, ye fule," said the judge easily.

The admiral, after seeing his brothers retire, had

---

[1] *Ciamar a tha sibh :* How are you ?
[2] *Cha'n eil :* I have not.

paced upon the terrace, for he liked the fresh air
and a smoke before bed. The night in these Highland hills, drenched as they were in silence, fascinated
him doubly because of his long absences from them.
At last he went to his room, and found his wife still
making her preparations for retiring.

" Well, mam," he said affectionately, " and is the
room to your taste ? " He placed his wig on a stand
and commenced to take off his coat.

" What do you think of her ? " Elizabeth asked in
her high querulous manner.

" My mother," said Colin, " thank God, is as well
as ever she was."

" But Mrs. Scipio ! "

" Oh—her ! " said her husband. " Well, mam,
every man to his taste."

Mrs. Colin regarded her thin features in the table
mirror.

" I hope," said the admiral gravely, as he un-
buttoned his waistcoat, " that Archy doesn't try any
indecent flirtations with her. He is too fond of a
new face—a man of his rank and position ! "

She looked at him gratefully. " Do you think
she is pretty ? I think she is."

" Any milliner or opera girl looks as well," said
Colin, removing his shoes. " As I said, every man
to his taste, and I prefer a lady of rank and breeding."

Mrs. Scipio Campbell appeared on the next morning
like a slender beam of sunshine. When first her
mother-in-law saw her Cydalise was gazing at the
full-length painting of Mrs. Captain Archy which
Scipio had so suddenly commissioned, and the old
woman was gratified by the young woman's praise

of it. Mrs. Captain Campbell endorsed thoroughly her son's choice of a wife. Cydalise had a distinguished if not a commanding presence, and her birth was equally of distinction.

The red-haired Mor Campbell of Uillian had been succeeded by the blonde-haired Joann Campbell of Barrill, and now the dark-haired Cydalise Cœur-de-roi was lady of Duisk. Mrs. Captain Archy had once hoped that Scipio would choose a Campbell, but now she saw no ground for complaint with his choice.

Already Cydalise had brought two young Campbells into existence, and Mrs. Captain Archy knew that in the course of nature there would be more.

" What's your name, sir ? " Drumgesk demanded gruffly of the timid-eyed four-year-old boy.

" Francey," said the child, shrinking.

" What ! " the judge exclaimed.

" François was the name of my wife's father," the general explained. " He has my own name as a second name. Emmeline is called after Lady Lexborough, whose husband's interest is invaluable."

" Well, Skip," said Archy, after a pause, " there wouldnae hae been muckle harm in remembering your father and mother, surely. There's nae Campbell smell in these names."

And, he added to himself, no Campbell brawn either ; for the little twins were pale-skinned, delicate creatures, nervously chattersome, and seldom happy away from the stolid, big-bosomed Juno. The mother was a favourite, nevertheless, and often spent an hour in the nursery, where she told them stories and conversed with them, using French in her speech to Juno that they might absorb that language.

But with her new relatives she conversed in perfect English, with a slurring accent that kept attention to her words. At table the talk was animated and lively. Mrs. Scipio and her two brothers-in-law found many common topics of discussion. With Colin she could discuss West Indian life and her native island of Martinique—which he had once assisted to bombard. Archibald Crubach was fond of French literature, and there he found Cydalise intelligent, and willing for instruction. Her mother-in-law had surrendered the premier position without demur ; Cydalise presided with a dignity that was peculiarly her own.

In the evenings the ladies sat by themselves and discussed various topics of conversation. Mrs. Colin had many friends in London and at court ; but Cydalise was unacquainted with them. She did not know any of the great Campbell ramifications, and Mrs. Colin was surprised at that, especially when Cydalise confessed that she thought her husband's family might be like her own, small and select. Lady Drumgesk retailed to her items of fact connected with the society of Edinburgh, which was greatly occupied with etiquette and dealt largely in genealogy. Cydalise listened courteously.

" You will remember, mam," said Mrs. Admiral Campbell to Mrs. Captain Campbell, " Georgiana Campbell, the daughter of old Gortonronach ? Her mother was of Stronalbanach's family, a daughter of old Dugald who had the lawsuit for Drimnaguie, but the Campbells of Bellachroy proved their right to be nearest heirs male."

" Wasna she a sister of Colin, of the Argyll

Regiment, who slauchtered Captain Loverance on
Leith Links ? " Lady Drumgesk inquired. " I've
heard Drumgesk come ower the story, for he tried
the case when it came afore the Fifteen."

" Gortonronach's younger brother married Margaret Baldalo, of the Riccarton family, and the
title would have fallen to her had not the fifth lord
taken the field on the wrong side and been
attainted. The fourth Lord Riccarton's mother was
Ann Campbell of the Glenorchy district, a near
friend of my own and connected with the Campbells
of Glenlyon. I think her brother Donnachie went
to Jamaica. Maybe you've heard of a Duncan
Campbell in Jamaica, mam. He wouldn't be far from
you," said Mrs. Captain Campbell to Mrs. General
Campbell.

" No, madame. I did not meet him."

" You were right, mam, about the murder of
Captain Loverance," said Mrs. Admiral Campbell to
Lady Drumgesk, " and it was all because of Captain
Loverance's connection with Murray of Broughton,
whatever it was. But I know there was some
rumour connecting it with Lord Dumbarton, then
living in France. Of course, the Dumbarton peerage
is dead now, and I suppose the last lord had a weari-
some time—perhaps some of your friends in France
knew Lord Dumbarton, mam. He would be well
known there, I daresay."

" Perhaps, madame. I have not heard them speak
of him."

During these talks Mrs. Captain Archy knitted,
and the admiral's wife did crochet work. Lady
Drumgesk preferred sewing, keeping beside her a

large Cumnock-hinged snuff-box to which she had
frequent recourse.

Before retiring, the four ladies generally played
quadrille for a time.

On arrival at Duisk the general's coach, apart from
himself and his lady and the children, had brought
the negress, the slender fair girl who was the lady's
French maid, and the general's man-servant. Now
appeared a further detachment which included a
man-cook of London birth, a governess-teacher for
the children, and a great number of boxes which
contained a portion of the lady's wardrobe. Cydalise
appeared in perpetual changes of attire ; each day
revealed a new creation in silk, or muslin, or satin.

Mrs. Captain Campbell was anxious that the young
woman should be instructed in the supervision of
the household and dairy, and suggested that an early
day be fixed for initiation into these details. Cydalise
evinced some surprise at these requirements, but
contented herself with a vague promise of attention.
Her mother-in-law, with kindly seriousness, persisted.

" Later, madame," Cydalise said.

Some festivities had been proposed in the way of
housewarming, and they were to occur soon, for the
two younger brothers could not hope to remain at
Duisk indefinitely. The reunion of the families had
been carefully arranged in honour of the new house,
but Drumgesk particularly had work awaiting him.
A bevy of local lairds and ladies appeared for dinner.
The ladies, after leaving their lords, made conversation with Scipio's wife. They were mostly
Argyllshire women of proud extraction and plain
living, and some of them had never been out of the

county. They did not conceal easily their curiosity in Scipio's wife nor their wonder at her splendid gown. The conversation lagged. After a time it was renewed ; local topics were discussed, local alliances and deaths, and Cydalise latterly found herself to be the only person who was not speaking.

Meantime the male guests were drinking and grew drunk. The general boasted of the beauty of his wife. A neighbour declared that he could have found handsomer on the Braes of Lorn.

" Have you seen my wife ? " said Scipio scornfully. " Here ! " he shouted to the servant, " inform Mrs. Campbell to come down."

Cydalise showed alarm at the summons. She passed quickly into the dining-room, to confront through a haze of smoke a line of staring faces. Scipio commanded her to come closer. When she did so, slowly, he placed an arm around her waist. " There," he declared with a hiccough, " is the finest woman in the world," and he added a compliment which was an insult.

Cydalise, on leaving them, ran up the stairs and past the drawing-room and up to her own apartment. But before reaching it she paused, holding to the balustrade, and stood for a little, thinking. And then she returned to the ladies. Mrs. Captain Archy had been apprehensive, and inquired if Scipio was unwell.

" It is nothing, madame," was the reply. " He is as usual."

There was no man fit to go home that night, and hurried arrangements were made for providing the visiting ladies with accommodation. The men guests remained in the dining-room as they had fallen. Drumgesk and the admiral retired in a state of tipsy exaltation. Scipio was carried to his room, intoxicated.

On the day following life in the house resumed its usual routine, and the first week of reunion at Duisk had passed.

" Did I mention," said the general suddenly, " that I met Jock Don in London ? You mind Jock Don ? " He was surprised by the savage spasm that crossed Drumgesk's face. It was there, and then had vanished.

" Aye," said the judge. " He lamed me."

" Old Cambus Don made Jock," said Colin. " And Jock's a general officer."

" He is home on furlough," said Scipio. " He made a name for himself in Yorktown, I believe."

" He made a nickname for me at Duisk," said Drumgesk. " It will outlast my reputation and out-live his."

" Did you meet him ? " Mrs. Captain Archy asked Cydalise. The young lady said no. " He is my nephew," said the old lady, " but the Dons don't come to Duisk."

" As a matter of fact," Scipio said, " I felt sorry for him—he seemed lonely. I invited him here, and he should be due soon."

In the lower regions of the house Peggy Mac-Lachlan presided, at a wage of four pounds a year. At the one long table in the kitchen the staff took their meals, and, seated at the head of it, Peggy sat dumb with misery. Some curious skirmishes had taken place under her eyes which she had not understood and was not greatly curious about; they concerned precedence, and the net result of the battles was that the French maid Antoinette, the Englishwoman named Barrett who was the children's governess, and the general's valet John Gray, a native of Fife, sat nearest her, none of whom could speak a word intelligible to her. Barrett and Gray had at first shown some resentment at being seated with the Highland servants, but latterly lowered their dignity and quarrelled with each other with some zest. The former had an additional grievance, as she should have had her meals in the nursery, she thought; but there the children were too powerful for her, and ate happily in the presence of the shining-faced motherly Juno.

Of those strange intruders Peggy felt most liking for the girl Antoinette, a fragile creature, willing to please, and often they conversed feebly in a language of signs and smiles. Antoinette was the loneliest of all at Duisk; apart from her mistress, only Juno and the children could understand her. Juno was in her way a linguist, having in some fashion picked up a knowledge of French and English, and a little Spanish.

The building of Duisk House had seemed a strange and ominous change to Peggy, but the correlative result, as now before her, was cataclysmic. A tradition, a system, and a creed of life were shattered.

The old Duisk had been the hub of a little kingdom, the heart beat of a domain. The long, low house and its clustering farm steading had typified the life patriarchal, where the laird met his retainers and dependants in dignified and mutually respectful inter-

course. Of the time of Colin Buie she had few
memories of her own, but she had heard during many
a winter *ceilidh* of the old man's assured sway, and
long back in Morvern her mother had spoken of
the times in Uillian when Mor Campbell had been
there and Neil the fiar, and of Duisk before the
MacLachlans had lost it.

And now this great square house stood in place
of its thatched predecessor, and broad drives led
to its portal, and the farm buildings had been razed
and replaced by a quadrangular stable with a clock
tower, and a new steading built a thousand yards
away and out of sight of the house. And around the
grounds—grounds! what was the need for grounds?
—a high wall had been erected to keep people out.

And strange English-speaking people had arrived
as servants : coachmen and footmen and valets who
tried to be free with the Highland girls. And they
all touched their hats when they spoke to Scipio
Campbell, and called him ' sir '. ' Sir '—that was
one English word she had learned the meaning of.
Sasunnachs, with their mean servile ways! Peggy
thought of them with contempt. Scipio Campbell to
her was Scipio Campbell; either that or Duisk.

And there, inside Duisk House, were miraculous
carpets and pictures and mirrors; and everything
was light and airy, and there was a hush that must
be preserved at all costs. And she, who might have
been the *bean-an-tighe* of the old Duisk, was the
housekeeper of the new one!

The very furnishings humiliated her, for she was
uncertain of some of their uses.

And what had happened to those three brothers

who had once used good Gaelic among themselves
and now did not choose to speak it.   They were
none of them old men, and yet they all looked so
old; old, proud, and domineering.   She could recollect the new lamed Archy, not yet called crubach,
crossing from Barrill in a rowing boat, and cursing
fretfully.   She could remember Colin, running wild
about the shore.   And one was Drumgesk, with his
grim, drunken, sarcastic face; and the other was
stout, proud, drunken, and an admiral.

And Scipio.   She remembered his irresolution in
the hall, and his handshake, and treasured the
moment.   He had spoken to her several times since,
in the old tongue, which he had forgotten a little,
and he sometimes puzzled for the right word.   But
he had asked kindly for her comfort, thanked her
in a grand yet simple manner for the care she had
taken of the house, and said that his mother had
mentioned her frequently in her letters.   It was then
the old Scipio she had known who had spoken.   Yet
the night before she had seen him in his fine clothes
being carried dead drunk to his room, and he would
have choked had she not loosened his cravat.

She accepted his courtesy with humble thankful-
ness.   She was his servant, she told herself.   Yes,
she thought, with sudden fierce resentment, and his
cousin as well.

Scipio Campbell of Duisk !   She, *she* was Margaret
Campbell of Duisk, and of Uillian ; and Margaret
MacLachlan of Duisk, if necessary, and her forbears
had ruled these lands where she was a menial when
those Campbells had been scribbling on scraps of
parchment.   Campbell of Duisk !

Admirals, generals, judges ! and old Joann Campbell running about them with anxious pride like a
hen around a trio of hogsheads ! The dark-eyed
woman quivered, and then smiled with the satisfaction of secret knowledge. And they had brought
their coaches, and horses, and attendants of all kinds
and ages and nationalities and colours, and they had
brought the neighbourhood in to drink with them
and admire them, and they flaunted their fine clothes
and their rich jewels, and they brought their wives,
their wives, the pinched Campbell women of Cantire
and the fat *cailleach* of the Gordonach and this light
slender creature from the other side of the world,
this *bean-shith*, this mother of weakly brats, this
woman in golden silks and rose-coloured satins and
ermine wraps, this young thing who knew nothing
about a house and cared less, who stepped daintily
on the garden paths that had been made for her,
and who left the rich food placed before her un-
touched, who had been seen early in the grey dawn
sitting at her window, who was so proud that she
spoke to none unless they spoke to her, who had
everything that the world could give or that a woman
or a wife could demand, who was so young, and who
must be so evil, and who was beautiful.

Mrs. Scipio Campbell ! who had descended the
stairs one day alone and met her face to face . . .
coming down the stairs, slowly, lest she stain her rich
soft draperies, and who had stopped and stared with
her strange proud stare and spoken in her foreign
tongue.

"What race is this of mine," thought the dark-
eyed woman angrily, " that the rich and the powerful

speak alien tongues, and even those of the *Gaidhealtachd* when they grow great ignore their own ?
Surely it is slaves that we are when our tongue is
fit only for the herdboy or the shepherd, and when
strange people come into our land expecting us
to know their tongues and scoff because we do
not ! ''

Mrs. Scipio Campbell ! standing there in the
shadow of the passage with pearls around her neck
and the red glow high on her cheek-bones and the
scent on her shining attire, to be met with Gaelic
words, and to turn away and ascend the stair again,
and sit with her white hands on her lap and the
false smile on her evil, beautiful face !

III

General Don paced the stone quay at the Rudha
to pass the time until a supper was prepared for him.

He had but disembarked from the Greenock packet,
and after engaging a room at a near inn had passed
out to breathe a fresher air.

The tall slender figure in the bottle-green redingote
and the shining top boots who picked his careful
way with the aid of a cane was a subject for surmise
to the fishermen loitering on the quay.

The air was chilly, and cold gusts swept up Loch
Fyne, spreading a ruffled surface on the waves. The
hills were changing to their velvet black mantles
of the night, and near-by in the village where the smell
of fish was heavy on the salt air dim cruisie lights
were glowing against the darkness.

A man detached himself from the group and came
forward diffidently to the soldierly figure. '' Is it

Colin Buie's grandson ? " he asked. " I was at Duisk, then, at the farm."

In the years Don had been at Duisk with his mother and her father he had learned his Gaelic, and he had not forgotten it. He spoke to the questioner pleasantly, asking after his well-being, and commented on his own long absence.

" There have been changes at Duisk, I was hearing," said the man, and he told Don about the new house and the new lady who had come to rule it.

" I met General Campbell and he told me of his marriage," said the officer. " I have not met Mrs. Campbell."

" And your mother," said the man with the natural courtesy of his kind. " Will we not be seeing your good mother again in the district ? "

" I don't think," said the general, " that Mrs. Don will care to travel so far."

In the morning he obtained a little horse for the seventeen-mile ride to his destination. General Don travelled alone, for the frugal habits of his early upbringing had remained with him. He had come directly from Edinburgh, where he had visited his mother and heaped money and presents on her, for this conscienceless rogue, who had used his profession as a means of personal aggrandisement at all costs, had a deep and simple affection for the cold hard woman who had borne him.

The tall slender man had been evolved by the rigours of soldiering and the refining influence of politer pursuits from the bully-faced youth of yore. The bully face remained, and was badly scarred by small-pox, but it had been moulded by the habit of command and lightened by cynicism. General Don had sloughed the drawbacks of a sullen youth and passed triumphantly in the ardours of war and genteel gallantry.

Now as he left the salt loch behind him and pressed rapidly to Kilmichael and the Sceótnish valley his face was shaded by the recollection of vanished days and darkened by a thought of bitterness. In time, he grew amused, and laughed. " The big Hieland stot ! " he said aloud.

As he rode beside the Add he saw two figures ahead of him ; an old man and a young. He glanced at them in passing and drew up, gazing at the elder man with a look of gladness.

" Do you remember me, Uncle Dugald ? " he said, and raised his hat. " I am John Don."

The old man's cheeks flushed and his eyes glittered. " I remember you ! " he said. He raised his stick menacingly. " Go you on your road, from me and mine. It is an ill day when the hawks gather."

Don was silent, and looked intently at the speaker. Then, checking the words that had risen to his tongue, he laughed and put his horse to the gallop.

Mrs. Captain Archy's vexation had been great when she learned of the invitation to Janet Don's son, and although she felt that the moment was inopportune for protest and that she had no longer any say in the choice of guests at Duisk, her annoyance was none the less sensed by her son. The admiral was indifferent ; as the youngest of the brothers he had never had much reason for dislike of the Dons. Drumgesk was silent on the matter.

But they all mustered a show of welcome when

the general made his unimposing appearance on his tired and dusty hack. From a window Scipio had announced his cousin's approach with an explosion of laughter. And the sight of Don, walking his exhausted little beast at a slow pace up the approach, was not imposing. They crowded to the door.

"But where's Sancho Panza ? " demanded my lord of the visitor.

Any hostility that Mrs. Captain Archy had cherished disappeared in the gallantry of Don's salutations and his solicitude for her health. His profound courtesy created an immediate impression upon the ladies, and the critical brothers inwardly admitted that Don was a fine gentleman. Standing in their midst his height was increased by the slenderness they had not got ; his manners were easy, his mien composed.

"I did not imagine," said Elizabeth Campbell to her husband that night, " that your cousin General Don was a gentleman of such elegance and refinement."

"He was telling me," replied the admiral with some animation, " that old Lord Cambus Don died last week. This gives Jock a vote in Midlothian, and Mr. Dundas will be anxious to know him. I wonder if Jock could be of use to us. If Elizabeth is going to marry Otway, mam, his interests could be better promoted by two men than one, and Jock's word would supplement mine."

Lady Drumgesk, on retiring, remarked to her husband : "They say that Cambus Don's estate is worth ten thousand, land and money. General Don is a man of breeding and refinement, Archy. Is it Craig's Close where his mother resides ? "

H

" Aye," said the judge, " and we'll let her bide
there."

" But, Archy——"

" It's an odd thing," said Lord Drumgesk thoughtfully, "how a nickname sticks to a body after a'
thae years."

Mrs. Captain Campbell had sent for Peggy before
retiring, relative to some arrangements for the day
to come. She was loquacious. General Don had
charmed her.

" You won't remember his mother, Peggy ? "

Peggy had seen her in the week of her arrival at
Duisk, but recollection of Mrs. Don had faded.

Mrs. Captain Archy checked some remark she was
about to make. " But the son is greatly changed,"
she said reflectively. " The army has altered him.
And he has inherited a considerable property from an
uncle. I wonder how that will affect his mother."
The old lady preened herself with satisfaction. " The
late laird would have been very pleased. Two
generals, an admiral, and a Session lord under one
roof, and all his grandsons !

" By the way, Peggy," she resumed with some
hesitation, " I was making a suggestion to Mrs.
Scipio that she might take over control . . . exercise
supervision over the household. In Martinique,
where Mrs. Scipio comes from, the ladies don't supervise as they do here. I suppose it is due to the
climate. My son explained as much to me, when I
remarked to him about it. And he explained our
Highland system to Mrs. Scipio." She paused, in
some uncertainty. " Mrs. Scipio at last assured me
of her willingness to oversee things. She tells me

that she descended to the kitchen quarters. Is it the case, Peggy ? ''

Peggy assented.

" Well," Mrs. Captain Campbell continued, " . . . of course, Mrs. Scipio speaks French and English, and, I understand, a little Latin and Greek. But of course she has no Gaelic. That is to be expected.

" She tells me, Peggy, that when she spoke to the housekeeper—to yourself, Peggy—that she spoke in English . . . was it English she used, Peggy ? ''

" I suppose it would be."

" And that you did not understand. Of course, it's very awkward. But the general and myself are very anxious that Mrs. Scipio should conform to our traditions, for although the general has seen so much of the world he has the old ways at heart, and they are the best ways ; and of course Mrs. Scipio did not fully realize at first what was required of her. She is a most distinguished young lady and will fall into our ways perfectly, but the customs of creole society are quite different. And of course I was disappointed when Mrs. Scipio told me of your inability to understand her. She made a strong point about that. I was thoroughly vexed, Peggy, as she had at last consented to do what was wished." The old lady looked at Peggy helplessly. " You understand, Peggy ? ''

Peggy understood.

" And of course," Mrs. Captain Archy proceeded incoherently, " the difficulty is to know what to do now."

" If Duisk's wife," said Peggy, " is not keen to be doing her duty as mistress of the house, or of doing what a proper wife should do, and is wishful to make me the reason for not doing her duty, it would be better for me to leave the house and you can get a woman in place of me who knows the English tongue."

" Not leave the house, Peggy," said the old woman decidedly. " That will never happen. But we could get another woman to act as housekeeper ; a woman with the English. And you could help her."

" My father's daughter will not wait here to be insulted," said Peggy fiercely, " nor to be made the fool by Scipio Campbell's wife."

" Peggy——" the old woman began tearfully.

" If she is a Campbell now, let her learn the Gaelic and be a proper Campbell. Let her get her bows and flattery from her foreign servants and not from those who lived in this country before she was born." She left the room stormily, the old lady's pleading words in her ears as she closed the door. " And that's Joann Campbell of Barrill," she thought bitterly, " who was the wise keen woman, and is now a coward and an ingrate." She ran down the stairs, her heart passionate with anger, and at the landing stood back to let the four gentlemen pass her on their way up. Their faces were inflamed by liquor ; Drumgesk was eructating. Don came last, and she glanced at him curiously. Another cousin ! Another of Colin Buie's successful breed, with fine clothes and an English tongue in his head. In her own room she stood, dark and sullen, and stared fiercely into the outer darkness. She felt lost. She thought forlornly of the days of her arrival at Duisk, and after the old laird had died, and when Scipio

Campbell had asked her to be his wife. That night
returned to her memory and she knew he must remember it. Those had been happy days, she thought
vaguely, and the memory of the low thatched house
of Duisk was pleasant in retrospect. She had been
a young thing then.

Her world had changed.

In the morning General Campbell came to her.
His eyes were red and heavy, and his breath was rank.
He inquired the state of her health with perfect
courtesy, and spoke for a moment or two about her
late mother.

" She was a fine woman," he said latterly. " Is
it Kilmichael she is in ? Kilneuair is it. Perhaps
you will allow me to place a stone to her memory,
and it could seem as if you had erected it."

" Dugald Leitch did that."

" He did ! " exclaimed Scipio. " And why, I
wonder."

" Perhaps," she said, " that was because his son
had died as suddenly as my father, and he felt a
sympathy for Peggy Bheag."

" Perhaps," said the general latterly. " My
mother," he said after a moment, " tells me that you
are displeased. I know the whole business, Peggy,
and I understand. Well, Peggy, there's no need for
you to worry——"

" I am not worrying, Duisk."

" I daresay not," he agreed. " You understand,
I won't permit a slight affair of this kind to cause
unkindness. You will do as you have been doing,
and that's all there is to it."

" I think, Duisk," she said, " I should go." She

watched him keenly while listening to his promises
and expostulations. " He is afraid," Peggy thought.
She consented ultimately to remain, and listened to
him tramping up the stone stair.

" She has beaten them all," she thought.

The French maid knocked at the door. She entered
brightly. " *Blath, blath,*" [1] she said in greeting.

Peggy smiled. " *Tha e blath an diugh,*" [2] she said
encouragingly. This young girl, at any rate, had
shown some spirit and gained much fun in picking
up a few of the words. But Antoinette's Gaelic was
exhausted there. She made some signs to suggest
that her mistress had a headache, and retired with a
bottle of vinegar.

" Yes ! " thought the dark-eyed woman, " if she
thought more of her house and did her duty she would
have fewer sore heads."

Upstairs, General Don was consolidating his con-
quest. That he was a charming and agreeable man
was felt by all the ladies, more so as he divided his
attentions with perfect equality, unlike their husbands, who had the habit of talking exclusively to
Cydalise. With Mrs. Captain Archy he spoke of old
days at Duisk as though there had never been any
friction ; with Lady Drumgesk he could discuss the
intimate details of Edinburgh society ; Mrs. Colin's
London friends he knew ; and he had been an attaché
at the British Embassy in Paris.

" Mrs. Scipio's uncle was a councillor of state there,"
said Mrs. Colin quickly. " Was he not, mam ? "

" Yes, madame."

[1] *Blath :* Warm.
[2] *Tha e blath an diugh :* It is warm to-day.

" Perhaps General Don made his acquaintance."

General Don looked from one to the other. " I know many of the French nobility," he said.

" He was Monsieur de Ferney des Ilettes," said Cydalise.

" Was it Monsieur Paul de Ferney or Monsieur Laurent de Ferney, madame ? "

" Monsieur Paul, sir."

" I knew him perfectly well, madame," said General Don. " His son, I remember, married Mademoiselle de Saint-Valery."

" Pardon, sir ; it was Mademoiselle de Saint-Verge."

" That is correct, madame," said Don. " It was Mademoiselle de Saint-Verge."

" You will feel quite at home now," her mother-in-law said smilingly to Cydalise, " as General Don is acquaint with your relatives."

" General Don," said Don, laughing, " ought in duty to make madame acquaint with his. Has madame not yet met the Leitches and the Mac-Tavishes ? "

Cydalise repeated the names mechanically.

" I expect," interrupted Scipio's harsh voice, " that the Leitches and MacTavishes are too much occupied with their own affairs to bother with us, just as we're too busy to bother with them."

IV

Cydalise walked in the garden.

From the high terrace nearest the hill she could see the loch very clearly and the hills beyond it, and, near-by, the big grey house.

Her dress was long and flowing ; it was of white

muslin, and a pale blue sash caught it in at the
waist. A large picture hat protected her face from
the sun.

She walked slowly, but did not stop, turning at
each end of the terrace and retracing her steps. The
day was oppressively hot ; the scents of the flowers
came to her in warm sensuous waves ; at inter-
vals there was the insistent humming of a questing
bee.

There was no expression on her face—there seldom
was, save in the moments when in company she
broke into quick, high laughter. But the set, intent,
distant look that was always there might have been
described as expression. Narrowing to the cleft chin
from the absorbed, amber-flecked eyes, her face
looked very young. The golden tint of the skin
exaggerated its softness and youth, but as usual the
high dabs of rouge on her cheeks made all allure
ridiculous.

She stopped at last, standing in the shadow of the
doric temple and looking lochwards. It was cooler
here ; there was shade, and the stonework seemed to
exhale a cold aura. She heard the click of a gate,
and looking through the window in the little building
she saw her sisters-in-law entering the garden.

In the path to which she fled there was privacy.
It was narrow and had been gravelled lately ; following it, she came to the burn, the Dubh Uisge that
had given the lands its name. It came down from
the hill-side in a clear, brown, transparent rush, full
of the spirit of the peat, leaping a little fall and
flowing rapidly.

Standing on the bridge and gazing at it she felt a

sense of peace. At no distance the burn was hidden by the tangled fern and bramble bush and brush-wood that bordered its descent. Bending over, she could discern the stony surface of its bed. Cydalise smiled to her distorted reflection. She glanced around her, still smiling; the sun was throwing brilliant shafts upon the water, dappling the grass with the shadows of the leaves. She saw her husband advancing along the path.

Scipio was wearing a red coat and white buck-skin breeches; his head was uncovered, and the heat had embellished the surface of his yellow face, making it shine.

" I wondered where you had gone. I was afraid you had lost yourself. Are you not tired, Cydalise ? "

" No; I am not tired."

" The ladies thought you were lost. You were away so long. They thought they saw you in the garden."

" I was there."

" Cydalise," he said abruptly, and she raised her eyes to his. " Are you not contented ? "

" I ? I am as contented as ever I was."

" I believe you ! "

Cydalise made a movement to return.

" At least," he said, " you could show more interest in the guests we have. You could show more gratitude for my mother's interest in you."

" Before I came here I knew very little of the name of Campbell and nothing of the name of Gordon. And because of that, because of that, your brothers' wives suspect that I have no name of my own. You bring General Don here, and madame your brother's wife would set a trap! But this has been from the beginning."

Scipio made an impatient gesture with his hand. "If that is all——"

"If that was all! I thought you would have resented these insults to your wife; I thought you would have preserved your own privilege there."

"By God, madam," he cried, "you make me pay for them."

"But why should I have expected you to resent them! Did you ever do so?"

"Cydalise," he said, and caught her arm, "we could be better friends than we are, I'm thinking."

"Ah yes," she said, turning her head away from his, it was so close, "but we cannot be, it seems."

"Cydalise, I have brought you here, proud of you, to the house I have built for you, and I have shown you with pride to all my friends."

"Yes; you did that."

"I have denied you nothing. I have done everything for you. Cydalise, if I said what was in my mind I would call you ungrateful."

"I am ungrateful."

"I want you to act like a wife, and not a *cocotte*."

"I was a *cocotte* when you showed me to your friends, but I was a wife when I gave you a son and daughter."

He clutched her wrist sharply, and she winced. "So long as my mother, or Mrs. Colin Campbell, or Lady Drumgesk are in my house, my wife is expected to display courtesy and interest in them, and she shall. Do you understand me? Do you hear me, Cydalise?"

"Yes," she said faintly. "Let my wrist go."

" You will make me a joke for my servants and a laughing-stock before my brothers."

" You are hurting me."

" Do you understand me, Cydalise ? Will you do as I desire ? "

" Oh yes," she exclaimed. " I have, always."

" Come, madam," he said, finding pleasure in her tears, " we have arranged to go a jaunt, and you must be gay and cheerful." He crooked his arm ; she thrust her own through it and they returned to the house together.

Cydalise had time to change her dress before the carriages came to the door. There were two, Scipio's and the admiral's. The Drumgesks and the Colin Campbells were in the first coach ; Scipio and his wife and Don followed in the second.

Turning south and leaving the loch, they bore inland, rolling slowly along the rough rutted road. The bracken growing above the ditches looked shrivelled and lifeless ; the sky was blindingly blue. A fly entered the rear coach and buzzed ceaselessly about the window pane. Cydalise watched the broad flat valley and the rising hills.

Don was sitting beside her and her husband opposite, and they talked animatedly. After a time their conversation lagged, and Cydalise saw her husband's disapproving glance fixed on her.

" A village ! " she exclaimed immediately.

" That's Kilmartin," said General Campbell. " Many a time I've been in Kilmartin. There's the castle, Cydalise, on your left. Yes, very old. I know every inch of this countryside," he declared contentedly.

" It's a bonnie country," said Don, regarding the landscape with a dispassionate stare. " But the roads are bad for coaches. Do you like our Highlands, Mrs. Campbell ? "

" They are very beautiful. I like high hills. I hope to climb them."

" Yes," said General Don, " but beware of the adders, madame. They are poisonous, and they come out in this hot weather. They like the sun."

" I remember once, when I was a boy," said Scipio, " cutting one in two with the stroke of a whip."

" That needs a deal of skill, I should think," said Don.

For a time there was silence, and they listened to the whirring of the insects in the hedges. Mrs. Scipio saw a bird in the sky. She wondered what kind of bird it might be.

" An eagle," said her husband. " They're rare hereabouts."

" It will have come from the north, doubtless," said General Don.

Cydalise remarked that the landscape on her right was unusually flat for that countryside. It was more like what she had read of the Netherlands.

" Why yes," said General Campbell immediately. " That's Moine Mhór—the Great Moss."

" On the edge of it," said General Don informatively, " is Dunadd, where our early kings were crowned."

Mrs. Campbell thought that the district was full of interest.

" So are the people, madame," said Don. " They

are a proud high-minded race hereabouts, and you
will see plenty of them to study where we are
going.''

" Where are we going ? " Cydalise asked.

" We are going to Kilmichael Fair," said her
husband.

Shortly the coaches drew up in a little village, and
the passengers dismounted. The amusement they
had decided on was a cattle market of importance,
which was held twice yearly and was attended by
farmers for many miles around and by dealers from
the south. All was bustle and noise ; the place was
a mass of frightened animals, the air was full of their
protesting voices. A gathering of many human
types was present : finely dressed men of substance
whose heads were kept on the stretch by their high
cravats ; men who mingled in their person the dress
of the farmer and the aristocrat ; men in homespun
and Kilmarnock bonnets ; men in plain cloth kilts ;
men in the garb of fishermen ; all there on business
or for curiosity. There were women in plenty, in
red skirts and tartan plaids, with sun-tanned skins
and shrewd eyes and soft Gaelic speech who had come
either to assist their husbands or to deputise for them.
There was the continuous sound of bagpipe music.
There was a gang of gypsies offering to sell amulets,
play reels, or tell fortunes. An atmosphere of anticipation and jollity was present.

The Duisk party made a way through the lively
throng, stopping occasionally to laugh at something
that amused or to exchange greetings with the greater
personages present. But the heat and confusion
grew oppressive. Cydalise felt tired, and wearied of

the people who appeared miraculously to welcome and felicitate her.

"Here ye are, leddy! Cross my loof wi' siller and I'll gie ye as bonnie a fortune as ever cam your way in the sooth, for I ken weel ye're no' sib to thae Hieland stots," cried a big-boned gypsy woman to Lady Drumgesk.

"Is she no', my lass?" said Lady Drumgesk's husband. "Aweel, she creeps' wi' ane. Tell your ain fortune, hinny, and see if ye'll no' swing in the tow ere lang."

"It's auld Drumgesk o' the Fifteen," exclaimed the woman's mate with surprise. "It was him that hangit Gideon Faa, that was ca'd Cheat-the-widdie."

"Aye!" said the judge, "but he changed it to Craigagee afore I was by wi' him!"

"Noo, bonnie leddy!" said the woman in a wheedling tone to Cydalise, who was coming last in the party. "Gin ye cross my loof I'll spae a true and kindly weird, for nae handsome leddy but speirs tae ken the future."

Cydalise looked hesitatingly around. She found Don beside her. "What does she say?" she asked.

"Would you like your fortune told, madame? It would be amusing."

"I trow the bonnie leddy will hae a winsome fate in store or my name's no' Betty Boboon," said the woman.

Cydalise slipped a silver coin into her hand.

"Is the gentleman biding here?" the gypsy asked.

"I had better," Don said to Cydalise. "You will not understand her Lowland speech."

The woman balanced the outstretched hand with

her own. "There was a muckle country ayont the sea," she said, "and a braw big sodger and a sair lack o' gear.

"There were twa fine ships and aicht aroun' them like an amber carknet.

"There are two men and a blude stain langsyne dried.

"And there's a muckle toun ayont the sea, and a boat tae gang there, and rowth o' singing and dancing and pearlings.

"And there's an axe forbye, but the haft o't hasna been hewn.

"And the bonnie leddy will leeve tae a lang and happy age, wi' mony bairns aroun' her knee, and a' thing crouse and canty, and the moose will ne'er leave her meal-poke wi' the tear in its e'e."

She called blessings after them.

"I understood a little," Cydalise said.

"She promised you every happiness and a long life," said Don, bending down with a smile. "She said there had been a foreign country and straitened circumstances, and a voyage in a ship with convoys. And I think she prophesied a sea journey for you, with a good deal of happiness at the end of it."

The others of the party were out of sight. Cydalise grew anxious. "We had better find them," she said.

"You are tired, madame," said the general. "The noise and the heat . . . we will leave the crowd for a little."

"General Campbell is perhaps looking for me."

"He will find us, surely. But it is not your place to look for General Campbell in this crowd of beasts."

She looked at him quickly. " Come, madame," he said, " and allow me to assist you to a quieter place. I am afraid for you in this rabble."

Her misgivings vanished, and she laughed when she saw whither he was leading her. " But this is a churchyard ! " she exclaimed.

" Graveyards are quiet," said Don. " That is their property." They passed into the enclosure, and after a little they sat upon a heavy slab. Opposite them was a headstone. It read :

DONALD LEITCH
Tacksman of Uillian
died 17 July 1754
aged 24
In Hope of a Glorious Resurrection.

" He was my cousin," said the general. " He was murdered."

v

From where they sat they could see the gentle hills in front of them, the afternoon sun giving them a green varnished look, and where, further up the glen, they rose to dim but greater heights. To them came the sounds from the fair, muffled, and mingled with the raucous crowing of a cock near-by.

Cydalise contemplated the little kirkyard in silence. It was unutterably peaceful after the stir without. Without movement of her head she could study Don closely, as he sat a little in front on the far side of the slab. He seemed lost in thought.

She watched him curiously, his heavy pock-marked face, the lines of decision at his mouth and nostrils, the dark shadows under his eyes. He had the grand manner. His eyes, she remembered, were penetrating and mocking, but now, as he turned his head to her, they were almost gentle.

"Yes, madame," he said, although she had not spoken, "he was murdered. Were you satisfied with the spae-wife?"

"Why was he murdered?"

"It is difficult to tell."

"He was very young."

"Very young."

Cydalise gazed again at the stone, already bearing the weathering of years, and shivered involuntarily. "It was cruel," she said.

"Sudden death was not uncommon in the Highlands. It is uncommon now. My uncles—your husband's father and his father's brother—they were murdered. And, as I said, our cousin lying here."

"Was he my husband's cousin?"

"Your husband's father, and my mother, and *his* mother, were of one family."

Cydalise was much surprised. "Was your mother a Campbell of Duisk, sir?"

"She is," said the general, smiling.

"There are different kinds of cousinship," she said naïvely, "and I did not imagine that was yours."

"Oh yes, madam; I have the blood of the hawks in me. Part of it. Not hawks," he added quickly, "for we have a saying that hawks don't peck out hawks' eyes. Wolves, perhaps."

"And why wolves, sir?"

"Wolves feast on their own disabled."

"To be eaten in turn, sir."

Don laughed outright. "Madame, you are not a proper Campbell of Duisk; not yet."

I

" Mrs. Campbell, my husband's mother, told me that the last wolf was slain up there," she said, and made a vague gesture to the north.

" Well, that's odd, for she has given birth to three. And there," he said, pointing to the headstone, " lies a cub of the tribe, slain young."

" Then there is a legend of the wolves, sir ? " she asked, and looked at him questioningly.

The general laughed again.   " You are sympathetic, madame. You have the eyes of one."

" What is the story ? " she said.

" It is a trivial story, and wearing with the years." His gaze turned to the intent mien of Cydalise, was fixed for a space.   And then he said lightly : " There was a tribe of wolves, madame, with a grey old wolf at the head. They left their own den for a better, and drove the enfeebled pack that was there away. But they did not gain their new lair without loss, for the old she-wolf of the tribe and two of their young were slain.

" They were prosperous there, and fattened, and the cubs of the pack grew up and were strong. They rejoiced savagely over their own strength. And then one day a cub of the tribe was slain. He was found worried to death. And none knew the name of the slayer.

" But the old grey wolf was very sorrowful, for the cub, although a half-breed, was his grandson and very dear to him. And he broke up the pack in his grief and left the lair he had conquered, and after a time he died, full of years and grief and iniquity.

" He had grown strange after the death of the young wolf, and he turned off the daughter-wolf that

had been his right hand and her half-breed cub with
a farewell that contrived to hide a snarl. They went
to a distant place, this mother and her half-breed son,
and there the son grew up.

" This mother and son, although savage, had certain
virtues and were attached to each other. But there
was always a strange barrier between them, madame.
They wondered, and they were embarrassed.

" Now, they thought much of the lair by the loch
side, and the reason for its abandonment. And the
mother wolf was worried. And one day, when they
were both absorbed in certain thoughts, the mother
spoke the question that was in her heart. That was
a terrible moment, madame.

" But this particular wolf-cub was innocent of what
she had been fearing, and gave his denial on honour,
and the mother was satisfied. She is a very shrewd
creature of prey, and had reasoned things out very
clearly. But her offspring at that time had not yet
learned to blood his fangs. The reassurance made
her very happy.

" Evidently they had been banished. Riding here
to Duisk I had confirmation of my fancies."

" But why," she asked wonderingly, " should there
have been that suspicion ? "

" Oh, madame, how can I tell ? "

" But who should want to murder ? "

" It is an inheritance, perhaps," he said gaily.

" But," she exclaimed, " why should they pick on
one ? "

" He was not a real member of the pack," said the
general lightly. " He was like this poor fellow here,
he was a half-breed. So much less sacrifice ! "

" General Don," she cried urgently, " who murdered him ? "

" On my honour, madame, I have no idea. One can deduce, as the she-wolf and her cub did. But in this world, and in this district, it is better not to be a Campbell at all, than to be half one."

Cydalise turned questioning eyes on him, but the general's gaze was on the distant throng. " Perhaps, madame, we should return," he suggested.

She took his arm and they passed out of the enclosure. " Some things are hard to forget," she said.

" We forget easily, sometimes. Even General Campbell's memory fails. He forgot to inform his wife where we were coming to, I noticed." Her cheeks still burned when they mingled with the crowd.

General Campbell had not for a time observed the absence of Cydalise ; when he did, and saw that Don also was missing, he contented himself with the reflection that they were not far away. He and his brothers—this was a great day for them. They preened and strutted inwardly, maintaining by an effort a pose of outward composure. The men of command were adolescents again, eager to show themselves to their neighbours as big men of affairs.

" I wonder," said Admiral Colin to Drumgesk in an aside, " if any of the MacTavishes Duin are here."

" Donnachie'll be ower busy drumming awa' at the rhymes."

" Well, it's no concern of mine," said Colin, " whether or not. But I don't think Scipio is over keen to meet them."

" He's like yoursel," said Lame Archy judiciously,

" he's no' keen on a body unless they're useful to him."

" Where is Scipio's wife ? " Colin inquired, glancing to where his brother and the two ladies were chatting to a little fat man with a laced waistcoat.

" Losh ! content yoursel," said the other.   " You've a wife of your ain."

" Archy," said the admiral confidentially, " can you make anything of her ?—I mean Cydalise.   She is a confounded handsome girl.   But it's a confounded queer union."

Drumgesk grinned maliciously.

" Oh, I know ! " said the admiral.   " You are as fond of her company as I am, Archy."

" You sodgers and sailors are a' blude and nae brains," said Archy Crubach enigmatically.   " It taks a lawyer to see through a stane-wa'."

Lord Drumgesk and Admiral Campbell had both been charmed by Mrs. Scipio, and their devotion to her conversation had been exercised under the watchful eyes of their spouses.   Both these loose-living men honoured their wives, and they respected Scipio Campbell's wife, but they found her presence irresistible and had each in his way attempted a harmless flirtation, Colin nervously and Drumgesk with zest.   Cydalise could reveal a sense of humour and a spasmodic gaiety when speaking to them which froze when speaking to the ladies or her husband. Cydalise Cœur-de-roi was an elf of enchantment compared with the proud-faced Elizabeth Campbell, but Colin in his best moments of allusive flattery sometimes felt rather than saw the suspicious face of Elizabeth Campbell at his shoulder.   It was like bearing down to capture a barquentine and finding a hostile three-decker to larboard. Drumgesk, the hero of a hundred sculduddery escapades, the participator in countless Canongate bacchanals, found a gay pleasure in the exchange of *mot* with the little creole while his fat wife was at his side. Sophy did not comprehend the meaning of half his speeches; he knew that. From the twinkle in her eyes, he was certain that Cydalise knew, too.

"She's a nice wee lassock, spoiled a wee, and gey lazy," said the judge tolerantly, "but Scipio's no' taking her the right way. I daresay he kens a' about revetting and shooting, but there's a lot he doesna ken about women."

"Look!" said Colin.

Drumgesk followed the line of his brother's cane. He saw Don and Cydalise coming from the graveyard.

The ladies were growing wearied. When Mrs. Scipio and Don appeared a return home was suggested. As they moved in the direction of the carriages they came face to face with an old man, grey-locked, grey-faced, with keen unswerving eyes. He was dressed in dark clothes of a homely material, but had the undeniable appearance of a man of culture. With him was a young man in his twenties, tall and ruddy.

Pretence was impossible. Scipio held out his hand, exclaiming: "Uncle Dugald!"

The old man ignored it. "General Campbell," he said quietly, "I ended all intercourse with Duisk twenty-eight years ago. I do not intend to resume it."

The gloss was off the day's outing; several onlookers had heard.

" Well," said the admiral irritably, as he assisted the ladies in and followed Drumgesk, " Scipio has made a fool of us all."

" It was a toss-up," said the other philosophically, " and he was afore you."

In the other coach Scipio sat with his wife and cousin, biting his lips. He was shaking with fury. At length he said, unable to control himself further : " A fine thing when one of His Majesty's general officers gets a cut from a country parson, from the owner of a few acres of hill—acres that were left him by my own grandfather, and that are mine by rights ! "

" The old gentleman apparently nurses a grievance," said Don to Cydalise. " He is our uncle, Dugald Leitch, father of the Donald who was murdered. I was showing Mrs. Scipio Do'l's grave."

" How like ! " said General Campbell with an effort. " Yon youngster must be Do'l's son. It was his very image." After a time he said : " What made you go to the churchyard, Cydalise ? "

" I was tired," she said. " I lost you, and so we went."

The laird seemed mollified.

" I hope, Mrs. Campbell," said Don, " that your last visit there is a long way off."

" I intend to prepare a family mausoleum in the policies," said Scipio.

" I hope it lies empty for long enough," said Cydalise.

" So you saw Do'l Leitch's grave," said the general presently. " What does it read ? "

" The name and date," said Don.

" Nothing about being a grandson of Duisk ? "

" No."

" They're a dour lot."

Despite the lessening heat General Campbell's face began to perspire. He looked hot and irritable, and commenced fanning himself with his hat. Cydalise watched his neck swelling over his cravat with a sense of discovery. She wondered if General Don was perspiring also ; if he was, he had not got the length of fanning himself.

" Were you interested, Cydalise ? " her husband asked.

" Yes, very," she said animatedly. " So many animals."

" There are more black cattle in Glassary than ever there were," he said. " And a lot more sheep. It's sheep, sheep, sheep."

" What is the reason for that ? " asked his cousin.

" You'll mind, Jock, how the farms used to be worked by anything from four to eight families. It was a bad enough system, except that it kept them all employed. You can imagine eight generals in command of one army ! The effect was the same. But now it's one farm one tenant. It was tried with the black cattle at first, and it proved a success. And for the last twenty years there's been a craze for the black-faced sheep. The old white-faced local sheep give the better wool, but there's not enough body in them. I kept in close touch with affairs through my doer. At Errachan Mor, where there were six families of the local folk, I've got one man now for a tenant. He's a Border fellow. Of course, some of the native folk are hard pressed for a living, and I daresay they'll have to emigrate. But, as I said, the younger lads could take the King's shilling. Yes, there's been great changes in Glassary, laird and crofter. I can remember . . ."

Cydalise gradually slumbered.

She awoke with a scream.

As in a dream, she saw the two men towering curiously above her and the windows at an oblique angle. Scipio, cursing furiously, was trying to balance himself and open the door at the same time. He stumbled out, and Don clasped her closely round the waist.

" Do not be alarmed, madame," he said gently. " A wheel has broken."

She looked up wonderingly at the pock-marked face. He repeated the caress, and was gone.

In a second the coach was eased up to the level, and she descended. The brothers were running back, and the ladies were hastening in their wake.

" Are you hurt ? " her husband asked tenderly. He was trembling. " You look so pale."

" It was nothing, nothing whatever," she assured him.

Scipio took her hand gently, and then released it. His brothers had come up.

" Mrs. Campbell is fortunately unhurt," said General Don. " But it was a close squeeze."

VI

It was singular that, of the six children of Colin Buie, four still survived, not one of them holding any kind of communication with Duisk.

Mrs. Janet Don was eighty-two, and at that age she vacated her eyrie in Craig's Close in the High

Street of Edinburgh and set off to Cambus Don, of
which her son was now the lord. Eighty-two years
old, bleak, cold, and composed, she took control of
that mansion with the same ease as she had of Duisk,
and after twenty-eight years' repression of command
resumed that command with the ardent spirit of a
girl.

Eilidh MacTavish of Duin remained there ; became
a matriarch. Ann Leitch the younger had given her
grandchildren, and now the grandchildren themselves
were parents. Eilidh was seventy-one years of age.
Habit had erased the old days from her active
thoughts. She thought sometimes of Inveraray, with
regrets for the irreclaimable past, and would glance
compassionately at the stiff old man who had been
a gay wooer then, but at Duisk she had been seldom,
and as seldom thought of it.

Colin Og, who had been so bewildered and delighted
by Do'l Mor's little Angus, now at the age of seventy-
five found these feelings renewed in contemplation of
Angus's little Neil. Colin was nervous, questioning ;
wondering at things with the timidity of a little child.
His memory was good but confused, and fraught with
irrelevancies. Thirty-six years had gone since the
passing of his mother, and he had never ceased to
miss her. He knew that his father was at Inveraray,
and expected him back daily.

The minister and the minister's wife treated him
compassionately. Dugald and Anne were living to
a healthy old age, not without worries. Do'l had
become a dim, sad memory. The other sons, Dugald
and Colin, were ministers of far distant parishes.
Ann was at Duin. But the pretty Isbell, now nearing

her fifties, was with them, and her son Angus had married Mary Ferguson from Knockalava, and had little Neil and Dugald and Angus.

The times were hard. There had been a potato famine ; barley and oats were not thriving in a district subject to long spells of wet weather and an occasional overflowing of the Add. Strone had a subsidiary farm which was in the tenancy of six families who wrung an existence from the soil they had been bred on. They held it communally, as Scipio had explained to Don, using the crude implements of the period, yoking four Highland ponies to a home-made wooden plough and walking backwards over their ground, dragging the beasts towards them. There was no fencing of any kind ; the children herded the cattle, keeping them from the scanty patches of grain. This condition of things was general over the countryside.

Yet the people were content. The system was bad, but it sufficed. In the great new house of Duisk there might be grandeur and debauch and dissatisfaction. In the modest slated house of Strone there were a few luxuries : some good furnishings, a collection of books, candles, china. In the low thatched houses of the petty tenants the peat reek ascended from a hole in the roof, a ladder in the sole apartment permitted the hens to rest on the beams above ; the inhabitants slept in stifling box-beds ; at nights a travesty of light came from the rush floating in the oil cruisie to expire in the thick haze from the peat, and there was one book in the house—a Bible. And there was contentment.

There were evenings of *ceilidh* when neighbours

foregathered and stories were told, and one would relate the tale of the last wolf seen in the district and the woman from Braevallich who had slain— and been slain by—it. And there would be reminiscences of the few who had gone to the Stuart support in '45. And perhaps there would be surmise regarding the great canal that was proposed for Crinan. And then there would be singing. Into the terrifying and wonderful silence of these hills would break the magic music of ' Crodh Chailein '.

They were content. They were living the lives that their fathers had led and, as they expected, their sons would lead. And soon it would all be swept away.

Dugald Leitch was approached by a stranger for a lease of his lesser farm. He was offered a higher rent than his six tenants combined paid him. The ground was to be used for the grazing of the black-faced sheep.

He refused the offer.

" My days are here by the will of God," he said, " but if I were to turn those families from their ground I would be an emissary of Satan."

Other proprietors were doing what he would not do, and some of the native portioners were going to North America. Campbell of Duisk was doing so, and the old families who had been on the lands of Duisk so long lived in a state of trembling.

Duisk was more frequently in Dugald Leitch's mind since he had seen the brothers Campbell and Don ; and Do'l Mor more frequently also. Once or twice, when he was on the main road during that week, the great emblazoned coach had passed him, two little pale children and a great black negress inside. The negress had become the wonder of the district.

Dugald related these things to his wife. He told her about the children. "Neil there is worth four of them," he told her with satisfaction.

The outings for the children had been the suggestion of Cydalise, who had hoped that she might contrive to go with them. Scipio approved of the idea, which permitted the flaunting of the coach where it would most excite comment, but he vetoed the mother's desire, having an inkling of her real intention. "We must entertain our kin," he said finally. "Send Barrett or Juno with them." That night he had another gathering of friends, but was able to stagger to his room.

In the morning Cydalise did not appear for breakfast, and the ladies were incensed at this mark of disrespect to them. They were of the hard school, and did not take breakfast in bed. Cydalise came down late and walked in the garden with her mother-in-law, who talked of the children. The air was doing them good, Mrs. Captain Archy thought. They were in love with the place. They were becoming more spirited every day. Were any of the Cœur-de-rois delicate ?

Cydalise did not think so. The foreign climates had not helped the children, but they were constitutionally strong, she believed.

"They are coming on," said old Mrs. Campbell. "Four years old."

Cydalise made no answer, as she felt that none was expected.

"I wanted particularly to speak about the children," Mrs. Captain Archy said presently. "You know, of course, that Lady Drumgesk has no children, and nothing short of a miracle will allow her to have any now."

" It is a pity."

" Yes ; and Drumgesk will go to her sister's children. It will be lost to us."

" Ah ! " said Cydalise with sympathy.

" Barrill goes to Archy, and I suppose after him to Colin and Colin's children. Colin has three daughters but no son. I am sorry about that, mam, for Barrill will go to Colin's eldest daughter Elizabeth, who, I hear, is to marry Captain Otway of the army. I had rather she married a Campbell.

" But it is of yourself I wish to speak," said the old lady with some hesitation. " I have only one grandson of the name of Campbell. Francey will follow Scipio. Of course, Francey may marry and have a dozen sons in time. Who can tell ? But both Francey and Emmeline are unused to our climate. It will be a great shame if Duisk should fail for males and go to some possible Otways, as Barrill will go."

Cydalise stood still. " Do you mean, madame, that you imagine François is dying ? "

" God forbid, my dear. But we need more heirs."

Cydalise raised her arm and regarded it. A discoloration was visible there.

" Oh ! " the old lady exclaimed, " what a dreadful mark ! You must be in pain."

" It is nothing, madame. It was a fall."

" No wonder you weren't at breakfast," Mrs. Captain Archy cried generously. " We were all wondering."

Cydalise smiled. " It will mend, madame."

They continued to pace the garden for a time. Mrs.

Captain Campbell reverted to the subject of heirs.
" You will consider this ? " she urged.

" Yes, madame."

" You understand how very important it is ? "

" Yes, madame."

" I am sure it is Scipio's dearest wish."

" Oh, madame, do not talk to me any more about
it," the girl answered wearily.

General Don had not yet seen all the improvements
made by the proprietor.   In the afternoon they drove
out, with Cydalise and Archibald Crubach.   General
Don had suggested that Mrs. Scipio might accompany
them, and the Crubach had invited himself.   The
others of the house party were driving round the shore
to Barrill.

It was in a light open carriage drawn by two horses
that General Don sat beside Mrs. General Campbell
with his cousins facing him.   As usual when Cydalise
was present the talk between the soldiers was plati-
tudinous.   General Campbell pointed out the various
alterations he had made as the carriage rolled by the
shore road ; General Don praised them all.

" You have come to a beautiful country, madame,"
he said latterly.

" Aye, there's worse than the Campbell country,"
said Archibald contentedly.   " ' It's a far cry to Loch
Awe ', mam, which means anything you like."

" It means different things to different people,"
Don observed.

Drumgesk was completely happy.   His lawyer eyes
had not been idle in the last few days, and he watched
with the amused detachment of the man of the world
and the jealousy of a race-proud gentleman.   These

feelings were struggling in him for mastery, but he was content to be silent meantime and observe what he told himself was a comedy.

Sometimes he would think of his brother Scipio in a mood of surprise, wondering how he had risen to such rank and eminence. Yet Scipio was admittedly a brilliant man in his own sphere, a dashing soldier and an organizer. The judge consoled himself with the reflection that love is blind. Had he been in Scipio's place he would have either cleared Don out of Duisk or shot him. He would have preferred the latter, for Lord Drumgesk was a lamed man, and he contented himself with the thought that Scipio would have to shoot Don. His hatred for Don was an old one, and it had strengthened with the years. Here before him was his hated cousin working his own ruin.

Archibald Crubach, therefore, laughed and jested. The afternoon was cool and sunny ; Cydalise had become unwontedly gay, and General Campbell responded to her humour with pathetic eagerness.

Don professed a wish to return by Errachan Wood, if madame was willing. Cydalise confessed that she had not yet passed that way. Scipio demurred.

" It is an eerie place," he said. " It is said to be haunted."

His wife evinced a lively curiosity.

" It was there," said General Don, " that our cousin, poor Do'l Mor, was murdered."

" I should like to see it," she said.

The carriage was turned off the main road and on to the grassy cutting that partitioned the wood of Errachan. The trees were dark and sombre there, and only an odd fern grew in their needle-carpeted and dusky flooring. Nothing broke the hush apart from the soft thud of the horses' hooves; once or twice in far recesses a glimpse of greenish-yellow sunlight slanted an attenuated triumph.

"Where," asked Cydalise, "is the spot where he was slain?"

"I will show you," said General Campbell, and he caused the carriage to be halted at the place.

They all stared silently where he indicated. Cydalise shuddered.

"Drive on," said Scipio. "I told you, Cydalise!"

"Who was the murderer?" she asked him with an effort.

"He was not discovered," said he.

"Mrs. Campbell, what would you do with him were he found?"

"I would hang the villain," she cried.

"That's a job for you, Archy," said Don.

"The hanging of a man costs nae sleep," was the response.

"I wonder," said Don, "if the killing of one does. There you are, promising hanging! It might have been Scipio or me!"

"We don't hang generals," said Drumgesk. "It would be ower muckle expense of rope."

"Lord Ferrers was hanged," said General Don.

"Lord Ferrers was a fool," said General Campbell.

On leaving the wood they came into the sunshine again. A feeling of heaviness deserted them, and they were all merry. Scipio promised to take his wife to the hill-tops on the first clear day for seeing the panorama of country.

"Where would these hills lead to?" she asked.

K

" To Loch Fyne, if you kept straight across."

" I must say I'm fond of the Loch Fyne kippers,"
said Archibald. " The Loch Fyne *sgadan*—the wee
fat curly darlings."

" Is there a road across the hills to Loch Fyne ? "
General Don asked. " I never knew. I know there
are tracks."

" There are the old roads," said Scipio.

" Not good for horses, of course."

" The farmers use them."

" The hills would be awkward for horses, I suppose,"
said Don.

" The back road by Loch Leathan goes to Kirnan
on the Add, and then up the river as far as Darnirnach, I think. After that there's a lump of hill
between the valley and Loch Fyne, but it's no great
stretch of a walk. It would be too far for a jaunt.
It would tire the ladies."

" I suppose," Don said, " that it would lead to
nowhere, in the long run."

" It leads to Loch Gair, the fishing place."

Cydalise was amused by the list of names. " And
where does Loch Gair lead to ? "

" To Otter Ferry," said her husband smilingly,
" and to the Lowlands, and to the wide world beyond
Duisk."

VII

Peggy entered the nursery to satisfy herself that
the maids had performed their duties.

The children were there, with Juno. They ran to
her, holding her hands.

They had won her over from her initial dislike for

them. They had seemed so pale and delicate and pinched—proper subjects for a woman's sympathy. But they had been the children of Cydalise.

She had been unable to maintain that aversion. For they were the children of Scipio, as well.

She smiled, saying words that they did not understand, and they chattered to her in a language foreign to her. The black smiling Juno nodded companionably.

The nursery windows were at the side of the house. Peggy, as she raised her head from the children, saw Cydalise and General Don walking in the shrubbery beyond the garden. She left the children at once and returned to her duties. Ashamed as she was of her feelings she could not help them. Had Cydalise been actively hostile to her she would have welcomed such a manifestation ; Peggy had the additional humiliation of knowing that Mrs. General Campbell treated her not as a person who might have stood in her shoes but as a paid servant with an unintelligible speech.

Mrs. Scipio Campbell, apart from the incident of the household supervision, had never thought of Peggy. As she strolled on the gravelled path with General Don her mind banished the thought of Duisk and its exhaustions in the pleasure of listening to the slender officer. She heard, with exquisitely attuned receptivity, his gentle and allusive speeches, and felt rather than saw his distinguished air and supercilious bearing. He was like a creature of fine Arabian breed, she thought, and the others three tramping bulls.

"I came to Duisk with reluctance," he said presently, "and I leave it with regret. You have made me very happy, madame."

"General Don—I shall be sorry when you go."

"Madame, you will have interests at Duisk ; your home, your husband——"

"My husband."

"—Your children."

"Yes," she said tonelessly. "That is all."

"You have the love of your husband, doubtless, madame——"

"General Don," she said, "I have." He was surprised by the sincerity in her voice. And then she added : "But I pay for it. I am tired of a drunkard's blows," she said languidly. "Men love, and they expect tolerance for coarseness and forgiveness for cruelty. Yet, in spite of that, they love. It is a great price to pay for a flight from poverty."

"You were poor, madame. I can imagine it. The penalty is hard. Madame, I am sorry for you."

Cydalise turned her eyes to Don's. The man's were serious, with a sincerity that seemed perfect. She echoed his words tremulously.

"It is a penalty to be enclosed here, for life perhaps, in this lonely countryside, away from cities and all the pleasures and gaieties that people of quality should have. I am sorry for you, madame, for you are a prisoner here for ever. Your existence is ended. I am disloyal to my good cousin when I tell you this, but I am very true to you. But you will have the companionship of half a dozen ladies in the neighbourhood, and of your husband's mother, and you will receive an odd visit from Lady Drumgesk. Those absurd Campbells !" Don laughed angrily, and flicked his cane at a fallen leaf. "The women of your family have ornamented Versailles. If you are fortunate, madame, you may receive an invitation to Barrill."

" I could not stay here for ever," she exclaimed, and her eyes widened with terror at the prospect.

" You know that General Campbell intends to retire. You and he will remain here for ever."

" When will you return to Duisk, General ? "

" Never."

" I am sorry," she said falteringly. " Your attentions have been very kind."

" I have hated Duisk," he said composedly, " for many years. Fortune was kind when I resolved to return, for I have had the joy of knowing you. It was not fortune. It was fate, I fancy. But I shall never return, madame. I have been used to better company than that of a trio of upstart boasters. Madame, you will learn to accommodate yourself to them. You are reluctant, I perceive. But you will learn. You will have to."

" I have my children," she said unsteadily.

" Your children—and I believe that you will have many more," he replied brutally "—will compensate for the interest of the ladies and the attentions of your husband. Madame, forgive me. I am your cousin too, in a fashion, and I feel from the bottom of my heart for you. When I leave Duisk, madame, I carry with me the memory of your lovely face, of your gentle heart. A soldier's prayers are a mockery, perhaps. Yet they are sincere. You will have mine, madame. I hope I may have yours."

Cydalise was pensive for the rest of the day ; she remained much in her room, and there her husband found her. She looked at him with the vague feeling that she was regarding a stranger. He was so big and masterful and sure of himself; so yellow of face, so red of eye, so strong of jaw. His hair was unpowdered and loosely arranged; his scarlet coat was open at the neck. He approached diffidently and gazed down at her in silence.

" Yes ? " she said, finding his stare unbearable.

" Let me see your arm," he said gently. " I am vexed, my dear. I have been worrying ever since."

Her nerves jangled with relief. " Oh, let me alone ! " she cried rapidly, and her slurring speech was accentuated. " You are a brute." She rose quickly from her chair and left him.

The next two days passed quietly enough. The third General Don had proposed for taking his departure.

" You'll have found a few things to amuse you," Drumgesk remarked as he limped in upon some talk regarding this.

" This visit marks an epoch in my life," said Don.

Scipio was gratified. " Well, each of us has done his best to entertain you, Jock, and you're welcome back at any time."

" Aye," said Drumgesk, " each of us our best, and in our ain fashion."

After her outburst of anger to him, Scipio was surprised by a sudden placability in Cydalise. Her eyes when he spoke to her shone kindly. She asked him to walk with her by the shore. On several occasions they went up together to the nursery and stayed there with the children for a little, and after leaving them Scipio would speak of their future, and the career he proposed to help François with, and the fine alliance that might come the way of Emmeline. Once or twice her hand met his and remained there, and the big man thought with a lump in his throat of his wooing of the slim young girl afar in North America and his pleasure when he won her. Of course he had bought her; she knew that, and so did everyone. But that was done daily, and the brides made no demur. He had not underrated the attractions of his rank, his talents, and his fortune. If he had been no longer a young man at least he had been an imposing one. At the time she had been flattered by his evident ardour; she had accepted him willingly.

And now, after these few years of continual estrangement, her old love was reborn. It was long since she had sought his company. The big man's heart was exultant. He talked incessantly of the future; of the importance he would attain for her sake, of the extensions he would make to the property, of the family that would come into being and grow around them. He sent to London for a gift of diamonds for her.

And he reverted continually to the subject of heirs.

She listened then, her lips parted slightly, her eyes intent afar, and would afterwards turn to him with a quick birdlike movement of the head and a wondering expression. And once she kissed him voluntarily on his wide firm mouth.

" You have been very good to me," she said. " I have been foolish, sometimes, perhaps. But why do you strike me ? "

" I'll never do it again," he said.

The invitation to the gentlemen came on the day before Don's departure. It was to Ardaneilan, ten miles up the loch. It would be a drinking bout, undoubtedly. Don declined. " Tell Ardaneilan to forgive me," he said. " If I'm leaving Duisk to-morrow I want to leave it with a clear head."

" Postpone the day, Jock."

" The packet sails once a week only, and I cannot stay another."

The three brothers departed in the evening. Scipio had not been keen to desert his guest, but his brothers were loth to miss a night's entertainment.

General Don made himself gracious to the ladies for the remainder of the evening.

At one in the morning the festivities at Ardaneilan flickered out. Some of the gentlemen had lost consciousness. The Duisk brothers were very drunk and were not willing to move, but their carriage was at hand. They were helped in and driven off into the night, their host being incapable of bidding them farewell.

The cool air that flushed in through the open windows revived them. The brothers recognized their location when the carriage passed between the pillared entrance of the avenue, but they were silent and surly, for their heads were sore.

Peggy admitted them. She lit three candles in the dark hall, but they were not too able to carry them, and she preceded her cousins up the stairs, slowly, to give them time, and after lighting each to his apartment retired.

She had reached the hall when she heard General Campbell calling on her, and she hastened noiselessly up the dark stair. His head was thrust over the balustrade and he called down : " Where is Mrs. Campbell—Mrs. Scipio ? " in the Gaelic.

Peggy stared wonderingly up at him, seeing his features grotesquely altering in the spasmodic motion of the candlestick he held. She knew he had drunk too much and thought he rambled.

" She will be in the room," she replied humouringly. " Go you to your bed and sleep, Duisk."

" Where is my wife ? " he cried peremptorily. " Her bed has not been slept in."

She completed the ascent of the stairs, echoing his last words. Taking the candlestick she glanced in, and saw that it was as he said. " She is gone," she exclaimed in astonishment.

Drumgesk appeared, crossed the landing and limped hurriedly into another room. Figures appeared from everywhere, questioning.

Drumgesk returned. He was sobered. He said something hoarsely.

Scipio gave a great roar of rage ; it whirled down the well of the house and left a silence. He was in that other room ; they heard him stampeding. He reappeared, dreadful to see and hear.

Peggy listened, shuddering. Her gaze moved from one to the other, to the men, their wives, their mother. Colin turned furiously on the general. " What kind of woman is this you've brought into the Campbells ? " he shouted. " Did you lift her from the stocks ? "

" Horses, God damn ! " cried the laird, and blundered heavily down the pitch-black stairway. His brothers followed. Peggy saw them pass in the faint glow of the light she held, which cast an eerie glimmer on their descent. It was not three men of rank and breeding whose faces she saw thus. It was three clansmen of a deadly clan, three fierce and savage faces, the masks of environment and composure fallen ; three men in whom instinct was uppermost, lustful for blood and hot for revenge.

Mrs. Captain Archy was on the verge of collapse, and had to be assisted to her room. " Oh, my poor Skippy," the old lady moaned. " My poor, poor Skippy."

VIII

" I'll go by Sonachan," said the general as he swung himself into the saddle. " Go you two by Kintraw and Kilmartin."

" Ask by the way," said Colin, holding his horse with difficulty, " for fear it's a blank choice. And take a groom."

Scipio turned on him a livid face. " Will I speir of every cottager the whereabouts of my wife ! And one man can shoot a whitterick."

He wheeled his mount and dashed into the darkness. The thud of the hooves passed into silence.

Scipio, as his steed bore him north by the shore of the loch, was goaded by a thousand pricks of rage and humiliation. He had one mood only : to slay. Even the thought of his wife faded from his mind and he fed on his shame alone, forgetting who had evoked it.

The maddened man had one dreadful moment of lucidity when he saw himself, not as what he had considered himself, but as obtuse, stupid, and blind, the detestation of his wife and the dupe of the smooth-

tongued man whom he had honoured with his
hospitality.

Don : whose mother he had hated and who had
hated him. Don : whom his own mother had bade
him keep from Duisk. Don : whom he had invited
to Duisk with the simplicity of a fool and the unthink-
ing kindness of a man of honour ; and who had repaid
him with the theft of his wife.

The thud of the hooves on the dusty cracked surface
of the road was music. Onward they sped, past
Ardary and the long slopes of Meall na Sroine, past
Durran and through the awesome shades of Eredine.
Round the bend of Kames, where Innis Sherrich sat
blackly on the black water ; past Innischonnell,
scowling darkly in the night—onward they sped.
The horse was sweating under him ; the white foam
from its mouth flecked against his face. He spurred
it anew, and they dashed like phantom creatures by
the loch, through the silence, in the night.

Dreadful spasms shook him, contorting his face to
an image of their meaning. His hand clutched the
pistol butt. He smiled. The recrudescent passions
of his race possessed him. He would have blood ;
the blood of both. Blood that would close all mouths
of scoff, that would cleanse his dishonoured name and
wipe all memory away of his dearly paid complaisance.

The face of his cousin mocked him as he rode, the
smiling pock-marked face of Don. Scipio laughed
aloud, thrashing the gathered rein on the animal's
neck. It would be over soon ; it would soon be all
a memory and a tale of red appeasement.

He stopped, and strained for other sound than the
exhausted breathing of his horse. Lorn slept serene,

its hills scarcely defined against the sombre sky.   He
heard the faint and startled twitter of a bird, and
nothing more.   With a curse he stabbed at the
heaving flanks and galloped on.

Colin and the Crubach had left in the opposite
direction, and galloped together the three miles to
the southern end of the loch.   The admiral was an
indifferent horseman, but despite the difficulties of
management he raved without pause against the
woman who was Scipio Campbell's wife.   Drumgesk
was silent.   At the Ford of Annagra they separated,
Colin to press through the passes of Craigenterive
and Kintraw on the chance that the fugitives had
arranged escape by the Atlantic shore.   " Shoot the
man," said the admiral as they parted.   " She can
be sorted later."

Drumgesk had no intention of following Scipio's
instructions to head for Kilmartin.   He despised his
brother's plans, and had formulated his own.   He
turned on to the back road which ran between the hills
and led in any case to Kilmichael, but was shorter
in length.   It was an indifferent road, and there was
little to guide him, but he knew every yard of it.
At this hour the loneliness of the valley was intimidating, but Drumgesk was not superstitious ; he was
more apprehensive of a stumble.   But he rode fast
despite of that.

The rancour which Archibald Crubach had cherished
all his life against him who had lamed him had seemed
so near the satiety of revenge.   Scipio, he had been
certain, would call Don out.   No man could fail to
see how things were going.   Drumgesk had thought
so, content to wait until his brother realized how

matters stood. Fighting was the trade of soldiers, but, judge or not, Drumgesk would have challenged Don and tried to kill him without a moment's hesitation had Cydalise been his own wife, for Drumgesk was a good Campbell. But it was not his honour that had been at stake ; it had been Scipio's. And Drumgesk realized that his expectations of Don's downfall had been shattered by the obtuseness of Scipio Campbell and the dexterity of John Don.

He was enraged ; mortified by the blow to his law-sharpened insight, remorseful that he had not warned his brother even while feeling against Scipio a species of savage contempt.

Drumgesk was a man who delighted in low life. His opinion of women was as low. But coexistent with that contemptuous outlook was a deep reverence for his mother and a profound respect for Lady Drumgesk. They were women of lofty morality. It was pleasant to know that the females of one's own family were such as a man could boast of. It was the essential difference in Cydalise to these women that had been the attraction for both Colin and Archibald. She had possessed a certain manner, indefinable, that marked her as apart from the women of his name.

Drumgesk knew now what she resembled, and all his good-humoured tolerance for the slender Cydalise was dead. He hated her. As he rode through the darkness he hated her. The frequenter of disreputable howffs was lost in the Highland gentleman, outraged in his family pride that the names of the pure women of his race should have been soiled by

association with this foreign intruder among the
Campbells of Duisk.

He rode past the little Loch Leathan and came in
time to Leckuary, where the road went down the
Add valley to Kilmichael and on towards the port
of the Rudha. But he left the road there, and after
fording the river hastened along its upper reaches.
Looking eastward he observed the faintest tinge of
grey above the rim of the hills.

He derived some consolation from the thought that
she had run away with Don.   There was still satisfaction to be got from that, and the judge smiled grimly,
for his satisfaction would be a bloody one.   It was a
chance to repay an old wrong and to avenge a new
one.   Drumgesk smiled again as he thought of the
consternation of his brethren of the Fifteen.   The
possibility of standing trial before them in his own
court on a charge of double manslaughter amused
him, and he laughed outright.   They would have a
hard job to convict Archibald Campbell.

By now he had left the river side and was riding
over the broken and hilly land to the east.   He grew
impatient, for the going was slow, the ground being
a mingling of marsh and mound.   But the day was
growing lighter, and the air was sweet, cold.

Of the routes pursued by his brothers and the
possibilities of them he did not think.   He was certain
that he had taken the true course, suggested by the
apparently idle questions of Don some few days before.
He passed the end of Loch Glashan, a loch in the hills,
fuming, for now he was compelled to walk the horse
both from the nature of the ground and its exhaustion.
As he advanced, the sudden change in the sky came,

like the opening of a shutter. A flush overspread it,
the dawn was bearing on its course. Drumgesk
mounted the last ascent pantingly. In the morning
light, five hundred feet below, shone Loch Fyne.

It was silver in the light of dawn, and on the far
side the heavy masses of Cowal dipped deep in reflection. Beneath, Loch Gair jutted from its parent
loch like the thumb of a hand. By its shores were
clustered the low thatched cottages of the fishermen, and on its surface were the herring boats at
anchorage.

The Crubach gazed on this lovely and peaceful
scene, his eyes roving questingly. His mount started,
and he saw silhouetted on a ridge a half mile distant
the form of a riderless horse. He then reverted his
gaze to the village that looked so diminutive from
where he stood, and shortly saw some figures appear
from the shadow of a house and walk towards the
shore. They were invisible again, behind a screen of
drying nets. Once more they came in view, stepping
slowly along a jetty. Two of them he recognized.
They got into a small boat which rowed them in the
direction of one of the smacks.

Drumgesk then prepared to descend the hill, confident of yet intercepting them. If he could not stop
them at once he could follow them by road either up
or down the loch and get them in good time. He
paused, and reflected on his intentions. It was easy
enough to do what he contemplated, and congenial
. . . and the name of his family would ring through
three kingdoms.

He knew Don's character and reputation, and he
made a guess at the girl's. He knew them better

than they knew each other. That mutual knowledge they would learn in time. It was an ironic thought, and he relished it deeply. For a long time he strained his eyes, until the little vessel had sails up and was making slow way into Loch Fyne, heading to Otter Ferry, which, as General Campbell had told Cydalise, led to the wide world. Reluctantly he gazed, torn between an elemental thirst for instant vengeance on the fugitives and the perception that their punishment would be the more cruel if self-inflicted.

He turned at last with stifled regret. " Let her gang," he said aloud, and led his beast for rest and fodder to Darnirnach on the Add.

IX

Of the brothers, Admiral Campbell was the last to return to Duisk. He had gone as far as Asknish ; his horse had lamed, and with another mount he had returned half-way when a false report sent him speeding down by Loch Craignish. In a suppressed fury he reached Duisk, where he was met by the sight of the French girl Antoinette weeping her eyes out on the front steps with her possessions lying about her. Scipio had thrown her out.

The brothers met in conclave. General Campbell had decided on going south and forcing his cousin to a duel. Admiral Campbell advised his brother to obtain a divorce. Lord Drumgesk explained his new convictions.

" So lang as you don't divorce her she's a worried woman and Don's a puzzled man. Forbye, he'll soon weary of her."

His counsels were unpalatable, but Scipio had a great secret respect for his brother's brains, and they prevailed.

Scipio then destroyed everything that reminded him of Cydalise. Barrett, whom she had engaged, was dismissed. Juno, who was a souvenir of America as well as a reminder of the dead pointer, was sold to a Glasgow merchant, and the children were heart-broken over their loss. But the children, too, could not be borne by their father's sight for a month to come. The coaches were sold, the English serving-men dismissed ; two horses only were kept. As a last irony the diamonds he had destined for his wife arrived. He retained them for the sake of grinding them under foot. The rich dresses of the fugitive woman were burned ; her toilette ornaments, her trinkets and jewels, were cast into the middle of the loch.

Drumgesk reflected that her cosmetics might have suited the admiral, but he did not say so.

A new agony tore at the injured husband's pride. On consideration he would have been better pleased had the elopement taken place anywhere than in lonely Duisk—in London, for preference, where the escapade would have been chiefly known among his own set, which was cynical and freethinking. A challenge and a decree would have cleared the business up. Here in Glassary—ever since the cottagers had been wakened wonderingly to the clatter of hooves in the night, and Dugald Leitch had seen two mounted shapes flash past his window at Strone to be followed later by the distinguishable figure of Drumgesk—the whole countryside of every class and rank was cogni-

L

zant of the general's shame. And Scipio was acute enough to guess that some of his servants had probably observed more, and more shrewdly, than he had, and that nothing would be lost in the telling that would lower him as an officer and a man of honour.

He was too proud a man to explain the seeming poltroonery of his inaction, and his character would have lost by his stubbornness had not the far-seeing Crubach dropped a word to his mother that she should talk to her neighbours, and talk often.

Lord and Lady Drumgesk sped away in their calash, and Admiral and Mrs. Campbell in their coach, and they arranged their halts in such a manner that they could pass through Inveraray without stopping. After that Scipio and his mother were left alone with the children.

For weeks the general did not leave his private policies. He knew that his own dependants were full of surprise at the man who could not keep his wife. They were full of derision, he guessed, against the man who allowed his wife to be plucked from under his nose.

Mrs. Don, in her mansion of Cambus Don, was stricken. All joy departed from her. The elopement added fuel to her ill-will against the Campbells. Her Jock had been ruined by the light intriguing wife of the boorish Scipio who had so often flaunted her. Her Jock had been ruined. She sat in the fine saloon of Cambus Don, her heart black against Scipio whose wife had been the means of ruining her Jock.

On the Leitches the news had no effect. " The

hawks gathered," said the Reverend Dugald, "and the hawks fought."

But on one person the effect was profound. To Peggy MacLachlan the flight of Cydalise was triumph. Her heart lightened and she felt strangely young. She was one with Mrs. Captain Campbell and her two Scots daughters-in-law in that she represented the steadfastness of womanhood. In her was embodied the old Highland tradition, its gravity, its truth and loyalty. She had refused Campbell of Duisk, and she still loved him. She could forget his drunkenness, his overbearing manner and his vulgarity of life, and now saw something infinitely pathetic in the shamefacedness and disgrace of this big brave Highland soldier. All things apart, he was of her kind, her Gaelic race, her type of mind.

She had refused him. And he had taken that young foreign slip of a girl as the next best thing, she told herself, and he had surrounded her with luxury and grandeur and all that money could buy. But she was not of the race, not of the type. And she had failed him, and left him.

It was Peggy's triumph and the vindication of her race. She was happy, secure, and there were no more English and Lowland servants in the house, and no more of the Sasunnach tongue.

She felt strangely drawn to the two children. They seemed no longer to be the children of Cydalise ; they were Scipio's only. And she felt a mother's tenderness for them. They, poor wondering brats, had been placed under the governance of a minister's daughter from Craignish and were thorns in her flesh, missing the ample amiable Juno and saying so.

At last the general chose to visit them. He stamped slowly up the stair, and on the landing he met his housekeeper, who had been with them. He stopped before her, fidgeting, and after clearing his throat asked if they were well. She said they were, and stood aside to let him pass.

"Well, Peggy," he said slowly, "there have been changes in Duisk." And he smiled with a ghastly pretence at ease.

"There have been better, Duisk. And there have been worse."

He nodded heavily. "It seems we are back to the old style," he said, and passed in to see the children.

She was pleased, glad of his acknowledgment of the fact. She almost told Mrs. Captain Archy what he said, but preferred to treasure the words. Mrs. Captain Archy did not greatly regret the absence of Cydalise in spite of the disgrace it had brought. She had begun to find Cydalise difficult. Also, she now had the exquisite felicity of having her son all to herself. She could inquire into the condition of his wardrobe and rate the servants for not having sufficiently good fires for the general, and hers was the delight of strolling with him in the garden or on the avenue, supporting herself on his arm and a stout stick and talking fondly and timorously of himself and his future. He contemplated a return to army life, and Mrs. Captain Campbell feared for the day.

Her husband had been murdered, his brother murdered, a nephew had been slain, a son crippled, and a son humiliated. She had ruled two large estates with profit and assurance, she had explored every possible avenue for the aggrandizement of her offspring, and the acid blonde woman who had grown into a white-haired benevolent old chatelaine felt well rewarded by this monopoly of her eldest son. She was happier than she had ever been.

She showed great fondness for the little François and Emmeline, despite her son's periodic aversions to them. She evinced the liveliest interest in the three daughters of her son Colin, and their marriages. The eldest, Elizabeth, married George Otway, an army officer; Janet, the second, became the wife of Admiral John Bowmaker, an elderly friend of her father's. In 1784 the marriage of the youngest daughter, Leonie, had precipitated a crisis.

Leonie, a girl of eighteen, had fallen in love with and eloped with Æneas Cattanach, the penniless scion of an Inverness-shire family. He had vague prospects of a post in the East India Company's service, and that was all. The Campbells were furious, and her father was determined to have the marriage annulled on the grounds that the girl was a minor and had been coerced.

Mrs. Captain Archy intervened. If the marriage was a love match let it stand. Her own marriage, she declared, had been one of love, and she sent the young couple her blessing and a substantial gift. Admiral Colin was enraged by his mother's interference. She and he met to talk things over; he remonstrated angrily, and she gave the admiral the best dressing down that he had ever received and desired that he would not come into her presence with a face done up like a play-actress's. She forgave him within the hour—he was her son—and the marriage of Leonie and Æneas stood good.

Soon after, Mrs. Colin died, and the admiral lost no time in choosing a second wife.   She was twenty years his junior, ' Caroline, daughter of John Deverell, Esq., in the county of Salop, an agreeable lady with a fortune of £10,000,' according to the newspapers, and within the year she had presented him with a male heir. The boy was named Augustus after a peer of his father's acquaintance who had influence with the Prince of Wales and the Duke of Gloucester.

"Dawm me," exclaimed Drumgesk blankly when he heard of the child's name on returning from the sentencing of a batch of prisoners to transportation. " Dawm me, whaur dae they fin' the names ?   There's a François, an Emmeline, a Leonie, and an Augustus. I've better names for my dogs. We used to be a' Colins and Archys and Neils and Calums in Argyll, and I doubt thae youngsters 'll never be Campbells. My grandfather would turn in his grave if he heard them."

But Mrs. Captain Campbell was delighted.   She had not relished the thought of the younger Otways— several of whom were now in existence—or the young Bowmaker ruling in Barrill.   She foresaw François in Duisk and Augustus in Barrill, and a long line of real Campbells following them.

The birth of her newest grandchild she did not long survive, and Drumgesk inherited Barrill.   At Scipio's desire his mother was placed in the burial-ground constructed in the policies of Duisk, and the brothers paid homage to her memory.

Sacred to the Memory
of
JOANN CAMPBELL OF BARRILL
Daughter of Archibald Campbell of Leck
and Relict of
Captain Archibald Campbell
ob. 8 May 1790.
Fame craves to Trumpet the Merits
of
This Amiable and Accomplished Female

Felicity, seek thou the yews !
Affliction now usurps the scale.
Let Consolation's homely muse
Pour forth her meek and artless tale.

The demands of decency had brought the aged
Reverend Dugald, despite his failing health, to the
burial, and on a further occasion he saw the memorial.
" They mean well," he observed when telling his wife
about it.

Drumgesk closed Barrill House, and was seldom
there, and Scipio now found himself alone. With
dismay he saw the few friendships which he had
hesitatingly renewed ended by death or bankruptcy.
Estates were for sale, and men could not live for ever.
He supervised his property, shot the game on it, and
fished the loch. He gained some excitement from a
lawsuit. He had ceased to feel the smart of the
flight of Cydalise ; it faded with the years—two years,
four years, eight years—and the neighbourhood was
not now a terror to his wounded pride. But he felt
unutterably lonely.

News of his kin came to him by the newspaper or
the information of Peggy MacLachlan. Mrs. Janet
Don died at Cambus Don, leaving instructions for

her burial at Kilmalieu, and so triumphed in the end.
Later, an advertisement in the same Edinburgh
newspaper announced that Cambus Don was for sale.
The elder MacTavishes and Leitches passed away
and slept the long sleep with their kindred in Kilmichael. There was left Colin Og. He remained in
the care of his grandnephew at Strone, but as though
bewildered by the disappearance of those most dear
to him, his life flickered out without resistance, and
the last of the family of Colin Buie Campbell was
dead.

On consideration, General Campbell resolved to call
at Strone and offer his young relative his condolences.
He was curious to know if Colin Og had left anything
behind him that should revert to Duisk. The general
had purchased a new carriage with no associations,
and he took the children with him. The drive did
not produce very pleasant memories to his mind, for
the last time he had passed that way in a carriage
he recollected very clearly.

He had some business to deal with on his own
property of Uillian, and instructed the coachman to
proceed slowly to Strone with the children. This
business settled, the general then paced after the
vehicle, head bared, and enjoying the sweet valley
air and the fresh spring sunshine.

The carriage was halted where the track led up to
Strone. " Where are the children ? " he inquired,
and the coachman said they had started playing with
a boy from the farm and were round the bend on the
road.

" The rascals ! " thought the general, and walked
forward to call them. His son and daughter were

there, and another boy who stood apart and regarded them with some surprise. François was crying.

The general inquired the matter. "That little boy and Francey quarrelled," Emmeline explained, "and he struck Francey."

"Well," said the general good-humouredly, "what's the reason for tears, sir? The lad there didn't cry when you struck back."

"I didn't strike back," François sobbed.

"What!" said the general.

"Francey didn't strike him," Emmeline chimed in approvingly.

Scipio stared at his son. "You took a blow? And you didn't return it? Your father never did that in his life." He brought his hand against his son's head with stunning violence. Torturing surmise showed suddenly on his livid face. "If he *is* your father."

He roughly ordered the weeping children into the carriage and at once returned to Duisk.

Thereafter, Scipio found a cruel pleasure in the taunting of his son. He suspected François of cowardice; he jeered at him for his timidity when riding a pony, for his awkwardness in climbing the hills, for his clumsiness in handling a boat. He found a thousand barbs with which to pierce the boy's heart, a thousand jests to gall his mind. François lived in a state of terror, and in the terror slowly germinated hatred. He was a slender, pale, delicate boy, and his sister was of a similar type. The general would regard his heir with angry contempt. "There's not enough fat on him to make a penny dip," he thought. Scipio's treatment did not tend to improve the lad's delicate nerves and constitution. By the time he reached his twelfth birthday he was a timid wreck, buoyed only by the hysterical consolation of his sister and the compassionate kindness of Peggy Mac-Lachlan. In the end the general packed him off to a school in Berkshire. " He's not much of a Highlandman," he said. " We'll see if he becomes an Englishman or what."

He treated Emmeline with kindness because of her gentle appealing ways, and after the departure of François the general's empty heart opened slightly for affection. For the next three years they were together a lot, and Scipio was very good to her. Emmeline adored him and feared him.

" Peggy," he said once, " do you think she resembles me much ? "

But there was trouble abroad. The head of Louis Sixteenth fell. War was declared. The outbreak of hostilities was as the sound of a trumpet to General Campbell, pining for something to do, and he offered his services to the War Office and was ordered south. He was a changed man the day he left Duisk, with the old set of the shoulders and the old gleam in his eye. He was then turned fifty-eight years of age.

FOUR

I

EMMELINE was fifteen years old when General Campbell volunteered for active service. During her eleven years' residence at Duisk she had witnessed numerous changes, at first with the callous indifference of a child. Now she had grown more grave. The death of Mrs. Captain Campbell, the departure, first of her brother and then of Scipio, left her the sole Campbell in the house. She had the company only of her governess and the staff.

The great lonely house terrified her. She would waken at nights, crying with fright ; the governess would find her shivering with nameless fears. Winter came, and her agonies multiplied. At length the governess wrote seriously to General Campbell, who was then in the Netherlands, about the nervous condition of the girl and blamed the solitude of the house for aggravating her trouble. He replied at once, instructing that Duisk be closed and maintained in the charge of Peggy MacLachlan, and that Emmeline be sent to Uillian.

Although Scipio at times had impressed upon Cydalise the antiquity and grandeur of his family, he had never mentioned Uillian. The long sojourn abroad that had imposed a new set of values upon his aspiring mind had made him ashamed of the old house. On his return, going there on business

171

with his doer, he had marked it, its long straggling appearance and thatched roof, and determined its instant demolition once the tacksman's lease expired; and the departure of Cydalise did not cause him to alter his intention. He decided to farm Uillian himself, but instead of razing the old house of Mor Campbell he superimposed a story on it and a slate roof, enlarged the windows, erected two small wings, and felt with some satisfaction that Uillian was now a gentleman's residence. Other improvements he effected at leisure : the formation of a lawn, a shrubbery, and a gravelled approach, and the insertion above the doorway of a stone bearing the arms of Campbell of Uillian quartered with those of Campbell of Duisk.

It was to this small mansion that Emmeline was transported, with the minister's daughter from Craignish to hearken her lessons and a woman from Duisk to do the cooking.

She was delighted with Uillian; there was no huge house to fill her timid mind with ghostly alarms, no dark loch to threaten her when she gazed from her bedroom window at nights. Uillian looked across the Add to Kilmichael, at the entrance to a cleft in the hills. It was a cosy place, with plenty of people at the farm buildings a stone's throw from the house. Emmeline would go there and feed the hens and stroke the velvety noses of the horses and see the cows being milked, although she always kept a safe distance from these last, for she was afraid of cattle.

Everyone around was pleasant to her, for they all knew of the exploit of Cydalise, and were full of pity for her abandoned daughter. Her father, too, had regained all his old prestige by returning to the army. It was felt now that his disregard of Don had been from contempt only, and Scipio's ride to war at his years had brought the general a second and increased glory. Emmeline would talk of her father to anyone who would listen, an easier matter at Uillian, where, from its nearer position to intercourse with the world, everyone had some English. "He is a fine man, Duisk," they would tell her approvingly. "He is a real Campbell." The people would speak in the little cottages at night with high admiration of Campbell of Duisk, and make hazard at the wild night of the departure of Cydalise and General Don, for, long since, from widely different parts had drifted reports of Scipio arriving, hatless and livid, at Cladich in the morning; of the rage-scarred face of sailor Colin as he raced by the shores of Craignish; and how the Crubach had been seen in the grey dawn on the hills above Loch Gair.

At Uillian the governess, Marianne Turner, became curiously happy and vivacious, and after a time when she and Emmeline took walks in the evening they would be joined by the schoolmaster. Miss Turner was in her middle thirties and he of a similar age. Emmeline was at first surprised by the amazing change in the customarily grave woman's demeanour, but was able to solve the reason in time, as Miss Turner, thirsting to speak to someone, confided to her charge that she thought the schoolmaster a model of a man. The young girl did not share that opinion, as Mr. MacInnes seemed to her only a nice but boring

person, but she appreciated the extra freedom that
the romance granted her, as, no superior power being
there to supervise her actions, Marianne would leave
her charge by herself for a time while she and Mr.
MacInnes sauntered in the dusky twilight.

Emmeline found a tremendous delight in being
left to herself, and Marianne, observing that no harm
had come to her pupil in the evenings, would now
permit her to stravaig alone in the daytime, for she
did not share the girl's fondness for tearing across
fields in the wake of a barking terrier. In one of
these harmless pursuits Emmeline came to the lands
of Strone.

It was a young man who was there, in the angle
of a field, repairing a broken harness strap. Hearing the rustle of her dress he glanced around, and
seeing her standing in the gap of the hedge flushed
and abashed, he smiled and spoke. His manner was
shy in spite of his greeting, and Emmeline gained
more confidence in face of it. Her dog had entered
the field, in any case. She gathered the folds of
her skirt together and stepped lightly over the dry
ditch.

" Such nice horses ! " she exclaimed, and patted
the shoulder of the off beast ; it turned its head
and nuzzled her hand.

" They are very quiet," he said. " This one,"
nodding to the one she was fondling, " is fond of
children."

She looked at him. He was dressed in simple
working garb, and was wearing neither coat nor waistcoat. His features were blunt and much tanned by
exposure to the open air. The general cast of them

was attractive and enhanced by the mass of thick hair that clustered over his brow. His body was sturdily built.

" Well ! " she said, " I am not a child. What is your name, my man ? " she asked the big brown animal.

" Her name is Flora," said the young man.

" Are you the ploughman ? " Emmeline asked in some confusion.

" I suppose I am," he replied.

" How old are you ? What is your name ? "

" It is no business, I'm thinking," he said, " of strangers."

Emmeline was cowed immediately, and said : " I am fifteen, and I am Miss Emmeline Campbell of Duisk."

" We are neighbours, then," he said. " It is at Uillian you are living. Do you like this side of the country ? " She said she did. " Your father is the big general," he said thoughtfully.

" He is winning battles over in France," she said, " and will help to put the new French king on the throne."

" If you ever want to gather the honeysuckle," he said, " there's a place up the burn there. You needn't be afraid of the cattle, for they won't harm you. They tell me you are afraid of the cattle."

Emmeline continued to stroke the horse. " Do you get a good wage ? " she asked presently, glancing at his homely clothes.

" I never got a wage in my life." She was incredulous, and loudly blamed his simplicity. " This is my father's farm," he explained.

"What is your name and how old are you?"
she demanded obstinately, as he was only a poor.
man.

"My name is Neil Leitch and I am eighteen years
old," he said.

The next time she was that way she encountered
the youth's father Angus, the posthumous son of
Do'l Mor. He regarded her critically, remembering
his grandfather's unexplained aversion to the Duisk
family, but he spoke kindly to her as she was so
young, and she returned often to Strone.

In Uillian Emmeline gained health and developed
a passion for climbing. She would join with the
people in their ascents to the peat moss on the hill-
tops, watching the men as their farrachans cut cleanly
into the black stringy fuel. It was cut when the
weather was fine, and the turfs spread out to the
sun. Then they would return on a later day and
pile the dried peats into stacks. There was much
gaiety and laughter among the grown people and
the children, and they would all descend to the valley
singing. Later the people would return to the moss
and fill creels from their own supplies. Emmeline
liked to accompany them. She was full of innocent
pleasure in the prospect from the hill-tops; there
was rapture in wild scurries over the soft turf, amid
the bracken, and the pleasure of drinking from an
ice-cold spring.

She grew reconciled to the absence of the general
and François because of these delights, for she guessed
that her father might not approve of them and that
François might not participate in them.

"It was your brother Dugald who struck my

brother one day years ago," she said once accusingly
to Neil.

"It would do him good," said Neil seriously, "and
it came better from a cousin."

Emmeline had some vague recollection of seeing
a family chart at Duisk with the Leitch name on
it, but she had not connected it with the Strone
family. The revelation gave her much pleasure.

Miss Marianne Turner was soon able to acquaint
the general with the news of her approaching marriage
to Mr. MacInnes, and begged him to arrange for
another person to assume her duties. The information arrived when Scipio was considering new plans
for his daughter's future, and settled his intentions.
He had Emmeline removed to a school for young
ladies near London where she would acquire the
accomplishments suitable for her rank and sex, and
be near him on his leaves.

Miss Turner conveyed the girl to London—a jaunt
which provided the future bride with reminiscence
for the remainder of her life—and Uillian likewise
was closed.

There remained only Peggy MacLachlan. She
stayed in Duisk, guarding carefully its parvenu
treasures and acquiring what scraps she could of
the language she hated from the parish minister or
the doctor. She was ageing visibly, and had grown
a little aloof in demeanour. The things she had
wanted to take place had happened, and on consideration she saw little joy to be derived from that.
The onrush of progress had been stemmed, but only
temporarily, she knew. François would come back,
Emmeline would come back, full of strange hostile

M

ideas. Already the daughters of sailor Colin had
paid visits to Barrill with their families, and from
there had made furtive visits to the house of Duisk,
peering, peeping, and asking questions. And Scipio
would return in time.

She heard accounts of the great things he was
accomplishing in the war. He would return grander
than ever, more foreign, more remote. Scipio Campbell, whose father had been slain in her mother's
presence in Glenshira at Kilblaan!

Once they had been very close. But what kinship was there now between the old proud general
and his old plain housekeeper! They had been two
trees together in the same soil; and he had stretched
to an exceeding height and borne storm and misfortune, and flourished despite them. And she had
lingered in his shade.

She had no grounds for complaint, she told herself sadly. She was at Duisk, as a MacLachlan
should be. She was secure, and privileged, and
trusted. What better could the left-hand daughter
of Neil Uillian hope for? What better! And she
would study her ageing face in the glass, seriously
and intently, and pass then to her duties, dully
conscious of frustration.

II

On volunteering his services Scipio had obtained
a command in the Duke of York's expedition of
1793. Landing at Ostend, he had taken part in
those engagements at St. Amand and Famars that
were followed by the occupation of Valenciennes.
In the excitement of war his late lassitude of spirit

vanished ; he felt younger, his old habits of resource and organization were reborn.　He proved his mettle and the mettle of his troops during the varying successes of the campaign and for the first time for years enjoyed some peace of mind, found amid the roar of cannon.

In these surroundings, in the rigour of battle, in the pomp of command, amid the rough comradeship of his hard-drinking officers, General Campbell had returned to the sphere most suited to him. They were the natural sequel to his Indian and American campaigns, and sometimes, so greatly did his present environment impress him, he felt that the domestic disappointments intervening had been overrated in his mind.

In the winter of the next year, following the setbacks at Lille, the army retired into Westphalia and in March embarked at Bremen for England.

Emmeline by that time was in London.　The general leased a house in Dover Street and made a habit of entertaining a select company of friends for whom the second Mrs. Colin Campbell acted as hostess, the admiral being on the high seas.

Mrs. Colin's stepdaughters were invariably with her.　The eldest, Elizabeth, in her early thirties, with a hook-nosed predatory face, pretended to live in a state of constant financial worry.　Her husband, Captain Otway of the infantry, had taken part in the recent campaign without being under the actual command of General Campbell.　Mrs. Otway could see no reason for an uncle of high military rank doing nothing for a husband of indifferent prospects. She made much of Scipio.

Her sister Janet had chosen a wiser destiny. Her features, so like her sister's but irradiated by the gift of beauty, had easily enough captured the heart of rich elderly Admiral Bowmaker, and in gratitude for the comforts he had lavished on her and for his long and welcome absences on duty she had presented him with a son, Thomas.

A jealousy had grown in Mrs. Otway's heart, consequent on Janet's child. There were four young Otways, the youngest lately born, but the little Cæsar and Colin and Archibald and Elizabeth would not have the financial backing that the little Bowmaker would have. Mrs. Otway had chosen the names of her second and third sons with some discretion. Her father was visibly pleased by the choice for her second boy. The name of the third was a tribute to childless Drumgesk. She had been confident that the Barrill property would descend to herself, but with the birth of her half-brother Augustus her dreams in that direction had vanished into space. She could only hope that her Uncle Archibald would remember her own Archibald with a legacy, and that her father Colin would not forget any of the little Otways.

" If," said Captain Otway, " you have two uncles, and one's a general and another's a judge, and your father's an admiral, and I can't get a little decent promotion with all that, I'll be shot."

The faithful Elizabeth, therefore, mapped out her own plan of campaign and kept General Campbell well reminded of her presence, and did not forget to impress her stepmother, with whom she maintained the most amiable friendship, that a word from

her to Scipio regarding Captain George Otway's future
would not be amiss. Mrs. Otway had moments of
despondency, but they did not last, and she never
showed them. She awaited eagerly the return of
her father, wherever he might be, Corsica, or Deme-
rara, or Surinam. After all, surely Admiral Campbell could do something for his own son-in-law.

The admiral's youngest daughter, the gentle Leonie
whose runaway marriage had incensed everyone save
her grandmother, was the mother of young John
Campbell Hamilton Cattanach. She had been the
first of the sisters to wed, and her son was now a
lad of ten. Leonie's husband held a secretarial post
in the East India Company which he had obtained
through the offices of his maternal uncle. The other
sisters had regarded Mr. Æneas Cattanach with a
good deal of contempt because he was not in either
of the fighting services and his position was not unduly lucrative. Leonie, on her part, seemed quite
satisfied, and at her husband's urgings wrote long
letters describing the charms of the little John Campbell Hamilton Cattanach to Mr. John Hamilton, the
child's grand-uncle, whose talents had lately raised
him to a governorship in India.

In the society of his female relatives and military comrades Scipio relaxed. Emmeline was still
at school, and would be for some years, but she was
frequently in his company and that of her cousins.
In the end she felt that the general's was prefer-
able. She was awed somewhat by the unswerving
stare and set smile of Mrs. Otway. Mrs. Bowmaker's languid airs and polite appraisement humbled
her, and she grew to think of Janet in terms of the

coiffure of jewels, plumes, and lace with which that lady decorated her head. With Leonie she was always at ease. Leonie was gentle and had a sudden and sweet smile, like the sun breaking through clouds. But Mrs. Cattanach's conversation veered constantly to the fascinations and clevernesses of the little John.

Scipio was different, and enchanted the girl. He was so big and brusque, his voice was so harsh, his look so searching. And yet he was unceasingly kind to her. They would drive out together and he would listen patiently to her animated chatter; often, if she revealed naïvely a desire for some object or trifle it would arrive for her on the following day. On one occasion only had he been angry, and that was when she had told him innocently of her visits to Strone. He had grown forbidding then, and the girl had shrunk from him. But on the next day he had explained his reasons.

" The Leitches are our kin, certainly. They are of an old stock of landowning physicians, of a Campbell and MacLachlan connection. We Campbells and they were social equals. My grandfather increased our position, and I have done even more. The Leitches have sunk. They are in difficulties, my agent tells me. Angus Leitch died last month—he was drowned in Loch Fyne. The new Leitch is very young. Remember, Emmeline, that you are a lady, and must not associate with those not of your own rank."

Scipio was brightened by the return from the West Indies of his brother. The admiral appeared not in the perfection of health, and it was observed that he powdered and rouged more vigorously than before.

The Caribbean and the rum out there had not been kind to him, but he was eager for further service in view of the remarkable opportunities afforded by the war in Europe. While waiting for further commands the two brothers drank heavily together, but between them they gained Otway his desired promotion.

" By the way," said Colin later, " I met Hew MacLachlan, who is at the Home Office, and he was giving me some odd news that had come his way. He got it from one of the government agents in Paris. It's about your wife, Skip."

Scipio stared at him thoughtfully. " Well," he said at last, " we'll hear it."

" Do you know where Don is ? "

" No."

" I do. He is in Norfolk. He married Gilwell the nabob's widow. She is worth one hundred thousand. They were living in Venice. The troubles abroad frightened them, and they scrambled home last month."

" Where is *she* ? " said Scipio.

Colin said that Don and Cydalise after their flight from Duisk had proceeded to Switzerland, where they had lived for a time by the shores of Lake Geneva. General Don had later proceeded to Rome, alone, as he had wearied of Mrs. Campbell's company. It was from there he had instructed the sale of Cambus Don, and his movements in the years thereafter were uncertain until his arrival in Brussels, where he had won the heart and fortune of the widowed Mrs. Gilwell.

Cydalise had gone to Paris, being rapidly reduced

to poverty following Don's desertion. The English
agent had made her acquaintance in the summer of
1793. At that time she had descended to an irregu-
lar mode of existence, and her connection with the
agent was of extreme value because of a channel
through which she could obtain information. She
had become suspect during the Reign of Terror, and
a charge being lodged against her, Cydalise was
thrown into the Saint-Lazare. She was beheaded
a week before the fall of Robespierre.

The admiral was surprised and slightly scandalized
on seeing his brother weeping. His own feelings
when he heard of his sister-in-law's execution had
been of family shame and satisfaction commingled.
He mumbled some words of consolation. Scipio
raised a haggard face.

"You might have spared me that, Colin," was
all he said.

For a week there was no spirit in him.

At the end of it he sought out an old friend and
had a close talk, the result of which appeared in
the newspapers some days later. There it was stated
that on the morning of the 26th September, 1796,
General Scipio Campbell, C.B., accompanied by Sir
Frederick Gwynne, had met General John Don, who
was seconded by Francis Silkstone, Esq., of Elling-
ham, in a meadow on the outskirts of Thetford, and
had shot him. The deceased officer, it was remarked,
had been the cousin of his antagonist.

III

Shortly afterwards General Campbell was appointed
to the supervision of troops being trained in the

Eastern Command and he disbanded his London establishment. In the ardours of hard work he determined to forget the sight of what came constantly before him, and that was a scaffold.

The Campbells were all pleased that he had at last avenged the slight on his honour, and Drumgesk was delighted. Colin did not reveal even to the judge the details of the disreputable later career and fate of Cydalise, but the story of the flight was so widely circulated that Scipio's vengeance was at once attributed to that. The only member of the family who was not too certain of the justice of her father's act was Emmeline, who had liked to consider him as mounted on a prancing horse and waving a drawn sword, and shuddered at the thought of him standing before another man and blowing his brains out. The eighteen-years-old girl did not yet know that her mother had run away with Don ; she had a vague belief that her parents had disagreed and that Mrs. Campbell preferred to reside abroad.

The sight of Don's spread body on the grass had given Scipio no great satisfaction, for his grief was greater than any other feeling. It was then he had realized the fidelity of his heart to Cydalise during fourteen years, a fidelity which his shame and wounded pride had stifled. He could not evade the memory of Cydalise. The recollection of her was constant with him. And, he thought, they had been so very near each other but three years before, and it was at that very time she was passing to her death. He thought of her as he had so well known her, with a sense of baffled love. He might have tried to

understand her better, he reflected. What Don had
completed perhaps he had begun. Her face, so curiously mingled of childishness and sophistication, came
before him continuously. For two more years the
man threw himself into his work with savage concentration.

Emmeline, whose education had been completed
and who was residing in London with her uncle and
aunt, wrote begging him to allow her to be with
him. She hinted that London was not agreeing with
her—nor was it, from the point of harmony with
her surroundings—and Scipio, misinterpreting her
meaning, believed that she was unwell and promptly
sent her off to Uillian that she might benefit by
what he termed native air.

His military duties had not been permitted to interfere with General Campbell's keen appreciation of
his interests as a landowner, and he had been constantly apprised of matters at Duisk by his factor.
The grasping character of his race which had stood
him so well in India had increased with the years,
and every change at Duisk had been effected with
the intention of drawing greater revenue. Under the
system of single-tenant farms which he had favoured
many of his old tenants had been compelled to leave,
either going to the coast to practise herring fishing or
emigrating. Many of the younger men had joined
the army, as a short cure for all questions. As a
final economic stroke he forwarded instructions that
Peggy MacLachlan should go to Uillian as cook and
housekeeper to Miss Emmeline. From there, General
Campbell wrote, Peggy could make periodical visits
of inspection to Duisk, and the people at the home

farm would always take care that the Big House
didn't run away.

Peggy was startled by the slender girl who descended from the coach one May day at Uillian.
Emmeline was now twenty, and the facial replica
of her mother, but she was fair-haired, and her eyes
were blue and candidly ingenuous. In the girl's
appearance was a fragility, a lack of animal vigour
that might have come from spiritual rather than
physical sources.

In Uillian, where she had told herself would be
found every desirable sequestered peace away from
her intimidating relatives, Emmeline was at once
lonely. The society of her school companions, the
interests of a large city, had intervened between her
last residence there as a young girl, and now the
place had none of the attractions suitable for her
age and fancies. Her tastes were not excessive;
she liked reading novels of the romantic type, she
had acquired a fashionable love of nature, she was
fond of poetry and sometimes attempted the com-
position of it. And she was full of sentimental
dreams.

She found herself alone in the house with a woman
of almost seventy whose English was ridiculously
mispronounced, and, with the exception of a child
of twelve who came from the farm to do odd jobs,
that completed the household. (Emmeline, indeed,
was solicitous that so much work should devolve
on Peggy, but Peggy said she could do it.) She
found herself strolling aimlessly on the road or by
the river-side, with tender appreciation of the scenery
around her and yet conscious of a vague lack. The

society of the landowning families which had been
plentiful in Colin Buie's day, was now almost non-
existent owing to the changes, and such families as
there were had little interest for her and found no
interest in her.

By the end of the first month Emmeline had
determined to desert Uillian with the earliest excuse
possible. But her resolution waned, for much as
she liked General Campbell, she was afraid of him,
too. She continued to correspond with him and
François, and they both wrote frequently to her,
Scipio's letters full of sense and information and
comments on public affairs, and François' generally
with a peevish ring in them, as they had always
had.

She paid a dutiful visit to the graves of Mor
Campbell's kin, urged thereto by Scipio's coat-of-
arms, and she observed on another stone the name
of Angus Leitch of Strone, whom her father had
said was drowned. He had not been forty at the
time of death. Despite the general's injunctions she
wondered whether she should call at Strone. She
remembered the family quite well, and it seemed
ill-bred to ignore them. For a time she hesitated,
ultimately visiting the house one evening. The
widow was there, and two of the sons, Neil and Angus;
Dugald, the middle son, had enlisted.

The June dusk came quickly, and it was dark
when Emmeline left the house. Neil escorted her
back to Uillian.

" It was very kind of you to think of us," he
said on the way. " You have the old spirit of kinship, surely."

"I would have been ungrateful had I not," she said. "Your father was always kind to me. You will miss him."

He said yes. Emmeline laughed suddenly. "Do you remember, when I saw you first, I asked if you were the ploughman? That was five years ago. And you said you were."

"I am everything now, since my father died. It is a very hard struggle. It was a bad crop last year."

"And what does that mean?"

"It means ruin, sometimes."

"But that won't affect you much," she said. "You own Strone now. Land is a good investment. General Campbell always says so."

The young man laughed. "General Campbell will have sixteen thousand acres, counting Uillian. And I have four hundred."

"And how many people do you pay to work for you, Mr. Leitch?"

"I pay none. Angus helps me. There was another farm, but it is sold, and the families that were there are gone." He spoke simply, without adding the information that Strone was mortgaged and on the verge of passing from his hands.

"Is it the case," he added suddenly, "that your father fought and killed a man called General Don? I have heard my great-grandmother talk about him. Well, I seem to have plenty of great relations, for his mother was a Campbell."

"Perhaps," she said rashly, "my father might do something for your interest were he to know of your difficulties."

"Perhaps he would, but I would be refusing it,"
he said.

"Of course, General Campbell has a great many
calls on his interest, and when he uses it he expects
gratitude in return."

"I can understand that those who go and beg
hat in hand will always be most ready with the
flattery. But it would be a strange thing, surely,
to force a favour where it has not been asked and
demand praise where it will not be given."

Emmeline was incensed and taken aback. It was
both natural and picturesque to show a friendly
patronage to this young man who was both a poor
farmer and a poor relation. She had read something similarly circumstanced in one of her novels;
in it the poor relation's gratitude had been touch-
ingly profuse. The reply of Neil Leitch was unexpected, and it was not merited by the condescending suggestion she had made, a suggestion all the
more precious as she knew in her heart that General
Campbell would scarcely approve of it. He might
be three years older than herself, this muscular rustic
farmer, and he was a good-looking intelligent individual, but he was not a gentleman, and she was
Miss Emmeline Campbell of Duisk.

"I think, Mr. Leitch, I can manage to find my
way home now, thank you," she said coldly. "It
was kind of you, and I am much obliged."

"I will see you to your own door," he replied
calmly. "My grandfather was murdered in the
woods at Duisk and I am not going to have you
murdered on the road at Strone."

"Who would murder me here?" she said pettishly.

"That's what my family asked yours, I am told. And none could answer."

Emmeline said nothing, and they walked in silence till they reached the by-road to Uillian. There he took her hand to assist her over a rough part but relinquished it at the convenient moment, bidding her good night at the door. She knocked, listening to the sound of his shoes in the darkness, and as soon as Peggy opened the door rushed up to her own room.

She opened the window cautiously and strained her eyes, but he had become indistinguishable with night.

"He was rude," she thought. "He was insufferably rude."

In the morning Emmeline chose a book and walked out. She crossed the fields and, coming to a spongy patch of ground, saw the myrtle growing thickly. It was the badge of her clan. She plucked a sprig and pressed it to her nostrils. The strange, compelling perfume of it puzzled her. It was so different from that of garden flowers, so remote from the elegant essences of the drawing-room. She stood questioningly, gazing on the sombre little plant and breathing its fragrance repeatedly. Then with quick light steps she passed to the little dell she had been told of, where the honeysuckle grew in its season. It was there, and around her was hazel and birch, like a canopy over the mossy bank whereon she sat. The sky was a light clear blue, and there was a hint of sunshine. Near-by was the undertone of a burn; on the hill-side facing were the sheep of Strone.

Emmeline drew towards her a spray of the yellow blossom. It was pregnant with sensuous melancholy —she released it, gazing vacantly ahead and seeing nothing.

She felt vexed at something. She was uncertain of what it might be—was conscious only of a vague dissatisfaction, a formless ache. She was gifted with a sense of grievance, and leaned her slim frame back against her extended arms and pondered dreamily. For a long time she sat so; then she shuddered, and her eyes glanced at the book that lay beside her. It was open, showing an engraving of a fine gentleman bowing over the hand of a slender lady, with a balcony, a curtain, and a lake in the background. Emmeline gazed at it long, and then her eyes reverted to the sheep on the farther slope and the swelling heights beyond, and her ears heard the subdued gurgling of the burn. On an impulse she thrust her face to the ground, smelling the cold sweet soil.

She raised her head, listening intently, and drew breath rapidly between her teeth. She rose, smiling with a smile of secrecy, and started the ascent of the opposite slope. In a little she had reached a place where the valley lay before her. Beneath was a group of buildings; a man was working in the nearest field.

As she returned to Uillian she wondered at the loveliness of the country. She had scarce noticed it before. In the afternoon she walked by the side of the Add, and in the evening strolled on the road.

On the afternoon of the next day she chose a dress with care, and tended her hair carefully, and

examined her face in the glass with anxious attention. With parted lips she studied the reflection,
and felt pleased, and after a final glance ran lightly
down the stair, humming a tune. And she made
at once for the place where the honeysuckle grew.

As on yesterday afternoon he was on the hill,
and she accurately judged the distance between his
descent and her walk to the lower track. He flushed
when they met, and looked awkward. Emmeline was
not certain what to say.

"Do you not tire?" she asked at last.

"I do not tire very easily. I go to bed early,"
he said.

Emmeline examined his face with possessive interest. His blunt, strong features were deeply sunburned, although not deep enough to hide his blushes.
Over his cheek bones grew a few fine golden hairs,
clear against the tan.

"You look very strong," she said.

"Yes," he admitted. "I can make no complaint
there."

After a thought she said: "There are no Neils
in my family. Were you called after some one?"

"I was called after my mother's brother, Neil
Ferguson at Knockalava."

"Oh," she replied politely.

"Are you fond of this part?" he asked. "I saw
you this way yesterday morning."

"I go this way in the daytime," she confessed,
"but I would be afraid to be alone here in the
dusk."

"Och," he said, "there is nothing to be afraid
of."

N

" I was afraid," she said, " and that is why I keep to the road in the evenings."

Emmeline had learned something about farming routine, and she waited until an hour after the evening milking before going out. They met on the road between Uillian and Strone. He was accompanied by a collie.

" I did not think you would have been out to-night," he said. " The evening has a nip in the air."

" I like the cool air," she replied. " I can walk much farther when the air is fresh."

" If you would like to take a turn——" he said hesitatingly. They strolled together over the fields.

The valley hills were clear in the evening light as though pencilled in strong strokes, and in the air there was a shivering that was of nature and not of cold—the suspense that lingers before the twilight. As they walked together they discussed the merits of his dog, and he told her of its peculiar qualities and virtues. Emmeline knew occasional moments of disquiet in which she questioned her hardihood in disobeying her father's commands and descending from her station, but the voice within her of Scipio Campbell was muffled by another that may have been Colin Buie's, for she argued that her companion was her cousin—her second cousin, once removed, as she had proved from the chart she had constructed that forenoon. In these moments of doubting defiance she would turn to him half pleadingly, and he would at that moment hurriedly avert his gaze from her.

" As we are cousins," she said, " it is nice to think you are going to show me the places around here."

"I'll be the pleased man," he said, "—except, of course, not in my working hours."

"Would you like to be a rich man?" she asked impulsively.

"I would like to be able to keep Strone, that was my grandfather's father's."

"And is that all!"

"It is not money that counts most in this world, I'm thinking," he said gravely. "It is maybe peace of mind. But it would be fine to help those who need help . . . my father's cousin Donald MacTavish Duin—he had to sell Duin two years ago, and he is losing on a small farm he leased in Knapdale, and in a few years' time he will be a crofter."

"And is he your cousin?"

"And yours too!"

Emmeline was surprised and slightly annoyed. "I did not know I had relatives in that station of life."

"His family and mine were in Glassary before yours was ever heard of," he told her with relish. "His mother was Ann Leitch. She was a very handsome woman, I'm told. She was a sister of my grandfather, and their mother was a Campbell of Duisk."

"It would be from there," Emmeline said naïvely, "that she would inherit her beauty."

"I will not just say that," he said seriously, "but we cannot tell." He assisted her to jump a burn in their course; they leaped together, she laughing joyously up to him. "But you are not wanting in good looks, Miss Campbell."

In the minutes before darkness they lingered, un-

willing to hasten their return. Emmeline found that
night, which lessens the span of eyesight, increases
the sense of smell. The pungency of peat that clung
to his home-spun garments was strange but comforting. She laid a timid arm on his sleeve when
darkness grew complete, and he asked her to place
it through his. She kept on telling herself that she
was Miss Emmeline Campbell of Duisk. In the
hedge-lined road to Uillian she stopped.

"Neil," she said, "—it seems strange to call a
cousin ' Mr. Leitch '—Neil," she repeated falteringly,
" perhaps what I said yon evening angered you, and
perhaps I should not have said it, but I really didn't
think."

" It was myself that was too quick with my anger,"
he said in a low, unsteady voice, "and I should
not have been."

" But Neil," she said piteously, " you are sure
you're not really angry. Because if I thought you
were I would be very, very unhappy.

" I have been worrying," she added breathlessly,
" ever since, because I was sure I had offended you,
and I am positive that General Campbell would be
angry with me for offending you, and I am certain
—oh, you're not angry, I hope." In her anxiety
she clasped his lapels. " And you may call me
Emmeline."

She then felt his strong arms around her, and
commenced weeping on his breast.

IV

In the companionship of the other girls at the
school for training young ladies Emmeline had con-

cocted many imaginary romances, her own particular hero being a young gentleman who would have
dark raven hair, a pale and rather melancholy cast
of features, and ardent eyes. She had favoured this
type so much that sometimes she was almost convinced that such an individual, known to her, existed,
and she would imagine them driving in an open cur-
ricle on a sweeping drive that led through undulating parkland to the palladian mansion that was his
home, a little spaniel frisking beside the vehicle.
She had seen pictures very similar. Her existence
thereafter was to be one of gentle sentiment—re-
clining in an arbour, loitering by a terrace balustrade, feeding swans on the lake, the dark-eyed dark-
locked husband always hovering near her in varying
postures of devotion.

In reality, Emmeline secretly feared men. She
had reached her twentieth year without losing the
timorous respect that she had felt for them when
she was twelve, and to be alone with one was an
ordeal almost too much for her. The shy, fragile
girl, while listening to the part love-stricken, part
mercenary chattering of her companions, had known
a secret bitterness, conscious that she was unskilled
in the arts in which her compeers in age were proving
so adept, and fully aware that she would never have
the heart nor the audacity to practise them. With
a feeling of complete strangeness she had heard
them discuss the eligibility and prospects of young
men of their acquaintance, wonderingly asking herself what the future could hold in store for such as
her.

Neil Leitch was the antithesis of all that she had

considered as ideal in a man. His hair was not
pomaded, his waist was not slender. He did not
wear the highest of high cravats, nor silk hose, nor
bunches of heavy seals. He did not even pretend
an extreme of reactionary loyalty and powder his
hair as a defiance to the spirit of the age. He had
no park, he had not even a spaniel.

Could Emmeline's dismissal of reserve have been
foretold to her, she would have been twitteringly
angry. Scipio in his occasional homilies had only
rounded off what the ladies' school had taught her,
and, although the girl's opinion of her own personal
merits was small, she was able to balance her short-
comings there by admitting the importance of her
social position.

She did not think greatly of the status of her distant kinsman. Strone was a farm-house, and much
less pretentious than most of the farm-houses in
Berkshire or Surrey. The acreage of Strone was
small, its soil indifferent. The connection of its
owner with the Campbells of Duisk was remote, remote enough to be ignored. And thinking of these
things and thinking of Neil Leitch, Emmeline knew
that she was in love with him.

Her isolation at Uillian, the knowledge that she
had still fewer opportunities there of giving and
gaining the affection that others gave and received,
and the constant admission that she was doomed
by her own temperament to a loneliness that the
years would augment, had stirred in the girl's starved
heart a feeble despair. That heart, which had never
known other than the most timid flutterings of admiration and shyness, had told her with unfaltering

truth that she loved Neil Leitch. It was an immediate attraction, irresistible, to be withstood for a
day alone. Emmeline had wilted under the blast
of this sensation. She knew feelings foreign to her
of strange and beautiful delight. The young farmer,
so strong and calm and unpolished, so different from
the young gentlemen whom she had met at the
admiral's house, so quietly proud and calm with the
calmness that is loaned of nature, so like nature
and unlike the urban elegance she had looked upon
—she loved him.

She had been unhappy in her loneliness, and now
she was swooningly happy. She had been resentful
against the partiality of a fate that had made her
diffident, and now the world was a place of wonder
and delight. She blushed whenever she thought of
her unmaidenly confession, and quivered careless of
it when she thought of his response. She loved him,
and he loved her.

Nor could she have disregarded convention and
modesty had she not been firmly convinced of his
social inferiority. Her conviction of his humble
status had strengthened her resolve.

Emmeline could not understand how or why she
had come so suddenly to idolize him, why he constantly monopolized her thoughts, or how the sight
of him sent vague tremors of rapture to her heart.
She did not know, and she ceased to care.

The young owner of Strone had never before seen
anyone of the beauty and appearance of Emmeline
Campbell. He had been stirred by her before ; that
was five years gone, but the meeting was a pleasant
memory and had remained very fresh. Despite his

own words to her and despite the inherited dislike which his father had attempted to instil into him, Neil was secretly proud of his family connection with the three old brothers who had achieved so much. They were like all Campbells, he reflected, greedy and grasping; still, they were great men. And the unconscious arrogance of the fifteen-years-old Emmeline had not dispelled his respect for the Duisks; during the struggling years he had treasured the incident.

Now she had returned, slender and delicate-looking, like a flower; beautifully attired, and with mannerisms and gestures that were novel to him in women. The sight of this bewitching creature had angered him beyond measure; he had been as courteous as possible, but his instant subjection could only be interpreted by a gravity that was sullen at the core. She was beyond him in all the amenities of life. She was not beyond him socially—the Campbells of Duisk! his own forefathers had owned land in Glassary centuries before—but she was rich and exquisite and tender-bred, and he was poor.

In one other thing only was he her equal, or indeed her superior. He could feel pity for her, knowing the story of her abandonment by her mother. That story had been revived by the killing of General Don, the news of which had swept through the district with great credit to her father. But her mother had been no kind of a mother or wife. He pitied her.

That fact made the girl a subject for honest compassion. But he needed none of that to stir his feelings. Emmeline could perform that work herself.

Their passage of words that first night on the road to Uillian had given him tremendous pleasure; each word of hers had been like a cruel little stab in him, and he had endeavoured to give her one or two in return. That fragile creature handling daggers!— the words she had spoken overthrew him.

Up till this, his twenty-third year, Neil had never been in any other company than his own. He had never found the time.

A goddess had appeared in Glassary, trim, gentle, and elegant. And lo! her appealing eyes were raised to his, her sweet lips were parted in a smile for him, her diffident and touching kindness was for him alone. Neil was bewildered by this inexpressible joy. His days were days of exultation, his evenings hours of unutterable delight.

Together they walked in the gloamings, by the river, by the hillfoots, on the paths that led to the sequestered little clefts of the burns where the bats would flit silently about them and the waters sing a melody of their own. Like the spirits of two alien worlds they met and walked together; or like the embodied mood of what had remained with that which had been torn from its ancient habitat, had been removed, but had returned.

They walked, silent most frequently, in a daze of happy wonder, not seldom questioning the fortune that had brought them together and the future that would be in store. Confidingly she would throw her arms around him and press her lips to his in the moment of parting, and he would grasp her in his strong arms as though it were their last. In their hearts was unselfish love, and perfect innocence.

V

Admiral Campbell had always made a point of keeping on the friendliest terms with his brother the Crubach. This was not difficult, for the brothers had always agreed, but Colin was never forgetful of his children. It was family knowledge that Barrill was the judge's absolutely and that he might devise it how he chose. There was no likelihood of the Crubach willing it furth of the family, as he was too good a Campbell for such an eccentricity, but the actual legatee of Barrill was unknown, and Archibald had too keen a relish of his relatives' anxiety to make a disclosure.

Drumgesk could hold more liquor than the sailor, but once, having had two hours' start, he grew incautiously communicative and divulged the possibility of making the youthful Augustus his heir. "He's a nice wee laddie," he said unsteadily. "No' muckle harns in his heid—he'll tak that frae his mither—and fit only to be a drucken murderous sailor like yoursel. But he's a Campbell."

Colin was well pleased with this revelation. But knowing that Archibald Crubach, like himself, could display a cunning changeability in many things, he was uncertain that his brother's decision was final, and constantly impressed upon his family the necessity of being pleasant to and writing frequently to their Uncle Archy. What effect these letters had upon the shrewd old judge was doubtful, but in the spring of 1798 his wife died, and Drumgesk passed to her sister's family. Archibald therefore determined to spend his summer vacation at Barrill, and as there was little suitable society left in his native countryside he invited the admiral and all his connections to visit him.

Such an invitation was a command. Colin himself was on the retired list, a retirement hastened by an argument with his superiors at the Admiralty, and was easily able to take his grievance and his wife north. Colonel Otway and Admiral Bowmaker were not free, but their wives were, and Mr. Cattanach urged Leonie not to lag behind. The ladies arrived with their families complete. Only the young Augustus, now twelve years old and a midshipman in His Majesty's Navy, was uncertain of his engagements. He was at Portsmouth. Admiral Campbell felt that the non-appearance of Augustus would be a tragedy, and by a judicious word in the right quarter he obtained a big leave of absence for the boy.

The lonely old judge was secretly delighted to have so many relations—twelve all told—to amuse him while at Barrill, and thoroughly enjoyed the deference he received. " I've met some polite people in my time," he solemnly told his brother, " but your wife and dauchters are the very mirror of good breeding." Colin was pleased, particularly by the regard which his brother showed for the little Augustus. This feeling was sincere, Augustus being a likeable manly lad.

Scipio had desired them to visit Emmeline, and he wrote his daughter requesting her to prepare for their visit to Uillian. There was a distance of ten miles from Uillian to Duisk and Barrill, and neither of the brothers was inordinately anxious to travel that length in a heated coach for an afternoon visit.

Instead, they deputed Mrs. Admiral Campbell to take
Emmeline an invitation to come and stay at Barrill.
She went gladly, being a pert inquisitive little lady
who did not care to miss the chance of seeing any
person or any house, and she took Mrs. Otway and
Mrs. Bowmaker with her.

At Kilmichael the coachman inquired the direction, but mistakenly drove past Uillian and farther
on. And there the ladies observed Emmeline and
Neil walking on the road.

The carriage was stopped and the ladies descended,
to Emmeline's inexpressible dismay. With an effort
she recovered sufficiently to introduce Neil to them
as a relation. Abashed, he made an excuse and left
them, and the girl took the ladies to Uillian.

Mrs. Admiral Campbell and her stepdaughters made
Neil the chief subject of their conversation on the
return journey. All the ladies were English bred ;
they had vague ideas that they were in a yet savage
country. They did not doubt Emmeline's statement
that Neil was connected with the family, but were
unanimous that his appearance was awkward and
vulgar, although, as the stepmother suggested, he might
be one of the old type of uncivilized mountaineer
chiefs. On one point they had no doubt whatever.
Their sharp female eyes had detected a romance.

"I always said," Mrs. Otway declared, "that
Emmeline was not so shy as she pretended."

"Still waters run deep," Janet observed.

"I wonder," said the admiral's wife, "if General
Campbell would approve of the object of Emmeline's
affections."

The Campbell brothers were advised of the romance

when the ladies reached Barrill, and that day a letter was forwarded post-haste to Emmeline's father.

Scipio's fondness for Emmeline was based mainly on the vague reminiscence of her mother that she was. For François he had never conceived a similar liking. During his heir's sojourn at school, college, and university the father had paid François occasional visits, with a forlorn hope that he might find something in his character that would wipe out the memory of his son's timidity. But he could find nothing. François also resembled his mother in feature. He was fair, however, and effeminate, and nervous. The old man could not stomach him. The admiral had suggested once that François was reaching the age for a commission.

"No—no," said the general abruptly. "Not that." Colin remonstrated. "The family's not secure enough —we must have heirs," said Scipio evasively.

He was afraid that his heir would disgrace him.

It was because of his aversion to François that Scipio, when offered a baronetcy shortly after Emmeline's return to Uillian, declined it. Colin had been wroth.

"Think of the additional prestige to our family, Skip!" he urged.

"Aye!" rejoined the other with involuntary bitterness. "And think who would inherit it."

He accepted a knighthood of the Bath instead.

In their meetings François had betrayed as much nervousness of the general as Sir Scipio had contempt for him. He was still at the university and the problem of what to do with him after that had begun to occupy the general's mind.

"I'll send him to bide at Duisk," he thought latterly. "It's all he's fit for." He determined to settle the young man's future at their next meeting, and that occurred soon. François listened in agitated silence.

"Sir," he said, when the general had concluded, "I have something very important to say. You may not approve of what I have done. It is done, though."

"Is it the army, eh?" asked Sir Scipio, with a faint gleam of hope.

François hesitated, and then blurted out: "I'm married."

The old man scrutinized him for a stupefied moment. "You damned calf," he was able to say in time.

He lost his temper, raved, hurled curses and blasphemies at the young man, who stood silent and trembling. "You!" cried the general bitterly. "You lily-faced scared cuckoo. *You* marry!" He stared fixedly at him, and then broke into derisive laughter. "It could only be a third-rate trollop who would take the like of you. Who's this that got you in tow?"

With a black brow he heard the young man's stammered recital. He had married six months ago; his wife was now enceinte. She was a lady, a doctor's daughter.

"I'll investigate all that in proper course," said the general dryly, when the young man's pleadings died away. "There's a wheen doctor's daughters going the rounds. Get out of my sight."

He did investigate, and the result was more soothing to his feelings. The bride was a year younger than François. Her character and her family's was irreproachable. The general was undecided for a time. At last he called on the young erstwhile Harriet Scott, who was yet residing with her parents, people of Lothian extraction. She was a dark, handsome girl, and it was evident that she and François were much in love. Incensed as he had been by the secrecy of the marriage, the general on reflection decided that it was the best thing that could happen to the young man. If fit for nothing else, he might be as well domesticated.

"What did you see in him?" he could not help asking the young wife, but she was not quite sure.

It was following this event that Sir Scipio received the tidings from his brothers. He had written the day before to both Barrill and Uillian announcing that François was wed.

Colin had sent full information, and the name of Emmeline's friend filled the old man with rage and ancient memories. He obtained immediate leave of absence and posted to Argyllshire with utmost haste, arriving at Uillian like a whirlwind.

Peggy received him at the door, astonished. He saluted her. "Well," he said heavily, "you might have taken the means of letting me know how things were going." Observing her questioning look he said: "I have just heard that Emmeline is likely to make a fool of herself with the young man in Strone."

"And what can be more natural," she replied. "It is very natural, and they are kin."

"Circumstances have altered, Peggy." He pulled

off his redingote and handed it to her. " It would be most unsuitable."

" I'm thinking, Duisk, that it could not be better, for many reasons," she retorted.

He was silent, and then inquired for Emmeline. She was in the parlour, in a state of terror at his arrival. " Emmy," he said menacingly, " what's this I hear ? What's this you're doing behind my back ? "

Crimson with shame, the girl flung herself into the old man's arms, and the general's manner softened. " Well," he said in a quieter tone, " you're a foolish little pigeon and there is no sense in you. But it must stop."

" But it can't, sir ! " she exclaimed, scarce conscious of what she was saying.

" Why ? " demanded Sir Scipio apprehensively.

" I love him," she sobbed.

" Tach ! " said the general with relief. " Ere you're much older you'll discover a wheen bankrupt suitors at your knees. But you'll find men of property, too." He silenced her protests. " I never thought you were eident to be a poor farmer's wife and churn butter, and milk cows, and muck out byres."

" He's a landowner, sir."

" Aye, he's all that ! "

" He's a cousin of ours, sir."

" We're related to half the folk in Argyll," he said derisively. " Look well at every bare-footed laddie you pass on the road, for you can cry them cousins. But that doesn't alter the fact that they have nothing and we have Duisk."

" Oh, sir," she cried pleadingly, " you should under-

stand and forgive us, for you must have loved my
mother.''

This plea, which Emmeline had thought was certain to have an effect upon her father, did have.
He put her away from him, but gently, and the
girl saw a wae look in his eyes. But he said latterly :
" No, Emmy, I won't have this nonsense. It would
make us ridiculous. He's a fortune hunter. His
people got Strone from mine, even. It would be
against all laws of order. It would be *un*natural.''

That evening one of the ladies in Barrill exclaimed
that smoke was rising from the chimneys of Duisk
House. " Skip must be home,'' said Colin. " He
has come quick, for his age.''

" He'll be at Uillian,'' said Drumgesk. " But
he'll be hauling the lassie ower there on the morn.''

The judge was fairly accurate, for General Campbell, deciding that Uillian was close enough to Strone
to be the jumping-board for any folly, was having
Duisk prepared for his occupancy. He had meantime sent instructions to François to come north
with his wife, to ensure that Emmeline would not
be left unwatched when he returned on the expiry
of leave, and while at Uillian contented himself with
keeping a strict eye on the girl.

On the second day of his stay at Uillian the old
soldier walked abroad. The forced stages of his
journey had proved tiring, but with a night's rest
the general had regained his usual vigour, and was
an imposing figure of a man, erect and burly in his
many-caped coat, three-cornered hat, and shining
top-boots, as he paced slowly up the road. The last
five years had wrought a change in Sir Scipio Camp-

o

bell, who was sixty-three, and not old for a Highlandman; the change was in his face. His eyes
were yet challenging and his jaw firm, but the skin
had slackened and hung loosely from his cheeks,
yellow and fleshy.

Old memories, going back to his childhood, of this
place crowded in his mind as he picked his way with
the aid of a cane. He had always loved Uillian,
as he had loved Duisk, and as he loved Glassary.
He had done no service to the district and had been
indifferent to the common good. But his love for
the countryside was apart from that. Sir Scipio
would not have connected the two.

He grunted with satisfaction on seeing a figure
ahead. It was a young man in a field near the roadway. The general did not hasten his pace, but
stopped as he came close to the farmer and signed
with his cane for him to draw near.

Neil did so. At the fence he stopped and gazed
down, but although the road was four feet lower Neil
felt that this bleak-faced old man was towering over
him.

"Are you Neil Leitch?" Sir Scipio said curtly.
The young man assented. "I understand that there
has been communication between Miss Emmeline
Campbell and yourself. It must cease."

"Who are you?" said Neil unsteadily.

"I am General Campbell."

Neil had never known the confusion of sickness
of heart and pain and humiliation that was now
his. He stared dumbly at the old man who stood
so surely and looked so contemptuous.

"It will not cease," he muttered.

" Your pretensions are greater than your prospects," proceeded the general cuttingly. " I know that Strone is mortgaged. I know very well. I have purchased that mortgage. If you pester Miss Campbell further I shall foreclose."

Scipio need not have asked the young man's name. As he left the dazed and stricken Neil he thought: " How like ! " and then his thoughts reverted to François.

Satisfied that he had settled this unfortunate wooing for ever, he took Emmeline to Duisk on the following day. He had not told Emmeline that he had taken over the mortgage on Strone, which, because it had once been Colin Buie's, he had long wanted to add to the neighbouring Uillian. It was a lucky coincidence, and he reflected that providence had aided him fortuitously. He was certain the threat would be a telling one on Leitch. But Sir Scipio did not for one instant think of using a threat of that kind for the control of Emmeline. That would have lowered him in his own dignity, and would have been insulting to a gentlewoman.

He said as much to his brothers when they met, and Colin applauded his views. Drumgesk was strong for a marriage. " After all," the judge said, " she could maybe gang faur and fare waur."

" Have you seen him ? " said Sir Scipio disdainfully.

" He hasn't," said Colin. " The young man has no standing."

" He's a kinsman," said Archibald Crubach obstinately, " and he's of the auld local stocks, like oursels. Neither of you hae muckle room to talk, I'm thinking. Francey has mairret a doctor's dauchter and Elizabeth mairret George Otway."

"Doctors have access to the best society," Sir Scipio said.

"So have midwives," said Drumgesk.

"What's wrong with Otway?" asked Otway's father-in-law stiffly.

"He's the son of a Suffolk saddler," said Drumgesk with relish, "and fine you ken it. And he ca'd his auldest Caesar to pretend he was sib to some pedigreed Irish squires, and he's as muckle sib to them as I am to the Czar of Muscovy."

"That's a thing my brother might let lie," cried Colin hotly.

"Losh!" said Drumgesk contentedly, "you're a bonnie brace o' blude-letting blades. You'll be threeping next that I'll disgrace you, for that I learnt my English in Edinbro insteid o' picking it up frae a wheen tarry-tailed sailors or a puckle o' murderous redcoats. Awa' back to the rouge-pots, Colin my lad. You were ower rushed this morning, and you'll no' look your best afore the weemen."

No persuasion nor badinage would shake Sir Scipio's resolve. But, to the admiral, Archibald Crubach's words had given alarm. He had counted on the Crubach's cherished hatred for Cydalise being renewed for her daughter, but Drumgesk had since been told of the mother's tragic end and he had watched Emmeline during her visit to Barrill with a sense of compassion. The old judge pitied the timid-eyed love-racked girl who was so alien among the others and whose mother had died so lately by the axe. The fact that she was in innocence of her

mother's folly and fate seemed to add to her forlorn
condition.

Colin was fearful lest the wayward old Crubach
should choose to make a stand for Emmeline and
Neil, for, were he to promise Emmeline the rever-
sion of Barrill, Sir Scipio would grasp at the chance
on any stipulation.   Colin placed Sir Scipio's mingled
dislike and aversion for all the Leitches to the bequest they had got of Strone.   The general could
mention none of them without impatience.   But
were Emmeline to obtain Barrill on her marrying
Neil, Strone in a sense would revert to Sir Scipio's
influence.   Colin was torn by apprehension.   He got
Drumgesk alone.

" Archy," he said straightly, " what do you think
of this François' marriage ? "   Drumgesk did not
reply.   " If François Campbell inherits Duisk and
has heirs," continued the admiral bitterly, " my
Augustus will be cheated of his rights."

" I'll not say aye or no to that, Colin," Drumgesk said slowly.   " You're ower late in the day to
speak of it."

" I think Scipio might at least . . . if I had done
proper I would have held my tongue on one condition."

" And what condition ? "

" That François and Emmeline remained unmarried.   You don't need to care, Archy.   You've
no children to think of."

" And why did you not speak sooner ? "

" Lord, Archy," said the other sincerely, " it takes
a hard man to tell a cruel fact to his own brother."

" Aye, so it does," said Drumgesk slowly.   " We

couldna well tell him that—not but that he kens
his own thochts."

"François is a milksop," said the admiral viciously.
"It's a scandal. I've nothing personal against Emmeline, for she's a woman, but she is François'
twin."

"And in the line of inheritance. Francey is delicate, you think? He'll maybe no' last. Emmeline's
a gentle lassie." The judge looked shrewdly at his
brother. "You're feared I'll leave Barrill to her.
I can see that."

"I am, Archy. François at Duisk and Emmeline
at Barrill!—no shame on me."

"I'll leave Barrill to Augustus. That's my promise."

"Well, I'm relieved," said Colin frankly. "That's
plain talk."

"It's Campbell talk. I'm not deaf to the rights
of my family. I wish," said the judge regretfully,
"that you had backed me ower that Neil Leitch
business, but you fighting men are blin' as bats. I
mean this," he said, "that Emmeline has a chance
yet of inheriting Duisk, in spite of François' marriage,
and this Leitch business would have eased our minds
at the expense of our pride. For Neil Leitch is the
grandson of Do'l Mor, and Do'l Mor, at any rate,
had the blood of the Campbells of Duisk in him."

VI

With the reopening of Duisk House, Peggy Mac-
Lachlan was kept busy, but not busy enough but
that she could assess the changes wrought in the
master of the house.

She was grey-haired now, and not quite able to walk so fast as formerly. Her manner had sharpened perceptibly. She had shrunk into herself.

Sir Scipio Campbell had passed still further from her sphere. He was aged, like herself, but with such difference! His ordinary tone was cold, his manner aloof. He had forgotten her, surely; forgotten that he had once proposed to marry her and had sobbed for comfort for his terrors. To young Scipio Campbell she had meant anything, but to Sir Scipio Campbell she was an old and faithful servant.

With a difference! But what constituted that difference was now ignored by him. He was too great and too secure.

Yet she had her moments, brief but splendid. When the young François arrived with his young wife Peggy had foreseen a return to the regime of Cydalise. Mrs. François Campbell was palpably amused by the lame English that Peggy had learned so reluctantly and laboriously.

"We Highland people, mam," said the old general to his daughter-in-law, "have a reputation for courtesy that extends to learning the English tongue. Were you in France you would be expected to know French."

Peggy was hurt because the young married couple had not shaken hands with her on arrival. It was an ordinary courtesy in the country. The Campbell brothers never omitted it. And she was mortally insulted when François called her by her second name.

"MacLachlan!" exclaimed Sir Scipio, who was present. "Pray, sir, who is MacLachlan?"

François innocently indicated the person so named.

The general's face grew savage, to François' puzzled
alarm. Peggy thought he was about to blurt out
something; two things she could think of. But he
calmed himself.

"You're an innovator, Mr. Francey," he said.
"Mistress Peggy, maybe, will permit you to use her
Christian name in future."

Peggy was grateful for these small defences. They
were all that Scipio Campbell would probably extend
to her. But once he called her into his room.

"I'm getting on, Peggy," he said, without preliminaries, "and I hope to see further service abroad.
Either may finish me quickly enough. Well, Peggy,
you've been a valued friend . . . I have never regarded you as a servant, Peggy." She bowed her
head humbly at the admission. "You have been a
friend, a kinswoman, a confidante. Well, life has
been queer enough for both of us.

"I want to say this," said the general, "that I'll
arrange with my man of affairs that you'll not want
in the event of my death. A man can put no trust
in his heirs."

"Thank you, Duisk, but I would be rather wanting
it," she said.

"Yes, I know," he replied with a trace of sadness.
"I'm as Highland as you, and I understand. Nevertheless, I'll do it. If it will give you no pleasure it
will me."

Although she had shown no desire for a pension
Peggy was grateful for the thought. Certainly, her
history and his had been mysteriously connected ever
since her mother had met Neil Uillian, ever since Neil
and Captain Archy had lost life in Kilblaan in Glen-

shira, ever since Scipio had returned in white horror from Errachan—and mysteriously, too, were connected the lives of the seed of that minister Master Dugald who had placed the stone to her mother's memory, Master Dugald and his young Do'l Mor, and Do'l's son's son Neil over whom the gentle Emmeline was weeping her eyes out.

Blood was strewn across the pages of that triple history, and she reflected superstitiously that more might still be shed. Whether Neil's or Emmeline's, or, for that matter, her own, she could not think ; nor did she wonder greatly. She had been bred in the old pre-1745 tradition, in the tradition of the clan system, and the honourable shedding of blood was no great crime in her eyes. Scipio had thought so too, surely, or he would not have slaughtered General Don.

She was used to seeing the active young ladies from Barrill appear with the ostensible purpose of keeping Emmeline company. The brothers would come and drink, and it was like old times. Or Scipio and Emmeline would be rowed across to Barrill. These visits were a torment to the pining Emmeline, for the only people at Barrill she cared for were old Drumgesk and the little Augustus ; perhaps because they liked her. Augustus was anxious to take her to Crinan, where they would get a sailing boat. He was proud of his nautical knowledge and desirous of showing off on the open sea. " Loch Awe's a dub," he would say contemptuously, " and no use to a naval man." Lord Drumgesk preferred to challenge the girl to a drinking match with brandy punch. But her smile was very wan.

" You're no' quick in forgetting your beau," he said to her unexpectedly as he limped by her side in the garden at Barrill. " Well, my lass, you're young and you'll forget."

Emmeline's throat contracted, as it always did at the thought of Neil, and she could say nothing.

" Your daddy's no' keen on it, and you'll hae to abide by that," he said paternally. " But it's a grief at the time. I've suffered it, when I was a callant."

" Uncle Archy," she said pathetically, " I haven't seen him since my father came home . . . and he may —he may be dying." And she commenced to sob hopelessly.

" He'll be keeping a weather eye on his sheep, mair likely, and if he's a wice man—hai! you young deevils, what ploy's this ? "

They had rounded a hedge to find the young Otways and John Cattanach hammering patiently with stones from the shore at the sundial. Archibald Crubach was proud of the sundial. It was a Gordon possession, of rich workmanship, eight feet high, and had twelve faces. He had removed it from Drumgesk to Barrill in his wife's lifetime, and felt justifiably proud of his adroit foresight. With an oath he made for them and caught Caesar Otway on the legs with his cane. The children stampeded, laughing with assumed bravado. At the gateway Caesar made faces at him.

" Croopak ! Croopak ! " the boy shouted tauntingly.

Drumgesk's lips tightened, but he said nothing.

" Here's Gus," he exclaimed contentedly, when they left the garden by the shore path and saw the little midshipman busy with a boat. " I like that laddie.

He's a rale wee man." Augustus came running.
"How many Frenchmen hae you killed the day,
sir ? "

" I was at Crinan, and I saw the workmen making
the canal, and I rode there on a horse," the boy
announced triumphantly.

"Losh !—if you're onything like your faither on a
beast's back . . . was't a boat you were after ? "

" For to-morrow. You can't back out, Emmy,"
Augustus exclaimed, suspecting a lack of enthusiasm.
" You know you promised me, and I know all about
sailing boats."

" Can you swim, sir ? "

" Yes, Uncle Archy."

" Emmy can't."

The boy was disgusted. " I won't need to swim,"
Emmeline said gently. " Augustus is a good sailor."

" Sure I am, Cousin Emmy. And I'll take Francey,
too, and Francey's wife, for that matter. Nobody
at Barrill will trust me," he added disconsolately.

" Aweel, you'll be able to practise on Emmy as a
start," said the judge. " I hope this is nae game to
run awa' wi' the lassie. You wild sailors arena to
be trusted."

Emmeline's inability to find pleasure in the companionship of her sister-in-law puzzled her, for she
had looked forward to the arrival of François' wife
with a satisfaction that was a compliment less to
Harriet than to François. But when young Mrs.
Campbell appeared the satisfaction faded quickly
enough. Harriet had the egotistic self-complacency
of the newly married woman. Despite her kindly
manner she was careful to impress upon Emmeline

that the wife of the heir to Duisk was of more importance than the heir's sister, for she believed in getting any little difficulties settled immediately. And her complete proprietorship of François was humiliating enough to his sister.

François ran at his wife's heels in a fashion that Emmeline resented, without knowing why. His uxorious submission seemed almost indecent. And he no longer had much time for the sister who had adored him—indeed, he spoke to her repeatedly in sharp terms, telling her that she had almost brought disgrace upon the family, and would have lowered the dignity of the future owner of Duisk had she contracted a *mésalliance* with a fortune-hunting unbred farmer. Emmeline preferred the forthright commands of Sir Scipio to the huffy remonstrances of her brother.

" There is one person who has not been consulted," she told François tearfully, " and perhaps will have different ideas." He disdainfully asked her who that person was, and she said it was their mother.

" Our mother ! " he exclaimed. He regarded her thoughtfully, and then said : " Do you not know why your mother isn't here ? "

" My mother is abroad, but I'll find her," Emmeline declared with weak obstinacy, and the man, with a weakling's cruelty, told her that her mother had disgraced them both by running away with another man.

" Oh, it's not true ! " she cried, trembling.

" Ask your father ! " he said, with a grin. " Jack Sallerton told me. It's true enough. And you want to do something the same," he finished brutally.

" And what did *you* do ? " she asked, crimson with shame and indignation.

"Do? What d'ye want me to do?"

"Oh, Francey, you were a coward. Had any man said that to my father's face——" With a bursting heart the girl ran from the room.

Emmeline had forgotten all about Augustus in her new sorrow, and was surprised when he appeared at Duisk on the following day. She was willing enough to implement her promise, but Sir Scipio vetoed that on account of her sex and her previous unacquaintance with the sea. He told Augustus to take François, and the two young gentlemen drove off to Crinan in the Duisk carriage.

When the cousins departed Emmeline remained for a time with Harriet, but excused herself and sought the garden. Her brother's words had roughly swept away the cherished illusions of years, but she found herself surprisingly composed ; her lips trembled, but no tears fell. She felt very grateful for the delicacy of Sir Scipio, who had kept this information so carefully concealed from her, and reflected naïvely on the fidelity of his kin and dependants. And she felt a great sorrow and pity in her heart for the vanished Cydalise Cœur-de-roi.

Her memories of her mother were very vague, but they were dear to her. She could recall an impression of a sweet oval face and wonderful perfumed clothes bending down to her, and not much more. There were no pictures of Mrs. Scipio Campbell visible in Duisk House, and to her surprised remarks on that her father had always replied with calm evasions.

In this time of her grief and loneliness Cydalise became doubly dear to the girl. She wondered what temporary estrangement had impelled her mother to such a tremendous step. Sir Scipio—what were his thoughts about his wife ? Emmeline thought forlornly on the tragic consequences of this power which she herself was now experiencing. Sir Scipio surely had loved his wife and must surely understand his daughter's capacity for love. Perhaps Sir Scipio would relent in time to her and to her mother ; concession to one, forgiveness for the other. Emmeline shuddered, not very hopefully seeing her father in that benevolent rôle. Inaction was tormenting ; she left the garden and walked in the further shrubberies, coming to the bridge and leaving the path to walk by the margin of the burn.

"Emmeline ! "

She stood, dazed by the rush of gladness, and then ran forward to the embrace of Neil.

"It is you," she said deliriously. "I knew you would come." She submitted to his clasp with quiescent pleasure. "I knew you would come," she repeated. "Oh, I was so unhappy."

"I wanted to see you," he said simply. "And so I have come to see you."

"I love you, Neil," she cried distractedly.

She led him from prying eyes, among the thicker bushes and the wild wood. All her despondency was gone from her ; she laughed frequently, with an exhausted rush of breath from the lungs, half hysterical ; her eyes gazed seriously into his, her lips smiled. She responded ardently to his ardent caresses.

"You will not leave me again, Neil. Promise me that you will never leave me again. For everyone is against me."

The young man groaned. "This is for the last time."

"But, Neil," she exclaimed, "you are not trying to be false to me, surely! Surely you will not go away from me!" Regarding him with the hurt expression of a child, she said : "You said you loved me, Neil."

"I love you too well to cause you harm," he answered slowly. "It is better, perhaps, that you and I should part."

She clung to him frantically. "Oh, Neil."

"Emmeline, why is it that things are so hard for us, and that you make things harder? All this has been misery for me, for it cannot last. I know that now. But I could not bear not to be seeing you. I had to come, Emmeline. I could not help it. I crossed the hills. Look!—I am wet to the knees. I left Strone, and I thought that I was dying." He stared seriously into her upturned face. "I wish that I were dead.

"I have been working those days, Emmeline, slaving at Strone, and my heart is breaking. I wish I had never known you. If I had never known you I—I would have peace of mind, maybe. But I can never be free of thinking of you, Emmeline. Because of what I suffer."

"But Neil," she said sweetly, and holding to him confidingly, "you love me well enough to be my husband, do you not? You said so once. And, oh Neil, I was so ashamed and so happy when you told me that. And you are not afraid of my father, are you? You would not be afraid to take me to Strone in spite of my father's anger, Neil? I will run away from Duisk if you desire it. For I will always do anything that you want me to do, and you cannot ask more of me than that."

" The day you come to Strone, Strone will be mine no more. Sir Scipio Campbell has the power and would drive us out. He told me so."

" But is it fear of losing Strone that makes you so changed, Neil. Surely you cannot put your land before my love ! "

" I put my honour before my love, and it is not a beggar's wife that you should be," he answered sombrely. " General Campbell told you, surely."

" No, Neil, he did not. But if he had it would have not made any difference to me. For if I ran away with you he would forgive in time. My mother ran away—I learned that yesterday, Neil—and I am sure that my father has forgiven my mother."

" I know she ran away. The whole country knows."

She was surprised, but she said : " I didn't, Neil. But they will agree again, and my mother will come back. It would be unnatural were she never to come back. I would like to have my mother near me, for I have never had her near me. My father will forgive her, and perhaps forgive the wicked man who enticed her to go with him."

" He can afford to forgive General Don. He killed him."

This final revelation left the poor girl stunned. And with that fond fancy vanquished, her resolution left her and she commenced to weep hopelessly.

" Emmeline," he said tonelessly, " your father is too great a man, too mighty, too proud, too good, to

have any kind thought for me and mine. He will
marry you to a man with money, and he will be
satisfied though the man breaks your heart with his
cruelty. General Campbell can be easy there, for he
can always console himself, knowing the man was rich
and powerful that he got for you. If General Campbell drove you from his house without a penny or a
blessing I would take you gladly, if he would leave
us alone in peace. But he would not do that. He is
too great and mighty a man to leave such as I am to
fight a fair fight. Oh, Emmeline, you believe me
and understand me? You know that I am not false.
You know me, surely. What right has General
Campbell to be proud. Is it of the lands his father's
father stole, or of the murder that was done on my
father's father here, or of his cousin that he keeps
as a humble servant to him, or of his lame brother
who loves to hang men, or of the old sailor wreck of
a brother who loves to paint his face, or of himself,
who leads men to slaughter, who drives his tenants
from their homes, who waits like a cat to pounce on
the lands of poor bankrupts, and who allowed his wife
to be taken from under his roof? He drives about,
smiling, bowing, and thinking much of himself and
his upstart race, and his heart is rotten. He is your
father, Emmeline. Obey him! Oh, Emmeline," he
exclaimed with a sob, "what evil have I done that
I should have come to know you!"

"You will not desert me, Neil," she cried in sudden
terror.

"It is too much altogether," he replied. "But I
could not bear not to see you again. Kiss me again,
and I will treasure it."

" Neil."

" Hush," he said, disquieted by the tragic look in
her eyes. " You will forget, and I shall try."

" Neil."

" Oh, calm yourself," he pled, alarmed.

" Neil. Look !—see that flower I have trodden
on. It is broken."

He grasped her meaning. " It is not broken. It
is bruised. The sun will raise it. It will rise again."

" I shall never," she said sadly. " No sun can raise
me. Go now, and desert me."

But he did not go with that dismissal, for she clung
to him, weeping with the fear of perpetual separation.
Recalling his last strength of resolution, he loosened
her grasp and turned to the hill path. There he
stopped and looked at her for a little ; and was gone.

Left in what seemed to her a tremendous isolation,
she latterly wandered to the verge of Errachan Wood,
and on the grassy marge of the cutting she sat in
miserable thought. The world had dulled in the close
of her brief hour of exceeding gladness and exceeding
grief. At once she had grown in stature of thought
for knowing both love and parting.

The afternoon sun slanted westwards, but she remained sitting in the silence. By turning her head
she could see the chimneys of Duisk, a patch of loch,
the shadowed hills and the sun-touched hills. Above,
the sky was very blue.

As the sun descended behind the further hills of
Lorn, the yellow glow slipped higher up the slopes.
The wood itself had darkened and grown cold. An
eerie sense of glamour grew upon her ; she remembered the ominous reputation of these haunts

and was seized by terror. She rose and fled, the fear
passing as she neared the house and her own personal
agony returning. Sir Scipio was at the door and
asked her where she had been so long, but she passed
him without speech and hurried to her own room,
to its silence and her tears.

VII

It was a drive of about eleven miles between Duisk
and Crinan, which village, on the shore of Loch Crinan,
provided the nearest sea anchorage. On the route
Augustus rattled away cheerfully to his cousin, but
secretly considered that François was a very dull stick.
The twenty-year-old heir of Duisk seemed not much
interested in the conversation of the twelve-year-old
heir of Barrill. He listened with an air of languid
superiority, regarding the landscape with bored and
supercilious eyes. To him, Augustus was a chattering
boy.

To Augustus, François was rather a muff. He felt
quite old in experience to the young man and indeed
inferred as much, to the open amusement of François.

"Wait," said Augustus, "till we're out at sea, and
I'll show you a thing or two."

The prospect was not exhilarating to his companion,
who had only consented because Sir Scipio had taken
for granted his willingness to deputise for Emmeline.
He saw small sense in travelling eleven miles for the
sake of a few minutes' sail, and said so.

It was a little sailing boat that the midshipman had
commissioned, easily negotiable by two, which two,
François believed, would be his cousin and the fisherman who led them to it. It was then that Augustus

explained they would man the boat unaided. Provisions and a bottle of wine had been brought in the carriage, which was to await their return.

The Campbells had some difficulty in understanding the explanations and warnings which the owner offered them in broken English, but the boy deduced that they were to avoid the tides and rocks at the entrance to Loch Craignish, at right angles to Crinan loch. To these exhortations Augustus paid serious heed.

" A good sailor, Francey," he observed wisely as they left the loch with a favouring breeze, " never ignores common sense."

Faithful to his principles, the boy kept the little boat wide of the dangerous currents that eddy around the shores of Craignish Point, taking a very live pleasure in alternately bullying his cousin and bragging. In wider water they felt a stiff breeze. The boat bore swiftly before it, to the boy's inexpressible delight. " She's a beauty," he repeated continually. " She's a little beauty."

François was infected to some extent by his cousin's enthusiasm, and as he was acting under command he could not help an intelligent interest in the duties of seamanship. Beyond Craignish Point a panorama was presented them that, in any case, would have aroused the admiration of the most obtuse.

Southward lay the Sound of Jura, fringed on its east by where the soft slopes of Knapdale were overlooked by the mountains of the hinterland, and west by the splendid heights of Jura Island spearing the sunny sky. North lay the tangled isles that fringe the passage to the Firth of Lorne : Scarba, Luing,

Shuna, thrown there as a bulwark from the heavy forces of the Atlantic Ocean to Netherlorn. On this magnificent spectacle of sea and mountain the sun shone benignantly, a clear golden sun that traced the shadows of the racing clouds upon the mountain sides. The salt smell of the sea, the sense of rapidity and exhilaration lent by the boat's motion, the billowy curve of her sail, spray-drenched and sun-glistened, made them shout and laugh, full of a vivid comprehension of existence.

"Oh, Francey, I believe I could make a sailor of you."

"You could make a hungry man of me. I'm ravenous."

"Well, fall to. But if I give you a shout be ready to jump. But I won't eat till you're finished. Why did you not bring Harriet, Francey ? "

"She wasn't quite able," said François evasively.

"All my sisters are frumps. Not one of them fond of the sea, and their father a sailor, Francey ! It's not natural. A man has no patience with them. Well, maybe it's because they're just half-sisters. Lord ! when I'm an admiral of the fleet won't I just scare the Frenchies ! "

François laughed, taking a drink from the bottle and filling his mouth with the Duisk provisions. His hair was blown awry, his neckcloth was loose, his eyes sparkled and when he licked his lips he could taste the salt on them. He glanced appreciatively at the surging water, deepest blue, foam-flecked, and grinned, showing all his teeth. " I used to be afraid of the sea," he said.

She was now in the centre of the sound, moving

with inimitable grace. " That big island," said Augustus, " must be Jura. I've heard my father speak of it. I wonder," he said, pointing to Scarba, " what the name of that one with the high peak is. It's like a mountain surrounded by the sea. Francey, what about touching it ! "

" Will we manage back in time ? " François asked doubtfully.

" Sure we will ! . . . with this breeze. We'll head her for it, Francey. What a lark ! My father will get the surprise of his life. We'll call it Emmy's Isle."

" What's that strange noise ? I've heard it for a time."

" A kind of roaring noise, Francey, isn't it ? "

Augustus hastily wolfed some of the food and had a drink from the bottle. He had little time for food, for the boat heeled under a sudden rise of wind. " She can go, can't she ? " he asked when the vessel righted. " Jervis couldn't have done better, Francey."

" That was close, was it not ? " François asked anxiously.

" Sure it wasn't ! You land fellows don't know about those things. One lurch and you think she's sinking."

François was reassured. And the sea, rough as it might be and broken now by squalls that spread the surf fanwise in pitted levels, carried so much of joy in its glistening stretch that his heart rejoiced again. The little vessel was heading for the strait separating Jura and Scarba.

" I never thought there was always that curious roaring at sea."

" There isn't," said Augustus scornfully. " There

must be something, somewhere. Not here, anyway.
Look, Francey!—we'll head for the passage. It'll be
sheltered, and I'm keen to land on the island there.
Sure I am."

Scarba, fourteen hundred feet above the sea, was
towering now to starboard.

In the protection of the two islands the gusts were
broken. The small boat moved under easier sail,
but not with any slackening of speed.

" I think," said Augustus, " we'll tack and make
for shore. No—I see, I think there's better anchorage ahead . . . we'll get in the lee-shore yonder.
Wouldn't my father, and Emmy, and Sir Scipio blink
if they knew we'd gone so far! Two days' sail to
America, Francey my boy!"

Augustus was gleeful, and ingenuously proud of the
seamanship he had displayed before this full-grown
cousin. He expatiated at length on the variety and
experience that a man gains who ships in the King's
Navy. François listened indolently, smiling with
secret amusement at the boy's naïve boasting.
Withal, he felt a secret envy of the self-assured little
Augustus. It was pleasant, seeing the green slopes
and the shores gliding past, to watch the steady
movement of the water and to hear the glucking of
it against the keel.

" Francey," said the boy suddenly. " I've made
a discovery."

" Have you ? " replied François lazily.

" We're running with the tide."

" That's all the better, I suppose ? "

" Yes. But if it's very strong . . . I think we'll
tack about. You see, there's some strength in that

tide. We don't want to land on the other side of
Jura. We'd have some difficulty in getting home,
and our people would grow anxious."

" Is there danger ? " asked François anxiously.

" Danger the deuce !   But by the time the tide had
turned it'd be getting dark.   It's a strong ebb.   And
it's flowing west to the Atlantic.   I didn't think of
that."

" Isn't that a confounded roaring ! "

" Here, Francey, lend a hand.   By Jove, Francey,
if I were Admiral Jervis I'd give you the cat, sure I
would.   She's a handy little craft, is she not ?   A little
beauty."

Under altered sail the boat swung sideways, splash-
ing against the tide, and trembled.   For a moment
she swung irresolute, and then slowly veered to her
original route.

" Well, that's strange, Francey."

The sail was hanging loose.

" Here, Francey, get a hold there."

" What's that deuced roaring ? " François demanded
irritably.   " Do you hear it ?   You must be able to
hear it."

" I hear it all right.   It must be breakers," said
the boy breathlessly.   " I'm hanged, but this tide
is too strong, almost."

" We can't spend the night on Jura," François said
with decision.   " I've no wish to sleep in a cottar's
cabin."

" Here ! we'll try again.   I wish that we'd thought
of oars."

Unresponsive to their efforts, the little craft swung
on with the swift ebb.   And now she was moving

more rapidly, treading the water with a quick jerky action.

"That sail's useless," said the midshipman,—"till we make the open sea, at any rate.   That sound is a bit louder."

"There surely won't be danger!" François exclaimed.

"Devil a bit of it.   This is an ebb tide and makes for open water. We haven't a danger of running on shore."

"That sound!"

Augustus looked ahead.   He was quite composed, and slightly thrilled by the thought of spending the night on a strange shore amid strangers.   Beyond the islands was the open sea, stretching limitless. "Why!" the lad exclaimed after a time, and very slowly, "there's a—look, Francey, what is that strange disturbance right ahead?   Can it be porpoises?   No."

François followed the direction with his eyes.   It was directly in the course of the boat.   He could see at some distance an agitation on the surface of the water.   It was broken, ruffled.   He gazed at it with vacant speculation.   The roar that he had heard was growing louder.   Suddenly he shrieked.

"*It's Corryvrechkan!*"

The lad turned to him inquiringly, and blanched, for the dreadful horror in his cousin's eyes aroused a nameless one in his own dauntless heart.

"Corry—what's that, Francey?"

"It's—the—whirlpool."   François sat limply in the stern of the boat and stared with haggard eyes.   "It's the whirlpool."

"But a whirlpool!" said the boy uneasily.

" What's wrong, Francey ? " The sight of François'
terror infected him. " What's wrong, Francey ? " he
demanded urgently.

" I heard about it," François babbled incoherently.
" It's the whirlpool—the awful whirlpool. It's
death."

The dull roaring, the savage growling of captive
beasts, the rumbling of continuous cannon, grew
louder in their ears.

Corryvrechkan—the whirlpool of *Coirebhreacan*,
death-bed of unwary seamen, of countless ships ;
Corryvrechkan, needle monolith of rock rising from
ocean bed, above and around which the ebb from the
sound and the swell from the ocean eddy in a whirl
of horror ; Corryvrechkan in loud-mouthed rage,
roaring to the isles and the waters its dread defiance.

Already the tumult was more visible, the noise more
angry, the tide more swift. They glided in a smooth
rapidity most terrible by its suaveness, awful in its
immediate silence.

" Francey ! " cried the boy, and knelt at his
cousin's side.

François placed a trembling arm around the boy's
shoulders. " It's death—it's the whirlpool—it's
death," he repeated mechanically.

" Francey," cried the boy pleadingly, " sure it can't
be. You must be wrong to hoax a man. It's a joke,
Francey."

François gazed faintingly on the water. It was
glassy, and, beneath the surface, in greenish depths,
and further beneath in olive-coloured depths, and still
further in dark profundities that were like hell, were
small crystal bubbles, small and white, moving,

bursting, forming, arising from an inky abyss and coming into vision, rising and bursting, but always, as they rose, moving with the course of the vessel.

" My wife ! "

" Francey," the boy cried imploringly, " are you serious ? You're not—Francey, Francey, *Francey,*' he screamed, tugging at his cousin's sleeve. " Francey, a man can't go like this and leave his mother. Oh, Francey ! " The boy thrust his tearful face against the man's. " Francey, I'm not afraid to die—a man shouldn't be afraid to die. But not this." He threw his arms around François' neck and they clung to each other.

The roar was louder, savage, impatient.

The boat's sail flapped loosely, with a wet slapping sound. The boat moved swifter still.

Ahead of them that tremendous cauldron boiled in its agonies. Into the air, to dizzy heights, clustered spray shot tremblingly, poising like gems in the rays of the sun, dissolving in its fall.

François Campbell screamed. The words he shouted, as they left his throat, dissolved in that louder element. He screamed again, like an animal in pain ; his voice gibbered wild repetitive pleadings, he clutched Augustus in a frenzied embrace.

" Francey," cried the boy. " Francey, should we pray ? Oh, Francey, I'd hate to go before the throne of God without a prayer, and I used to make fun of them. Oh, Francey, my poor mother."

He turned a wild glance to the surrounding water, now ruffled, restless, and flecked with foam on its countless diminutive peaks. For a moment he stared at it, vacantly, and then the full conception of imminent death broke upon him with all its horror. He shuddered uncontrollably, a sob broke from his pallid lips, and he leant his head on François' shoulder. "Save me," he cried imploringly.

Augustus saw his cousin's head fall back, saw his cousin's eyes closed and the veins about them blue and heavy. The iron grip relaxed.

In his isolation the lad muttered a prayer. He kept his pallid face directed to the terror straight ahead, his flaxen hair waving in the wind, his lips parted, his eyes wild. The surface was now a bubbling mass, the falling spray wet him, the vessel quivered violently. He bent and kissed his unconscious cousin's face.

The boy started to cry, thinking of his mother. He closed his eyes then and prayed again, hearing the while that insatiable artillery in his ears, until it stopped suddenly, and all things with it.

VIII

Late that night the coachman returned to Duisk. Sir Scipio was not unduly alarmed, and when he sent a note across to Colin he stated that doubtless the young men had beached the boat farther along the coast, at Carsaig, perhaps, or Kilmelfort.

But when they did not put in an appearance on the following day the general felt that it was incumbent on him to make inquiries. He rode alone to Crinan and found the fisherman in whose boat the Campbell sons had set to sea. The man was in a state of agitation. A vessel had arrived that hour from Scarba for provisions, and those in it had a tale to tell. A shepherd, not of the party, had seen a small

sailing craft carried helplessly on the ebb tide through
the Gulf of Corryvrechkan. The boat had passed near
enough for him to distinguish the occupants, a man
and a boy. He had sworn that the whirlpool
swallowed them up.

This information put General Campbell in a frenzy
of alarm. Hoping against hope, he determined to cross
at once to Scarba and question the shepherd, and he
set off immediately. Before doing so, he despatched
word to his brother of his fears and intentions.

The weather had changed overnight. A blustery
wind blew with showers of rain, and the sky was
threatening. In Scarba the people gazed on the
proud old man with compassionate eyes. Sir Scipio's
face was grim and set, and they guessed his errand.
He desired that the shepherd be brought to him, and
paced by the shore impatiently, gazing across to his
own countryside and listening to Corryvrechkan's
roaring.

Rain fell in a sudden heavy downpour. He was
invited to enter a house for shelter, but preferred to
walk in the open.

It was almost two hours before the shepherd came,
and he brought the doom of General Campbell's
tenuous hopes. The description of the boat—corroborated by its owner, who had crossed with him—
the description of its two passengers, left Sir Scipio
in no doubt. Was the man positive that the boat
had gone under? Yes, he was positive. He had
discerned two men on the Jura hill-side opposite;
doubtless they had seen as well, and would vouch
for his statement.

Refusing food but accepting some whisky offered

him, Sir Scipio resolved to return at once to Crinan.
The voyage was fraught with danger. A gale was
blowing up the sound, and rain spattered before it,
cold and stinging. The general sat upright in the
stern, his coat wrapped about him, immobile.

At Crinan Admiral Campbell was awaiting him.
He had been prevented from attempting the passage
by the refusal of anyone to risk craft or life, and had
watched the return of his brother with a presage of
certain disaster. Sir Scipio was stiff, and had to be
assisted from the boat, and walked with difficulty in
spite of his brother's aid. Neither spoke.

They entered the carriage, where the general pain-
fully unfastened his wet coat and threw it from his
shoulders. He was blae, and shivered frequently.

" Well ? " said the admiral at last, very wearily.
His titivated complexion was in ghastly contrast to
his eyes. " I suppose it's ill news."

" They're in Corryvrechkan, right enough."

" Yes."

" It was trustworthy evidence, Colin. And we can
get more."

" Yes. Evidence."

" Your wife will be sore hurt by this, Colin."

" Yes. Sore hurt."

" Never mind, Colin. We're older now. Less time
to grieve, Colin."

" Oh," cried the admiral in a voice of agony, " he
was the pride and joy of my heart. The wee laddie."

The news of the disaster threw the two households
into frantic grief. The suddenness of their deaths,
their youth, the hopes entertained for them, and their
drastic closure, left everyone in a state of stunned

disbelief. And the thought that their bodies were
pitching in the wild inferno of the whirlpool, never
to be recovered and laid quietly amid kin, embittered
the poignancy of their loss.

That night Harriet gave premature birth to a
female child.

In the midst of the confusion that preceded the
birth of his grandchild Sir Scipio paced on the terrace.
He was in a tumult of doubt and despair. The death
of François had grieved him more than he could have
thought possible, and that of the little midshipman
meant even more. He walked with impatience,
anxious to know the result of what was happening.

Peggy it was who told him that the new-born child
was a girl.

" A girl ! " he exclaimed incredulously. He turned
away with visible rage. " Then there will be no more
male Campbells of Duisk."

The old woman smiled, tauntingly, he thought.

" No more Campbells of Duisk," he repeated,
astonished.

" It has been great trouble for nothing, then,"
she said simply.

He glanced at the great house, shadowy in the
darkness.

" It would have been better for the Campbells if
Colin Buie had been content with Uillian," she said.

" How is my daughter ? " he asked abruptly.

" She is very poorly, crying for her brother."

" And the mother ?—and the child ? "

" The mother is not well."

" Aye ! " he said. " Scipio Campbell can wear
them all out, it seems . . ."

She said urgently : " You are ill, Duisk, I see.
Get you to your bed, for you are ill."

" Well, Peggy," he said, laughing slightly, " this
is no night for feasting, Peggy. I'll see my daughter."

He went directly to the room of Emmeline, who lay
upon her bed, stricken. The hysterical girl clung to
him and sobbed convulsively. Her week was full.

Sir Scipio comforted her, and the girl finally lapsed
into quiet moaning. "Never mind," he said gently,
" we'll have good times yet." He left her and returned
to inquire after the mother. The doctor was grave.
The child was well, he said, but the mother's grief
had told against her. Mrs. François was in danger.

" Doctor MacIver, this is the time for you and not
for me. I'll sit up for your news." He asked Peggy
to bring whisky punch to the dining-room. He was
shivering, and his limbs trembled.

" Duisk," she said, laying her hand on his shoulder.
" Duisk, get you to your bed, man."

" I have no mood for it," he replied languidly.
" You're not asking me to sleep in all this horoyally,
Peggy ! "

" I will not have you sitting here, Duisk, in the
state you are," she cried passionately. " Let the
others be as they like, but go you to your bed."

" Do I look ill ? " he demanded, smiling. " I was
never ill in my life."

When morning came Mrs. François was dead, and
Sir Scipio was in a fever caused by his exposure on
the sea.

The rain had recommenced, a heavy warm downpour that stabbed vertically at Loch Awe and glist-
ened on the trembling sprays when the intermittent

sun gleams struck. Half-way down, the hills were masked in veils of mist; oppression weighted the atmosphere. From Barrill the dull-eyed inmates saw the façade of Duisk, indistinct, with all blinds drawn but one.

Dull-eyed. And dully questioning when they learned that Death, as it had struck at Inveraray years before, had struck with a trident thrust.

The sture old judge, dumb in grief, the bereaved father, unrouged, uncomforted, gazed with surmise and speculation, with the shadow of fate heavy against them and superstition in their eyes.

Confusion was in the house of Barrill, the sound of women's sorrow. In Duisk there was silence and death, with death still unappeased.

Upstairs, Sir Scipio lay silent. His face was scarlet of an unnatural tinge, and his eyes shone brightly. They could see a glimpse of hill and sky, and he was content with that. He lay quite still, without desire to move, and feeling a foreign ache in all his body and a strange fever in his blood.

Dividing his attention between the infant and the invalid, the doctor came and went, silently. Peggy was seldom absent from Sir Scipio's side; he smiled gratefully when he saw her, but did not care to speak, for he felt very tired. Roused from her absorbing woes, Emmeline sat by his side and gave him his physics, and cooled his forehead.

With evening the general grew worse, and MacIver, who was not leaving the house, ordered that he be watched all night. Peggy returned to the sick-room, where Emmeline was, and whom she bade go and rest for a little.

Q

Left alone with Sir Scipio, Peggy placed more logs on the fire, and after trimming the candles sat by the ill man's bed. He had lost sense of his surroundings and lay with closed eyes, breathing stertorously. The shadows from the leaping flames in the grate and from the candles cast combating light and shade; they flickered on the invalid's face, giving him an uncanny look.

Inevitably her mind went back to that night when she sat by the bed of this selfsame Scipio, the bedside of the young handsome Campbell of Duisk moaning in terror. How many years since?—forty years or more. The woman gazed on the old man's face with careful scrutiny. Scipio Campbell! She found herself shaping her lips to his name. In her heart great sorrow swelled for him, who was so overriding and proud, and who was so alone. Doctor MacIver—Emmeline Campbell—what did they know about the treatment of this sick man! That was her duty, her right, her prerogative. She would sit by his bedside all night, and gladly; she would sit by his bedside all week, all year, and they would all know that Peggy MacLachlan knew what was meant by the claims of kinship. She leaned forward and gently smoothed the sheets at his neck. Yes; she would show them all, and shame them and their foreign speech and foreign ways. Let François die, and the little Barrill laddie die, and the wife of François die; let them die. She knew what was her duty in this hour of weak tears and womanly grief. She knew her duty to Campbell of Duisk.

She was one of them, and but for one accident these lands would have been hers, and but for another she

would have been their lady. Weak François !—
timid-eyed Emmeline ! She smiled scornfully. They
were not the children that a Campbell of Duisk should
have. Campbell of Duisk should have had a dozen
of children, strong tall lads, fair-haired, kilted, roaming
the hills from dawn till dusk, fishing the lochs, hunting
the deer. Sturdy limbed lads who would speak the
Gaelic, and not thin pampered creatures who talked
a southern tongue and could travel only in carriages.

Ah, Scipio Campbell ! she thought pityingly, you
lie there, in the midst of grandeur, on your priceless
bed that gives you less comfort than the hedge-side
gives the tinker, with your starred coat there that can
warm you less than the plaid that warms my shoulders,
with your cheeks wrinkled and mine smooth, with your
gold that cannot cool your brow and your pride that
cannot ward off illness. You lie there, alone in the
midst of your splendours and honours, and the woman
who would have been your true wife and the glad
mother of your heirs sits watching you ! The *cailleach*
Peggy ! She smiled with the barren mirth of despair,
but it faded in a surge of apprehension, for she feared
that he might die.

' No more male Campbells of Duisk,' she. thought,
and leant forward to see how he fared. No more
male Campbells of Duisk. How bitter to the three
old brothers !—and she remembered ironically how
little their race had cared for the MacLachlans of
Duisk. And in fifty-two years' time the ambition
that had been paid for with three lives had ended with
another three. She moved dreamily to the window
and stood there for a long time, gazing on dark loch,
dark hill, dark sky, and a gleam that would be Barrill.

Archy Crubach and Colin would be sitting up lamenting for the loss of the child. Her heart was sorry for them; they were her kin, and were men among men, at least.

"Cydalise."

She turned sharply, looking to the prone man. His lips moved, he breathed deeply, and sighed. Peggy crossed to him and wet his lips and forehead with water. "Rest you, Duisk," she said.

"Cydalise," he said again, restlessly. His head moved from side to side; his eyes opened, scrutinized her without recognition. She spoke soothingly, but he did not hear. "Cydalise," he repeated again.

More urgently she spoke to him, hoping to calm the fevered brain with the mere harmony of sound. He heard, apparently, and in an attitude of vacant expectation waited.

"Sleep now," she said. "Sleep now, Duisk."

A low agitated pleading broke from the man's lips; a spate of words, endearing, appealing, sorrowing. His voice rose; desperation was there, and a sob of despair. Into his speech came continually one word, the name of his wife, and it was like a dagger to the woman who listened. It sank away in muttering. Again it grew louder, hoarser, and always the word came: "Cydalise."

Yes! she thought; a doll in silk and scents! He lies there and calls on her, and she threw him off like an old shoe!

The repetition of that name, articulated with such sweet appeal, with such fond humility, was intolerable to the woman. She left the room, hastening to the room of Emmeline.

" Sit by your father," she said.   " I am not well."
She departed downstairs to her own room and barren
vigil in the darkness.

Emmeline had not slept, and welcomed the opportunity of sitting by the sick-bed.   She was not afraid,
although the room was eerie and full of shadows, for
others were awake in the house, she knew, relative to
the death and the new-born child.   For a little Sir
Scipio was silent, and she did not venture to speak,
even although his eyes were riveted on hers.   But
in time his hands began to play with the coverlet,
and he showed restlessness.

" Where are my lads ? " he called sharply.

Emmeline started, and watched her father with
some alarm.   She hoped he would not attempt to rise.

" My own lads," repeated the general impatiently.
" Damnation ! " he said in a low fierce tone, " send
those Dorset yokels out of here, and bring up my lads
in the tartan.   Hai, lads ! you see those Frenchmen
on the height ?   They're two to one and that's well
matched.   Put ' Baile Ionaraora ' on them, piper,
and your day's fee will be a silver set."   Sir Scipio
struggled up in bed, his features tense and set.
" Now, my lads, this isn't swaggering on the High
Street of Edinburgh, but we'll show those fellows
. . . Cydalise," he ended on a plaintive tone, sinking
back on the pillow.   " Cydalise, my dear, why have
you left Duisk ?   Why have you left Duisk ? " he
continued in a surprised tone, " why have you left
your house and children ?   Oh, my dear, come back
come back . . . " his voice sank to a whisper of
horror " . . . no-no, she is dead, and I dead with
her.   That's right !   That's my wife, gentlemen, and

here's her husband. Though her sins were crimson she is my wife. Now, sir, a quick despatch. Is she shortened ? Ah, dear God, they have not taken off that beautiful head ! Is it off ? Is it truly off ? Then here's mine, and let them kiss in the basket. Die ?—not die with my wife ? It is no death that, I'm thinking, and I am Campbell of Duisk. We Campbells are not feared of the face of man, or the edge of an axe for that matter. Oh, Cydalise ! " he cried in a dreadful cracked voice, " I won't believe that tale. My wife ? It's false ; my wife's beyond reproach. Is it Mrs. Campbell of Duisk ? . . . then shear us both."

Emmeline clasped her father's hands in an agony.

" Yes, Cydalise, you're there," Sir Scipio said at once in a tone of utter tenderness. " I shot him for your sake, and the reek of his blood was incense in my nostrils. How can I judge you, I that must be judged ? Had you let me know, my dear, had you told me of the hunger and the sorrow and the cold . . . yes, I'd have forgiven you. For I, too, have sinned. You did not know that, Cydalise," he said gladly. " No. No one knows. Peggy knows. You know her—Peggy. Peggy MacLachlan. For I told her, when I was weak. For I saw him once, in the gloaming, come out from under the trees . . . pale and grey. And he looked at me. He looked, looked, looked. Without a smile, Cydalise ; and I thought his eyes would have burned me through. I think I saw through him, he was so pale and grey. It was then I told Peggy, my cousin Peggy Mac-Lachlan, Neil the fiar's daughter. Yes, I told her. But she was faithful."

Sir Scipio heaved a deep sigh. "So you see,
Cydalise, I cannot blame, and I am telling you this
that you will feel no shame in gazing at me, for I
have done folly also. Yes. But you are dead,
Cydalise! The Jacobins—did they slaughter you?
Did they not? So much the better; I was told they
did. Yes, you are here and I am happy. Hold my
hands tight, my love. Yes, we will live again at
Duisk, and I shall make you happy. Did I not tell
you?" Sir Scipio laughed with pleasure at his
revelation. "Yes, Cydalise. I, too, have sinned.
'Judge not, lest ye be judged.' I give forgiveness,
for I want it. And you will not hide your darling
face in shame from me when I tell you that I killed
Do'l Leitch in the wood of Errachan."

Emmeline screamed: "Peggy! Peggy!"

"I killed Do'l Mor, Cydalise," the general repeated
triumphantly, "for Scipio Campbell was never the
man to thole a blow."

FIVE

I

A YEAR passed.
Admiral Colin Campbell and his wife were back in London, attempting to forget in the interests to be found there what they could not forget.

Lord Drumgesk was in Edinburgh.

And General Sir Scipio Campbell was with the army in Holland, where the British and Russian troops were combined against the French and Dutch.

In Duisk House Emmeline remained, with the infant heiress Harriet.

Once again Peggy MacLachlan had seen the tide roll back from Duisk.

She had seen the burial of the young Harriet Scott, short time loved and buried remote from her own kin ; she had seen the brothers from Barrill roll round the end of the loch and speed past Duisk like hawks in mourning ; she had seen the sailor's daughters and their broods pass by, preoccupied and serious, to their England and its ways. And she had seen General Sir Scipio Campbell, pale, weak, and broken, drive from Duisk as though pursued by the Furies.

" It is the third time you have gone away, Duisk. Will you come back ? "

" I'll come back," he said, " when I am dead."

In her heart she despised the broken Emmeline ;

Emmeline, who now shared the secret and who clung
to her like a frail ghost. What if her mother had
died on the block !—there were plenty of Highland
people alive whose fathers had died likewise. What
if Scipio Campbell had killed his man !—it was long
ago, and no business of his daughter's. Had Neil
Uillian killed his man would she have shrunk from
him ?—she would not ! She would have dared all
Scotland for her father's sake. But this poor weeping
creature . . .

Peggy was glad that a full-length portrait of Sir
Scipio hung in the dining-room. Often she gazed
on it.

She loved Scipio Campbell as she had always done,
and that knowledge of Do'l Mor's murder had not
had power to weaken. The repulsion born of his
stammered confession on that far-away night had
died within a month. But the strength of her own
fidelity made her under-estimate that of the fragile
timid Emmeline, and she did not imagine what
effect the last revelation had made upon the girl.

General Don had been shot in a duel. But Do'l
Mor had been murdered. Even that difference might
have lessened in the girl's mind in time had not Neil
Leitch been Do'l Mor's grandson. The realization
had stricken Emmeline with horror. She, the murderer's daughter, had walked with the unavenged.
It was unnatural. There was injustice, surely, in
that the bloodstained Campbells of Duisk should be
so rich and prosperous and their wronged kin
struggling with ruin.

That Sir Scipio should have threatened to complete that ruin raised a revulsion in her against her

father. It was the threat of a savage—callous,
brutal ; and he had made it with bloodstained hands.
Emmeline could not conceive the perversion that
evil makes in the mind. She could not realize that
Sir Scipio, having wronged the Leitches, rather than
make attempt at reparation, found a bitter pleasure
in adding to his misdeeds, in driving the barb further
into his conscience.

The big arrogant gentleman, knight, general, laird
—her father—a murderer. Emmeline brooded over
the knowledge with idiotic intensity. It was incredible. And she would think—unable to reconcile
the two—of his tender pleadings to the vanished
Cydalise Cœur-de-roi. Horror overcame the wretched
girl when she thought of her mother, hazarding
vague and innocent guesses at her later life, seeing
vividly the torments of her bloody death.

Emmeline had lost her brother in the Gulf of
Corryvrechkan, had lost her lover, had lost the fond
hopes of reunion with her mother and had been
offered a tragedy to replace them, and had had all
her best conceptions of her father shattered. In the
hour of parting with him she had swooned, and he
was gone when she recovered. And the general
returned to his trade with that picture of revulsion
in his heart.

The girl felt that she had become the target of an
evil destiny, and the belief was natural enough. On
all sides her idolatries and presumptions lay fallen ;
she was isolated, unutterably alone.

With less fell knowledge she would have turned to
Neil Leitch. But she could not now. Gradually
she shaped a reason for events, and she saw in the

destruction of her idyll the expiation for the family
sins. She had asked Peggy with surprise in what
way the old woman was related to her, and Peggy
told her, calmly, of the earlier night of blood.
Emmeline was sickened. Blood was spread on the
ramifications of her race. Surely the Campbells
throve on it. To cleanse the stains from the house of
Duisk she would never venture near Neil Leitch
again, and thus offer the oblation of her heart to
appease the thirsty gods of Duisk.

She sensed Peggy's cold contempt for her agonies
—and what comfort could she gain from that woman,
nearing seventy and white-haired, who declared with
conviction that Scipio Campbell was worth all the
rest of them put together ?

" My father is a monster," said the girl, pale as
death, and trembling violently.

The old woman regarded her with scorn. " You
are no true Campbell to say those things. The dead
of your race will rise against you. A monster ! He
is a man."

II

And General Campbell, in these days, was in North
Holland, amid his troops, with his whole world dead
and rotten.

He thought sometimes, with wonder, on Peggy's
unquestioned fidelity, and how easily she might have
broken her silence.

But it was with wonder only, and a sense of
gratitude. His heart was in Paris, in the Place de
la Révolution. It was there, with all his love, his
thoughts, and his memories.

How much he had been drawn to Emmeline because of that evanescent resemblance, the living shadow of a vanished substance! But that also was done and by with, and now there was the army left, which was killing legalized.

He knew now that his own home was forbidden him. He had known Duisk as a young man, eager and violent; he had known it as a husband, fooled and robbed; and as a parent, anguished and exposed. He reflected that life might have been kinder to him.

Sir Scipio had returned to the bottle, and was comforted no whit by it. Of all his pursuits he had found satisfaction only in the din of arms, in marching, in bivouacking, in hearing the incitement of war music and the grave orchestra of artillery.

Of his race he would be the last soldier. Of the ultimate inheritors of Duisk he did not care to think. That property had gone from the Campbells, and in that strain he had written to his brothers. From Edinburgh Drumgesk had replied announcing his approaching marriage.

Sir Scipio was grateful.

Meantime, his abilities were taxed by the efforts made to drive the French and their Dutch allies out of Holland. Already, six years earlier, he had learned the value of the desperate revolutionaries, fierce Frenchmen with a sense of wrong in their hearts, and backed now by the obstinate courage of the native troops of Daendels. For several weeks, ever since the Duke of York had landed the army at Helder Point and effected a junction with the Russians, there had been constant manœuvring and

skirmishing among these dikes and canals, on those
long flats that ruled out the more spectacular elements
of surprise attack or ambush, and left only cam-
paigning in an open country, against fanatical
opponents, amid a hostile population. He was quite
satisfied. Only his great pull with high authority
had given him a command ; there were many younger
men, with influence also, who had desired it. But
the royal duke had welcomed him. Moore and
Abercromby were friends and men of judgment. To
have enjoyed this campaign Sir Scipio would have
served as a subaltern.

He had been active in the repulse of the enemy
from the first positions assumed by the British
troops on progressing from the Helder. Then had
followed the anxious advance by the sands at low
tide from Bergen to Egmond, with Colonel Mac-
Donald's men protecting the left flank on the sand
dunes above. Egmond had been gained with considerable loss of men on the way, and once there,
some confusion had arisen in the minds of those in
command as to the next step.

In the council of war that had been constituted
for the strategy of this campaign General Campbell
had no say. He was junior to Abercromby, Pulteney-
Murray, and Dundas, who were lieutenant-generals,
and he had to content himself with his own private
opinions on the tactics of invasion, having a perfect
confidence in his own ability to act either on a
preconceived plan or the necessity of the moment.

The disorders that had broken out among the
allies were grave enough. The civilian population
were sullenly resentful against the licentious soldiery

who had come in the guise of saviours. They sold
the British troops their cattle,.hired them their canal
boats, and among themselves hoped with a fierce
desire for a republican victory. The support of the
British by their Prince of Orange left them unmoved.
They were aware of the dogged courage of their own
countrymen under Daendels and of the determination shown by Brune's Frenchmen in the assault on
the allied positions, and fervently desired the early
expulsion of these uninvited troops of the English
king and the Russian despot.

Over a stretch of miles the allied troops had
advanced during that day when Abercromby led his
men along the Bergen sands. Inland, the French
had retreated slowly, fighting for every village, every
farm, and when they retired at length to their own
lines of defence it was with the Russian commander
in their possession.

The new commander of the troops of the Czar was
well aware of the Duke of York's contempt for him
and his army, a contempt generally expressed under
the influence of liquor. Nor did the allied rank and
file fraternize any better. Their regard for each
other was similar, but less respectful, to their regard
for their foes.

Facing hostile troops, amid hostile peasants, with
hostile allies, and under continuous drenching rain,
the royal duke and his council of war, complete with
Russian representatives, debated each move in the
plan of campaign, aware that time had been hopelessly lost in disembarkation, in advancing, and in
consequence meeting with unexpected resistance.

At Alkmaar, over twenty miles from the place of

landing, the duke had set up his headquarters, wedged in the peninsula of North Holland, with the whole of the Netherlands still unconquered.

The campaign had been mismanaged, but Sir Scipio Campbell was happy.

Once again he heard the thunder of artillery, the jingle of accoutrements, the unmusical message of the bugles. Once again he was facing the troops of France, those revolutionaries now tenfold hateful to him, those ragged scum whom he hoped to ride down under the hooves of his horse. Each new day was a reminder of Cydalise ; each new day helped him to forget Duisk. He asked himself why he had ever returned to that cursed place on Loch Awe, why he had ever forsaken this element of death and battle where he was at home.

He was on horseback now, in the early dawn, watching his troops march past. The rain came down in sheets, drenching them to the skin. General Campbell, a resplendent figure in plumed hat and braided greatcoat, bestrode a great grey horse that shook an impatient head at the downpour. Grouped behind was his staff, wishing that their commander had chosen a stance farther back in the protection of the little village church.

The rain stung the brandy-reddened and forbidding features of Sir Scipio, but he seemed oblivious of it. He was motionless but for his eyes, which moved alertly over the marching men as he wondered what spirit the uncertain fighting and the pelting rain had left in them. Advance was planned between Alkmaar and Boccum, preparatory to the grasping of the key town of Beverwijk, and already there was fighting on the flanks. Above the steady swish of the rain sounded the distant rumble of cannon.

The men marched stolidly, deploying into line as arranged. Sir Scipio had his orders; near-by a French corps was securely posted and was to be dislodged from its positions.

A battalion of Highlanders came next. The skirl of the pipes startled his charger. He soothed the restless beast with voice and hand.

" I heard," he said, turning to his aide-de-camp, an Argyllshire Campbell like himself, " that Colin Campbell, Blarbuie's son, fell yesterday."

Captain Campbell assented.

" It will be a sore grief to his father," said the general. " I've known Blarbuie all my life, and I'll write him to-night."

He spurred his steed and galloped forward, followed by his staff. Mounting an incline that commanded a stretch of the country in front, he asked for his spy-glass and scanned the positions with an eager eye.

The roar of artillery now sounded along the lines, mingled with the sharp crackle of musketry.

The countryside was broken by beltings and patches of woodland, intersected by deep rain-filled ditches on the flats. Against the trees the drifting cannon-smoke melted into the drifting rain-vapour. It was impossible to see clearly the course of events.

Sir Scipio hastened to an advanced site. There he was among his men, and from there surveyed the full course of battle, sending instructions along a two-mile front.

Battle raged all afternoon on those green and

undulating pastures, in that drenching October day.
A quiet countryside, broken by the raucous roar
of warfare, the screams of mangled horses, the
groans of dying men. Cavalry swept forward, heavy
dragoons on massive chargers, and spiked the enemy
guns.

" It's hard going," observed the general, mounting
another horse in place of the slain grey. " We can't
win battles at fifty men a yard."

Careless of his person, he rode along the lines,
despatching orders to his brigade commanders and
the generals commanding on his flanks. The French
fire was now slackening.

" I informed Generals Singleton and Ripley that
I am advancing, providing they can do likewise. It
will have to be careful going, or we'll be outflanked
in the woods." Sir Scipio dashed the drips from his
hat. " I think the day's ours," he said. He fumed
at the delay in answering his messages. " I should
have had word from them long since," he said.

Favourable tidings reaching him, he set his lines
in motion. The din of cannon recommenced; in
less than a mile's advantage the advance slackened.
The troops were facing broken strips of wood, and a
red-hot rain of fire raked them from its protection.
It was late afternoon by the time the artillery had
dislodged the enemy, and the attackers were dis-
inclined to make further attempts. They were exhausted by the constant deluge of rain, by the constant deluge of gun-fire. Behind, the ground was
strewn with the bodies of their comrades, the ditches
were full of them. Murmurs of dismay arose, and
General Campbell rode along the front.

R

" Now lads, we're not going to let our comrades carry all the honours of the day," he shouted. " It needs one more effort to knock the fight out of those Frenchmen, and you're the lads to do it." To his subordinate commanders he despatched orders for a general advance. " If this try doesn't pull things off, Campbell, I doubt some of these lads will run."

Anxious because of the signs of twilight, Sir Scipio signalled for a general assault. The reinforced defenders were ready : Frenchmen with a strange new belief in the sacredness of their cause and fairly willing to die for it, men hardened by long exposure and privations in days anterior to war. From an elevated stance the general surveyed the fortunes of battle along the lines. He saw his troops advance valiantly, hesitate, and weaken.

For a time there was a confusion of hand-to-hand bayonet fighting, a shambles of rain-soaked horror. Into the wet ground dripped wet blood ; prone bodies lay, bloody faces saturated by the shining rain. There was the cessation of all order, and what had been warfare between opposing armies had become fighting between man and man, regardless of bellowed orders, of repetitive commands.

The cannon-smoke trailed across the flats like ghosts of wrecked balloons, the air was rank with the acrid smell of gunpowder.

By now the sound of cannon was heavier. Anxious horsemen dashed up with tidings, and the general's face grew livid.

" Singleton's men are on the run, and so is he. Gentlemen, instruct brigade commanders of a general retiral. Captain Smith, inform Sir John Ripley that

I am retiring in alignment with General Singleton."
He wheeled his horse and sped forward amid the
frenzied masses. With difficulty the troops were
forming into an approach to order. The bugles
continued to sound the Retire. The retreat was in
danger of becoming a flight ; a regiment of dragoons
dashed back through their lines in wild disorder, and
the infection of that haste put men in panic.

" Steady ! " roared the old man, riding coolly
through the confusion. He knew there was small
chance of immediate onslaught from the damaged
enemy in front. Were some calm diffused among
his troops a retiral could be effected in proper order.
He feared only a flank attack from the positions
vacated by Singleton's men. He rode among his
men, composed and unshaken, despatching hurried
instructions to every point.

On his exposed flank the cannon of Brune were
beginning to rake the retiring lines, as he had feared.
Weary and disheartened, dragging tired bodies over
the rain-sodden ground, the infantry on the flank
were no longer able to face this fierce and unexpected
attack. General Campbell called for heavy cavalry,
and to inspire confidence in his panic-stricken men he
rode in front of them, bare-headed, shouting appeal
and command. The men paused, hesitated, and
disregarded him, continuing on their flight. Sir
Scipio fretted at the non-arrival of his dragoons.

" That lot's surrounded," he said sharply. He
indicated an isolated group, among the last to retire,
which had been attacked in the rear and against
which a detachment of enemy lancers was now riding
at the gallop.

"Those men are lost, sir!"

"Some of the Cameronian Volunteers."

"They haven't an officer left, sir.   I can see that."

"Some of the Argyllshire lads were drafted into the 79th," said the general slowly.   "Some Glassary lads among them.   I twitted Cameron about it."

"They haven't a hope, sir.   And, by God, they're putting up a good fight."

The next moment Sir Scipio was plunging across the intervening slope, followed by his astonished staff.   He dug his spurs into his horse's flesh;   he drew his sword, and dashed into the mêlée at once. Amid the welter of kilted bodies and victorious foes the old man appeared, bare-headed, fierce, terrible, slashing to right and left, his frantic charger trampling over enemy and friend.   And then a long lance was thrust through Major-General Sir Scipio Campbell's body.   He fell from the saddle, suppressing any moan of pain.   As he lay, he was pierced repeatedly by the savage victors, and died.   The sounds of conflict ceased, for all had now been slain.   And the tide of battle rolled backward, leaving Campbell of Duisk silent amid the silent kilted forms.

SIX

I

LORD DRUMGESK was a busy man, eager in the execution of his work, vigorous in the bacchic company of his friends. He judged and he drank; and between the two he allowed himself little leisure. Once he had liked leisure; now he was afraid of it.

As the years passed on, Lord Drumgesk saw himself with a vanishing list of acquaintances. Laugh and swear and drink as much as they liked, the boon companions were one by one being tapped upon the shoulder, and on receiving that grisly accolade they vanished to the dust. At times the laughter sounded hollow.

And on looking back upon the years of his life Archibald Crubach was left with a feeling of frustration. He was successful, rich, landed, honoured. He was envied, hated, flattered, and childless. Following on the deaths of his nephews he had chosen a successor to Sophy Gordon with the hope that a male Campbell might be born to carry on the line of Barrill. But Marianne Murray, the sturdy thirty-year-old Perthshire laird's daughter whom he married, died shortly of fever, and Drumgesk accepted widowerhood with fatalism. He had a premonition that his last marriage would be the final outstanding event of his life.

261

Alone in his house in Castle Street, he sent for
Emmeline and the child Harriet, now under the
guardianship of himself and his brother. Emmeline
went willingly to Edinburgh. She would have gone
anywhere, if only to leave Duisk.

All spirit was gone from her, and she was not
exhilarating company for Lord Drumgesk; but the
judge had not been expecting that. He clung to
her in a pathetic fashion, and so did she to him.
He had gauged accurately the intensity of her affection for Neil Leitch and was sincerely sorry for the
girl. Perhaps Sir Scipio also had judged it accurately,
for the handsome fortune he left her was conditional
on her never marrying any of the descendants of
his grandsire Colin Buie.

She was changed greatly; there were no lines on
her young face, and nothing marred its fairness. It
was the expression of it that had altered. The
pleading timidity of yore was replaced by wan
inquiry. Drumgesk was solicitous. Once he asked
her if she cared enough to let the money go and
follow her heart. She was disturbed by the question,
and evaded it. The old judge, softened by the years,
hinted that he would see Leitch decently placed, and
it was then that she confessed her determination
never to see Neil again. He was surprised, and
thought her mercenary, although her inconsolable
pining did not support that belief; but Emmeline
could not explain her real reason.

"Oh, Uncle Archy, you cannot understand," she
cried in a passion of unpent grief. "It is the
thought that we are parted . . . and will never meet
again."

" Aye," said the old man slowly, " and you're both
alive. I had mony a love affair, Emmy, and one
near garred my heart to break. But young lovers'
partings arena such terrible things, Emmy. I recovered, and in time I mairret Sophy Gordon. And
Sophy Gordon's deid. She was a very fine woman,
Emmy.

" When I was a callant of twenty I was gey fond
of Sandy Campbell, that was in the same classes as
me. We were a daft pair, and up to a' the tricks.
And then Sandy Campbell died o' the small-pox, and
he lies buried in the Canongate. I went ae day to
his grave and stood at the foot o't. It was a brech-
ling day in June, and I could feel the heat in the
soles of my shoes. I stood at the foot of the grave,
Emmy, and I grat like a bairn. I felt like I was
committing a sin, breathing the air and feeling the
sunshine, and knowing that Sandy was dumb and
deid aneath the grass for ever. He was fond of a
joke and a laugh, and he would never laugh again.
That's grief, Emmy, because death parts us for ever.
It's the only begetter of grief. The sun shone doun
on the grass, and Sandy Campbell was boxed aneath
it. I'm not ower sure of another world, but I'm
hoping there is, for there's a hantle lot o' folk I'd
like to meet again. Death is a terror, Emmy, for
it shears our friends like grass. Of two friends, it
is better to die first, for you suffer less. No, Emmy,
Neil Leitch is alive at Strone, and Strone isna the
Canongate."

" But your friend was a man——"

" Aye, Emmy. ' Very pleasant hast thou been
unto me ; thy love to me was wonderful, passing the

love of women '—the loves of two men are founded
on more than the loves of a man and a woman.
They are founded on the turn of a phrase, on a
chance confidence, on the pleasure of walking
thegither in silence. The sighs and pantings o' a
lad and lass are gey puir stanes to build a friendship
wi'. Death is the enemy, as you'll learn in time.
My love for Sandy Campbell and his for me were
things we took for granted. It was only when he
passed afore me that I kenned what's meant by love.
And God forbid that you ever stand by the grave of
a friend, kenning that he's dumb for ever. You'll
be a rebel then, and I fear you'll doubt God. But
from then on you'll no' fear death. But death is
the enemy."

One there was who knew as much. She was at
Duisk.

In those days Edinburgh was not dull. It was
lively with garrisons, the coming and going of soldiers,
the stir of recruiting, the knowledge of great events
abroad. The years passed, slowly at first, later with
gathering rapidity, until Emmeline recollected with
some surprise that her father had been dead six
years. She began now to lose the horror with
which she had formerly thought of him; perhaps it
had never been very strong. Her mind reverted
frequently to him, his high look, his unquestioned
grandness, and she would remember gratefully how
kind he had always been to her save in one thing.
The girl reproached herself sometimes for having
thought angrily of Sir Scipio, but the relationship
between Do'l Mor Leitch and Neil Leitch would yet
assert itself. Her love for Neil was very lasting.

Emmeline was not anxious to return to Duisk, but she hungered for information of a kind. It was useless to write to Peggy, for Peggy had never learned to write. That the Leitches still held Strone was all Emmeline knew, for no foreclosure had been effected, thanks to Sir Scipio's death and her influence over the judge. But a young native of the parish, having settled in Edinburgh, had occasion to call at Drumgesk's house to request a reference of character, and Emmeline seized the opportunity for questioning him on several things.

She learned then that Neil Leitch was married.

The information completely unnerved her, and it was not until she had sought out the suppliant at a humble address near the Cowgate that she was able to hear further details. That the wife of Neil had been Phemie Fletcher and was connected with her husband in some fashion through the MacTavishes was all she learned.

Emmeline brooded over the news with despair in her heart. Resigned as she was not to think of marriage with Neil, she had never thought possible that he would not do likewise. Her abnegation was to have been of a partnership. She had certainly never suggested as much to Neil, but that he should contemplate marriage with another had been unthinkable. All at once she felt remote from reality; the stream of life was passing by her. Neil Leitch of Strone, on whom she had lavished all her heart, had given his own to someone else. It was a betrayal.

When the first spasm of grief was past a strange new resentment against Neil formed in her. She, a gentlewoman, had cheapened herself, and lo! she was nothing compared to some country byremaid. A mood of pettish bitterness against the young couple lodged itself in Emmeline. The Neil Leitch wedded to Phemie Fletcher was not the same Neil Leitch that she had known, surely. He was a stranger; not the Neil of Strone who was sprung from the Campbells of Duisk, but a mere farmer wedding with one of his own kind. She tingled with the desire to hurt him, to show her love by harming him. She hoped fretfully that he would still fail to prosper and that she might hear him say so, that she might say: ' I told you so! '

In this jealous mood Emmeline's devotion to her distant kinsman remained unchanged. He was as dear to her as ever; but she could not bear to think of another woman sharing his life. That the young man might have married for a number of reasons apart from love—from umbrage, from necessity, for economy—did not occur to her. Neil, in fact, having realized that the young lady from the Big House was out of his life for ever, had with difficulty banished the face of Emmeline from his memory, had dismissed his love for her as a hopeless dream, and had latterly married the smiling Phemie Fletcher from Cairnbaan, whose mother had been a MacTavish, the daughter of the poet Duncan of Duin.

It was during this passion of resentment that the Edinburgh house was informed of the death of Peggy MacLachlan. The passing of General Sir Scipio Campbell signalled the end of his cousin, but the bodily frame of that strong spirit was strong, too, and six years she took to follow in his wake. They were

years of silent and sullen grieving. Latterly she
grew garrulous and would speak aloud, scarce conscious of her words. " I could have been the wife of
Scipio Campbell," she would say, to the amusement
of those who heard. " I know something about
Scipio Campbell that King George never knew," she
would say mysteriously. " It was a long journey,"
she said at the end. " The road was rough and it
forked in two."

The funeral took place from Duisk to Kilneuair,
where her mother was. It was a good funeral, and
the mourners who had gathered from the surrounding
district took turns at carrying the coffin. It was a
good funeral; there were frequent rests on the road
for refreshment and eulogy on the dead woman's
merits. Her connection with the Campbells of Duisk
and with the half-forgotten MacLachlans of Duisk
was discussed, and her straight forthright nature was
praised, and her fine spirit of hospitality; and it was
regretted that in later years her manner had altered
perceptibly, for she had grown a little thrawn. It
was only when the mourners arrived at the graveyard that they discovered the absence of the coffin.
Search was decided on, and such as were able returned as they had come, to find it on the top of a
dyke where it had been left at the last tasting,
those behind thinking it had been taken in front
and those in front thinking it was being brought in
the rear.

She was buried in a corner of the enclosure, in a
new grave, as her mother had been placed in a family
lair which was now full. No one thought of erecting
a stone to the memory of Peggy MacLachlan, and

her few possessions were passed to a half-cousin whose right to them was doubtful, the deceased woman having no relations according to law. Very soon the mound sank and the nettles flourished on it, and there was nothing to indicate who lay there or what that person had been. She had served the Campbells of Duisk for fifty-one years.

II

During these years there was continual corres-pondence between the Campbells of Edinburgh and London; occasionally the surviving brothers met in Edinburgh, talking wistfully of old times and the days of their youth. The meetings of Archibald Crubach and Colin were fraught now with a melan-choly. Many mutual friends were gone; their family hopes were shattered; the brother to whom they had been sincerely attached was buried in far Holland.

They would part reluctantly, yet not without a secret relief, for both found forgetfulness apart from one another in the society of heedless friends. When Admiral Campbell returned to London he won solace of a kind for the dead Augustus. Yet he could never keep from thinking of the age his son would be were he alive—nineteen, twenty, twenty-one . . .

But the presence of his wife and daughters could remove that ghastly shadow from his mind. In their company, in the discussion of their plans and ambitions, he was able to gain a relieving interest, his wife and he mutually allaying their mutual sorrow.

The three daughters of Admiral Campbell had been shocked by the death of their half-brother, but once the horror at his tragic end had passed they could only simulate grief. They had been grown women before the boy was born ; they had seen little of him and could not be expected to feel his loss as his parents did. And to one of them the death of Augustus had opened up a new future.

Elizabeth Otway, immediately after the first terrible news of the Corryvrechkan tragedy, had visioned her sons installed at both Duisk and Barrill. The birth of the little Harriet had been a bitter surprise to the ambitious woman, for she had not been aware that Mrs. François Campbell was enceinte, and Emmeline she considered a frail creature with no great prospects of life. But at any rate she was certain of Barrill. By the clause in Malcolm Campbell's will the two estates could never be conjoined.

Mrs. Otway's husband had reached the rank of brigadier when he fought at Maida in 1805, but Mrs. Otway was not content with that. Her sister had command of a fortune placing her above all cares and economies, and the knowledge of the luxuries lavished on the young Tom Bowmaker filled Elizabeth with vicious impatience. Old Admiral Bowmaker had a house in Park Lane and an estate in Sussex—a grand palladian house, pillared, winged, and collonaded, with grounds in the latest style of park-like disposition—and the very sight of Lanshanger Place roused Mrs. Otway to impotent fury.

"You see!" she said to the seventeen-year-old Caesar as they drove away from the mansion on one of their not infrequent visits, "your cousin Tom Bowmaker will come into all this." She surveyed the finely timbered slopes of verdure and the avenue of elms with disconsolate eyes. "And you've got nothing."

"That's father's fault—not the Bowmakers'," Caesar protested grumblingly. He had a good share of the Campbell features, with a suspicion of his father's addiction to obesity. "If once I get into the army I'll maybe show the Bowmakers a thing or two."

"You'll go into no army," the mother snapped.

"But I want to go into the army," Caesar insisted.

"You'll wait your time and go into Barrill," said Mrs. Otway conclusively. "Is Tom Bowmaker going into the navy ?—no ! Yon milksop couldn't manage his hands at table far less a ship. Your Aunt Janet is not risking Tom's life, for sure. The big clumsy booby . . . yon boy should be well thrashed. There's nothing of the Campbell in him, at any rate. One fighting man is enough in one family, and your father is the soldier in ours, Caesar."

"Well, Admiral Bowmaker is the sailor in theirs."

"Bah ! " said Mrs. Otway elegantly.

The contempt and jealousy that Elizabeth felt for her second sister was altered to simple contempt for her youngest sister. She regarded the unpretentious establishment of Mrs. Cattanach with unconcealed pity ; she always felt that Leonie had been a fool to marry for love, and she said so, both to Leonie and the younger Otways. These indiscretions were repeated to Æneas Cattanach, who was amused. "Elizabeth is a meddlesome woman," he said indulgently.

"I don't like her to say those things," his wife said with some resentment. "I don't want to be nasty, but——"

Cattanach, a thin-lipped saturnine man, smiled. He could not imagine his gentle partner being very nasty to anyone.

"—but Elizabeth is very trying," she said.

"Elizabeth was giving advice to Janet Bowmaker, I hear," he responded. "Your father was telling me, who got it from his wife, who got it from Janet. And if Elizabeth can't hold her tongue she'll be less at Lanshanger in the future."

"She likes going to Lanshanger."

"Yes; like a crow."

"She was criticizing John to me . . . after she spoke about you. She says John has no manners, and that he is stupid."

"I've seen some stupid brats," said Mr. Cattanach, "but, believe me, I've never seen such ignorant, misbehaved, hobbledehoy youngsters as those young Otways. They would break the heart of anyone except your sister, and I'm hanged if she isn't proud of them. Mark me, those children will give her a heap of trouble some day."

"She is going too far," Leonie said nervously.

"We can leave Otway himself to deal with her," Cattanach remarked peaceably. "I thank my stars I'm only her brother-in-law," and he retired to write a letter to his uncle, Mr. John Hamilton, in India.

The condition of mind that bade Elizabeth find faults with the branches of her father's house was reflected from neither her father nor his wife.

Admiral Colin was delighted that Janet should be so well provided for and that his Bowmaker grandson would become a wealthy squire; he was sincerely proud of the reports he had received of George Otway's fighting qualities and was hopeful that further promotion would be in store for that officer; and he was quite well satisfied with his quiet, capable Cattanach son-in-law, and, while admitting that Æneas's position in the East India Office was not spectacular, he shrewdly guessed that more might be got from it in the long run than from either army or navy.

Colin, as the years passed, went less to Scotland. Only Drumgesk was there to attract him north, and now the rouged old sailor could think of the bibulous heavy features of his brother with a sense of terror only.   Drumgesk was a reminiscence of past youth, past hopes, past revenges.   He reminded Colin of old days at Duisk : of Mrs. Captain Archy, of Colin Buie and the fatuous Colin Og, of dead Do'l Mor and the pursuit of Cydalise Cœur-de-roi ; and of his slain brother and hero, Sir Scipio Campbell.   Drumgesk with his purplish heavy face and powdered hair, in the long sitting-room in Castle Street, in the dim candle-light, growling and guffawing with little runs of melancholy in his speech—a changed Archy Campbell from the Archy who had hunted for birds' nests in the woods of Barrill in the long sweet days of boyhood !   And as for Emmeline and the young girl Harriet, the daughter of François— Admiral Campbell had no sentimental thoughts for them, and only the ordinary courtesies.   He knew, or he thought he knew.

And so the visits of Colin Campbell to his own country grew less, and the brothers maintained their connection by correspondence. They had aged much recently, most from their heavy indulgence in liquor, and their letters reflected the gloomy nature of their meditations. Only in the thought of the augmented glories of his family did the admiral gain any satisfaction. Himself was rich with prize-money, Drumgesk was rich with that of litigants, Scipio had left a fine fortune. The house of Duisk, founded by Colin Buie, was rich in everything save male heirs. He visioned a baronetcy and lieutenant-generalship for Otway, and a line of Otway-Campbell baronets of Duisk ; he imagined a political career for Tom Bowmaker, and a Lord Lanshanger of the future ; he hoped for a high place in the civil government of India for the young John Cattanach. He would retail with pride the words of Royalty when he had surrendered his brother's insignia of the Bath, and how Royalty regretted that Sir Scipio's son had not survived to assume the peerage destined for his father. Admiral Campbell had bowed in grateful silence, but how gladly would he have asked the august and portly Presence to confer that honour on himself with remainder to his daughters' heirs ! Lord Duisk —Lord Glassary—Lord Campbell of Alkmaar ! Colin would sigh sometimes for his courtly pusillanimity. He had no wish for rank for himself, but it would have been a grand jump for the Campbells of Duisk. In these visions he would disregard the prior rights of Emmeline and Harriet, so strangely was his mind set in one particular. He would often speak on these matters to his wife.

s

Caroline, a complete comfort and resource to the
old man, shared his views to an extent.   She likewise
never could forget her lost Augustus, but, unlike
her husband, she had less interest in her husband's
grandchildren and would sometimes inquire with
asperity why Tom Bowmaker and the Otway boys
were not destined for the fighting services to fit
them for the future. *Her* boy had been in the navy
almost since birth.   The admiral was not averse that
his grandsons should take risks, but his daughters
were.

Despite the old man's suggestions neither Elizabeth nor Janet would permit of their sons having
commissions bought for them.   " Hang it ! " said
Colin to his elderly son-in-law over a glass of port,
" it looks bad for me when every man in London
asks me if Tom's going into the navy.   The boy has
traditions to maintain."

But Admiral Bowmaker could only reply that his
wife wanted Tom to hunt foxes and not Frenchmen.

Elizabeth was more direct.   " Caesar must run no
risks, father," she answered his protests with finality.
" He has Barrill to look forward to."

" Isn't there Colin and Archy, too !   You've three
sons, Elizabeth, and there's wonderful chances just
now."

" To be shot ? " she snapped.   " I can't afford a
commission, in any case."

" I'll pay," said her father. . " To hear you speak,
you'd think Otway was fighting for nothing.   He's
not like our distant relatives in Argyll who are
'listing as privates in the army."

" My husband's pay is keeping him, his wife, and his four children," she hinted. " I'm not like Janet and Leonie, with one boy apiece. Who are the distant relatives ? "

Colin laughed. " You remember Emmeline's beau ? —you saw him, I think. He married a farm-girl, Archy wrote me."

" That's a relief," she said thoughtfully. " Emmeline almost disgraced us."

" And, you know, the Duisk estate held the mortgage on his property. He was in difficulties. Apparently they overwhelmed him, and his farm, Strone, has lapsed to Duisk. And he has 'listed in one of the Highland regiments as a private."

" He was a very distant relative."

" He was."

" When did he marry ? "

" Lately, I think. So you see, Elizabeth——"

" I wonder," she remarked, " if Uncle Archy did this of his own accord. He would scarcely do it to a relative. It's the only thing he is sentimental about."

" It's a matter of business," said the admiral easily. " And lawyers are not sentimental, at the best of times."

" From what I've seen of Emmeline," Mrs. Otway said, " I fancy she has a good bit of her mother in her—from what I've heard about her mother."

III

TO

MAJOR-GENERAL SIR SCIPIO CAMPBELL OF DUISK AND
UILLIAN

Knight of the Most Honourable Order of the Bath
This Memorial is Erected.

To an Ancient Family *he added* LUSTRE
On an Honourable Profession *he conferred* VALOUR
And over the History of His Country *he shed* FAME.

HE

Was UNERRING in his JUDGMENT, HAPPY in his DOMESTIC
SPHERE,
And GENEROUS in his PRIVATE LIFE.

To the Gracious Condescension of his

SOVEREIGN

To the Pleased Applause of his

COUNTRYMEN

And to the Admiring Approbation of

EUROPEAN GENERALS

Is added that Fraternal and Disinterested Love *due to a*
VALUED AND RESPECTED BROTHER
from
HIS DEVOTED AND BEREAVED KIN.

Nat. 1st April 1735
Ob. 16th Octbr 1799

He made the name of BRITON glorious in THREE CONTINENTS
&
Was slain while at the Head of his Troops
Near ALKMAAR in the NETHERLANDS.

In the private burial-ground at Duisk his brothers
had erected the memorial to the dead general. It
stood for all to see in its grandeur of marble, corin-

thian' pilasters, scroll-work, wreaths and urns, and
the cold cenotaph was now all that Glassary would
ever know of Scipio Campbell.

For the years were passing and the elders of the
district with them, and to the children who were
growing up the great general of Duisk would be but
a tale for winter nights, with speculation for the
future of the great empty house.

In Glassary the years pass slowly, and change
comes as slow. But it had come with greater expression than usual latterly; between Crinan Loch
and the Rudha, where Ardrishaig is, the canal was
being built that would shorten the sea route to the
western isles by many weary days. Already in the
district there were signs of activity, presaged by the
new waterway. On Loch Gilp, near to Ardrishaig,
the village was growing that in time would form the
burgh of Lochgilphead, and to there the ruined
farmers and crofters of the landward parts were
flocking, either to pursue the herring fishing or to
find work on the new canal.

The system of part-tenancy of the farms was now
demoded, and those who had lived by that system
perforce had to try another. To the sea-shore they
went, settling in the hamlets at the water edge, at
Minard, at Kames, or at Lochgair, there to com-
mence a life of which they had little experience, and
no incentive other than the master urge of existence.
Or they toiled patiently on the foundations of the
canal, wondering sometimes what they would do
once it was completed and thinking with hopeless
acquiescence of America beyond the ocean.

For now the social system of Glassary was altered,

and there remained two principal classes. There were the High and the Low.

There were still farmers, of the large united acreages ; there were doctors and ministers in the district. But the gradation of rank that had simplified existence by ennobling man's race and dignity was now no longer. There were only the native inhabitants who had bread to seek with anxiety, and those other native inhabitants who had managed to retain their estates, to augment them by the possession of their neighbours', and who found the outward symbol of their dignity by methods such as Scipio Campbell had found by the building of the new house of Duisk.

There was the Gentry and there was the Peasantry.

Neil Leitch of Strone had found all things against him. Misfortune had fallen upon every effort to re-establish the security of his house. With the final blow, when Strone was taken from him, he had been past grieving. He departed to Bellanoch with his mother, his wife, and his son Colin, and he who had been a laird of a kind became a labourer at the canal.

He had not blamed the trustees of the Duisk heiress for taking what they were entitled to take ; rather had he been surprised that they had forborne so long. Yet he had known bitterness that on him of all his race had come the final misfortune ; that of the two families, who should rise so high as theirs !— and who should fall so low as his !

Working furiously, he had thought galling thoughts, glancing across the intervening flats of the Great Moss to the hills above Strone, and to the hills above Craigenterive, and to those hills which indicated

where, on the loch beyond distant Duisk, frowned
the castle of Innischonnell. With all those places
his family had been connected ; his family, that had
known this district before the Duisk Campbells had
set a foot on it . . . and he would return to his
work with voiceless protest.

Once, after his final leave-taking of Emmeline,
thought of her had been an anguish to him, and for
months that condition of mind persisted. He had
not then seen how he could ever possibly erase the
memory of that sweet pleading girl from his mind.
Her absence was profound and awful. He had been
stunned, and for long he had gone about his work
with the miserable indifference of the bereaved or the
forsaken, feeling that life had no more to offer him
since it had withdrawn from him his beloved. He
could not then forget her ; and he did not want to
forget her. All his reflections were set on the brief
moments of that forlorn courtship, sweetest because
they had been so short.

And then she had come less frequently into his
thoughts. He observed as much, unwillingly, and
he forgot her still the more. She receded a little,
grew indistinct ; the sharp clear vision of her faded.
Strone was present, though Emmeline was not. To
Strone he had turned, and slaved on it.

Yet half-reluctantly he had married his relative,
the willing Phemie Fletcher, who also was descended
from Duisk, largely urged by his mother, who wanted
a good managing woman to aid her son in the years
ahead. This marriage had been one of humble class
convenience, for Strone required a helper and Phemie
was glad to have a husband. For a time he could

scarcely believe that he had become a married man.

That fancy also passed, and with it passed the final yearnings for the grace, the elegance, the distinction, that had been Emmeline Campbell. He was wed to the vigorous hard-working Phemie, who preferred the Gaelic, who was so matter-of-fact and tireless, who had presented him with a small male Leitch.

It was then that the blow had fallen, and Strone, the gift of Colin Buie, was withdrawn by Colin Buie's seed.

In the thatched one-roomed cottage at Bellanoch that had two small openings in the walls for light and was so low that he had to stoop in entering, Neil abode with his mother who had borne him, and his wife, and the son his wife had borne ; and the grandson of Do'l Mor started afresh.

It was there that the chill Phemie Fletcher had contracted while working in the fields in the rain developed, and it was there that she died.

He had regarded her corpse, composed in death, with unbelieving surprise. Was that Phemie Fletcher ?

" She was a very good woman, mother," he said. And he felt his heart go away from him.

On the following Sunday he walked ; he walked in a frantic state of mind, hardly aware of his route, until he found himself at the grass-grown approach to Duisk. Up the silent avenue he paced, his mind filled with a conflict of emotions, and he stood at the place where he had bade Emmeline farewell. There emotion left him. He contemplated the spot without

feeling ; his visit had cleansed her from his mind for
ever.   A second life had commenced for him since
then and had been closed by the death of Phemie
Fletcher.   And now he would start upon a third.

"It is a long time since you were at Knockalava,
mother," he said on his return.

"I am not caring to see it again," she said.   "So
many of the old friends are away."

"Would you not like to go back to your brother
Neil ? " he asked.   "He would be glad to have you,
and you could take the young one with you.   For I
think I will go to the soldiering."

Almost a month later he bade farewell to his
mother and son and walked across the hills to
Inveraray, where he took the King's shilling.   As he
entered Inveraray by the south road a carriage containing Miss Emmeline Campbell and Miss Harriet
Campbell rolled round the shore from the Lowlands
and took the sharp bend for Glenaray and Lochaweside.   The street length separated the two.

Emmeline had kept herself well posted in the
doings of Glassary.   She was older and more sure of
herself.   And she had learned of Phemie Fletcher's
death.

Her ostensible reason for returning to Duisk was
to give Harriet a change of air ; she was not certain
of her real reason, but the death of Neil's wife had
excited her strangely.   Of the straits to which the
Leitches had been reduced she knew too well, and on
the road from Edinburgh she had some misgivings
as to how Neil would now look.   She remembered him
as the lithe young farmer ; would he be changed ?

Did she want to marry him ? she wondered, and

laughed nervously. Surely not ! It would be the
talk of the country. But the unerring fidelity of her
affection for Neil, that had survived all her resentment and malice, could not be lightly put aside.
The wonder of that brief summer idyll had impressed
itself too strongly upon her heart. The years, which
had obliterated the memory of it from Neil, had but
beautified and consecrated it in the impressionable
love-hungry heart of the daughter of the impressionable and love-hungry Cydalise Cœur-de-roi. It was
folly, she knew ; she knew it was madness . . . and
what man had she met since then who could cast a
shadow on the picture of Neil Leitch of Strone, three
and twenty years of age, tanned by the Glassary
sun, with the fine golden hairs on his cheek bones ?

And the carriage jolted over the rutted road by
Loch Awe, and the young wide-eyed Harriet asked
innumerable questions, and Emmeline sat in trembling and expectancy.

In Duisk there had been preparations for the
ladies' visit : airing and warming, and from Kilmartin
a woman had been requisitioned as temporary cook
The sight of the well-loved scenes gave Emmeline a
reminder of her former bliss. Without many preliminaries, after questioning the Kilmartin woman
about some of the local changes, she said : " And
the Leitch family, which was at Strone ? " She
assumed surprise on hearing that the young wife was
dead and inquired negligently for the husband.

All that night Emmeline lay awake.

The ironical knowledge that she had missed him
by hours at once awoke the most ardent feelings in
her heart for him. All doubt was banished. And

all hope with it, for not only were the risks of war to be combated, but the woman had explained his reason for enlisting. It had been grief for his dead wife.

" Ah," she thought in an abandonment to agony, " he has done this to hurt me. He knows it hurts me. He cannot forget me. He cannot. I know he cannot. And he hurts me because he loves me."

IV

The newness of Duisk House had gone, and it now sat maturely amid its matured policies. Invisible from the public road because of the high boundary wall, its privacy was enhanced by the tall trees of Colin Buie's planting and the pleasaunces laid out by direction of Sir Scipio.

To Harriet this fine place was a delight. The child had not before been in such a mingling of freedom and splendour, and it was with incredulous awe that she heard Aunt Emmeline tell her that it would be all hers some day. She could not understand that.

In the care of her aunt or her governess she passed happy days in scrambling about the shore, or in the woods or garden. And would stand admiringly before the full-length portrait of Sir Scipio in his uniformed glory, pleased that her grandpapa had been such a splendid man. As yet, there was a dearth of family portraits at Duisk; there was the general's and Mrs. Captain Archy's. That of Cydalise had vanished, and only a miniature of the elder Harriet and a silhouette of François existed to guide the girl to her parent's features.

Young Harriet Campbell presumably was like the unseen Cydalise, for she resembled Emmeline and her father, although with a difference. For the darker complexion of the Scotts was distinguishable on her face, and an occasional obstinacy that was reminiscent of her mother. At present, she was a lovable child, full of kindness and vivacity. She was the only distraction that Emmeline had at Duisk.

So much good had the change performed on the child that Lord Drumgesk determined she should return to Duisk every summer. He had let Barrill House to a retired Campbell officer for a lengthy time, and saw in this plan his opportunity for an occasional jaunt home. For a period of years, these years when Europe was a battleground, when Napoleon was making and unmaking kings and breaking enemy armies like reeds between his fingers, the old judge in his seventies and the young woman in her thirties and the child returned annually to the quiet of Lochaweside. There were no changes, the Crubach would think, as he gazed at the immemorial hills, the suave water, the billowing clouds; no changes, save in the heart of man.

He found a sardonic irony in being with these two, the daughter and the granddaughter of Cydalise Cœur-de-roi. He would study them solemnly, and then smile. If they knew! His rancour against Mrs. Scipio had never abated; but to her female descendants the old judge would not extend it. Emmeline had done much for him in recent years, and the little child's talk was diverting.

Often he questioned his own conclusions, for there was something strangely familiar in Emmeline at times, some course of thought, a phrase, a belief, that struck an intimate chord in himself ; something typically Campbell. He would regard the gentle fragile young woman and recollect her passion for the lad at Strone, and ponder with cynical relish on her ultimate act in that idyll. It had been so Campbell-like.

So Campbell-like, also, her eager turning to the past, snatching the bitter pleasure of remembering what was gone for ever. Lord Drumgesk realized that her love for Neil Leitch had been no girl's fancy, but a woman's devotion profound to the point of cruelty. She had met young men enough in her long sojourn in Edinburgh, and, although she was no longer very young, her fortune was sufficient to attract men at any time. But she had shown interest for none of them. There was pathos in such abnegation, and humour as well ; but life, Archibald Crubach felt, was a tragedy played by comedians.

Even the growing Harriet in time was aware of the occasional remoteness of her aunt from the vivid things of the day, and expressed her observations outright. Emmeline was vexed that a child should notice her absorptions, but consoled herself. The war could not last for ever, surely. There would be no preoccupation in her mind when Neil Leitch returned from Spain. She would ask him to marry her.

Once she determined to visit distant Knockalava in the Add valley, far among the hills. She restrained herself from going ; she did not want to see the son of Phemie Fletcher and she did not want to hear anything that might blur her picture of Neil Leitch.

In the spring of 1812, Mrs. Otway, hearing through her father the date of the annual sojourn in Duisk, wrote to Emmeline in so pleasantly melancholy a tone, with such expressions of her fondness for Argyll and her dearest wish to see it again, that Emmeline suggested she should be invited for a visit.

" Let her come," said the judge.

" And her family ? "

" Let them all come," said the judge.

Elizabeth arrived with her three sons, Caesar and Colin and Archibald. The eagle-faced woman presented the trio, their ages ranging from eighteen to twenty-four, with all the pride of a mother.

" You're getting gey fat, Caesar," said Drumgesk, surveying the eldest with a smile ; and Caesar was certainly fleshy for his age.

" The years show differences," Caesar's mother interposed. " The Otways are inclined to stoutness."

" But no difference in me, Caesar," cried the old man with a laugh. " I'm still *crubach*."

The Otway visit was a welcome diversion, and everyone enjoyed it. The young men were charmed by the place, and, as Elizabeth pointed out, well they might be, for, whatever the Otway inclination to embonpoint, the Campbell looks were stamped on their features. " My sons are Campbell in all but name, Uncle Archy," she said.

" And that's easily altered," he replied agreeably, and Elizabeth was pleased.

Despite that it made her outlook to her relatives so intolerable, Elizabeth was at her best when planning for her family. In the past winter she had won a brilliant triumph with the marriage of her

daughter Elizabeth to Captain Philip Rooke, a young
man of great inherited wealth.   Aided by the younger
Elizabeth's charm and looks, Mrs. Otway had cleared
all obstacles to the capture of the young plutocrat,
and she had left a round dozen of defeated mothers
in her wake.   With her daughter provided for, and
her husband risen to general officer's rank, Mrs.
Otway felt kinder to the world.   She could now
think of Mrs. Bowmaker with more charity ; as for
Mrs. Cattanach, some unfortunate events had brought
about a complete cessation of all relationship.

Her object in visiting Duisk was less to see that
place than to see Lord Drumgesk on his Highland
heath.   She was aware of the judge's promise not to
leave Barrill to any of Sir Scipio's descendants—her
father had told her of it long ago—but the years
that Emmeline had been with her uncle caused Mrs.
Otway much alarm.   She had shrewdly summed up
Archibald Crubach, and was convinced that, being a
widower and a former rake, he was a creature of
moods and impulses.   Common decency made her
admit that Emmeline had been a comfort to his
lonely old age, and could be expected to benefit on
his death.

"And she has plenty already," Mrs. Otway thought
disconsolately.

She was gratified, therefore, by the interest displayed by Lord Drumgesk in her sons, and by the
kindness with which the little Harriet and Emmeline
treated them.   "Be nice to Harriet, Caesar," she
said.   "Of course she is a child, but Duisk is hers."
She paused, thinking.   "After all, she is only five
years younger than your brother Archy."

Caesar grinned. " What about myself, mother ! "

" Duisk and Barrill can never be united. But it would be a good match for Archy, or for Colin."

Drumgesk found Caesar gazing from the drawing-room window across the loch to Barrill. " I see you're haeing a vizzy at Barrill," he said conversationally. " Aye, you're right there ; it's a bonnie place. And I'll be loth when I hae to leave it ahint me."

" It is beautiful, from the distance, with the sunlight on it," said Caesar with what he considered man-of-the-world ease and elegance.

" Aye, Caesar, ' 'tis distance lends enchantment to the view,' as Mr. Campbell says. He is sib to us—his folk used to hae Kirnan ower the hills at the back of us. ' 'Tis distance lends enchantment to the view,' right enough."

" I wish," said the thirteen-year-old Harriet one day to the eighteen-year-old Archy, " that you and your people were always here. It's such fun."

Archy grinned mischievously. " You wouldn't say that if you knew my mother better. Have you met Aunt Leonie Cattanach ? Well, we're finished with them. Mother was giving Aunt Leonie some good advice, and John Cattanach—that's my cousin—he told mother not to insult his mother, for he is grown up now and quite the man. And mother and John Cattanach came to words, and mother boxed his ears." He laughed uproariously. " Gad, yes ; mother boxed his ears. And we've had nothing to do with the Cattanachs since. Grandfather is awfully upset by it. But, of course, we all stand up for mother."

"Have you quarrelled, then?" Harriet asked, awed.

"Quarrelled!" Archy cried. "It's not a quarrel. It's only a vendetta!"

On Emmeline, Mrs. Otway still cast a shrewd eye, but it was less suspicious since she had come to Duisk. There was no attitude of proprietorship in Emmeline to the judge. Seeing so, Mrs. Otway wondered if Emmeline could be managed in any way to her family's advantage. But her eldest son was ten years Emmeline's junior, and with his prospects of Barrill he might do better matrimonially. It was a pity, she thought, that Emmeline had not been younger, and then a match might have been arranged with Colin. Caesar at Barrill, Colin and Emmeline, Archy and Harriet. . . . She was unaware of the proviso in Sir Scipio's bequest to Emmeline.

"I was asking my father recently if he had made any dispositions of his property," Elizabeth said to Emmeline as they strolled in the garden. "He is very well, I am pleased to say, but we never know when we may be called."

Emmeline assented to the justice of the thought.

"I wonder," Mrs. Otway continued, "if Uncle Archy has done likewise. You know, Emmeline, you have been a great help to Uncle Archy. I hope he will remember you."

"I never thought of that," replied Emmeline without interest. "I hope Uncle Archy will live for long enough. And my father left me well enough off."

"I know, my dear, that you have no mercenary

T

thoughts, but it was admiration for the help you have
given Uncle Archy made me speak. Has he never
spoken at any time of his intentions ? "

" He has never discussed them with me at all,"
Emmeline answered with some impatience, " and I
have never thought of them."

" Uncle Archy must have a large private fortune."

" I suppose he will have," Emmeline agreed. " It
is a pity he has no children to inherit it."

Mrs. Otway laughed abruptly. " Some of us have
children and have no fortunes to leave them. Otway
is dependent on his officer's pay. I was glad of
Elizabeth's marriage to Rooke, but my sons have
no prospects."

" But Caesar should inherit Barrill, should he
not ? " Emmeline asked simply, and Mrs. Otway was
satisfied.

" But some people are very fortunate," she could
not help saying. " Tom Bowmaker came into a
large fortune last year. He came of age shortly
after Admiral Bowmaker's death. And he is develop-
ing into a complete rake, I hear. I was vexed with
Janet ; she showed so little grief for her husband's
death. Only my father grieved for Admiral Bowmaker. And Tom Bowmaker haunts the worst
gambling hells in London. He ought to be in the
army or navy, like a man. My boys are so anxious
to serve abroad, but we can't afford it.

" And my sister Leonie Cattanach is most in-
tolerant. Her son John is a spoiled big booby. A
big booby, Emmeline. But those only sons are
always the same. I can't think what his mother sees
in him. He was most rude to me, and instead of

Leonie rebuking him she took his part and ordered
me never to go near her house again. She must
have been mad, surely, for as you know Leonie isn't
in the habit of acting like that. And I was always
the best of sisters to her and was always willing to
advise her in the smallest trifle. And so she cast
her own sister out of her house for the sake of her
malicious big lump of a son. John Cattanach will
come to no good. He is a sarcastic sullen big booby,
squinting down his nose at everyone. And since his
father's uncle, Mr. Hamilton, was created Lord
Bressingham they have been very difficult, all of
them. I must admit that we were surprised when
Mr. Hamilton received a peerage, and it certainly
carries distinction, but it is absurd for the Cattanachs
to adopt airs because Mr. Cattanach's father's sister's
husband . . ."

More than ever, Emmeline was glad that circumstances had kept her in Scotland after Sir Scipio's
death and that her connection with Admiral Colin's
family was not constant.

In the year following the Otways' visit Lord
Drumgesk invited his brother and his brother's wife
and the remaining branches of their family to Duisk.
The Bowmakers, mother and son, were little interested
in Duisk, and excused themselves. But the raddled
old admiral and his wife were accompanied by Mrs.
Cattanach and her son John.

It was a melancholy reunion. Colin at seventy-
three had failed greatly ; he was old compared with
his elder brother, and his speech was on mournful
lines. Drumgesk regretted this last meeting with
Colin, for he felt that it was their last. He was

interested, however, in John Cattanach. Of all the Campbell scions, this slender young man had inherited most the magnificent features that had marked out the fatuous Colin Og and the faintly remembered Captain Archy as notable among men. The high proud look was his, the predatory nose and jutting chin.

"Man," said the judge with emotion, "but you're a real Campbell. Every inch of you."

The young man smiled dryly. "Is that a virtue, sir?"

"We have been envied by many. And respected."

"And hated," said John Cattanach.

"Sir!" said the judge.

"Those who want respect should give respect. My father got little respect from my mother's family, and what he once wanted we can now do without."

"Oh!" said Drumgesk, with a stare and a thought. "These are odd words to hear on Loch Awe."

"My lord, there are other places than Loch Awe in the world, and other families than the Campbells."

"Maybe," said the Crubach coldly. "I'll not gainsay you there."

He watched the guests depart from Duisk with a conflict of feelings; he strained his eyes until the carriage rolled from sight, answering the admiral's feeble waving, with a wrenching at his heart.

"Colin Ban Campbell will never return to Loch Awe," he said simply to Emmeline as they went in. "We had great times here when we were bairns. A' things change, Emmy," he said. ". . . Bar maybe the price o' rouge."

With the entry of the Allies into Paris and the exile to Elba of he whom they termed the Usurper, Emmeline brightened visibly. Drumgesk watched her with anxiety, for he had a shrewd idea of the changes that a military life works in a man, and particularly in a private soldier. He was certain that the return to Glassary of Neil Leitch, when he would return, would offer her the greatest disillusionment of her life. But he was content to keep silent, marvelling at the faithful channel in which her mother's inherited strength of feelings had chosen to flow.

And then the Usurper returned, and Europe waited for the final clash.

It came, when on that Sunday in June the Frenchman from Corsica and the Englishman from Ireland met for the first and last time. And at nightfall, amid the sixty-two thousand corpses strewn upon the battlefield was that of General George Otway, C.B., and that of Sergeant Neil Leitch.

SEVEN

I

MISS Harriet Campbell came of age in the summer of 1820, and at once assumed control of Duisk.

From her father and from her father's mother she had inherited the small delicate nose and the cleft chin of the Cœur-de-rois, but the dark arched eyebrows and the purposeful lips were the legacy of Harriet Scott. Perhaps both stocks blended in the eyes of Miss Harriet Campbell; they were amber unwinking eyes, very beautiful, and full of cold appraisement.

She was five feet in height and moved with a light motion that became her. Her figure was very thin, her hands too large and not shapely. When she was thoughtful or vexed she had a habit of drawing her lower lip back against her teeth.

Harriet's education had been completed with a visit to France and a season in London, granted grudgingly by Lord Drumgesk, who had felt impelled to send Emmeline with her. On attaining her majority, when by her grandfather's will she obtained full possession of the estate, she proceeded at once to Duisk, inviting the forty-two-years-old Emmeline to follow whenever she thought fit.

" She'll cause a heap of trouble, that one," said the Crubach, when she had departed. Emmeline

was troubled, and said nothing. In latter years
Harriet and the old man had not agreed well.

"How did she fare with Colin's lot ? " he asked.

Emmeline smiled wanly. " You know what women
are."

" I do that. A' smirks to ilk ither's face, and
daggers aneath their tongues. I thocht Caroline
wasna ower enthusiastic from her letters. Ah well,
I'm done wi' Duisk ; and thank God, I'm not done
wi' Barrill, though some wish I was."

Against all advice and entreaty, Harriet had declined to have a temporary chaperon, and for twelve
months she lived alone. She had command of a
large fortune, and Duisk went back to its first glories
again, with everything except the joyousness of
companionship.

But Harriet was not immediately caring for that.
She knew that she was attractive, was rich, was
young. The flush of expectancy was in her heart.
It was a complex heart, and there was a mind con-
trolling it, but it was not closed to the fancies of
romance.

The power that was now hers also had a fascination. She was queen of Duisk, lady of those jumbled
acreages, dictatress of the humble folk and their
futures. The hand that grasped the power was
steady, nor knew how to be otherwise.

In those solitary days in which she read, or painted,
or rode on horseback, Harriet planned a future life
at once satisfying and alluring. In that recent
visit to London, in those weeks in Paris, she had
been too aware of the interest that she had evoked
in men. The knowledge that she could attract them

had dulled her own active interest, but not her future intentions.   When the time came, when she grew wearied by her solitary rule at Duisk—and she knew that would be soon—she would return to the desirable world of fashion, and look around her, and choose a husband.   He would be clever, he would be fascinating, and he would be a nobleman.

Her recollections of the London visit were not of pleasure unalloyed.   For Admiral Campbell and his wife she had felt the courteous tolerance demanded by decency due to hosts; for Mrs. Bowmaker she had conceived an amused contempt, and for Mrs. Otway an active hatred.   There was something alien in all those women that aroused her antipathy; even Mrs. Cattanach was not immune from it.   It extended to Lord Drumgesk, and there had been fanned by contiguity.   She had wondered what might cause it, and not until she had settled permanently at Duisk and was making a masterful exploration of the house from basement to garret did she find the answer.   In a dusty lumber room she discovered a huge thin sackcloth package, very heavy.   She had it unwrapped, and there looked out to her the intent sweet features of Cydalise Cœur-de-roi.   Harriet did not need to be told the sitter's identity; she guessed instinctively.   But the artist's name, the period, the very frame, all proved it the companion to the painting of Sir Scipio downstairs, and an old man from the farm corroborated that.

" Ah," she thought, " no wonder I cannot bear those absurd Campbells."   And she had the painting dusted and placed downstairs, where it once more looked across to Sir Scipio.   Harriet then despatched an enthusiastic letter to Emmeline, extolling the beauty of her grandmother and the joy that the discovery had given her.

" The devil she has ! " said Drumgesk, when Emmeline told him that Harriet had caused the picture to be re-hung. For Emmeline's sake he added charitably : " I dare say Scipio was feart the sun would spoil it, and had it out of harm's way. He was gey fond of your mother."

" I can guess his reason," she said in a halting voice. They stared at each other questioningly, and then Emmeline told him of Sir Scipio's delirious confession of the death of Cydalise.

" Well," said the Crubach slowly, " I thought Colin and myself were all who kenned . . . keep a tight haud of your tongue, Emmy."

" And, Uncle Archy," she said falteringly, " did you know about Donald—about Donald Leitch ? "

" What about him ? " asked the old man sharply.

" My father murdered him," she said, and began to sob hopelessly.

Drumgesk raised a protesting hand. " No—no, Emmy. You mustna say that."

" But it's true—I know it's true," she exclaimed. " Oh, Uncle Archy, my father . . ." She laid her head on the old man's knees and he stroked it comfortingly.

" Think nae ill of the dead, Emmy," he said sadly, " for they've nae defending counsel. Remember, it was because of John Don that your father hid yon picture, and no' for what came after. Scipio Campbell wasna the man to scorn a hapless woman, and your mother was a gey prood lady when she left

Duisk. As for the slauchter of Do'l Mor, I'm no' surprised, and I aye suspected it." She raised her head and looked at him aghast. " It's an ill bird that fouls its ain nest, Emmy, and nae real Campbell will chatter to his brother's hurt. Come, lassie, content yourself."

" Uncle Archy," she said in a monotonous tone that held terror, " I lost Neil Leitch because of my father. When my father died I was resigned to the loss as a sacrifice for my father's crime. But I could not forget Neil, and I would have given up everything for him . . . and then he married." Her words came slowly and indistinctly. " You know that I am a murderer also. You know that, Uncle Archy."

" What havers is this ? " he exclaimed with assumed brutality. " Is this a' you've time for ? "

" I wanted to hurt Neil Leitch because I loved him and because he had married that woman, and you know who urged you to foreclose on Strone. And it was because of that his wife died of exposure, and because of his wife's death that he went to the wars, and so I surely murdered him."

" Emmy ! "

" Murdered him—murdered him," she repeated exhaustedly. " I murdered the man I loved. I murdered the man I loved, and murdered his wife, and stole their home, and made their child an orphan." She commenced to shriek. " And God will not kill me, for I must live and suffer. We are a race of murderers. We are all murderers. There is blood on all our hands." And she fell unconscious on the floor.

Unaware of the past that her letter had evoked, Harriet drew continual satisfaction from the painting of Cydalise. The absorbed expression that the artist had caught on canvas spoke many things to her; she tried to read the secrecies behind those mingled pigments, and tried to adapt herself to what she thought they required of her.

"Those Campbells!" she said aloud, staring at the picture. "I look a Cœur-de-roi."

Sometimes she would gaze across to Barrill, apprehensive lest Lord Drumgesk should decide to revisit his house, once more untenanted. She did not want any of the senior Campbells near her. She would have been glad of Emmeline, and, as for the Otway brothers, they had been pleasant enough and had admired her greatly, but she cared not for Drumgesk.

But the Crubach was never to see Loch Awe again. On a Saturday afternoon he met Sir Walter Scott at the house of a mutual friend, and Lord Drumgesk interested the younger man with reminiscences of life in the Edinburgh that was gone, and told memories of Robert Fergusson and Robert Burns and many others he had met and drunk with, and gave Sir Walter, who was interested in such matters, some legends about the Seer of Inveraray. Sir Walter was grateful, and deferential to the old man, for Archibald Crubach could assume the manner of the *grand seigneur* when he chose. But that evening the Crubach entertained a few boon companions in his own house. He was eighty-three now; the bacchanal was too much for him, and in the morning he was dead.

The mail conveying the announcement of his demise to London was passed on the road by that taking the news of Admiral Colin Campbell's death. The younger brother had wandered beyond the brink of his senility. He was buried in London, and Archibald in the Canongate graveyard in Edinburgh, next to the grave of Sandy Campbell.

The third death followed, as it had done twice before, but it was indirect, being merely that of Lord Bressingham, formerly John Hamilton, who had fallen a victim to the Indian climate.

The admiral's estate, after making a substantial allowance for the widow, was divided equally between his three daughters, a distribution that gave Mrs. Otway grave dissatisfaction, for she felt that the Bowmakers could have done without. The admiral had maintained considerable style in his mode of living, secure in the knowledge of his pension, and of the large sums of prize-money he had gained little was left. The amounts allotted to the daughters were inconsiderable, but the news of Lord Drumgesk's passing soothed Mrs. Otway, who felt that providence had taken a remorse of conscience.

Lord Drumgesk's will was brief and flawless. He left his gold watch set with diamonds, his silver dinner service, his portrait by Raeburn, and the sum of twenty thousand pounds free of any condition to Emmeline Campbell. He stated that as Barrill was his absolutely, without entail, and as Caesar Otway when a boy had taunted him with his lameness and as John Cattanach had thought lightly of the Campbell blood, he could not gladly bequeath the estate

to anyone of these two families ; Barrill estate, therefore, and what balance of his personal estate remained,
he devised to Thomas Bowmaker of Lanshanger,
Esquire, in the county of Sussex.

A savage passion of rage shook Mrs. Otway when
she learned of these bequests. For a time she could
not eat, nor sleep, and her heart was full of hatred
against everyone, even against her son. On the dead
Crubach, laughing from beyond the boundary, the
full force of her baffled spite was directed. That he
should have treasured some careless words, and
brooded over them, and nursed them in his mind
for a day of vengeance, was incredible, was maniacal,
was unendurable. That he had allowed her to keep
her fond illusions all these years, that he should
strike her with a skeleton hand, that her own son
should have been such a fool . . . Mrs. Otway was
over sixty now ; the strain was too much, and doctors
had to be called.

In her convalescence she brooded with the intensity of baulked ambition. They should have been
preparing to go to Barrill now ; in the commonest
justice of things Barrill was theirs by right. She
would have law ; she would fight for her rights, a
widow's rights, and for her son's rights. And that
of all the family he should have chosen the Bowmakers, rotten as they were with wealth ! The old
hanging dog !—the lame drunkard, the disreputable
night hawk ! The miserable old sinner that he was,
gloating over a revenge that he could not live to
see, a revenge on a boy's thoughtlessness.

During these past years she had been a complete
stranger to Leonie while maintaining relations with

the Bowmakers. Now she was done with the Bowmakers, and had lawyers searching out the will of
Malcolm Campbell of Barrill. But there was no flaw
there ; Barrill had been left to the Crubach absolutely.

In the days following this blow Elizabeth felt
almost kind towards Leonie. They had indeed exchanged some few words at their father's funeral,
and Elizabeth convinced herself that she would have
grieved the less had Barrill gone to the Cattanachs.
And then the contents of Lord Bressingham's will
was published.

The property of the dead nobleman was found to
be great, and it was left entirely to his nephew Æneas
Cattanach. And Elizabeth learned for the first time
that the Bressingham peerage had been conferred
with special remainder to Æneas Cattanach and his
heirs, provided they added the name of Hamilton
to their own. Leonie had become a peeress.

Mrs. Otway shed furious tears. She was estranged
from both her sisters ; she disliked both their sons.
And now the rich one of those nephews had whipped
the coveted Barrill from her expectant grasp, and
the other, the objectionable John Cattanach, had
risen from obscurity in a night, had become Honourable, with the succession to a barony.

And her fatherless sons ? " It is unjust," she
moaned. " My poor boys. The whole world is
against them." She rocked herself in an agony of
frustration, only partly consoled by her daughter's
marriage to Rooke. That couple was in Naples,
where Captain Rooke was military attaché. With
her hopes of Barrill dashed for ever, Mrs. Otway
drew pen and paper to her and wrote urgently to

her daughter, pointing out that something must be
done for her defrauded boys.

II

No one mourned Drumgesk more than the daughter
of her whom he had hated most.   The generous bequests had left her unmoved, and for a time she was
numbed by the loss of the old judge who had been
so feared by the Scottish jacobins and who had
always been gentle to her.   Inevitably she rejoined
her niece at Duisk.

Emmeline was no longer the fragile creature who
had romped on the hills of Uillian.   Already her hair
showed streaks of grey ; she was obsessed by an
unfleeing sense of guilt and by the feeling that she
was an accursed member of an accursed tribe.

Of Harriet's innocence of the family's dramas she
was envious.   Harriet had no cares ; she had been
born at the right time.

Not until the arrival of her aunt at Duisk did
Harriet feel lonely.   She had been happy in her own
solitude, but now the presence of her listless relative brought a new unpleasant melancholy into the
house.   The younger woman fretted under this strain,
and determined that at all costs it must go ; she
began to doubt her desire to have Emmeline with
her.   Nor did Harriet's correspondence lessen her
impatience with her kin.

" I have had letters from the three sisters all in
a week," she said satirically, " and they make a
diverting tale.   Janet Bowmaker is enchanted by
her son's luck, and grieved by his thought of selling it.   He is not interested in Barrill.   Leonie signs

herself ' Leonie Bressingham,' which is not the action
of a well-bred woman to a relative. Elizabeth's is
a model of venom."

" She will be hurt by the loss of Barrill," Emmeline
said indifferently.

" She has nothing to complain of," said young
Miss Campbell. " She is well enough off, in spite
of all her grumblings. Her sons are idlers, and have
never done a day's work. She has a thoroughly
good house, and her pension, and her father's legacy.
But she lives on wrongs. She has been unwell, she
says, and thinks Highland air would do her good."
Harriet laughed happily. " We must leave Duisk,
Emmeline, or we will have the Otways on my doorstep."

Emmeline wondered where they might go.

" To *their* doorstep, perhaps," said Harriet. " I
am afraid of Mrs. Otway's plans, Emmeline. She
looks at one, and smiles. And you know that she
is wondering all the time what use she can make
of one."

" She can make no use of us, surely."

" Caesar is heir to Duisk after you, Emmeline. I
don't suppose he will ever inherit it. Caesar is unmarried, and I don't know whether the choice is to
be you or me."

Emmeline smiled wanly.

" Tcha ! " said Harriet. " You shall see. But we
must leave Duisk. I wish to travel."

Her disinclination to receive Mrs. Otway coincided
with her boredom at Duisk, and the two ladies soon
journeyed to London, where they stayed with Mrs.
Colin Campbell for a time. There Harriet tasted

the delights of the fashionable world to which her fancies continually wandered. She was impartial in her relations with the admiral's daughters, and she and Emmeline visited Mrs. Otway at her house in Curzon Street, Mrs. Bowmaker at Lanshanger, and Lady Bressingham in Kent. Every courtesy was extended to the two rich Scots ladies, and the Otway sons were particularly attentive.

"Caesar is fat and sleek," Harriet observed to her aunt. "Colin is a vain villain, and Archy is very nice. Archy is a great improvement on the others."

Whatever might have happened was made abortive by the progress of the Duisk ladies to Paris accompanied by Harriet's uncle Robert Scott, a gentleman who, like the Otways, had never formed an inclination for work. The position of guardian on a foreign tour was outwith the boundary of industry. Mrs. Otway displayed the liveliest interest in the projected tour ; as the ladies expected to be in Cologne after some months, in pursuance of an interest in the Rhine evoked by *Childe Harold,* she insisted on writing Mrs. Rooke to ask that lady and her husband to have a rendezvous with them there. Captain Rooke and his lady were returning soon from Naples by the overland route.

Equipped with many introductions, the Miss Campbells spent a month in Paris, a period which tried Emmeline excessively and filled Harriet with delirious happiness. In the gay diversions of the capital and moving in the society of her compeers, Harriet knew that she was tasting the life most suitable to her ambitious temperament. She exulted in her

U

youth, her wealth, her attractions, and wondered peevishly why Emmeline could not do likewise. There were older women than Emmeline who were less well equipped yet socially desirable, and she urged her aunt to make intimacy with the dressmaker, the hairdresser, and the beauty salon.

Once, as they drove through what had been the Place de la Révolution, Emmeline burst into tears.

From Paris the ladies proceeded to Brussels, and thence to Alkmaar to pay their respects at the grave of Sir Scipio. And from there they diverted their course to the German Rhineland.

It was now midsummer; the Rhine valley lay in rich fecundity under the blazing sun. Nurtured in the romantic tradition, both Harriet and Emmeline lingered there gladly, passing the days in making expeditions with the handy Uncle Robin to ruined castles and ancient churches from their headquarters at Bonn or Wiesbaden or Heidelberg. Mr. Scott, who was fat and good-natured as well as impecunious, was well content with his duties as male chaperon, sleeping happily as the coach rolled by the shores of historic Rhine.

In August the party returned to Cologne to implement the promise made to Mrs. Otway. The arrangement was now found irksome, and Harriet discovered that in her delight in other things the Rookes had shrunk to little consequence. Mr. Scott, however, found amusements of some kind there, and begged the ladies to curb their impatience, which they did for a fortnight. At the end of that time Captain and Mrs. Rooke put in an appearance.

Elizabeth Rooke was seven years older than Harriet,

and much older in experience of the world.   Handsome and vivacious, with prominent features, golden
hair, and lively grey eyes, she had a charm of manner
that transcended all else.   She drew largely on her
husband's fortune for the clothes and jewels that
were necessary for her happiness, and he, a bomb-
headed young man with plastered hair, made no
protest, being idolatrous of his distinguished-looking
wife.   When they arrived at Cologne it was observed
that Captain Rooke was unwell, the reason being,
as Elizabeth frankly admitted to her relatives, his
fondness for northern stimulants in a southern
climate.   " His health is shattered," she said philosophically.

Harriet felt strangely inferior to her laughing kinswoman.   She would not admit superiority in Elizabeth's features, nor in her wit, but she recognized
an ease and composure that she had not herself
attained.   Perhaps, she thought, it was the result
of acquaintance with a court, even if it was only
the court of the Two Sicilies.

Indeed, the Rookes were at present bound for
another court, if one still smaller.   Her husband,
Mrs. Rooke explained, had formed a close friendship with the Hereditary Prince of Berg-Solingen,
then visiting the court of Naples, and they had been
invited to pay their respects at the grand-ducal court
on their road home.   " The late Grand Duke Caspar's first wife was the Princess Ottilie of Düren,
and the Hereditary Prince, who has since succeeded,
and is now the Grand Duke Nectar, is their only
son." Elizabeth spoke airily, as though well acquainted with the grand-ducal family, although she

had obtained all her information about Berg-Solingen from the wife of the Prince Nectar's equerry.

Harriet was reluctantly impressed. She admitted that she knew nothing about the grand-duchy of Berg-Solingen. Elizabeth explained condescendingly that it was small, but exclusive. " But why not come with us ? " she added hospitably. " I am sure you will receive the *entrée*."

The chance of mingling with a reigning family was soothing to Harriet's socially ambitious mind, and without any demur the Duisk party proceeded to Solingen in the company of the Rookes, Elizabeth explaining the niceties of court etiquette on the route.

" The Grand Duke Nectar is addressed as grand-ducal highness, and so are the members of his family. He has two half-brothers, but they are not members of the grand-ducal family. The elder, Paul, is the son of the Grand Duke Caspar's morganatic marriage with Paula Langensiepen, an opera singer who was created Countess of Windeck, and he is Prince of Windeck. The younger, Rupert, is the son of the Grand Duke Caspar's second morganatic marriage with Adelina Lesitzke, a gardener's daughter who was created Countess of Zelle, and Rupert is now Prince of Zelle. They were both raised to the princely dignity by their half-brother, who is quite fond of them. Of course, they are only noblemen, and are addressed as serene highness."

" They haven't come off so badly, to be an opera singer's and a gardener's daughter's sons," said Uncle Robin profoundly.

" The late Grand Duke was a very moral man."

"Have they estates to support their rank?" Harriet inquired.

"They hold commissions in the army," said Captain Rooke languidly, recollecting that his acquaintance with the present Grand Duke was caused by his facility for losing at cards.

On arriving at the capital it was discovered that the grand-ducal court had gone to Schloss Wupperthal, the summer residence. The five travellers with their servants put up at the best hotel, while the court chamberlain was informed of their presence, and there Captain Rooke was seriously ill. For two days and three nights he hovered in a condition approaching delirium, a condition which the hotelkeeper, who was well pleased to have such rich personages in his establishment, tactfully ascribed to the drainage of Cologne.

"It was confounded silly of me," the captain said to Mr. Scott when on the road to recovery. "I never mixed champagne and schnappes and beer before on an empty stomach, and the quantity was too much, although the quality was right enough."

By that time he had obtained a reply from the grand-ducal court, and if it was slow it was gratifying, for the Grand Duke, with vivid memories of his successes at écarté, had invited the victim and his connections for a limited stay at the *residenz*.

Schloss Wupperthal was a grand mediæval castle, a huge accretion of bastions and walls of enceinte surrounding a massive donjon, all poised proudly on a knoll and commanding the wooded slopes of the Wupper valley. As the coaches rolled up the winding road that led to the first archway Harriet thrilled with anticipation. She felt that the social delights of Paris and London paled in comparison with an introduction to the stronghold of a sovereign prince.

The miniature court, its restrictions, its formalities, remained long in her memory. From her bedroom window she surveyed the panorama of mantling woods and sloping meadows that quivered in the blazing sunshine. And again the fashionable glitter of the gentry and nobility was dimmed by the shabby grandeur of this old-fashioned regime, its indifference to change, its apparent security. She wished she were a grand duchess.

The Grand Duke Nectar was a man of fifty, tall in body, with a very small head and unkempt fingernails. He lived on bad terms with the Grand Duchess Maria Augusta his wife, and indeed they never spoke now, she preferring the privacies of her own wing of the castle. They had a son and three daughters and a household of barons and counts, baronesses and countesses, all very correct and dignified, and all extremely shabby.

Paul, the Prince of Windeck, a sturdy nobleman of forty, was a bachelor, and interested in genealogy. He assured Emmeline in excellent English that he was the leading authority in the science and requested a résumé of her family history. " You will be of the herzöge von Argyll. Eh ? " Emmeline was surprised, and replied that she supposed all Campbells were in some way ; she said she was of the line of Duisk.

" Ach ja," said the prince, nodding his head sagely. " Campbell von Duisk. You are of the ducal rank, Fräulein Campbell." He regarded her with increased respect. "It is a great family, the herzöge von Argyll."

That night Harriet appeared in her aunt's bedroom. "Emmy," she exclaimed in a rapt manner unusual with her, "I love this old castle. I mean, this is real rank and dignity—this court."

"Well, Harriet," Emmeline said, "we are not out of place here, I hope."

"Yes, but this is better than the society of London generals' wives or those Parisian dandies. These Berg people are so sure of themselves." She paused, and then asked abruptly: "What do you think of Prince Rupert?"

"Prince Zelle? I thought he looked very handsome in his uniform."

Harriet laughed mischievously. "He calls me Fräulein von Duisk. It is so funny. And he said his brother told him we were related to the Duke of Argyll. Did you say that, Emmy?"

"Certainly not!"

"He is twenty-nine and very poor, although he does not complain, because the Grand Duke is so nice with his brothers. Prince Rupert is most friendly, and not condescending in the least."

"A gardener's grandson does not need to be condescending to a general's granddaughter," said Emmeline.

"He is a serene highness in spite of that," said Harriet. "Emmy, I feel so sorry for Prince Rupert, because I asked Elizabeth whom morganatic princes generally married, and she said some nobleman's plain daughter, and then they would live in a small house with a tiny income to support them."

On the next evening there was a ball in the great
hall of the castle, when the gentlemen all appeared
in ornate uniforms of uncertain age and the ladies
in gay dresses of proved durability.   The grand duke
and grand duchess sat in state on a dais, without
speaking, and smiled with fixed urbanity on the
solemn-faced dancers.   The Prince of Zelle made
himself pleasant to the Duisk ladies.   A tall young
man, he had inherited his handsome looks from the
horticultural side of his family, and, like his brother
of Windeck, was an excellent linguist.

" You are the first ladies of Schottland I haf ever
known," he assured them seriously, " and I am very
honoured.   Herr Scott, your goot relative, is he a
relative of the Baronett von Abbotsford ? "   He
smiled triumphantly.   " Ach ja, I know !   I know
all of Schottland.   The Baronett von Abbotsford—
he is very much knowing of our Deutscher literatur.
I know.   I haf read *Marmion* and *The Lady of the
Lake* ; eh ?   And I know of Lucy Ashton and the
very goot Jeanie Deans and the tantzing Madge
Wildfire.   For he has written them—eh ?—although
he will not say.   Soon I com to Schottland to make
the visit—Loch Katrine, and Abbotsford, where I
will see the Herr Sir Walter, and Edinburg, and Schloss
Tantallon.   Goot ?   Ja.   And I will know your Highland dress, and the Clan Alpine, and haf the Highland food."

" Highness, will you be coming to Scotland ? "
Harriet asked.

" Ja," said the Prince agreeably.   " I haf long
wanted to com to Schottland because of the works
of the Baronett von Abbotsford.   I com next spring.

There is nodings I want better," he added conclusively.

" It would be a great honour to Duisk House," said Harriet immediately, turning to her aunt, " if His Serene Highness would consent to visit it."

Prince Rupert beamed. " Gnädige Fräulein, Fräulein von Duisk ! " he exclaimed. " This is your Schottisch hosbitality, of which I haf read."

" We have mountains in Argyll, Prince, and the scenery that you admire, and my niece and I would be very pleased," Emmeline said cordially. " You will see Inveraray."

" Ja ! " said the prince immediately. " Dugald Dalgetty and your ancestor the Markgraf von Argyll ! " And he laughed teasingly.

The Grand Duke Nectar and Captain Rooke disappeared together.

Uncle Robin Scott was engaged in a conversation of signs and smiles with an elderly dowager.

Mrs. Rooke was dancing with a stripling Spanish duke who was touring Europe to broaden his mind. She crossed to Harriet when Emmeline had accepted the gallant invitation of Prince Rupert to valse.

She had summed up Harriet as a determined, self-willed girl, and was amused by the excited glitter that showed in her eyes. After all, Harriet was so young ! she thought. A radiant, flashing apparition, she fluttered down gracefully beside Miss Campbell and asked her if she was enjoying herself.

" Oh yes," Harriet said. " I am."

" Court life can be very dull," Elizabeth said patronizingly, " and of course Berg is a trifle to Naples, or Turin, or Paris. But this is quite amusing."

" So many people," Harriet breathed happily.   " It is a spectacle, Elizabeth."

" A court has the resources of pageantry.   Ordinary society has not.   Well, Harriet, I have brought you here, and I'm glad you're pleased."   She glanced over the scene with the satisfaction of one who is admired and noted.   The grand ducal orchestra was playing a waltz by Hummel ; to the vaulted recesses of the huge apartment the music lilted a melancholy gaiety ; the swaying colourful figures of the dancers moved beneath the light of a thousand candles ; from dull gleaming frames on the walls dead kurfürsten gazed bleakly down.

" I am enchanted," said Harriet softly.

" You were not present when the Grand Duke's hunting circle arrived this afternoon."

" Prince Zelle was showing me the gardens."

" They are charming men.   See ! they have Saint Hubert's horn on their sleeves ; that is Baron Kohlfurth in the scarlet uniform, and Baron Papiermühle with the lady in white ; the tall fair man is Count Altenbau, and the red-faced officer Count Stöcken ; that is the Duke of Mangenberg, who is very rich. Baron Fühlingen, who is standing at the doorway, is too lame to dance, but his sister's husband, Count Worringen, is devoted to the waltz ; that is him with the wife of Baron Stommeln, who is dancing with the Countess Bedburg."

Harriet listened, or thought she did, her absorbed eyes seeing the hall and all its occupants as a bright incentive to her thoughts.   And her thoughts were also bright.   " Ah," she reflected, with sudden pity for Elizabeth's complacent enumeration, " she is the

military attaché's wife, the cavalry captain's wife.
She is content with counts and barons."

III

On the termination of their stay at Schloss Wupperthal the Campbells and the Rookes journeyed to
Ostend, leaving the Grand Duke Nectar richer in
the pocket.

Harriet was happy and lively, and talked incessantly of the court of Berg-Solingen, much to Emmeline's satisfaction, for at Cologne the younger
woman had planned a return to Paris with the
object of making acquaintance with a branch of the
Cœur-de-rois who had been in the country during
the Campbells' sojourn in the French capital.

But the attractions of the grand-ducal court now
outweighed the quest of the French vicomte and
his family, although Harriet had made use of the
connection, having informed the Prince of Windeck
that her grandmother's relations included the dukes
of Rocamadour and the marquises de Ferney. Emmeline was scandalized when she knew of this, and
frankly reminded Harriet that she had blamed Lady
Bressingham for vulgarity on a lesser occasion. " It
is different in Germany," the niece replied. " The
Germans attach great importance to titular rank."

It was a merry party ; Captain Rooke alone was
slightly dumped, as he had lost heavily at play, but
this fact kept him more sober than usual, and his
health was much improved when they set foot on
England. Drunk or sober, Captain Rooke always
received the sweetest affection and amiability from
his wife, and her fidelity touched Uncle Robin deeply.

" She's a fine woman," he said once with conviction. " A remarkably fine woman. If I had met a woman like that when I was younger . . ."

Indeed, Elizabeth became a favourite with all, and was particularly friendly to Harriet, giving any necessary hints for the completion of her social education. " But you must marry, my dear," she said. " You cannot enjoy the society to which you are entitled as an unmarried woman, as an orphan. You cannot wish Mr. Scott to be with you always, surely." Harriet agreed readily. " When you marry, my dear," Mrs. Rooke said winningly, " marry with wisdom. Choose a gentleman you know well—since childhood, if possible. And great wealth or great rank in a husband is not essential, and sometimes causes unhappiness, for a man of that type always finds other amusements. Rooke is the only exception I know."

Harriet expressed some surprise at her relative's points of desirability in a husband. But Mrs. Rooke only smiled winningly. Often she spoke of her relations, with tender affection for her mother and brothers, and without rancour for her cousins.

" General Otway's death was a great blow to mother," she remarked once with emotion. " We have only the satisfaction that he died a hero and a Briton. My brothers and I venerate his memory." She laughed with conscious embarrassment. " But Caesar has always been my hero, ever since I was a lanky little girl. He is so kind, so honourable, so affectionate."

" Family loyalty is very proper, I think," Harriet observed.

" It is Caesar's strongest virtue. He is so proud
of all his relations and of our mother's family. He
always mentions you in his letters to me with the
deepest sentiments of regard. He thinks so highly
of you, Harriet. I am afraid you have stolen Caesar's
heart, and he is so unimpressionable with women."

In spirit Harriet remained in the Bergische land.
Short moments of that brief stay recurred incessantly to her, fraught with rapture : watching from
an embrasure the changing of the guard in the court
beneath, hearing the sharp commands, the click of
heels, the rattle of accoutrements ; gazing from her
bedroom window on the valley sleeping so drowsily
under a golden moon ; wakening in the earliest flush
of dawn to hear the first clear twittering of the
birds, to see the grey mists lifting from the tranquil
river and the dreaming trees swathed in a cloak of
mystery ; walking by the river-side, on the hot dusty
road, past little cottages where great bunches of the
grape vine hung in dusky succulence, while, on the
farther bank, the sun-parched trees drooped branches
to the water's lip. Walking with the Prince of Zelle.

Since her visit to the Grand Duke's court Harriet's
outlook had not altered, but it had enlarged and
leaped ahead. The social successes she had promised
herself in England or in Scotland seemed on recon-
sideration to be small things compared to what she
coveted now. Her rank and wealth and attractions
would have placed her high in the course of things ;
she had never raised them to a sovereign rank. But
the vision of impressive progresses through Europe,
to continental courts, with the position of a princess
and a serene highness, now seemed actually possible.

She knew what her relations did not know, that
Prince Rupert was impressed by her.   What though
he was poor, was debarred from his brother's sovereign
privileges, and was merely a nobleman of no prospects !—he was Prince of Zelle, an imposing name,
and his disability of status permitted him to marry
almost where he pleased.

Harriet was the first Campbell of Duisk to whom
Duisk actually meant nothing.   All the earlier Campbells, even Emmeline, had been conscious of the
peculiar intimacy of ancestral soil, which is satisfying to the soul.   But in spite of her fondness for
the place, Duisk was simply a pleasure house to
Harriet, a landed appanage that gave her county
rank and influence. . She had gained nothing spiritual
from it, and had given it none.   Consequently, the
thought of uprooting herself from her inherited home
for the satisfaction of titular ambitions was a light
one ;   there she may have proved the recrudescent
power of her Anglo-Scottish mother's blood and of
her French-American grandmother's.

She felt quite able to love Prince Rupert, although
she might not have considered him apart from his
rank.   Discreet inquiries had shown her that even
he would be unable to give his wife his princely
name were she of a rank inconveniently lower to
his own.   Harriet was determined not to suffer that ;
it was because of that she had encouraged the style
of von Duisk which she pretended had so amused
her, and that she had spoken so freely of her noble
French connections and allowed Paul of Windeck to
believe in her close relationship to the house of Argyll.

All the girl's acquired or inherited breeding vanished

before these ambitions ; her thoughts shaped words continually before her eyes : 'H.S.H. the Princess of Zelle."

In London the Duisk ladies stayed with Mrs. Admiral Campbell preparatory to returning home. Only the Otway cousins were in town, and they called frequently at the house. One evening they dined, and Archy later asked Harriet about her travels. She was enthusiastic and eager to talk of them, more so as she liked the grave, thoughtful youngest of the brothers. They sat together in an alcove ; Harriet suddenly discovered his glance fixed on her in such a curious manner that she stopped abruptly.

" Harriet," he said awkwardly.

" What is it ? " she asked, her words attuned to his own lowered voice.

" I am going to be a soldier," he said inconsequently. " I can't go on for ever living on my mother's charity. It's not manly."

" I'm glad," she said. " I hope you'll have every luck, Archy, and I'm sincere."

" It's like this, Harriet," he said in the same low voice. " I—I like you."

Harriet did not answer, but her heart beat fast.

" I've always liked you, Harriet. But I couldn't tell you before. You've got so much and I have nothing. I wish you were poor. I'm not a fortune-hunter."

Harriet's gaze had been fixed on his hands, which were moving restlessly ; now she raised it to his eyes, and thought them very candid. " And what does this mean ? " she asked softly.

" It means a proposal," he said.

He was so handsome, and sincere, and so diffident, that her heart went out to him. She had always liked him and for a moment thought to accept him. Instead, she laid her hand on his and said sweetly : " I'm sorry, Archy ; I'm very sorry. I like you very much, but not so much as that."

Archy turned very white. " It's all right," he said with agitation. " You're not offended, Harriet ? " She shook her head, and her eyes blurred because of his dejected manner. On an impulse she touched his lips lightly with hers.

Her mood that night was mingled regret and triumph. Many a woman would have been glad to have him, she thought forlornly, gazing at her mirror, but she could not repress her satisfaction at having had a proposal of marriage. It was the first she had received.

Her second one came on the following day.

Old Mrs. Otway had other reasons than the desire to provide the Campbells with company when she arranged the rendezvous with the Rookes in Cologne. And it was at her mother's written desire that Elizabeth had frequently reverted to the discussion with Harriet of Caesar, his virtues and amiabilities. Actually, these eulogiums had made no impression on Harriet's mind other than that Mrs. Rooke was a very affectionate sister. Diverted by the amusements of Paris and the Rhineland, Harriet had almost forgotten Caesar and the expressed suspicions she had felt of his intentions for either herself or Emmeline, and she was surprised when Caesar asked her for a moment's privacy.

Caesar, now gallantly sailing through his thirties, had increased greatly in bulk. The flowered satin waistcoat that he wore emphasized his rotundity there; his blue coat with silver buttons stretched tightly across shoulders like an ox's; his hooked nose and projecting chin, his bold glance, diverted any feelings of absurdity, but already his cheeks were over-full, his chin showed signs of tripling. He bowed before her in silence, and then led her to a chair. Harriet sat, watching his hand stray caressingly over his pomaded black hair.

"Harriet," he said, giving each word and syllable its absolute value, "one of my earliest recollections is of seeing your dear mother some days before her lamented death. The demise of that excellent woman was compensated for, if it *could* be compensated for, by the orphan to whom she bequeathed her sensibility, her elegance, and wit. As a scion on the maternal side of that illustrious clan to which you belong, the fortunes of our family have always been the cherished ideals of my heart, and although disappointed of my own natural expectations by the dictates of posthumous malice, I have rejoiced that a collateral branch should be represented by one with the amiability, the inherited beauty, and the acquired elegance that are peculiarly yours. Yet the mind of a woman, however polished and spirited she may be, is not properly fitted to control the management, guide the policy, and make the decisions necessary for the continuous prosperity of a large and lucrative estate. Your lineage is honourable, your prospects are bright and your fortune is great. Have you ever considered what temptations

these endowments are to the unprincipled, the un-
scrupulous, and the needy ? No !—I realize that
you are too ingenuous, your mind is too unsophis-
ticated, your heart is too proper, to realize the snares
that are set for the unwary and the innocent. The
young and generous-minded girl is no match for the
fortune hunter, and only by placing her confidence
and heart in the possession of one familiar by repute
to her can she guard against the worldly subtleties
that surround her. Conscious of the refinements conferred on me by gentle birth, education, and the
worth that the heart alone bestows, I have no hesitation in placing these merits on a level not inferior
to the more substantial, more material possessions
which fortune has thought fit to grant you in addi-
tion to your natural virtues. In the union of all
these qualities by the alliance of our related families
you would have the protector that is the privilege
allowed to every woman and the happiness derived
from association with an admiring and devoted husband." He scrambled on to his knees. " I ask you,
therefore, for the felicity of your hand in marriage."
    Harriet broke into a peal of hysterical laughter.
    There was an awkward silence.
    " Rise, Caesar," she said, with instant agitation.
    " Harriet———"
    " No—no." She regarded his astonished face with
some concern, and nervously urged him to rise. But
his awkwardness in regaining his feet was too much for
her risibility, and again she laughed uncontrollably.
    Caesar's blank expression changed under that re-
vealing mirth. His breath came rapidly. He glared
at her. " Are you amused ? " he demanded.

"No—no. Forgive me, Caesar. I will never marry you." She added disarmingly : "You are kind. It is impossible. I am touched." He continued to stare at her, not speaking, and biting his nether lip savagely. He was so crestfallen that Harriet's sympathy fled again, and she could only add : "You took very long. Archy asked me in five seconds," before she once more burst into helpless laughter.

IV

"Ach, Sir Walter, it is very goot," said Prince Rupert admiringly.

The three men had descended from the sociable, and now stood on the road that curves round Bemersyde Hill. Beneath them was Old Melrose in the loop of Tweed, sylvan, sequestered ; beyond, the Eildons cleft the sky.

"It is a bonnie bit," said the buirdly, ruddy-faced man contentedly. "It's a bonnie bit," he repeated. He smiled with the boyish pleasure of one who has left the unexpected to the last. "These hills will outlive Dryburgh, Prince ; and Abbotsford, by the same token." His hand caressed the deerhound which had thrust a cold nose against his palm, but his gaze remained on the hills.

"I will haf many notes to take," said the prince approvingly. "Max." The equerry stepped forward obligingly. "Look !" The prince pointed down to Old Melrose. "It is like somdings. Eh ? "

"Ach ja, durchlaucht. It is like the Wupper," replied Captain von Elsdorff affectionately.

Prince Rupert laughed with glee. "If the goot

Sir Walter would com to Berg he would then see
the Wupper. Ach, Sir Walter, in Deutschland we
would be proud."

" Maybe," said Sir Walter with twinkling eyes,
" if I left my own country the folk here would keep
me out for good." The men and the hound entered
the sociable. " Walk them for a bit, Peter," said
he, and the carriage moved slowly while the visitors
commented on the panorama of borderland.

" It is an honour, Sir Walter," the young prince
assured him earnestly, " to be shown thus by the
gentlemans who has made them the world known."

" If they give me the credit, Prince, I hope they
will give me some of the profits ! "

" Ach ! " said the prince idolatrously, " it is the
world known. The goot ladies Campbell von Duisk
last year, they said so in my brother's house. You
know them, Sir Walter ? "

" I have met Miss Emmeline Campbell at her
uncle Lord Drumgesk's. You will be well received at
Duisk, Prince. It, is a large house, I am told, and
the Duisk family is very rich."

The Prince of Zelle, in pursuance of his intention,
was now in Scotland, furnished with ample introductions. At present he was lodged under the roof
of renowned Abbotsford, making excursions in the
company of Scott and his family to the places
memorialized in ballad and novel. This day he had
seen Melrose Abbey, and thence by St. Boswells
they had gone to Dryburgh. His host had left the
Bemersyde route for the return journey, as a surprise
for the young German's love of the picturesque.

The spring day was warm, and the trees were

leaved with foam-like green. The horses broke into a trot, and the carriage swung between sunny fields on the road to Abbotsford. The young prince talked continuously and effusively to the big ruddy-faced man in his fifties, whose serene poise, whose easy manners, marked him more as a cultured countryman than as one who was the praised of Europe.

Prince Rupert's next progress was to Loch Awe, and now Sir Walter was gently disillusioning him of his preconceived ideas of encountering savage clansmen. The young man, not unadventurous, was slightly disappointed, but heartened by the assurance of the hospitality he would get at Duisk. He remembered the ladies von Duisk with respect, and looked forward to seeing them in the midst of their tremendous mountains. Sir Walter told him of the brothers Campbell ; of Sir Scipio and Drumgesk, and mentioned that a grand-niece of theirs had inherited a fortune of two hundred thousand pounds on the recent death by a broken neck of her husband.

To welcome the honoured visitor Harriet had projected a family gathering, leaving out her maternal relations owing to Uncle Robin Scott's limpet-like disinclination to part from her after the foreign tour. The Cattanach-Hamiltons were unable to accept, nor did Mrs. Otway's health permit her to journey so far, but Caesar and Colin travelled north and so did the widowed Mrs. Rooke, whose husband's untimely death had occurred from a fall downstairs while he was attempting in a state of tipsy exaltation to light a cigar from a candle on a first-floor landing. Archy Otway was now in India. Mrs.

Bowmaker was never likely to go where the Otways were, and her refusal was not unexpected.

The Prince of Zelle was enchanted by Duisk and everything connected. He heard bagpipe music, he listened open-eared to conversations in Gaelic, he heard old songs, and saw old kilts ; he climbed the hills, he sketched Innischonnell Castle, he inspected the Crinan Canal, and heard Corryvrechkan, and fished in the fresh-water lochs and on the salt sea. And he made copious notes of all he saw and heard.

In the evenings there was genteel conversation to follow the excellent food and wine, and much good humour and courtesy. And the ladies and gentlemen were all quite willing to sing, the prince included, but particularly Captain von Elsdorff, who sang the songs of his native land in a voice compounded of virility and melancholy.

Sometimes driving expeditions were formed, and sometimes sailing excursions. Frequently delightful walks were made to picturesque places near at hand, when the ladies and gentlemen all strolled informally in couples or trios to find picnic awaiting them in a secluded spot and carriages for the return journey.

Harriet was thrilled. She was proud now of her fine palazzo and its impressive environs ; proud of the mountains, and of the loch, and of the Highland pedigree, which all charmed the romantic-tradition imbued young foreigner. Prince Rupert would see now that she was chatelaine of no insignificant domain, but a lady of birth and possessions . . . her mind was dizzied by the profusion of her ideas, and she trembled that a few short days would fulfil or shatter her ambitions.

Frequently he walked by her side in the garden,
discussing the writings of Scott and Goethe and
Byron, or reciting Bürger.   He never spoke inti-
mately, but the restraints imposed by his exalted
upbringing might be responsible for that, she reflected.   His manner was soft and winning, his looks
caressing ; when he discussed poetry his eyes were
bright with passionate fire.

That the prince was a most agreeable nobleman
was warmly endorsed by Mrs. Rooke, to whom Harriet
confided her admiration of the young man.   Elizabeth still affected the blacks of a bereaved woman,
but her inherent courage had enabled her to assume
a gaiety and animation that relieved her fellow-guests.
She said she admired the prince for the comforting
words he gave her in their walks together, and which
lessened her grief better than any religious adviser
could have done.

" He is a noble man, dear Harriet.   Most amiable
and accomplished."

During these days Caesar made a forlorn effort
to establish an understanding with Harriet, but he
found it hopeless.   In his heart burned a heavy rage
against his brother Archy.   Following Harriet's foolish
revelation he had thought that Archy had gained
her, and was incensed.   When he realized that his
youngest brother had no better luck a furious outburst of hatred had found vent against him.   He
would have gained Harriet, he declared violently,
had Archy not gone first and made his own proposal ridiculous.   Caesar had no personal modesty;
he could not imagine any woman not caring for him.
He was full of malice against Archy for making what

he declared to be his honourable intentions resemble
a family fortune hunt. A savage conflict had taken
place between the brothers, not to old Mrs. Otway's
benefit. They never spoke again, and Archy departed
to Indian service followed by his brother's curses.
Mrs. Otway secretly favoured Caesar. He was the
eldest, he was drunken and dissolute and had wheedled
many sums of money out of her, and was inattentive
to her, selfish and surly. His infrequent moments
of consideration to his mother consequently gave
Mrs. Otway the most exquisite satisfaction. On the
other hand, Archy had always been a dutiful son.
Mrs. Otway could accept his attentions as a matter
of course, and even reprimand him sharply for trifles
that she would not have found fault with in Caesar,
nor for which Caesar would have tolerated reprimand.
Archy departed for India, ignored by Caesar and
sped by the blackguardly foppish Colin with sarcastic goodwill, and Mrs. Otway sometimes thought
of him with pettish resentment, feeling that he had
wrecked the prospects of her Caesar.

Colin had followed these attempts of his brother
to rehabilitate himself with sardonic relish. His contempt for Caesar was unlimited and secret; his admiration for Harriet absolute. And he determined
to make a bid for the prize himself, at a later date,
for he shrewdly guessed that Caesar's presence was
a reminder to Harriet that would give no Otway
a proper chance.

He was more dandiacal than Caesar, and proud
of his slender figure. He was content to wait, confident that if Harriet failed him some other heiress
wouldn't. The two brothers were nevertheless en-

joying their sojourn, voting the prince a capital fellow
without pretentiousness and with good cigars. At
first they had wondered if he could be useful to
them in any way, but their sister had disillusioned
them there. Elizabeth was always quite willing to
further their interests and was perfectly good-natured
and generous with her brothers, even to giving them
loans which she knew they would never repay. For
that reason, perhaps, she continually counselled them
to contract good marriages, and while at Duisk she
hinted to Caesar that Emmeline might not be
unamenable.

"It's no use," he answered disconsolately. "I
can't propose to the whole family. She wouldn't do
it; but I'd have given her the offer if I'd thought
she'd bite." He grinned, thinking of the listless
Emmeline. "What an old hag she is becoming,"
he commented elegantly.

On the evening before the Prince of Zelle's departure Harriet brought some people of consequence
from a distance—there were few left in the neighbourhood—and the dinner was a farewell banquet
of honour to the distinguished guest. She had not
forgotten Mrs. Rooke's magnificence at Schloss Wupperthal, and now was a competing constellation to
that blazing lady. There was goodwill and good
humour pervasive, but hers was greatly assumed;
she was disappointed by Prince Rupert's inability
to make a decision. In a flowery little speech near
the end of the meal Caesar praised the prince's amiability and condescension, and His Serene Highness
rose to reply.

"It is not for nodings," he said graciously, "that

I haf com to Schottland, for to my own land I will take much bleasant memories. I haf seen the goot Baronett von Abbotsford, the goot ladies and gentlemans of Edinburg, and the very goot hosbitality of the beoble of Schottland. In the mountains of Argyll I haf seen the Highland beoble in their own land, and will take back the memory of their skeendoos and beebrochs and tartans. And I will com to what I will say when I will take back somdings else. In this beautiful house of Duisk, of the Campbells von Duisk, of the herzöge von Argyll, I haf found again a treasure that is more beautiful than your cairngorms. I haf met that treasure in my vaterland and I met it again in Schloss Duisk. That treasure is a lady, ladies and gentlemans, who is of the herzöge von Argyll and of a family that is a very goot family. It gives me much bleasure that I tell you this in the house of her ancestors and that she will be Fürstin von Zelle." He paused, and smiled mysteriously on the expectant faces. "The lady, ladies and gentlemans, is the very beautiful lady, the gracious Misdress Rooke."

At these last words, which swept all her ambitions away with the efficacy of a blow, Harriet was transfixed. The murmur of many voices, the preliminaries for a toast, recalled her senses ; she saw the smiling prince in a kind of haze, she heard the deprecating laughter of Mrs. Rooke. With an effort she added her congratulations to the rest.

"It is a romance, purely," the gay voice of Elizabeth was explaining. "Prince Rupert . . . friendly, Schloss Wupperthal . . . renewed . . . love, Duisk . . . tenderest messages of the heart . . ."

In her own room that night Harriet stood before
her mirror and surveyed herself. She thought her
face had altered curiously. At the age of twenty-
three! She stepped closely to the glass, and read
fury there. For a while she stood, watching her
features, thinking. And at length tears came.

" In my own house ! " she thought, and wondered
why she had been fool enough to ask any Otway
there. " A romance ! " she thought scornfully. " A
romance of two hundred thousand pounds ! "

v

Harriet was not heart-broken, but she felt deeply
humiliated. Thankfully she reflected that she had
confided to no one her plans—unless, perhaps, Mrs.
Rooke had suspected. That needle mind was able
for anything.

With the departure of her guests Miss Campbell
promised herself that no Otway would ever enter her
house while she was alive. Had it not been entailed
she would have sold it. The very name of it, so often
on the lips of the Prince of Zelle, had become
distasteful to her.

She reminded herself that there were other princes
in the world, although few so suitable, perhaps, as
the Prince of Zelle. In her mind the outward symbols
of rank repelled all else ; she desired to be a woman
of high title who could take a part in the world of
fashion and gaiety. And for that, she told herself,
she was willing to forswear love.

The new style of Mrs. Rooke was not soothing to
her feelings. From Paris, where the now married
couple had settled—for Elizabeth did not share

Harriet's romantic attachment for Berg—letters arrived full of the light gossip of the desirable world, and in Paris was born the little Princess Elissa of Zelle. " We have called her Elissa," Elizabeth wrote, " partly after my mother and myself, and partly after the Queen of Tyre." These letters filled Miss Campbell of Duisk with mortification, and with envy.

Without reverting to the Zelles, she spoke frequently to Emmeline of her desire to move in a livelier sphere, and spoke often of her distant relatives the Rocamadours and the Ferneys. To these longings her aunt could only offer a languid interest ; she had lost touch with the world, and indeed with everything, moving aimlessly about the house and grounds, finding a mild recreation in the poultry, and reading much. She would not have left Duisk unwillingly, only there was no place she particularly desired to go to, and least of all to Paris.

Later came the announcement of the birth of a son to the Prince and Princess of Zelle. " We have called him Rupprecht Ludwig Nectar," Elizabeth wrote, " after my husband, and in honour of the King of France, and my brother-in-law the Grand Duke."

It was not the society of London that attracted Harriet. She reflected that the highest circles there were strictly exclusive, and the rich greater peers of the British nobility were vastly fewer in number and more difficult to annex than the many impoverished nobles who thronged the continent. The glamour of foreign high-sounding names was intoxicating to her.

Emmeline privately ascribed these tendencies to

the plebeian strain of Harriet's mother. She could
find no other reason for the young woman's passion
for ostentation. The pity, the compassion that she
felt for her own mother was unmingled with that
idolatry of the Cœur-de-rois affected by her niece.

In time the Princess of Zelle informed them of the
birth of her second son. " We have called him Georg
Caspar Heinrich," she wrote, " in honour of King
George the Fourth, of my husband's late dear father,
and of the Duc de Bordeaux."

Harriet then announced her intention of travelling
abroad ; perhaps to Switzerland, perhaps to Italy.
Emmeline declined to go.

" Will you stay here, in Duisk, like a hermit ? "
the younger woman demanded. " Emmeline, you
are a fool to sulk like this."

" I am not sulking," said the aunt wearily. " I
have no wish to go anywhere."

" I shall close Duisk."

" Perhaps I can have Uillian."

" No, Emmeline."

" On lease, of course."

" No."

The two women regarded each other then, and a
flash of dormant energy showed in the older's eyes.
She rose with more determination in her manner than
she had shown for years. " I am glad that I have
not lived on your charity and that I have contributed
to the upkeep of this house. But you will not in-
timidate me to do your wish in this fashion, for I
shall take a house of my own."

" Go to a convent," said Harriet cuttingly. " I
said you were a fool, Emmeline, and so you are. For

you have never lived, and never loved, and never desired either."

" I have loved," said Emmeline, trembling uncontrollably, " and if I had never loved I might be eager to live. You gibe at me, Harriet, and you have known neither."

Harriet put forward her preparations for departure, and made her first step Lady Bressingham's, who introduced a middle-aged gentlewoman to act as Miss Campbell's *compagnon-de-voyage*. Equipped with Miss Cripps and with numerous introductions from the peeress and from Mrs. Bowmaker—she ignored the Otways—Harriet crossed the Channel on her quest of a husband.

A tumult of emotions had troubled Emmeline Campbell before her niece's departure. For a moment she, too, was glad that Duisk was to be closed, and was almost grateful to Harriet for her drastic action. The elder woman visioned unwillingly escape from the heavy memories of the past in some other part of Scotland, or in England ; anywhere away from Glassary. But Glassary was too strong for her. All her fondest recollections were bounded by these hills and lochs ; accusing memories, but tender. The conflict was painful ; she wanted to go, and decided to stay. But she preferred to go as far from Duisk as possible, and took a house near Ardrishaig, looking to Loch Fyne, and just over the parish boundary.

Before Harriet left, the two women had become reconciled, and now they corresponded. Harriet, like her half-cousin, delighted in detailing the pleasures of her social amusements ; they left her aunt mildly surprised. She could not understand the attraction

of these frivolities, that could give satisfaction neither
to head nor heart.

Herself, she grew inured to the new house, a comfortable gabled building with privacy. Thither she
had transferred her own furnishings—mostly her
Uncle Archibald's—and with her books and the company of a cook and a maid she whiled away the days,
summer and winter. She had no desire to go further
away ; she found sufficient to interest her in the
people of Ardrishaig and Lochgilphead, working people
all of them, and she grew closer to them in thought
and act, making acquaintance with them, finding
surprised wonder in their hard valiant lives, their
unconscious heroisms and sacrifices.

Loch Fyne—that great fjord whose herrings have
been famous for a thousand years, whose waters sway
between the soft kind swelling hills, whose beauties
are not of the savage nor of the languid kinds, but
are mysterious, having a charm that is of myrtle and
salt brine. Its waters bear the spectre ships of
immemorial fishermen, its waves beat coronach for
the men that are no more. The galleys of the kings
of Lochlann and of Albainn have trod its surging
waters, and the red beacons of warning have reflected
on its midnight wave. Along its shores have lived
the lowly toilers of the deep, through many centuries,
in their humble fashion, breathing the saline glamour
of its breath, fearing it and loving it, seeing it in the
wonderful dawn of birth and bidding it a sad farewell
when the sun of life is sinking. Loch Fyne, for the
sake of which alone the dead will gladly rise.

And gazing on that grey band of water, changing
with the sun and with the sky to gold and blue and

silver, the peace that the salt sea only can give was given to Emmeline. She would sit by her window in the summer evenings, watching the last rays of the sun gild the tops of Cowal and see against the further shore the fishing smacks from Lochgair and Stra'lachlan move slowly down the loch; so slow, they seemed immovable. The Ardrishaig boats would sail out then, passing so near that the active figures aboard were recognizable. Southward they would sail, towards Ardlamont, or perhaps some lingered up the loch, preparing to cast their nets off the Oitir. Night would come, and she would stroll down to the gateway, lingering there, and listening to the gluck of the waves on the pebbled shore, hearing the heart-piercing call of a seabird, smelling the cold saltness of the evening swell.

It was a fugitive peace that entered into her heart, but it came often. It had come from without, and at first slowly. From that great arm of greater ocean she was drawing a tranquillity that the fresh waters of Loch Awe had failed to give. She remembered that the father of Neil Leitch had drowned in Loch Fyne. Was it a token, from his watery sepulchre was the father granting absolution to her who had loved and wronged his son?

The thought was mystical, and so it comforted. Neil Leitch was dead and all the past dead with him. Regret would live while she had life, but it was no longer barbed with the bitter remorse of yore. She was strengthened by the knowledge of her fidelity, her love that transcended the momentary folly of vindictiveness and was throned in the sacred chambers of her heart. Neil Leitch was dead; and

Loch Fyne stretched forth an invisible hand, and assoilzied her.

In the repose that was gradually becoming permanent Emmeline was able to hear of her relations' affairs without envy or wonder. Thomas Bowmaker sold Barrill to an alien family, and no Otway would ever reign there. Colin Otway had drifted to Canada. The second Lord Bressingham was dead. The affairs of those people were of little interest, but she was more sensible to those of Harriet, whose ambitions had been fully gratified.

Reaching Paris on her travels, Harriet had not scrupled to renew acquaintance with the Zelle family, reflecting that any mortification she suffered had not been consciously inflicted by them. The house of her rich half-cousin provided a jumping off board for an entry to a desirable society, which was enlarged by the distant Cœur-de-roi connections whom she was careful to discover. Her good looks and reputed wealth, combined with the guaranteed relationship of the Princess of Zelle, provided her with a number of suitors, and Miss Campbell made a careful and deliberate choice.

On consideration, she was not anxious to ally herself with any of the young men who sought her. They were dissolute young men, and, however pleasant their company, she feared they would make intolerable husbands. But among the visitors of the princess was a relic of the *ancien régime*, the Duc de Sarge. He was over seventy, a childless widower estranged from all his relations, and lived in shabby pretentiousness. Of the pre-Revolution days he had tender memories ; he had been a courtier at Versailles and a dear friend

of Marie Antoinette. Harriet would listen to the
pleasant ramblings of the courteous old beau with a
sense of wonder. His had been a life, she thought;
and she felt sorry that he was so obviously ill, for
inherited and acquired ailments made it certain that
he had no great time to live. His high birth and
breeding and his low state of health generated in
Harriet's mind a definite plan, and she made her
desires known through a proper channel. The old
duke, who had never expected that a rich young
woman would offer her hand to match his age and
poverty, was perfectly agreeable to the match. She
joined the Roman church; they were married with
all the Zelles, the Cœur-de-rois, the Rocamadours, and
the Ferneys in attendance, and then the young bride-
groom and his young bride set off to seek romance
by the shores of Lac Leman. But, following on the
excitements of the ceremony, the rigours of coach
travelling proved too much for the nobleman, and
he had to lie up in an inn at Dijon, where he passed
away with courtly dignity.

In one stroke, and at no great expense, Harriet had
achieved the summit of her desires. Her late husband
had been head of an old if decayed family; he had
belonged to the ancient *noblesse*; he had been a
Frenchman. Against these facts the new name of
Zelle and Prince Rupert's equivocal descent seemed
small. The duchesse could feel sorry for her half-
cousin Elizabeth.

Dividing her time between the capital and Mon-
treux, whose attractions had been brought to her
notice by *Childe Harold*, Harriet lived the life that
her grandmother would have revelled in, and said

farewell to her Campbell associations; forgetting
Duisk, except as one means of income.

The large fortune that the Duchesse de Sarge had
inherited from Sir Scipio made her independent of
the revenues of Duisk, but not indifferent to them,
and in the changes that were refashioning the Highlands, and of which Harriet was kept cognizant by
her man of affairs, she was ready to do her part. Of
recent years the remarkable sporting facilities of the
Highlands had become widely known, and although
at first a great acreage of shooting could be leased
for a trifling sum, the increasing demand for sporting
lets had raised their value greatly. These changes
had occurred since Harriet's accession, and as neither
of the Duisk ladies were interested in grouse shooting
or deer stalking the moors above Duisk had been leased
for a number of years to strangers. In the landward
parts of the Duisk domain were still some scattered
hamlets inhabited by families who made a precarious
living by the manufacture of lint or weaving, and
whose rents could generally be met by the small
amounts laid aside from what they could make by
selling produce to the coast town merchants. The
houses were wretched thatched cottages, always by
the side of a burn, and destitute of any civilized
comfort, but they were endeared to their occupants
by all the indivisible ties of home life and recollection,
and their sites were such as to pleasure those of a
race never lost to the glamour of beauty. Sir Scipio
in his drastic alterations to farm tenure had left those
cottars' houses alone, and they had remained in their
oases of cultivated patch, surrounded by the bracken
and heather slopes and snugly sheltered from the

violent mountain gusts. Little disturbed those peaceful cottagers save the late appearance of the shooting
tenant and his dogs; they felt secure and happy,
they lived in the place where they had been born and
bred; serious, sun-tanned, they worked assiduously,
speaking their soft Gaelic tongue as their fathers had
done throughout the ages. If they had regrets, they
were only for the changes that had swept so many
from the communal farms—some of them, indeed,
were the children of the one-time farmers. For Miss
Harriet Campbell of Duisk, their landlord, they
entertained the liveliest respect and affection.

The incidence of grouse moors had brought the
fascinations of deer-stalking into prominence, and the
larger rents paid for the latter class of lets had induced
many proprietors to convert their estates into forests.
The district of Argyll proper, not alpine in the real
sense of the word, could not offer the attraction of
peak and corrie that would test the stalker's skill and
endurance, and fell far short of Ross or Sutherland
there. But there was a sufficiency of mountain and
broken upland in those lands east of Loch Awe, and
the factor assured his mistress that the deer would
breed freer and stronger there were it not for the
presence of man and sheep. In her *hôtel* in the Rue de
Grenelle the Duchesse de Sarge deliberated on his
figures and considered the accrued revenue that was
promised.

She instructed the clearance of all her property
that was suitable for deer.

And the cottars went.

They went unwillingly, disbelieving the order to
leave, and latterly declining to move. For that the

fair young Harriet would drive them from their
cherished homes was what they could not credit.
And not until strange men appeared, and they found
themselves with their few sticks of furniture beside
them and the thatched roofs of their cottages roaring
in a gush of yellow flame and black smoke, did they
realize that they had no homes.   Wild-eyed, sullen,
they trudged down to the valley to seek temporary
shelter from charitable kinsfolk, and on the way one
woman who was advanced with child was taken ill
by the roadside, and gave birth.   And she and the
child died.

A surge of anger shook the district.   And it was
heavy against the owner of Duisk, who was absent
and a coward, and who was a woman and had no
pity.   The changes in tenure had been resented,
the altered conditions of status regretted, but none
had occurred with the savage completeness of these
evictions.   Everyone was incensed, save Emmeline,
and she remained in ignorance, for none told her.
It was only the indefinable change of manner to
her that latterly made Emmeline curious, and she
mentioned her observations to the minister, who told
her the reason.

She was shocked.   That Harriet was living a gay
and selfish existence, indifferent to the sufferings of
her old tenants, filled her with angry resentment, and
at once she drove to Duisk, where, as she might have
realized, there was no one who could either help or
counsel her.   At the home farm she received details
of the evictions, now a month past, and was told
where the homeless people had gone, some to seek
employment for themselves and families in Lochgilp-

head, and some to Glasgow, and some were embarking that day for America. Fretting against the inhumanity that could disperse people like dust, she continued her course to Crinan.

At Crinan forlorn little groups were waiting to embark on board the tender that would carry them to the emigrant ship lying off Jura, whose snow-tipped peaks glittered like spears in the sunshine of this April day. They stood in dejected segments, exchanging with friends the last half-shamed words of affection ever to be exchanged on this side of the grave, and seeing for the ultimate time the native scenes that had been theirs since childhood. The men were drab in their coarse homespun, the tartan or bright scarlet plaids of the women heightened the melancholy scene with bizarre hues ; their spare possessions lay at their feet in bundles tied up in blankets. The children, bare-footed, were eager and tearful by turns, playing with the faithful collies from which they were soon to part.

All the traditions of a race, a language, and a system, the passionate loyalty of that race for the land and customs of its forbears, were to be shattered for ever by that boat making for the shore. The places sacred with ancestral dust would be no more enriched ; no more would the air be felt that was sweet with the scented myrtle. The cloud shadows would sweep across the hills, and none would be there to gaze on them. The peat moss would stay unvisited, and those turfs that had been promise of kind nights of ceilidh and a wealth of song and legend would never now be lifted. " Cha till sinn tuille,"—we return no more.

In the new cities of the new continents, and on the great plains and in the vast valleys of the Americas and Australasia and Africa, they are—the scions of those lost departed ; new worlds have been enriched by them, their vigour and their integrity, and an old world is impoverished.

Emmeline left the carriage and moved hesitatingly down to the shore.   She was suddenly afraid of those people, most of whom she knew.   What she would say or do or promise she did not know ;   she only knew that they must not suspect her of this cruelty, · that they must not hate her . . . she advanced towards them, and they grew silent and turned and watched her.   They did not regard her with anger, as she had expected, nor did they hurl imprecation at her as she had feared.   They simply regarded her, silently, impassively.

She stopped as though an invisible wall had stayed her movement.   For a minute the Duisk tenants and the Duisk lady stared at each other in mute surmise, and Emmeline understood that they had ceased to regard her as a friend.   Her heart failed her and she turned timidly away, and returned trembling to the carriage.   There she looked back ;   the tender was come.

Suddenly arose the sound of singing.   From the · shore it came, rising to the neighbouring heights, and the startled sea-gulls swooped low in joined protest. At first it was a lowly sound, quavering and uncertain. It strengthened, strengthened by the confidence it voiced, and the united tongues swelled into a loud pæan of praise and trust.   Like a glad chant it was, the chant of those whom danger cannot dishearten

nor tyranny break, whose faith is fixed in the eternal
and the immutable.

> " O God of Bethel ! by whose hand
> Thy people still are fed."

These people driven with ignominy from their
homes, forced to seek their bread in a far distant land,
parting at the moment, son and mother, husband
and wife, with but the vaguest hope of ever re-uniting,
were triumphantly reiterating continuous faith and
confidence in their God.

" Drive home," she said wearily.

Emmeline suffered the full meaning of this sight
some days later, when a young man, not known to
her, brought to the door some fish she had ordered.
His features were vaguely familiar, and she inquired
who the young man was, as she was wont to do.

" It is one of the tenants of Errachan Beg," the maid
told her bluntly. " He and his grandmother, who is
dead now, went there from Knockalava five years ago.
He is helping some of the fishermen until he finds
something to do. His father was killed at Waterloo
and his name is Colin Leitch."

After all, this eviction was only on a larger scale
what she herself had accomplished, she thought with
bitter self-reproach, and all her recent peace of mind
was fled. Harriet had done to this young man what
she, Emmeline, had done to his father.

" We are all evil," she reflected fearfully. " Every
one of us. We are savage animals."

When she inquired next about Colin Leitch it was
to learn that he had sought work some miles away,
and was helping in a fishing smack.

The anger over the Duisk evictions passed in time, not quickly forgotten, and Duisk estate was cleared of most of its tenantry to the augmentation of its value. The mansion was occupied in the autumns by the deer-stalking tenant. The grouse sportsmen had been content to lodge in the farm house, and Emmeline wondered what Sir Scipio would have said to this desecration of his house by strangers.

A new age was beginning, but Emmeline was unconscious of that. So slowly did change pervade the district that it was hardly noticed. A steamboat now ran from Glasgow to Ardrishaig pier; more houses were building in Ardrishaig and in Lochgilphead. There was great talk of the new railroads that were being constructed in the Lowlands. A young queen was on the throne. Everywhere there was activity, and every year was another dear and melancholy link with the past.

Among her own relatives the changes had been many. All the daughters of Admiral Campbell were now dead, as was his widow. His grandson Bowmaker had died suddenly after a life of careless extravagance. Leonie's son, the new Lord Bressingham, was deep in politics, had filled cabinet positions, and was expectant of a colonial governorship. In Canada Colin Otway had met Elsinore Moore, an actress in a touring company, and married her, to the rage of Caesar, who wrote a vigorous letter to Emmeline deploring the shame to his family name. And Elsinore in time gave birth to another Colin Otway.

Caesar also had married, and now, a gross mass of obesity, he lived in Somerset, for he found that a

handsome mansion could be got there for a moderate
rent.   He could live comfortably by economizing,
which he did by cutting his servants' wages and his
wife's dress allowance.   With the death to his hopes
of Barrill and the refusal of himself by Harriet, Caesar
considered himself an injured man, but no other heirs
had come between him and Duisk ; he was easy on
the score of Emmeline, and in time was satisfied that
Harriet would not marry again.

" She knows when she's well off," he would say
explanatorily to his wife, and the whilom Augusta
Guild would sincerely agree with him.

Drinking in the company of the neighbouring squires,
he would think morosely of Duisk, and to comfort
himself would sometimes beat his wife.   In the
ultimate kindness of Providence he had some faith,
for the death of Archy had evinced that kindness.
He wished that Harriet might die, reflecting that she
was eleven years younger than himself.   But he would
reassure himself.

" She can't stand the pace," he would say aloud.
" She's been frisking and frolicking in France all those
years.   Hang it ! it's bound to kill her soon."

Against his wife his rage would sometimes reach
insane proportions.   He had no children, his next of
kin were Colin and the actress's son, and he could
not forgive Augusta for that.

" I'll never forgive my brother for disgracing the
family," he would say confidentially to his acquaintances.   " You know my feelings in the matter, so
you can guess what my sister the Princess of Zelle
thinks about it, or my cousins the Duchesse de Sarge
and Lord Bressingham."   For Caesar, in his delight

at being able to roll these names off his tongue, would
ignore his animosities for the time being. Driving
home, he would keep thinking of Elsinore and her son,
and then unleash his anger on his wife.

Of all those aspirations and bitternesses Emmeline
was ignorant. Some of her relations corresponded
with her, and she was glad to hear of their affairs,
but it was a detached interest that she felt. They
had all become strangely alien to her.

With increasing years she had found it necessary
to keep a carriage, and would drive out in the summer
afternoons, an elderly slender figure with the air of
fragile sweetness that no sorrows had succeeded in
eradicating. She had become a favourite with the
people in the neighbourhood, and loved to stop and
talk to them of their families and hopes. Once, on
the high road by Loch Fyne, she stayed the victoria
to watch a group of children. It was a day of blazing
sunshine, the sea sparkled with a million lights, the
sky was blue and cloudless. The children had been
for peats, and came towards the road carrying their
little creels, singing and laughing the while. Miss
Campbell, from under her purple parasol, watched
them smilingly.

" But they are carrying very heavy loads, John,"
she remarked involuntarily.

" Och, they are used to them," the coachman
reassured her. " They will drop them soon enough
if they have the inclination."

The children came to the highway, and tramped
merrily on the white dusty road, barefooted and
happy. One child of about six was ahead of the
others. She was bareheaded, fair haired and blue

eyed, and she wore a little patterned pinafore. Her smiling little face and her sturdy bare legs were tanned deep by constant exposure, and the sunburn intensified the colour of her hair and eyes. She sang as she advanced, with a child's emphatic intonation :

> " Ishopel Leitch is my name,
> Scotland is my nation.
> Glassary is my dwelling place,
> A bonnie habitation."

" Is she not the wee sturdy ! " John exclaimed admiringly, and turned round with a smile to his mistress. But the smile had left Miss Campbell's face. She stared at the child with frightened eyes and motioned her to stop. The little one did so, gazing shyly at the lady in the victoria and screwing her face to keep the sun's glare from her eyes.

" Is your name Isbell Leitch ? " Miss Campbell asked gently. " Where do you live ? " But the little girl was overawed, and gazed mutely at the lady, her playmates keeping some distance away.

" Och, I'll have a word with her," said John jauntily, and talked to the girl in the Gaelic. She answered readily then, and laughed demurely.

" She's the daughter of Colin Leitch, who has a croft up the way there, Miss Campbell," he said, indicating with his whip. " These two lads are her brothers, she says. I mind Colin's father when I was a lad. He used to be at Kilmichael, and was killed when he went to the wars." He laughed in a pleased fashion. " Is she not the sturdy wee moor-achan ! And they'll always be keenest on the Gaelic."

Miss Campbell contemplated the child in silence.

Neil Leitch's granddaughter ! and she thought of all
that might have been. There was a divine irony,
surely, in that the poor descendants of that other race
should cling so desperately to the soil of Glassary,
transcending all fatalities, and grow strong and
straight in spite of their poverty, and that her own
strong overbearing race should have waxed rich and
secure, and was become effete, sated by the power it
had coveted, lost to the traditions that had nourished
it, and passing its exhausted strain to an alien and
unsympathetic line.

If the Campbells of Duisk had been false to their
traditions and the demands of their dependants,
surely they were paying the penalty in the contempt
with which their failing and oppressive race was held.
If the Leitches had been true to those traditions then,
verily, they had lost everything—and retained everything.

She started, conscious of the silence, and smiled
faintly. " Come here, my dear," she said, and the
child obeyed the gentle cultured voice unquestion-
ingly. Emmeline, her eyes wet with tears, kissed her.

Again the old terrible regrets tortured her as she
drove home, and she knew that her life had been a
barren one, that all existence had been epitomized
in a few short weeks of youth, and then had passed
her by.

For a long time Loch Fyne could never comfort
her. She thought continually of the granddaughter
of Neil Leitch, who carried on the spirit of whom she
loved and the spirit of this district of their races.
She felt remote and strange, apart from the people
among whom she passed her days.

The decades moved by : twenty, thirty years since she had left Duisk. The middle of the century was left behind and the years in front of it were overtaken. Men and women might come and go, but Glassary remained, and the sun shone and the rain fell in their appointed seasons.

EIGHT

I

IN the spring of 1860 Elizabeth Zelle informed her brother that Harriet was contemplating a long-delayed visit to Duisk. At first Caesar gave only jaundiced thought to it, but an unconquerable curiosity desired him to renew his relative's acquaintance. All his knowledge of Duisk was now gained through his sister, and that was slight.

Calculating when she would be likely to reach Argyllshire, he travelled from Somerset with his wife, not deigning to tell her his reason, as he suspected Augusta's capacity for holding her tongue. The late death that had been bringing Duisk constantly to his mind abetted his desire to see it again.

His wife and he had been dawdling complainingly about Ardrishaig for a week, Caesar keeping a keen eye on the steamer travellers who passed through the village, when at last he had the satisfaction of seeing a greatly changed Harriet Campbell being whirled towards her home, and after a discreet wait of two days he wrote to her stating that while revisiting old haunts he had been informed of her return.

Harriet laughed gaily on reading this ingenuous note, and at once answered, inviting Mr. and Mrs. Otway to stay with her.

" Say nothing to nettle her," he cautioned his wife on the way. " Those great women are easily angered, and she must be worth a good deal. I couldn't see her clearly, but she's been a train journey, a sea crossing, a train journey to London and another to Glasgow, another to Greenock, a sail to Ardrishaig, and that drive to Duisk, which, hang me, must be seventeen miles at the least, and if she's not feeling all out by this time, I'll be hanged." He lowered his hands, on whose fingers he had ticked off the stages of Harriet's journey. " She's a ticklish woman to deal with, if what Elizabeth says is true, although I can't put any trust in what Elizabeth says at the best of times, but she'll be a ticklish woman in any case, and please to remember that."

" Very well."   •

" She's sixty-one, and I'm seventy-two, and I've waited a cursed long time on her breaking up. It's a perfect scandal that women of frivolous propensities should keep other people out of their honest rights. *I'm saying*, it's a scandal that a woman like Harriet should keep me out of my *rights*."

His wife agreed meekly, and Caesar lolled discontentedly over the carriage. It was open, for the day was fine, and he watched the lonely stretches through which they were passing with greedy eyes. He felt that Lord Drumgesk and the Duchesse de Sarge had been crosses to test his manhood. A huge ungainly figure, his large red fleshy face surrounding a pursed scarlet mouth, he divided his arrogant glances between the landscape and his paunch, for he was already feeling hungry. The thin, worn-out woman with the white face and the subdued eyes squeezed further into her corner.

In the avenue of Duisk Caesar commented on the

evidences of neglect ; the gates were off their hinges, the avenue was grass-grown. But now the timber had increased in height and beauty, and what had once been two lines of modest trees threw the approach into impressive shade. A thick sea of fir trees frilled the hill-side.

"Caesar!" He stared at the dainty figure who greeted him, at her golden hair and marvellous complexion. Disappointment swept over him. Where was the wrinkled duchess he had hoped to see ? The women kissed.

"France agrees with you, Harriet," he said grudgingly.

"You were *so* good to write. I was so pleased." The duchess turned with a quick movement to Augusta. "Elizabeth has spoken so often about you, dear Mrs. Otway. What a delight !" She was brimming with courtesy and good-will, complimenting them on their appearance of health, and enthusiastic over their visit. She wore a black velvet crinoline dress with a great quantity of exquisite cream lace on her neck-yoke and sleeves. Her neck was encircled by a rope of pearls ; above that neck the lively features of this youthful looking woman whose light motion held a great dignity were the undeniable features of the amber-eyed Harriet Campbell. But it was a Harriet who had become a *grande dame*.

All day Caesar was both impressed and vexed by his relative and her active personality, and Duisk seemed to slip from beyond his grasp. She was like a girl. Sixty-one ! and he watched the fairy-like creature, studied her wonderful clothes, heard her light gay laughter, with a sense of bafflement.

z

" She'll see a hundred," he told his wife despairingly. " That life seems to suit some people. Painted and powdered like a doll. And she's as right inside as out. I watched her eating."

His eye would wander over the rich furnishings that Sir Scipio had brought and which he had counted on some day owning. There was no need for further hope, he told himself, and resigned himself to Somerset. And he heard with a jealous mind how Harriet had brought her French chef to satisfy her wants on this brief holiday, and he heard her maid running about with officious speech about " Madame la Duchesse." " She'll see us all out," he told his wife with a foul oath, for he was not particular with his speech before Augusta. " She's tough 's leather."

" You have been a long time away, Harriet," he remarked courteously as they walked in the grounds together, he with the aid of a stick.

" I meant often to return, but I never had the time. Duisk has no memories for me, or no happy ones."

" Have you had happy memories since ? " he asked enviously.

" I have had many. I have had a full life." A gleam of malice flickered in her eyes as she indicated the house of Barrill. He had already observed it— not the house that the Campbells had owned, but a great new structure in the fashionable Scots Baronial manner, a dark-red agglomeration of crow-stepped gables and corner turrets and great bay windows.

" It is called Barrill Castle now, I hear," she said. " A Glasgow family—the Allisons, or Allansons— merchants. It is a vulgar house."

" Bowmaker made short work of Barrill. Drumgesk would have been pleased ! The Crubach ! "
" I have forgotten all those things," she said.
" They seem so far away. And this house, when I
saw it again, seemed like a remembered dream. I
had forgotten Duisk—over thirty years—and I suppose that the district has forgotten me."
" I have never forgotten you."
" I daresay," she said indifferently. " And now ! "
and she pointed to the private burial-ground. " Sir
Scipio might have saved himself the trouble, for there
are only my mother and his mother buried here."
Colin gazed around him at the mural tablets. There
were two new ones, and he looked at one of them long.

To
the memory of
COLONEL ARCHIBALD OTWAY, —th Regt.
Killed at Chillianwallah
while fighting in the service
of his country
13th January, 1849.
This memorial is erected by his
kinswoman
Harriet de Sarge.

" I knew you were estranged," she said. " You
were very wrong. I liked him. He was a good man.
He was the best of the three of you."
On the other stone was graven the words

EMMELINE CAMPBELL
died 3rd August, 1858
aged 80.
God is Love.

" That wording was her own wish," she said. " She

was buried in Kilmory churchyard, beside Loch Fyne, as she desired."

"The Campbells are loth to use their own burying-ground," he commented caustically.

"Holland, Corryvrechkan, Edinburgh, London . . . and I suppose, in time, Père-Lachaise."

"You are not remaining here, then?"

She laughed, as at a jest. "I had Emmeline's private papers to examine. I am vexed that I never saw her again. We went our own ways, Caesar, and that is the proper thing to do. No, Caesar, I feel like a foreigner here. I sought happiness, and I found it."

"I have sought it too," he said sourly, "and I've never found it."

"It is a gamble, Caesar. Elissa, your niece, married for love. She is very unhappy."

"Her mother has never told me that."

"Why should she? Your brother Colin married for love, and he was an idle scamp."

"And still is, I'll wager."

"Colin has been dead for ten years."

He was incredulous.

"You are not grief-stricken, Caesar, but I see you believe. Yes, I have gone over Emmeline's papers, and they are full of surprises. Colin is dead. After all, we were none of us entitled to know, for we all broke with him. He was publicly disreputable. He corresponded with Emmeline to the end. All his letters are in my possession now, and they make a story."

"I'd like to see them."

"You never shall. But I'll tell you this much, that the woman Elsinore Moore made a good wife, and that

she kept him for years with her salary as an actress,
and it couldn't have been much. And he was a good
husband, I imagine, in his own fashion. He was a
poor creature, but men can be changed. During all
these years he kept up a correspondence with
Emmeline. It was to his own interest, for she helped
him a great deal. His wife died in Bristol, and he
remained there, like a dropped stone. And Emmeline
gave him an allowance for the education of his son.
What a mad world! I saw his letter of years back
begging her never to mention his condition or address
to any of his relations, because of the way they had
ignored his wife. He always mentioned Elsinore,
before and after her death, and was vindictive against
the Otways because of her."

"And the son ? " he asked involuntarily.

"The son is twenty-five, I think, and is in the line
of inheritance of Duisk. Emmeline treated him hand-
somely, and he should be grateful, but I don't suppose
he will be. He is in the Consular service, at Brindisi.
He will be waiting on you and me, Caesar ! "

"Well," he said thoughtfully, " I'm cursed sorry
to know that Colin's dead."

"Too late, Caesar ! And too late for Archy, also.
I liked Archy. I was vexed. I was vexed when
Archy was killed."

"Colin might have written before the end," he
blurted. "It was dashed inconsiderate. He could
have got me through Elizabeth."

"Emmeline probably had the same feelings for us
as Colin had, but she was too gentle to ignore us."

"Well, to leave all one's money for a charity, as
she did, is a big enough cut for any family."

" Yes," she said in a low tone, " I am glad that I left Duisk and stayed abroad. Relations are impossible. It is money, money, inheritance, inheritance, all the time."

Caesar was uneasy at the passion in her voice, but her mood passed. " You and I are both old," she said irrelevantly.

" I don't feel old," he answered. " And you don't look your age. You look forty, Harriet."

She smiled then. " Our contemporaries prove our ages, if our common sense won't. I read my age in you, Caesar. I read it in Elizabeth. I read it in John Cattanach. But he is still very young in heart, for he can still hate. He will not recognize your sister because of their mothers' feuds. Well, the Queen sends the great Marquess Cattanach as her ambassador to France for the continuance of peace and good will, and his first peaceful act is to cut his cousin ! A great blunder in a diplomat, but it keeps him young in heart."

They were at the burn, where Scipio had bullied Cydalise and where Emmeline had bade farewell to Neil. She studied the brown foaming water for a time, smiling at the past illusionary memories. " This place wearies me," she said. " I shall be glad to return to my own home."

He thought he detected a weariness in herself as she spoke these words, and was encouraged. But in the evening she was a gay talkative person, enchanting Mrs. Otway, who had seldom received such condescension from anyone. Caesar again took careful scrutiny of Harriet, from her animated and bedizened face down to her exquisite gown and dainty high-heeled shoes. And he felt that it was a losing battle.

"I'm hanged if I know how she stands it," he exclaimed disgustedly to his wife. He told her about his brother Colin. "He was two years younger than I, and very much healthier. And here am I! It all comes," he ended virtuously, "of my living a proper life."

Before the Otways departed Harriet reverted to discussion of Colin's son, and strongly urged Caesar to communicate with him. "Remember, Caesar, he will inherit this place, and it is as well to make sure he isn't a fool as so many of his connections were."

The Otways departed, Caesar taking with him a mood of disappointment. He had hoped that something to his advantage would have been gained by seeing Harriet. "Duisk lies empty ten months of the year," he exclaimed, "and we would be doing her a favour if she asked us to inhabit it for nothing. The place would have been kept in order. She's very tight. And, by Jove! she's well preserved."

Augusta meekly agreed with him.

Left alone, Harriet did not remain long in the house. She went through all Emmeline's papers again, systematically, and destroyed them all. She sent for her man of affairs and discussed all details necessary for the augmentation of her income ; and then there was nothing more for her to do. The weather changed, rain fell continuously, and looking out on the fretted loch she was thankful that a few more days would finish her stay. It was with relief that she left for France.

On the morning of her departure there was rain ;

but it ceased, and a watery sun shone, glinting the hills and the loch with thin gilding. The carriage wheels whished over the fine red sodden gravel of the avenue, passing between parks where the grass was long and drip-laden. She glanced out of the window. In the leafy branches the birds were singing salute to the tardy sun, which dappled the ground with gold.

Harriet leaned back, looking thoughtfully at the cheap upholstery of the hired carriage and listening to the vehicle behind that was carrying her luggage and her chef. Past the empty lodge, on to the public road, to Kilmartin, to Kilmichael, to Ardrishaig . . . she sighed, thinking of the weary stretch of miles.

" Well, Angelique, you have seen Scotland. Do you like it ? " With fervour in her piping voice the maid replied that she did, and the Duchesse de Sarge smiled absently. " It is a good country for sportsmen," she remarked in an unusual burst of condescension.

II

' DUISK.

' This first class shooting extends to about 16,000 acres, capable of yielding 500 brace grouse and about twenty stags. There are also black-game, pheasants, roe deer, hares and rabbits, and, in winter, woodcock and wild fowl.

' The house is beautifully situate overlooking Loch Awe. It is an excellent one, and contains 5 public rooms, 10 family bedrooms, 3 dressing rooms, 5 servants' bedrooms, kitchen, scullery, pantry, &c. There are also stables, coach house, harness room, keeper's cottage, with boat-house, capital kennels, and an excellent garden. There is a post office near hand.

' Loch Awe provides excellent trout and sea trout fishing, and good sport can be got on some hill lochs.

'Steamers from Glasgow and Greenock call daily at
Ardrishaig, from whence hire.'

The property so eagerly grasped by Colin Buie
Campbell, so gladly glorified by Scipio Campbell, and
in which had been epitomized their family pride and
ambitions, was now only of importance in a sports-
man's guide.

For the greater part of the year it remained lonely
amid its neglected policies. There was life not far
away, for during all the changes the home farm of
Duisk had never been abandoned, as its acreage, like
that of two other farms on the property, had not
encroached on the deer's territory. But when Harriet
had become Duchesse de Sargé and decided on a
permanent residence abroad she had relinquished it
to the tenancy of a stranger.

Apart from the people there, and the keeper, there
were none others near Duisk. In August the shooting
tenants and their guests arrived with much noise and
clatter, and for a time the place, like all other parts
of the Highlands, resounded with the banging of
guns. Strange folk, the tenants : officers of general
rank, occasional clergymen, peers of industrial and
territorial value, and odd tatters from all parts of
creation in whom the sight of fur and feather aroused
an abysmal lust to kill. Their querulous, or patroniz-
ing, and high-pitched voices shattered the Sabbath
still of Duisk. For weeks there was a confusion of
butlers, and footmen, and maids, and fat stomachs,
and narrow shoulders, and splay feet, and grinning
faces, and mailing of game, and hiring of post-horses,
and laughter, and complaints, and condescension.
And near the end of their stay a notice would appear

in the papers stating that 'Sir Philip and Lady Chauncey, who have leased the Duisk shootings for three years in succession, return to London on the 20th. Sir Philip, with his customary great generosity, has distributed a gift of rabbits to people in the district, and the fortunate recipients are truly grateful to the benevolent donor.'

And after the tenant and his guests departed, there was silence.

Rain and sunshine had weathered Sir Scipio's house, and around it its protecting timber clustered like a mantle of emerald velvet. It matched its surroundings, and had become Highland, and perhaps arrogant, for from its steady poise on the grassy knoll it gazed across to Barrill Castle with what was like disdain.

It was beautiful without ; and inside it was like a sepulchre.

The farmer's sister received a small fee for inspecting the house weekly and giving warning of damp or damage, and the farmer's son was paid a pittance for performing some essential work on the garden. Sometimes they would take visiting friends along the moss-grown pads to the mansion, and after studying the exterior admiringly the friends would be allowed to see the inside of the house, its covered furniture and pictures, and would talk in hushed whispers while their footsteps sounded hollow on the bare corridors. And they would look at everything enviously, marvelling that the owner never stayed there, even although she was a duchess.

It was a house, but no longer a home. It was a luxurious shooting lodge, a lifeless shell. It was the heart of a domain, and had ceased to beat.

The low thatched mansion of Colin Buie had given
life to the lands of Duisk and had drawn life from
them. But this lovely classic house, walled in so
forbiddingly from all around it, could only reflect the
setting sun from crimson tormented window panes,
like tears of proud appeal.

An alien thing when it had first been raised, Duisk
House was now rooted pathetically on Lochaweside
without the chance of effecting liaison. And its
owner, who bore its name and all that it represented,
had cut herself from its influence.

The elegant Duchesse de Sarge saw Duisk as a
means of income. In Somerset, Caesar Otway,
gradually ageing, saw it as a vanished dream ; and
in Bucharest Colin Otway saw it as a future down-
sitting.

The long-acquired habit of expectation would not
quite leave Caesar, resigned though he tried to be,
and every letter that came from his sister he read
hungrily for its news about Harriet. But Harriet
seemed always to be well. He would bite his lips
savagely, wondering why she wouldn't die. And he
felt with a sickness of heart that he was going to die
before her.

Everything that happened to his relatives was
galling to Caesar's frustrated ambitions. John Catta-
nach-Hamilton, who had sunk his father's peerage
in a marquisate of his own name, was a statesman
and politician of world renown, a cold, suave, polished
man with children to succeed him. And that was the
son of Æneas Cattanach, whose marriage had so
disgusted the Campbells ! The Princess of Zelle's
children he had never seen ; they were long since

grown, were middle-aged now and had passed far
beyond his ken, with grown-up families whose names
could be found in the Almanach de Gotha.   And as
for Harriet—she would be sweet and laughing in the
salons of Paris, shining at the Bonaparte court which
she had deigned to recognize, with scarce a thought for
Duisk ; Harriet, who had found his wooing so amusing.   His brow would darken then, and he would
reflect bitterly how little Duisk meant to her and how
much it would have meant for him.

Harriet, from Emmeline's papers, had supplied him
with his nephew's address, and Caesar got into touch
with him, a late sentimental tenderness for his dead
brother dictating his resolve.   In the years since then
a polite correspondence had been maintained by the
two Otways, although there was no immediate chance
of meeting.   Despite this show of friendship Caesar
could not restrain a feeling of jealousy against his
nephew, who was bound to inherit what he would
never.

The younger man had married in the summer of
1866, shortly before his appointment at Bucharest.
His wife, Clementina Hart, whose father was a retired
naval captain, bore him a son in the following year
who was named Colin, and, two years later, a son
Clement.

" There you are, mam," Caesar remarked with a
display of teeth, and threw the letter across to his wife.
" Plenty of children, eh ?   Damnation."

The death of the Princess of Zelle in the same year
saddened him greatly.   She was the living link with
a world which he had never seen but of which he liked
to speak, and his connection with which conferred

a certain éclat on him. None of the Zelle family
ever bothered writing to him, and he knew that
his relationship there was definitely ended. The
additional reminder that he was the last of his parents'
children filled him with melancholy.

These mournful musings were dispersed at one blow.

Elizabeth Zelle had closed her fashionable existence
before war broke out. When it did come there was
a check on social amusements that she would have
regretted had she been alive, and that the Duchesse
de Sarge, who still was active, did regret. Harriet
was in Paris when the Germans invested it. She
might have fled in time, but obstinately declared that
a siege was the one diversion she had never enjoyed.
Her taste was gratified in full, and in the ensuing
hardships her constitution, so long maintained by a
constant succession of interests, cracked.

At first Caesar was stupefied by the news of his good
fortune. He was now a man of eighty-two ; his lip
trembled, his hand shook, he smiled at Mrs. Otway
with ghastly pleasantry. " We owe the Bonapartes
a debt, mam. You are now Mrs. Campbell of Duisk."

His exultation was modified slightly by the full
divulgence of Harriet's affairs. Duisk, of course, was
his by right of entail, but the duchess, after the pay-
ment of all debts, had left little money, having latterly
converted her fortune into a settled annuity, and what
she did leave was bequeathed to Colin Otway, her
grand-nephew. From now on the lairds of Duisk
would be poor. But Caesar was not dejected. He
was Campbell of Duisk ! . . . although he was the
first to inherit not bearing the name of Campbell.

It was late autumn when the formalities were completed that allowed Caesar to assume his property. He then hastened with his wife to Argyllshire, having surrendered his Somerset home. After the forced journey he felt unwell, but his heart leapt at sight of the beautiful mansion and the thought that these piled-up acres were his. He had waited fifty years for them.

In pursuance of the entail's conditions he at once adopted the name of Caesar Otway-Campbell and matriculated his arms afresh, quartering Campbell of Duisk and Campbell of Uillian and Campbell of Barrill with Otway, of London. He conferred a fictitious animation on the place, keeping a yellow carriage with a pair of grey horses in which he drove about the roads, installing a gardener in the entrance lodge and retaining a cook and a couple of maids. And the house, now revealing the glories of its interior furnish-ings, grew warm and comforting. One who benefited greatly was the seventy-five year old Augusta, for her husband's manner to her was perceptibly im-proved, due to his change of fortune, and she found a great pleasure in being chatelaine of the fine mansion and Mrs. Otway-Campbell of Duisk.

" I've had a long wait for it," Caesar would say often, " and I'm hanged if I don't intend to enjoy it. I'm good for another twenty years. And so are you, mam, if you like to take the trouble." Occasion-ally he would walk with her in the garden, arm in arm, and she was pathetically pleased, and pleased also by any reference in the county press to Mrs. Otway-Campbell of Duisk.

The leaves began to drop, and the pathways and avenues were thick with russet and gold. A film of austerity was cast on the countryside : cold steel-like water, brown bare woods, stark hills. The days shortened, and were cold, and the flowers in the garden died. A new charm was revealed then, and it was heightened when the snow fell, and white drifts piled against the corners of the house, and a great hush was in the deep white-carpeted woods, under the white laden branches. Barrill stood redly out against its glistening background, and the loch looked very black. But the smoke rose from the chimneys of Duisk, and was comforting.

It was then that Caesar contracted a chill, having returned from a morning walk and omitted to change his soaked shoes. At first he made light of it, but his condition grew worse ; he took to bed and called in a doctor.

" Hang it ! " he exclaimed, looking about the apartment, which had been the bedroom of Sir Scipio. " I've never been ill in my life. I'll have to shake this out of my system, before the good spring days come in. Read me that letter Clementina has sent me."

The letter announced the death of Colin Otway at Bucharest, from cholera.

Caesar looked grave, and then after a little his features showed a measure of contentment. " I'm living them all out," he remarked. " Why, his boy can't be more than three years old. And I'll live him out as well, mam."

" Poor Colin," she exclaimed involuntarily.

" But, mark you," he said, " I'm putting up no tablet to his memory in that place over there. I'm not starting any more of that nonsense. No. But

I'll bury you there all right and put a handsome slab on you, I promise you that, mam.''

He turned much worse that evening, and Augusta and the cook Mary sat up by turns to watch him. At ten o'clock the bell was rung violently, and Mary, suspecting that something serious was wrong, answered it herself. Mrs. Otway-Campbell came out of the bedroom, weeping bitterly, and the kindly servant did her best to comfort her.

" Oh Mary," her mistress cried inconsolably, " I am no longer Mrs. Campbell of Duisk.''

BOOK THREE

DUSK

ONE

I

THE death of Caesar, the trident thrust again, signalized to Duisk the passing of the eighteenth century. Caesar, who had died in the age of railways and steamboats, had been born in an age of stage-coaches and sailing ships. He had remembered when men wore powdered hair and knee breeches and ornate clothing. Particularly with Duisk was his passing significant, for Caesar Otway-Campbell had talked with Sir Scipio Campbell, who had talked with Colin Buie Campbell.

With all the traditions, the meannesses, the quarrels, and the heroisms of the Campbells of Duisk he had been well acquainted. He had learned much about them from his mother and her father, and the rest he had discovered for himself. He had known much about Colin Buie's children, and General Don, and the Leitch relationship, and being an inquisitive man had unconsciously absorbed much family lore that had undoubtedly aided his desire to inherit Duisk. One or two things he had never known. He had been unaware of the identity of Do'l Mor's murderer, for only Peggy and Emmeline and Drumgesk had ever known that. And Admiral Colin and Drumgesk had never communicated their suspicions about Sir Scipio's children to anyone else. Nor had Caesar ever suspected; if he

371

had, he would have felt defrauded of his rights indeed.

With the death of Caesar all touch with the past was lost. The Cattanach-Hamiltons had become English, just as Caesar had become Scots ; they were a great family now, and the name of Campbell was merely a genealogical link to them. The descendants of Elizabeth Zelle were foreigners. Colin Otway, the child who was now the laird of Duisk, was a stranger in everything but descent, and only one-eighth of him was Campbell ; his father had never seen the place and had known none of his paternal connections ; the grandfather, the first Colin Otway, had cared little for the Campbells at the best of times and had early severed his connection with them.

The new owner, therefore, when he grew to manhood, would own an estate together with a family tree that could tell him nothing vital. Whatever intimacy would arise between him and his acres would be a thing acquired and not inherited, and to counteract that possibility was the alien education already in store for him.

Mrs. Clementina Otway had suddenly become a woman of increased importance, as mother of a landowner with a long minority before him. Immediately on her return with the children to England she journeyed north, and was impressed, delighted, by the place and its surroundings. Augusta was still there, reluctant to take her final departure, although comforted by the annuity that she would draw from the estate in future. Together they went over the house, talking and speculating.

" It is a lovely place," said Mrs. Augusta Otway-

Campbell wishfully. "One could live here for ever. And there is so much accommodation."

"Yes," agreed Mrs. Clementina Otway, "I am sure you will be sorry to go so soon."

The old widow surrendered then to the young widow, retiring to the south of England, and Mrs. Otway remained with her children. Burdened as it now was with Augusta's allowance, Duisk gave sufficient revenue for comfortable living, for the maintenance of a governess for the children and the retention of a carriage and servants. A small alert woman with the movement and eyes of a marmoset, Clementina grieved deeply for her husband, whom she had loved greatly, but she did not deny that providence had now become good to her in her thirtieth year.

She remained there until August, departing before the arrival of the shooting tenant like all the Highland lairds, with folded tents, and journeyed with the children to London. She intended to return when the season was over, and meantime renewed acquaintance with her own connections. Mrs. Otway did not return. In London she obtained the social intercourse which was not to be found at Duisk, and gradually the thought of going back there grew distasteful to her. The imposing mansion called her for a time, but she turned her thoughts away.

In the south was the stir and interest to one city-bred, as she was. The future education of the children had to be considered, and the appropriate school for the young Otways could only be found there, she believed. It would never do to keep them as savage barbarians on Lochaweside, growing up

ignorant of the polite usages of society, and she had
since discovered that Highland landowners of importance preferred English schools for their children.

So the young Colin and Clement in time took their
walks with their nanny in the open spaces of London,
and for holidays were removed to Worthing, a place
in which Mrs. Otway had implicit faith.

They stretched, were sent to school, grew more,
and went to college. Several times they were taken
north, and liked the house, especially the elder lad,
who was proud of the estate that he would control
on his coming of age, when he would assume the old
surname. He had designed to enter the army, as
had his brother, and Mrs. Otway had granted the
wish, although reluctantly.

No changes happened in these years at Duisk, for
there was little that could change. The hills and
lochs of Glassary—them man could not alter, nor
could he alter the sun and the sky. On the Loch
Fyne side of the parish there was industry with the
herring fishing, but on Loch Awe the world was quiet.
The seasons passed in their solemn dignity, and life
passed with them. The old traditions among the
people were being forgotten, and the old language
laid aside. The cities of the Clyde were attracting
the youth of the district ; the men to the shipyards
and the ocean-going vessels, and the girls to domestic
service. They left with regret, uprooting themselves
from their ancestral shores and valleys, but there
was no work for them at home. The old folk were
left behind in loneliness, and their humble homes,
when they were finished with them for good, fell
derelict. The nettle grew within the roofless walls,

and in the garden patch without the currant bushes
were choked by weeds.

On the twelfth of each August the banging of guns
was heard over all the parish, over all the county,
over all the land. The sportsmen had arrived, if
the people had gone.

Amid all these mutations the hills and the lochs
were changeless.

II

' An interesting ceremony took place on Tuesday
at Duisk House when Mr. Colin Otway-Campbell,
the young laird, who recently attained his majority,
was presented by the household staff and the tenantry
with a suitably inscribed gold watch and cuff links.

' Mr. Hector MacDonald, Uillian, the oldest tenant,
in handing over the gift on behalf of the subscribers,
commented on the friendly feelings which the Campbells of Duisk had always maintained to those on
the estate and the affection with which they were
regarded. He wished the young laird many years
in which to enjoy his possessions.

' In returning thanks, Mr. Otway-Campbell expressed his appreciation of the gift and announced
his great pleasure in being in their midst that night.
He regretted that circumstances had prevented him
being as often at Duisk as he wished, but the
home of his ancestors was always in his thoughts.
(Applause.)

' After the ceremony luncheon was served, when
the Rev. Angus MacNeish, in proposing a toast in
honour of Mrs. Otway, remarked on the long connection of the Duisk family with the district. During

all that period their watchword had been " Duty,"
and Mrs. Otway had nobly performed hers in super-
intending the early years and education of the
gallant young gentleman who was now taking control
of his ancestral estate. (Applause.)

' Mrs. Otway, in a neat little speech, gracefully
referred to the enthusiastic tokens of goodwill
observable on every countenance.

' Toasts were also proposed by Mr. John Mac-
Millan, Strone ; Mr. Angus MacCallum, the Lodge-
house ; and Mr. Dugald MacPhee, Post-office.

' The function concluded with the singing of " God
Save the Queen." '

III

Between his coming of age and the close of the
century Colin was twice at Duisk. He was abroad
on garrison duty, and his furloughs had been spent
mainly in England. Mrs. Clementina Otway suffered
much from rheumatism ; on one or two occasions she
had journeyed north, subsequently blaming Lochaweside for aggravating her ailment, and latterly nothing
would induce her to return thither. She was content
to know that Duisk was there, awaiting the final
retirement of her son, and meantime supplying him
and her with an income augmented since the demise
of Augusta.

In both her sons was a lack of stamina that Colin
Otway the first had not inherited but which Colin
Otway the second did inherit. Clement was a fair-
haired, fair-skinned and sentimental young man with
blue eyes that projected slightly, and his mother's
alertness of manner had not descended to him. In-

stead, he was languid, a natural attribute enhanced
by an affectation of manner that he considered distinguished, for Clement was aware that his grandmother had been an actress, and instead of finding
romance in that as some young men would have
done, he was thoroughly ashamed of it, preferring
the satisfaction derivable from his great-grandfather
Otway's military rank and Waterloo death, and from
his Campbell ancestry. There he gained the liveliest
pleasure, particularly in remembering that his dead
father had been a full cousin of the Zelle family. He
was sometimes sorry that it had not been necessary
for him to assume the Campbell surname, like his
brother. He was plain Otway. In the circle of his
mother's and his own friends—which was that of the
lesser official class, for the Otways had no acquaintances among the landed families—Clement would
introduce the great names of his foreign connections
with ill-concealed triumph.

"My father's cousin, Princess Elissa—yes, she
married the Duke of Rothenburg, yes;—yes, their
daughter is Princess Sangenheim, yes; of course,
she is my *half*-cousin only . . . yes."

Mrs. Otway with pleasure and mortification commingled learned of her elder son's approaching
marriage. Colin had met his future wife in India,
where her father held a command. The wedding
took place in the summer of 1897, in which year the
young laird's regiment returned home, and in a
pretty Berkshire church Victoria Dangerfield became
Mrs. Colin Otway-Campbell.

The best man was Clement, now a lieutenant in
the army, and one of the maids of honour was

Albertine Higgins, a friend of the bride. They met frequently at the newly-married couple's house.

Her own ill star or her lack of strategy had always militated against Albertine's secret hopes, and she had passed her nineteenth, twentieth, twenty-first, and even her twenty-eighth birthday without any man taking any particular interest in her. She was quite pretty in a fashion; she was always well dressed, and her tall, very slender figure showed her clothes to reasonable advantage, but neither at balls, nor croquet parties, nor at any of the recreations graded between, could Albertine hold the attention of a man. The realization was at first puzzling, and then she brooded over it bitterly, and at last grew quite forlorn. And she told herself with piteous self-analysis that their neglect was inexcusable, as she had always been ready to encourage their interest —which, indeed, was the reason for Albertine's isolation, for she frightened them with far too much encouragement.

She was an expert in needlework; she could crochet charmingly, and make seaweed pictures and flowers in wax, and she was very expert on the piano, her principal achievements there being ' The Battle March of Abyssinia ' and ' The Battle March of Delhi.' She sang with feeling : ' Juanita,' and ' Love was once a Little Boy,' and ' O Merry Goes the Time When the Heart is Young,' all out of the Globe Song Folio.

" Please play that little bit again, Miss Higgins," Clement would say enthusiastically, " It's awfully stirring," when Albertine would be rendering ' The Battle March of Abyssinia.' Thereafter, whenever

he was present, Albertine would play the part called
' King Theodore's March' thrice before proceeding
further.

Albertine liked Clement at once and unswervingly.
It was her nature to do so—she was quite willing to
reciprocate any gentleman's honourable affection,
and although discreet inquiries had made known that
he had no prospects other than what his military
career could offer, Albertine reminded herself that
she had none either, being one of a vicar's eight.
At least, if Clement would come to the scratch she
would not go to her grave under the slur of spinster-
hood.

Clement was a shy young man, so shy that
Albertine's persistent frontal attack had not alarmed
him as it had more wary contemporaries, and for a
time, while cherishing a fervent admiration for her,
he had thought so slightly of his chances with Miss
Higgins that he did not dare propose. But every
time he appeared Albertine was ready with ' The
Battle March of Abyssinia ' and a host of questions
about military matters on which she declared that
he alone could give her satisfaction.

" Bertie's making a dead set at Clemmy," Colin
remarked thoughtfully to his wife.

Victoria asked if something should be done to
hasten affairs.

" No fear," said Colin decidedly. " Bertie's carrying too many guns as it is."

Clement and Albertine were successfully wed in
the spring of 1898, and in the following year a son
was born to them named Colin Albert Clement Otway.
The initial Christian name was the father's choice.

"I want to give you the honour, old man," he told his brother with friendly satisfaction. "It was really through you that I met Bertie. Great Scott! I can hardly believe that a year ago I was never thinking of marriage, and here I am, a husband and a father!" Clement seemed quite bemused. "I was quite scared when I proposed to Bertie," he confessed, "for I know she was never thinking of me. But she was wonderful, by Jove!"

A century was drawing to its close and bringing up the past in retrospect. A hush might have fallen upon those closing years, as it does on the final minutes of any departing year, and the nineteenth century, ushered in amid the storms of warfare, would have been sped in an hour of peace. But there was not peace, and both Captain Otway-Campbell and Lieutenant Otway found themselves at the close of an era in South Africa.

Those were anxious years for the women of the family. Mrs. Clementina Otway, now in her sixties, aged perceptibly; she had never been reconciled to her sons' desires for an army life, and had hoped for peace in their time. Valiantly she read the papers, and would make pathetic suggestions to her relatives about ways in which the conflict could be shortened; and all her confidence in Roberts and Kitchener was not unalloyed by the feeling that she could do much better herself.

It was with relief that she learned of the stoppage of hostilities and the safety of Colin and Clement. With greater relief she heard of her elder son's decision to retire. He had been promoted major, had been mentioned in despatches and been decorated for gallantry. He wanted now to enjoy the seldom-known pleasures of his country estate. Old Mrs. Otway was overjoyed. She journeyed north with them for the express purpose of initiating Victoria into her Highland home. Clement and his wife were meantime proceeding to India.

IV

The tenant of the Duisk farm was Angus Mac-Lachlan, a man between thirty and forty years of age, and his wife was Mary MacDougall, a Kilninver woman. They had two children, John and Christina, aged four and two respectively when the new century dawned.

Little Jochkie and Kirsty lived in a world circumscribed in one fashion and boundlessly remote in another. Their first impressions had been of the spacious farm buildings erected by Sir Scipio Campbell for his personal gratification ; to them this world had been big enough. It was enlarged when they grew old enough to make little expeditions to the shore with their black cat Maisie, and there they would potter about happily, much to the disgust of Maisie, who preferred beiking herself in the wide quadrangle at the farm.

In time they went to school, some distance away, and tramped there patiently, but without much enthusiasm, through sunshine, and rain, and foot-deep snow. It was a small school, with a motherly middle-aged woman as teacher, and there were only fifteen pupils in it, although once there had been sixty. Jochkie and Kirsty liked Miss MacEachran and Miss MacEachran liked them, but the children

were always pleased when four o'clock struck and
they could go romping to their home among the
fields and trees.

They saw a huge jumbled countryside around
them, but they encountered very few people.

" Miss MacEachran is saying that there are over
four millions of men and women in Scotland," the
little girl told her mother disbelievingly, " but there
are not many atween Ford and Sonachan."

Any grievance that was hers for this was not
experienced by Jochkie, who had discovered that
school, at any rate, can furnish friendships.   For him
it furnished Neil Campbell, the son of the Duisk
gardener and lodge-keeper, and the two lads were
very close with one another.   They ran about together happily.   Neil was a dark curly-haired boy
dressed in a jersey and a grey tweed kilt.   The fair-
haired Jochkie wore a jersey and shorts, and both
boys were bare-footed.

" Jochkie," the one would demand earnestly to
know, " when you're a man and grown up, what
would you like to be ?   I would like to have a farm
of my own and have white horses, and a dogcart
to drive about in."

" I would like to go to Australia and make a great
amount of money, and then I would come back and
be the laird and live always at Duisk," replied John
with conviction, for he had grand ideas.   John took
the milk up to the Big House ; he was familiar with
it, he had conceived a great passion to live there
some day.

Sometimes he encountered the laird, or the laird's
wife, or both of them ; and he would glance up at

them shyly, touching his peak to the lady, and trot
on, wondering what it felt like to be great.

He profoundly admired the major, who always
smiled pleasantly to him and said : " Well, Jochkie ! "
with an abrupt but warm tone.   He thought it must
be wonderful to be a laird, and walk about in knicker-
bockers with a Clumber spaniel at your heels, and be
tall, and have a prominent nose, and sunken cheeks,
and a fair moustache.

" Who is that fine gentleman ? " he would imagine
someone saying, and could also imagine the reply :
" Oh, that is Mr. John MacLachlan of Duisk.   He
was in Australia and made a million pounds, and
bought Duisk from Major Otway-Campbell, and he
lives there with his father and mother and sister and
his friend Neilie Campbell."   And he would have a
horse to ride on, he decided, and prance along the
road on it, and be a perfect terror to tinkers.   Or
perhaps it would be discovered that he was the
major's nephew and that his mother was a long-lost
sister of the major's who had been stolen away by
tinkers, and then in course of time he would inherit
Duisk in a perfectly natural manner.

Occasionally his ambitions stunned him, and left
him very forlorn.   They were so tremendous in his
own admission, for he did not imagine there could be
greater houses than Duisk, and could not believe
that the King's palace was any bigger.

But his love for Duisk was tremendous also.   He
was always thrilled when he climbed over the stile
that led into the private policies ; his way then led
through a path between fine grown firs, and then past
a patch of parkland to the burn, and then round by

the rear of the garden to the back door, where
smiling rosy-faced Meg MacGregor would say : " It's
you, Jochkie ! " and maybe give him a jam piece, or
an apple, or—perfect felicity—a handful of preserved cherries.   He loved the policies of Duisk : the
fine big trees and the fir beltings, and the golden
sunshine that slanted through the leafage on to
thick lush grass.

Sometimes he met Mrs. Otway-Campbell, who
wore marvellous raiment and large shady hats with
sweeping feathers, and was wonderfully perfumed,
and always followed by two little Pomeranians, a
white and a brown one. Mrs. Otway-Campbell
would stop him, and ask how he was getting on at
school, and did he like it, and how his sister was,
and his father and mother, and how old was he now.
And he could scarcely answer, so abashed was he by
that beautiful high and sweet voice.   He would
stand by the roadside, awed, as the barouche of Mrs.
Otway-Campbell swept by with gleaming wheels,
two foam-flecked dock-tailed horses prancing with
spirit in spite of the bearing rein, a sallow-faced young
footman sitting on the box beside a red-visaged
coachman.

It was wonderful.

And then, in each July, the laird and his lady
went away to England, and the shooting tenant
arrived, and Neilie and Jochkie would be employed
as beaters when the guests were driving over the
grouse moor. The major and his wife would not
return until April, and he would hear his father and
mother talking among themselves about them,
although for a long time he was uncertain what they

could be meaning. He could not understand why his
mother spoke so pityingly of 'the poor major,' for
how could the major be poor, and why should he be
pitied ? And always his father would say at the end
with an air of finality :

"She'll spend him out of it."

What 'it' was, Jochkie could not comprehend.

"Mother," he said one day, throwing all secrecy
to the winds, "I'd like fine to own Duisk, and keep
you there, and have a carriage for you."

"Hear the laddie !" she exclaimed laughing, but
in a pleased fashion. "Well, son, if you can find
the money I'm thinking others will find the land
quick enough."

He was glad to hear her say that, thinking it
showed infinite confidence in his ability, and he
thought of her reply with a warm glow that day,
when he was playing with Neil and Kirsty by the
side of a little burn that was fringed with shelisters.

As they laughed and argued among themselves in
the warm July sunshine a great satisfaction stole
into his heart. He felt quite old, being now in his
twelfth year ; it would not be long before he was
making a great deal of money. Jochkie stood up,
looking over the surrounding whin bushes to the
great stately loch and its background of hills, lazy,
colourful, in the brilliance of the season. The water
sparkled, the sun glints shone on the long reeds by
the burn, and the air was full of the humming of
insects.

Then he saw the sight he loved. It was the Duisk
barouche, taking Major and Mrs. Otway-Campbell
home from their afternoon drive. The two spanking

B B

bays, their heads drawn back by the bearing rein, the glistening coachwork, the green silk green-fringed parasol of the lady . . . Jochkie stared fascinated. The equipage rolled towards Duisk, the dust settled on the white heat-cracked road.

" Mrs. Campbell has got four parasols," Kirsty said inconsequently, " and I've seen every one of them." She commenced singing loudly : " A parasol, a parasol, a bonnie bonnie parasol."

" My father says the Germans are trying to have a bigger fleet than ours," Neil commented.

On returning to Duisk Major Otway-Campbell had hoped to live there all the year round, with the exception of the shooting season. It would have been the first more or less permanent occupation that the house had known for over seventy years, with the exception of Caesar's short occupancy. He had badly required his mother's guidance at first, for his original feeling was of helplessness. He had been a foreigner in a lonely land.

Gradual acquaintance with the house and its associations, with the district and its traditions, had imbued Colin with a deep affection for Duisk. It became very intimate to him ; he cherished it as a possession of great value, he forgot that his name had ever been Otway and gloried in the name of Campbell. That great Argyllshire clan, so ambitious, so coldly acquisitive, also possessed the merit of transmitting a strain through the women of its race that was not quickly thinned.

The major was surprised that there was so little social intercourse in the neighbourhood, so unlike England. And the handsome Victoria Dangerfield found Duisk enchanting but dull. It was satisfying enough, perhaps, to own a great tract of the country-side, but the sacrifice of mingling with one's social equals was one penalty exacted for it. Mrs. Clementina Otway also thought so, for she had returned soon to London and stayed there.

But Colin became quite content to participate in the small functions of the district : bazaars, concerts, sales of work. His soldierly presence and courteous manners at these innocent gatherings was well partnered by the charm and courtesy of his wife, whose dresses were the awe and admiration of the countryside. No one within miles had horses like those in the Duisk stables, and when they became demoded Mrs. Otway-Campbell was among the first to own a motor-car. She was fond of jewellery, she was fond of excitement and amusements of all kind, she liked to spend the winter in London and then travel on the Continent before returning to Duisk. And she presented the bills for clothes and other trifles without comment to her husband, although, indeed, she never presented him with an heir.

" I don't think we can keep this up," he said once soberly.

" Can it not last our time ? "

He looked rebukingly at her. " Why ' our ' time, Victoria ? There are others to follow us."

" Just the Clement Otways," she said indifferently. " In any case . . . those Socialists and revolutionaries. There will be changes."

" I like to think I've been given a trust," he answered slowly. " After all, I'm just a life-tenant here."

" A life-tenant ? "

" Like those who were before me."

" Some of them didn't think that, did they ? " she asked sharply. " Your mother has told me that when Caesar Otway inherited he expected a great fortune, and discovered that the duchess and her aunt had squandered it all." She was indifferent to his protests, for she knew that his fine bearing masked a weak will. He might be a good soldier and a brave soldier, but the Campbell blood was flowing too strongly in his veins, and its virtues were allied with something else—with the accumulating decay that was the aftermath to generations of vigour, generated by gentle breeding and indulgence that had made the blood effete.

Victoria was quite fond of her husband, and admired his weaknesses as much as his virtues, for she felt she could well afford to.

The rents of Duisk farm and Strone and Uillian were raised, but the extra revenue seemed to make little difference.

" We've gone too far," he said haltingly. " We must retrench."

She regarded him for an incredulous moment. " I suppose we must," she said latterly. " We can sell Lord Drumgesk."

" Victoria ! " His tone was so pained that she felt sorry for him. " It's the best picture in the house."

" I know," she agreed. " It's a pity that Sir Scipio and his wife hadn't chosen a better-known painter. You should bless Drumgesk. Raeburns are valuable at present." She rose and regarded the

picture. Archibald Crubach's hard large features
stared down at her, his judicial robes falling from his
massive shoulders. " He was a handsome man," she
said absently. " He should be worth two thousand
pounds, at least."

" It's a wrench, Victoria," he said agitatedly.
" That picture's a treasure. It's a link with the
past."

" It's a mercy that the old spinster left it to Duisk
without restrictions," she murmured. " instead of
sending it after her money."

" She left the picture and the silver service."

" Was the silver service hers ? " Victoria asked with
interest.

The painting of the Crubach went, and so did
the dinner service ; and the proceeds of these sales
in time went, too. But Mrs. Otway-Campbell did
not slacken her spending. She was a natural squan-
derer, of the type that gets little value for their
extravagance. By 1910 what timber could be cut
down was felled, and in 1911 Colin found himself
faced with financial crisis. He told his wife so, with
unusual bitterness.

" I'm sure there must be a way out," she suggested
hopefully.

They had returned from the Mediterranean, and
Duisk, in these spring days, was at its loveliest.
His back turned to her, Colin gazed at the loch with
angry eyes. " I wish you would help me a little,"
he said.

The way out was found by the family lawyers.
Neither Uillian nor Strone had been included in the
entail of Duisk. Perhaps Sir Scipio had foreseen a

crisis when he kept these outlying possessions apart
from the larger property. They were put up by
public roup and sold, and the lands of Mor Campbell,
who had first set the family on the path of fortune,
passed from the family's hands for ever.

Despite her indifference to its future, Victoria was
fond of Duisk. She was proud of the old house, and
believed that residence there was good for her health
after the amusements of the winter season. She
hoped that Duisk would remain in the family as
long as she lived, at any rate.

Jochkie MacLachlan was now fifteen years of age,
and helping his father on the farm. As in any
country place, the news of the sale of the smaller
properties had aroused much surmise, and Jochkie
thought that Major Otway-Campbell was very
foolish to dispose of his land. His father smiled.

" Those big folk think they keep their affairs a
secret and that only a sale like that gives them away.
For years they have been selling everything in the
house that was valuable—pictures, silver, furniture.
They say that Mrs. Campbell's jewellery is false, and
an imitation of the real jewellery she has sold."

" If I had things like that," said Jochkie with
conviction, " I would be wanting to stick to them.
The major is very foolish."

" It is not the major. It is the wife. Tach!
What does she want with a French lady's maid, and
a footman, and a butler, and all those things. Before
she is knowing where she is she will have nothing.
But it is not that which is ruining them. She is a
gambler. And she thinks no one on Lochaweside
knows about it. The whole country knows about

it ! She gambles away there in France, where they
have public places for gambling, they tell me, and
she places her money against some number and she
loses it."

Jochkie sorrowfully suggested that the major
should stop her.

" He should ! " said his father, but the son was
too young to detect any cynicism. " The laird is a
good man and knows a horse inside and out. But
there are some things he isn't namely for."

" The minister was telling Neilie's father that the
Campbells have owned Duisk for nearly two hundred
years," said the boy with awe.

" Maybe," said the father. " And the Mac-
Lachlans have fished Loch Fyne for a thousand
years."

By 1913 Duisk estate was mortgaged.

Something like hatred against his wife was engen-
dered in the heart of Colin Otway-Campbell. His
long minority had made him a rich man when he
came of age, and his own mode of living, although
generous, would not have struck deeply into the
accumulated fortune. Victoria had gaily, idly, languidly, gone through all that. She had dispersed
the eighteenth-century treasures of the house, she
had felled its plantations, sold its auxiliary lands
—and what had she gained ? Nothing but the
memories of foreign gadding about and fevered
moments at the roulette table. *His* gain was thrice
bitter, for it was the acquired knowledge that, as
his love for his ancestral property had increased, so
had its adornments vanished. He had allowed them
to go, unable to check the careless extravagance of

the woman he had married, the woman whose vanity prevented her from giving birth to a child.

And even while he nursed a resentment most fierce because of its impotence, he was making preparations for their forthcoming continental trip.

They returned from it as they always had, his wife again enlivened and once more disillusioned, and himself poorer in heart and pocket. Lately he had told her that things could not go on as they were going. He had warned her repeatedly—exasperatedly, for she seemed quite unable to comprehend that her manner of life could in any way be altered. They would find money some way, would they not? she suggested brightly. She knew that Duisk was entailed, and the knowledge comforted.

" It is mortgaged," he repeated.

" Yes," she replied brightly, " but it is entailed."

What an empty-headed fool she was, he thought, and wondered why he had ever married her. He saw them, she heedless, he helpless, gaining celerity in their headlong progress down that slope of wastefulness ; he saw them, he, she, and Duisk, plunging into a final and irrevocable chaos of ruin.

In July of that year Mrs. Otway-Campbell made her usual preparations for departing shortly before the shooting tenant's arrival. But she was not destined to travel. For more than Duisk was involved, and more than Major and Mrs. Otway-Campbell, in a chaos of ruin immeasurably greater than that involving any Highland estate, and if not so final at least as irrevocable.

The major at once offered his services to the War Office, and was ordered south.

V

John MacLachlan, who was no longer called
Jochkie, and Neil Campbell joined the army at the
same time and for the same regiment. They were
both eighteen, and when war was declared they
enlisted as a matter of course. It was their duty,
they said ; their country was in danger.

At once they were thrust into a new strange world.
It was not so much among their comrades that they
found strangeness, for the Highland regiment in
which they were serving was composed of men
mostly of upbringing and antecedents similar to their
own. It was a battalion of crack men, clean in
wind and limb, and Celtic to the core.

The novelty came from without, and through the
eyes.

On a moor of gorse and sandy turf on the border of
Norfolk and Suffolk the battalion was undergoing
training for the battle front. There, in early morning, the sun slanted on the long lines of camouflaged
tents, the air was cold and aromatic ; to the far
horizon soldierly poplars stretched in squadrons that
grew mistier in recession. There was a charm in
waking to the teasing notes of ' Johnny Cope ' ; in
seeing so many hundreds of men around, in the same
situation, with the same sense of comradeship ; to
thrill, if detailed for special duty, at the sight of the
battalion morning parade and see the companies
marching severally to their drills, the hedged bayonets
glittering in the sunshine as the men wheeled and
counterwheeled.

It was a new experience, to be fraught in the

immediate future with danger, and at present rough, exasperating, humiliating, but enjoyable.

Lochaweside had been so lonely!

Darnham Cross Camp also was a lonely place, with nothing visible from its surroundings save the gilded dome of a mansion that had been built by an Indian prince, but in the canvas town that had been raised upon its sand was a little army, ten men to a tent, full of comradeship and health and good humour.

And in the evenings, after twelve hours' drilling, there was always talk about Argyllshire, for nearly everyone came from there, and the name was enough to bring a smile of pleasure to the face.

Two miles away was Graftonford, the small relic of a once-important town, with its lazy river that was so like the Crinan Canal, and its ruined abbey gateway, and its three fine churches, and the old coaching Bell Inn, impressive witnesses of the vanished ages. To the two young men, used to the white austerities of Ardrishaig and Lochgilphead, this redbrick village was at first revoltingly foreign, and latterly held for them a warm attraction. It was so neat, so trimly Dutch and spotless. And, when the battalion was on route march, little houses were passed by the roadside, red mellowed brick homes embosomed in roses.

The thoughts of Neil Campbell would revert then to the low white-washed cottages of Argyllshire, which he decided were far nicer. Yet those English houses seemed to be so much more comfortable, as far as personal comfort was concerned.

He loved the flat Norfolk scene, its screens of plume-like poplars, its lush meadows and bracken

wasteland. Neil would stand and gaze at the Little
Ouse, so placid that not a ruffle marred its surface.
A foreign country indeed! And then he would
think of the foaming torrents of his own country, and
the falls of Blairghour, and timeless Loch Awe, and
all his momentary disloyalty would fade in a spasm
of nostalgia.

"Those English," he said thoughtfully to John
MacLachlan, "know fine how to live. They all
seem to be bien and comfortable."

The friendship formed in boyhood had been
strangely strengthened during the months of training. They had made a host of other acquaintances.
They were on friendly terms with all the men in
their platoon; with those in their own section they
were yet more intimate. And this free and easy
intercourse with so many comrades was satisfyingly
complete, for it had not estranged them, drawing
them closer instead as the old bonds of affinity
asserted themselves. In their great mutual love was
the profundity of awe and gladness that a vast and
unexplored territory offers. There were constant
delights to be revealed, revelations of beauty to be
expected. And their love was all the deeper because
it was never spoken of, and because they were so
inarticulate. They would have been ashamed to
confess their feelings.

Theirs was to be the post of danger very soon,
and they looked forward to it, without foreboding,
but with a vague surmise. The risk was to be theirs,
so therefore they could disregard it. But those at
home, in a countryside bereft of young men, waited
with anguish for the day of embarkation, reading the

newspapers that the soldiers did not bother with, and finding in them a portent of the horrors that were waiting impatiently for their sons.

Whatever rigours John and Neil and their comrades would encounter were yet visionary, but the fathers and the mothers of John and Neil and their comrades were already suffering lone hells of agony and seeing no end to their forebodings.

For them the days àll passed in outward calm. They had their daily duties to perform, as they had always had. They saw few people ; the postman, an odd neighbour, an occasional aged tramp. In their hearts was the constant pain of anticipation, so familiar to the Celtic mind, as is the pleasure of the same.

There was the consolation of religion, to be found in the good Book and in the human heart. And to those people, nurtured among the hills and on a simple and trusting creed, a consolation was derived fleetingly from old immortal words. ' I to the hills will lift mine eyes from whence doth come mine aid '—words that have pierced to the heart how many generations, past and present, of country men and women, as, in their bare little kirks, they have seen the grassy slopes framed in the windows, heard the faint bleating of sheep ! Plainly apparelled, calm visaged, with no outward expression, no emotion visible—and with hearts torn by exquisite yearning, comforted by infinite trust.

In Argyll there had been fierce days, long past and still remembered. There had been clan feud and family resentment, and forlorn passion immortalized in scraps of song. In the blood of the Argyll people

—the highest evolved type of the Highland race—
there flowed the spirit of idealism and the spirit of
battle, mingled together. But the idealism was
stifled and incomplete, thwarted by the uneasy
manner of their lives. The aptitude for conflict was
now unleashed, but not at home.

Across the seas the guns roared and the battle
raged, more terrible than mankind had ever known,
as progress produced the flower of scientific invention.
The centuries had reached their nadir, and could
show how from the simple arrow and the primitive
spear had been evolved the grand terror of long-
distance guns, of submarine warfare, of death by
air, and the supreme magnificence of poison gas. In
these achieved triumphs the splendour of man was
sunk, and all his privileges. Battlefields : gigantic
whirlpools that sucked into their vortex the young
and the ageing, all armed, all uniformed, all shadowed
by the twitching shape of death ; all whirled into
maelstroms of roaring savagery whose reverberations
were heard in the lone outposts of Russia, in the
Swabian forests, in the vine-lands of the Angoumois,
and by the lone lochsides of the north. Until the
thunder would calm in time and the storm abate,
when those who had gone abroad could come home
again—such as were left.

TWO

I

NEIL CAMPBELL, before going to war, had
been apprenticed to learn motor-engineering,
and on his return from service he finished his time
at that trade. For a while he worked in Glasgow,
but he did not care greatly for that place, and five
years after demobilization he returned to his native
county. The countryside was being opened up in
a manner never dreamed of; Neil obtained a job
driving a bus, and settled in lodgings in Ardrishaig.

He was very happy there, as with the motor-
bicycle he had purchased second-hand, a run home
to his own people was an easy matter. He had
plenty of acquaintances in Ardrishaig, and numberless relatives to the fourth degree who could go
through the intricacies of genealogy in complete detail.
Every Saturday afternoon when his work was done
he left for home, where he stayed the week-end.

This Saturday in June was warm and tranquil.
As he left Loch Gilp and cut inland he was filled
with a sense of satisfaction which showed on his
serious, swarthy and sharp-cut features. He had
grown into a tall lithe man, active in movement,
with a quick eye and a slower smile. It was good
to be alive, he thought, as he neared Ford and the
head of Loch Awe.

After tea he strolled over to the farm-house.

Kirsty greeted him and asked him into the kitchen, where they sat by the fire and he lit his pipe.

"Mother is at Dalmally," she said in the tone used in speaking to a known friend. "She will be home on Monday."

He did not reply. The late sunshine was slanting horizontally through the window on to the big grandfather clock in the corner and the long range of tin dish-covers. On the window-sill a work-basket sat beside a great geranium whose flowers were blood-like in the setting glow. Through the open door was visible the plat of chuckie-stones on which some hens were languidly foraging before retiring, and beyond that the long sun-shot grass, and the bushes, and the loch.

Conjecture was in him ; he was thinking how long it was since first he had entered that kitchen. A long time, twenty-five years at least, and nothing was changed in it. The brass letter rack beside the mantelpiece was still there, and the alarm clock that would not go, and the big family Bible on the gate-leg table, with beside it the photograph of Uncle Donald MacDougall and the brass monkey he had sent from India. Nothing changed, surely, except man.

The atmosphere was drowsy ; he was lulled by the faint twittering of birds outside, and by the occasional mournful cluck of a hen, and the rustle of the bush that grew by the door. The peace was drenching. A black-and-white collie sheep-dog came in and recognized him. He stroked its head without speaking, and it lay by his side.

He looked intently at Kirsty, whose face was silhouetted by the glow from the fire. It was a calm, tranquil face, the hair drawn back from a high forehead, the eyes peaceful, the lips clearly made and firm. She wore a light print frock, fresh and clean, and the hands folded upon it were strong and beautifully shaped.

Aware of his scrutiny, she turned her head and looked at him. For a moment they stared so, and then she said : " It was good of you to remember, Neil. Mother was pleased."

He murmured some deprecatory words, and to cover his awkwardness picked up the newspaper that was lying on the table and read what he had already read elsewhere.

' MacLachlan.—In loving memory of our dear son and brother, Private John MacDougall MacLachlan, —th —— Highlanders, who was killed in action at Arras, on the 24th June, 1917, aged 21 ; also our dear husband and father, Angus MacLachlan, who died at Duisk Farm, on the 7th July, 1918.
> ' The trial was hard, the loss severe,
> To part with them we loved so dear ;
> We cannot, Lord, Thy purpose see,
> But all is well that's done by Thee.

Inserted by their sorrowing mother and widow, and by Kirsty ; Duisk, Lochaweside.'

' MacLachlan.—In constant memory of Private John MacLachlan, B Company, —th —— Highlanders, killed in action at Arras, June 24th, 1917. ii Samuel, Chap. i, Verse 26. Inserted by Neil.'

" It is nothing," he said in a hollow voice, and pushed the paper away from him. " Will you be taking a turn ? "

They walked to the highway, talking slightly. It

was pleasant there, beside the ferny banks and hearing the glucking water. They went down to the shore and stood gazing across to the shadowy castle of Barrill and to the crimson torment of sky at the back of Lorn.

The beauty of the evening fell upon their hearts.

" Poor Jochkie," he thought.

A motor horn startled them, and they turned to see a long low car nosing its way round the corners. In it sat an elderly woman, two young women, and a man. One of the young women was driving.

" There's the Campbells home from London," she said. " They wrote me they were coming, for they wanted me to find them a kitchenmaid. Mary and Annie arrived at the house this afternoon."

With the curiosity of the countryman he asked whom she had obtained.

" It is Martha Smith, poor soul. She is just sixteen, and her mother has had a terrible time with a big family. Her husband was a rascal, and left her. It was through my aunt at Dalmally telling me about them, and I thought it would be a fine chance for the girl, especially as she has not had as good an upbringing as other girls."

On their return she poked the fire into a blaze and set the kettle on. " The shepherd's wife is coming in for supper, and she'll be glad to hear all the news of Ardrishaig."

" I saw the advertisement of Duisk."

" Yes," she replied, and there was a note of regret in her voice. " After all those years."

" My father was saying that Mr. Campbell will be loth to part with it."

" The last time that they were at the Big House he called in here as usual, and he was telling my mother that the taxes are far too heavy. He was very sore about it. And they've been economizing, too."

" They don't know what economy is."

" And the estate was so hard hit during the war when no one would lease the shootings. And then there was an annuity to come off it for the colonel's widow, although she loses that now that she's married again. And they couldn't get a shooting tenant last year. It's a shame."

" They economize by giving my father a poor wage, and by cutting down their subscriptions to the local charities, and by letting the woods and the house go to wreck and ruin. But Mr. Campbell has his sports car, and Mrs. Otway has her London house and her big car, and they have a chauffeur for these cars, and Miss Campbell has her two-seater and is dressed to kill at any time, and if they would cut their expenses there they could talk of economizing."

" Still, Neil, they'll be sore at having to part with Duisk."

" They're only proud of Duisk because of the position it gives them, and because it supplies them with money. I used to think fine sentimental thoughts about them, too, before I went to the war and saw a bit of the world."

" My word," she exclaimed, laughing, " you're becoming a revolutionary, Neil, to say things about the Campbells of Duisk. And you a Campbell yourself ! "

" And that's more than they are, Kirsty. You'll
mind yon box of chocolates I brought last Saturday. It was tied with a tartan ribbon. Yon tartan
would be made in Switzerland, and it was just as
Highland as the folk up at the Big House. The
Campbells of Duisk are only playing at being Highland . . . although I'm sorry about Mr. Campbell's
arm. There are plenty of jokes and scoffs about
the Clan Campbell, but they were the finest clan
in the Highlands, and it doesn't matter if they were
greedy and grasping and all the rest of it, they
always stuck by one another. And the Campbells
of Duisk would be like that at one time, too, or there
wouldn't have been so many great people in their
family. But now ! . . . I'm a Campbell, Kirsty ;
a real Campbell. And I'm proud of it. My folk
have never been away from Argyll. We've been in
Argyll all through the centuries, and I'm determined
to stay in Argyll. I won't go back to Glasgow,
and I won't emigrate to please anyone. This is my
country, and I'm biding here.

" I don't like to meet any of the Duisk family
when I'm staying here. They're nice enough people,
but they're condescending. You know that they
think they're something above you. And why should
they think that ? The very name they're using isn't
theirs. They're not even as kindly in their manner
as the colonel, who was a good gentleman and died
like a man, as Dugald Dewar saw and can tell you.
They don't know what the Highlands mean. They
think they're Highland when they wear a tartan kilt
or a tartan skirt. They babble about the clan spirit,
but if my father Donald Campbell dared to contradict

Colin Otway-Campbell he would find himself out of a job. They say clan spirit and they mean servility. They don't mean to be nasty, but they don't realize, they don't understand."

" My, Neil, you're on your high horse now ! "

" They drove all their people off the land to make way for deer and make more money. And now they find that money is tight with sportsmen as with everyone else, and their deer aren't valuable unless someone is wanting to kill them. And when their land is taxed they set up a great howl, and talk about the loss to the Highlands of the old families, and wonder what will happen to Argyllshire then. After they've squeezed all the money they can get out of Argyllshire ! And they say they don't know what will happen to the people if the landed gentry have to go. It's a wonder there were any people left after the landed gentry were finished with them. They talk about the old families and the landed gentry and seem to think they are the same thing. When the landed gentry have gone the old families will still remain. You belong to one of the old families, and so do I, and so do most of the people in Argyll.

" I know that Scotland isn't England, and hasn't such good ground. But if you could see how many people can live in the English countryside, and compare it with here ! And we've got to have a quiet countryside so that the grouse and deer will not be frightened ! I used my eyes when I was in England, and poor Jochkie and I used to talk together about things, and when I was in Glasgow I got a chance to read books about the Highlands that told me things I never knew before, and had never imagined.

"I used to think the Campbells of Duisk were wonderful people, because they were gentry, and educated in England, and had no Gaelic, and spoke with a strange accent. And I thought at that time that I must be a third-rate kind of Campbell because I was poor, and poorly dressed, and because my father and mother always spoke to me in the Gaelic. I was ashamed because we spoke the Gaelic.

"But I know better now. I'm a Campbell, a real one, like my forbears.

"If Mr. Campbell was worth his salt he'd sell his motor-cars and buckle up his shirt-sleeves instead of going about complaining of the hard times. Every-one is having hard times. He's no exception. And he and his family will want for nothing. His sister is selfish and heart lazy, and will do anything in this world except work."

"But, Neil," she protested, "that's not fair. I wonder what Mr. Campbell would say if he knew that his lodge-keeper's son was talking like this! Mr. Campbell is a fine young gentleman, and he lost his arm at the war when he was Lieutenant Otway. And you couldn't get anyone nicer to speak to than his sister Elissa. At least she's always very nice to me, and last time she was here she came over to the farm, and asked me what I thought of her new jumper. It was beautiful."

"I know," he said with a touch of weariness, "they're all right enough. But in the long run they think they're a cut above such as you and me. The idea's ingrained into them. If they could only realize that it's the like of us who are pure bred. But I don't think they'll ever do that. I don't like the idea of being considered an inferior being by anybody, and the folk up at the Big House think that. In any case, I work for a living, and Mr. Campbell does nothing. The whole countryside is decayed, and the people don't know where to turn for a living, and Mr. Campbell and his like are doing nothing to better it. If they are the leaders of the county, as they claim to be, they wouldn't sit twiddling their fingers and lamenting the taxes. They would try to do something."

"And what would you want them to do, Neil Campbell?" she cried stoutly. "Would you want to turn the country into a playground for ignorant outsiders, like those Lancashire people I saw last summer in the Pass of Brander in a bus, wearing woollen tammies that were an insult and blowing on tin trumpets? Do you want to bring crowds of hooligans from the cities, to start works and build factories and make the place a ruin with their filthy swearing and drinking? Or do you want to build huge hotels and run railways up the Cruachan Ben, the way that they have done in Switzerland, as I know from pictures? Or do you want to organize winter sports for wealthy idlers who have nothing better to do, and have all the newspapers praying for snow like fools and never thinking that the native Highland farmers may be losing their sheep if it comes? If things like that were done I would go to America."

"I want to see Highland people on decent-sized Highland crofts, as they should have been long since.

I want to see the countryside thick with poultry farms. I want to see quick communication with the big towns for the transport of dairy produce. I want to see the Lochfyneside fishermen properly protected on their own ground by the Government instead of starving of hunger because the trawlers are allowed to steal their living. Our fishermen won't swallow their pride to take the Government dole, and the Government shows its gratitude by not protecting them! The peat in the hills could be worked to give hundreds a living. If they could set about it, the people in this country could make a living by selling eggs and honey alone . . . and I question if there's one skep of bees between Campbeltown and Ballachulish."

" Well, and whose fault is that ? "

" Maybe the bees would frighten the grouse. Here's the shepherd's wife coming."

II

" Oh, good morning, Donald."

The lodge-keeper turned round slowly—he was getting on in years—and saluted the young laird. " It is yourself, Mr. Campbell," he said. " It is a fine morning."

" You're all alone, I see," Mr. Otway-Campbell remarked. " Neil usually comes home at the week-end, doesn't he ? "

" He is away to church with his mother and the farm folk." Donald glanced politely at the girl who was with the laird, and Mr. Otway-Campbell said :

" Miss Anson is an old school friend of Miss Elissa's.

Donald has been with our family for a very long time, Hester."

"How do you do," Miss Anson said with a stare and a smile.

"You will be liking Duisk, I am sure," said the old man courteously. "I am sure you will be thinking there are few places like it."

Miss Anson laughed shortly, and so did the laird. "It is lovely," she conceded.

"How is Margaret, Donald? And Neil? Oh, that's fine. I'll be seeing Margaret to-morrow, I expect." Colin bade the old man good morning, and he, standing in his patch of garden, admiringly watched the progress up the shady avenue of the slender dark-haired girl in the knitted suit and the tall thin young man whose empty left sleeve was tucked in his jacket pocket.

"Who is Margaret?" Miss Anson was asking without preliminaries.

"She's the old man's wife."

"Thought maybe she was his daughter. Nice old man. Looks as though he had a will of his own. He's all hairy about the ears."

Colin said reminiscently: "He used to hunt me out of the garden when I came here as a kid to visit Uncle Colin and Aunt Victoria. I used to eat the gooseberries. He's a Campbell, like myself. He's a fine old chap, very faithful and very friendly."

"You inherited him with the house."

"And I'll have to lose him along with the house."

"Those eighteenth-century houses are very restful," she said, as Duisk came into view.

"I wasn't greatly struck by it at one time. But

it seems a shame now to part with it, for my family built it."

" Put up a fight for it."

" I can't. Even if I do get it sold, there are a lot of burdens that will have to be cleared off. It's lucky that Elissa is the next heir, for the breaking of the entail. I hope someone buys it soon. Things are getting desperate."

" Desperate, Colin ? "

" I mean that we're near the end now. And it's rotten for mother, and for Elissa, as well as for myself. It's those taxes. If I do get it sold I'll have to try some sort of business investment, and I know nothing about business. I've very few friends to help or advise me. And a one-armed man is no use to anyone in this world." He gazed down at the alert eager face rather forlornly. " No use to anyone," he ended abruptly.

" I don't know about that, Colin."

Mr. Otway-Campbell paused and took out his cigarette case. The girl placed a cigarette in his mouth and then put a match to it. She had an attractive face, with a pale skin and a flush of colour in her cheeks, and she looked up at him, laughing.

" Inferiority complex, Colin ? "

" I think I have. And, to crown everything, some anonymous hound has sent me a copy of a Socialist paper that's giving what it calls exposures, and it says we stole this estate. *Stole* it."

" Well, write to it, Colin, and give proofs that it was purchased."

" I've no proofs that I know of. It was granted to the family, I believe."

"That's perhaps the same as theft," she said with some shrewdness. "You'd better not write, Colin."

"I'm sorry it's likely to be your last visit as well as your first."

"Elissa also was saying that things were pinching."

"Was she complaining?"

"Hardly."

"There are other families in the same boat."

"Elissa was talking about looking for a job."

He was surprised. "Is there anything she thinks she can do? Elissa never discusses these things with me."

Miss Anson again laughed up to the face of her host. "She is talking of becoming a dancing instructress."

The young man frowned. "That's not a very high ambition."

"It's a fashionable ambition, Colin. And Elissa's a wonderful dancer. She knows all the latest dances."

"I can't stop Elissa if she wants to do a thing. She's twenty-three, and should know her own mind. I wish she would try to think better. If we're going to London for good, there's no need for Elissa to start and act the fool there."

"Babs Charleston—you've heard of her—Elissa knows her quite well, and——"

"I'm not interested," he said quietly. "People like us are doing our best to keep our place, with outsiders trying to pull us down. And some of our own class do their best to help them. If that's the limit of Elissa's ambition the sooner we're out of Duisk the better."

In the house they found Mrs. Albertine Otway
and Elissa reading novels. It was their main recreation .at Duisk. Elissa, who had preferred to alter
her surname along with her brother, was alike him
in appearance. They had the fair hair, the blue
eyes of their mother, but an indecision frequently
noticeable in the man was not apparent in his sister.
Elissa's features were sharper than his, and her
glance so direct as to seem impertinent. Nor had
her speech any trace of the mother's languid manner.

Life held no terrors for the laird's sister, although
it sometimes offered disappointments. She had
realized that all her future must depend on a successful marriage, and she much preferred living
where men were plentiful than in the solitude of
Duisk. The death of Major Clement Otway in
Gallipoli had been followed by that of Colonel Colin
Otway-Campbell in Flanders. Victoria had then
been required to vacate Duisk, and the mother and
daughter had spent some weary periods there which
latterly had been acutely worrying when the young
Colin Otway neared military age. They had then
retired to London, at which period Colin gained his
commission and was sent to the front. During the
last month of warfare the nineteen-years-old lad was
seriously wounded ; he recovered, minus an arm,
and for several years lived with his family on the
south English coast, near old Mrs. Clementina Otway,
who was living to a ripe age in a small house at
Eastbourne attended by two serving-maids almost
as old as herself. Mrs. Clementina Otway had drawn
a certain income from the estate all these years. Her
sons' deaths had been tragic blows to her, but she

had recovered with the lapse of time and was more or less prepared to live all her relatives out.

Albertine and Elissa had found the old lady's dictatorial ways trying after a time, and had removed to London, where the young girl felt that she had found her spiritual home. She was fond of company and amusement.

And there Mrs. Otway would say : " My daughter, Elissa ; she is named after my father-in-law's cousin, the Duchess of Rothenburg, who was the Princess Elissa of Zelle." She had learned this habit from her husband.

Yet, although the mother and daughter cared little for the house in Argyll, a sense of awe descended upon them when they realized that it soon might no longer be the family home. They returned this year with a sense of regret, as one does with an old friend taken for granted whose departure brings a wrench to the heart. And, at Colin's suggestion, they had invited Hester Anson, Elissa's old school friend.

It was perhaps this certainty of eternal parting, the snapping of the link giving them status and distinction that made them more alive to the traditions of the house than at any time before. And during the week Hester was shown over the house, having pointed out to her the few objects of art left in it by Victoria Dangerfield. Colin obligingly drew the guest's attention to a quaint family tree in the library.

" I have the same name as the first of the family," he said, pointing at it. " Colin is the family name."

" What does ' fiar ' mean ? " Miss Anson inquired, peering closely:

" I've no idea," he confessed. " But I could find out if you want to know."

" Oh, don't trouble. Don—Leitch—MacTavish," she read aloud. " I think that's a lovely name— Cydalise Cœur-de-roi. A Frenchwoman ! "

" Do you know, some antiquarian discovered lately her name in a list of guillotine victims in the French Revolution. It's a mystery. Of course, if she was in France at the time, a woman of Lady Campbell's position . . ."

" What a shame ! "

" Emmeline left all her money to endow a home. I'll perhaps be glad to get admission to it some day."

" Your family tree has got very thin, Colin. Just like a spinning top. Only Elissa and yourself."

" That's right ! Elissa and myself," he said with sudden bitterness. " And when Elissa goes her own way I'll be left, without my house, and with a string of names that mean nothing, and without an arm, and without a single friend in the world."

" Do you know, Colin," she said sweetly, " you are a proper ass. You keep on talking about having no arm and no friends. You have called to see me so often, and yet you will always term me Elissa's school friend. It was you who told Elissa to ask me here. She told me that in confidence. Now, Colin, we'll settle the business now. I certainly shan't refuse if you care to ask me."

His face twitched, he looked at her with pathetic eyes. " I can't ask you. It wouldn't be fair to you . . . although I'd like to."

" Why wouldn't it be fair ? " she asked calmly.

" My arm, and the muddle I'm in——"

" I never thought," she said rather forlornly,
" that I'd ever live to make a proposal to any man.
It's carrying woman's emancipation much too far."
" You'll marry me, then, Hester ? "
" Right-o."
They stared at each other for a moment, slightly
embarrassed, and then she suddenly threw her arms
around his neck and kissed him.

III

" Duisk is bought, mother."
Mrs. Otway turned to her son and regarded him
with stupefaction. " Bought," she echoed.
He fingered nervously the letter he was holding.
" Yes—and sold.   Well, it's all over now, I suppose."
The mother looked around the room in an incredulous kind of fashion.   " It's very unexpected,"
she said vaguely.   " Of course, it's what we're
wanting."
Colin sat down and expelled the breath from his
lungs with a rush.   " And that's the end of an old
song," he said.   " Yes, by private purchase," he
added in response to her question.
" How much are we getting for it, Colin ? "   He
told her.   " That's not very much," she said grudgingly.
" I suppose I'm lucky to find someone willing to
buy it.   We would have got three times as much
eight years ago.   Morrison writes me that this Mr.
Angus Fletcher has a family connection with the
parish.   His people were at Cairnbaan—you know
Cairnbaan.   He's very rich.   He made a fortune in
Burma.   Wish I'd gone to Burma, mother.   Well,

it's sold, anyway. And he wants to be in here by
Lammas."

"Lammas ? " she asked helplessly.

" August, mother.   Oh," he exclaimed in a sudden
burst of anger, "I wish I could keep my estate.
This is a place in a thousand. It's a place that
Hester loves, I know. When she and Elissa went
away on Thursday . . . I saw that Hester was sorry
to leave this place."

" Elissa was sorry, too," Mrs. Otway murmured
loyally.

" Elissa was quite relieved to get away. She's
not interested. She goes back to London as though
released from jail, and all that will interest her is
her share for consenting to break the entail. She'll
be quite happy just now."

" Of course, Colin——"

" I think we're done," he exclaimed with weakly
rebelliousness. " We're played out, and exhausted.
We don't seem to have any ambitions left. Elissa
has none, and neither have I. No wonder we can't
keep Duisk. This chap Fletcher has been abroad
and made a fortune, and now he's able to enjoy
the house we built, and the woods we planted . . .
and he deserves to. The Campbells started off all
right, but it's one thing winning battles and another
opening bazaars, and water always sinks to its own
level. If times had been better we could have put
up a fight for it. What's the use now ? I come
into a place up to the ears in debt, with a new load
of taxes every year and the ill-will of half the people
in the kingdom. People are asking what I and such
as I have done to justify our positions. Well, we've

always been willing to spill our blood for our country
. . . but I suppose they have done that as well.   If
the place had been sold before I came of age, before
I had ever returned here, I wouldn't have minded.
But Duisk has got a hold on me now.   I'm not
wanting to part with it.   I want to keep it, for your
sake, for my own sake, for Hester's.   But I can't.
Well, anyway," he ended wearily, " I'll instruct
Morrison to make the final arrangements for disposal,
whatever they are."

" Of course, Colin, we can't keep it up.   It's
impossible, and——"

" I know, mother.   But the feeling remains that
for a couple of centuries we've been here, that one
man got a grant of Duisk, and another built the
house, and they loved the place, and improved it,
and hoped that it would go down in the family for
centuries.   And they were a keen lot—you only need
to look at the chart and you can see that—and then
it comes to me.   And I'm parting with it ! "

" Your Aunt Victoria Dangerfield is a wicked
woman," Mrs. Otway exclaimed with unusual vehe-
mence.   " She helped to ruin this place and would
still be an annuitant on it had she not married Sir
Luis Miranda.   First the wife of a gentleman and
now the wife of a Jew.   And Lady Miranda had the
insolence to write and ask me for the Sheraton escri-
toire as a keepsake when she knew we were selling
out !   She must have overlooked it, or it would have
gone to Dowell's with the rest.   She's a wicked
woman."

" I suppose I was lucky enough to inherit anything," he said languidly, " as I wasn't born a Camp-

bell. If we had villages on the property with a
good tenantry things wouldn't be so bad. Tenantry
means a steady income. And ever since Uncle Colin
sold the part over at Kilmichael we've had to depend
almost completely on the shootings. Well, they've
failed us also. I can never understand why the
Highland people have such a craze for emigration.
There are the ruins of quite a few villages on the
estate, and they would provide a decent [rent-roll
to-day. The Highland people have such an absurd
craving to go abroad. It doesn't give the landowner
a chance." He did what his mother had done; he
glanced around the room, absorbing its height, its
light spaciousness, its symmetrically-placed windows
and Adam mantelpiece, with a sense of bewilder-
ment.

Albertine's fair faded features had shaped into an
expression of disconsolate sympathy, but she was
not quite certain what to think of his late born
affection for the place. He had not always been
so obviously attached to it, she thought with some
surprise, fumbling for a suitable rejoinder, and was
quite heartily pleased to hear a tap on the door
and see the matronly figure of the cook. " Yes,
Annie ? " she asked benevolently.

The servant advanced silently, and, as she approached, Mrs. Otway was alarmed by the grave
expression on her face. " What is it, Annie ? " she
demanded feebly. " Has something happened ? "

" It is something very serious, Mrs. Otway," said
the dark woman, gazing from the laird to his mother
with a world of regret in her manner.

" Has anything happened to Miss Elissa ? " Mrs.

D D

Otway exclaimed with sudden apprehension. " Oh,
Annie ! "

" What is it, Annie ? " Colin asked with some
impatience.

" Miss Anson's brooch has been found, Mrs. Otway."

" Oh, I'm so glad ! " Mrs. Otway exclaimed rap-
turously. " Have you got it, Annie ? " The cook
handed her the brooch, which was of gold with turquoise inlay. " Hester mentioned that she had lost
it, Colin. It is of no value, she said, but she treasured
it for sentimental reasons. It was her mother's.
How lucky it has been found ! We are awfully
obliged to you, Annie, and I'll tell Miss Anson that
you found it. Where did you find it ? "

" What did you mean when you said it was something very serious, Annie ? " the laird asked.

The servant looked from one to the other hesitatingly, distaste and indecision on her usually tranquil features. " It is not a very nice business at
all," she said latterly, " and I would never have
mentioned it had it not been for Miss Anson's brooch.
There was never anything like this happened at
Duisk before. Well, Mrs. Otway," she said reluctantly, " there's a thief in the house."

" A thief ! "

" Isn't it awful, Mrs. Otway ? "

" Who is the thief, Annie ? " Colin demanded,
astonished.

" It's like this, sir, that Mary lost some silver
that was in her purse last Wednesday, and she couldn't
think where it could have gone to, for she was certain that it should have been there. And then on
the Friday there was a ten-shilling note I had left

on the top of my table to take with me when I was going to the post office, and when I went to get it it was gone too. I thought that maybe it had blown off, for the window was open and there had been a good breeze. But by that time Mary had missed the silver brooch that had been her mother's and that she wouldn't lose for a kingdom. It was all very queer. And then, within the hour, I saw Martha coming out of my room where she had no business to be, and I just jumped to the whole business and yoked on her about it, and after denying it for a wee while she admitted the whole business. Never the like of it was known."

" Martha ! ' "

" Yes, Mrs. Otway ; Martha."

" Oh, Annie," Mrs. Otway cried incredulously, " this is terrible. A thief in the house—living in the house ! I—I—oh, I don't know what to think."

" Martha ; that's the young girl recommended by Christina MacLachlan at the farm ? "

" Yes, Mr. Campbell. She's the Dalmally girl."

" Isn't this dreadful, Colin ! It is scandalous," Mrs. Otway exclaimed tremblingly. " And to think that she stole Hester's brooch. Goodness knows what else she has stolen. I'll have to go over my things. And that she is working beside respectable girls . . . Annie, this is a case for the police. Send for the police, Colin. The girl is quite abandoned. I'm surprised that Christina MacLachlan got a girl of such a class for us. It is most inconsiderate. Most inconsiderate. She deserves no wages. What do you think, Annie," she said appealingly ; " don't you think this is a case for the police ? "

" She has had a very poor upbringing, Mrs. Otway,"
Annie replied apologetically, " and, indeed, her people
are little better than tinkers now.   But she seemed
quite a nice lassie, and is a good hard worker, and
I think it was maybe because she has so very little
in the way of finery that she was tempted.   It will
be a terrible blow to her mother, Mrs. Otway," the
cook pursued earnestly, " because Kirsty told me
that she is a good woman who has suffered a great
deal from her rogue of a husband."

" But the girl's a *thief*, Annie."

" Kirsty MacLachlan thought it would be a fine
chance for her, getting into a place like Duisk.   It
is a pity Martha has been so foolish," Annie said
respectfully.

" It is a case for the police," cried Mrs. Otway
indignantly.   She studied the brooch that she held
in her hand with wide-eyed astonishment.   " How
can we possibly explain this to Hester, Colin ? "

" How old is this girl, Annie ? "

" Sixteen past, Mr. Campbell."

" Colin, it's scandalous," Mrs. Otway exclaimed
hysterically.   " The more I think of it.   Such gross
ingratitude.   What do you propose doing in this
horrible matter ? "

Colin looked hesitatingly from one woman to the
other.   " It's most unfortunate," he murmured.

" It is, Colin !   But, of course, if Christina Mac-
Lachlan recommends girls of that class for our service . . .   I could tolerate almost anything, I think,
except theft.   It's most degrading.   It's so utterly
low and mean.   And we must protect ourselves.
We have to protect Annie and Mary.   We have to

protect your own future wife. Why, it's ridiculous. You'll have to do something, Colin."

" Of course I will," he said reluctantly. He glanced at his mother, surprised at her sudden and violent indignation. She was usually so languid. Aware that both women were awaiting his opinions or commands, he shuffled his feet awkwardly and coughed.

" I don't think this is a case for the police, mother."

" I don't agree with you, Colin."

" The girl has stolen nothing from you or me, mother. She stole Hester's brooch, and we've got it back. She has stolen from Mary and Annie. I don't know Mary's opinion, but I'm sure Annie doesn't want a prosecution. Do you, Annie ? " he asked appealingly.

" Certainly not, Mr. Campbell," she said firmly. " And Mary won't either, I'm sure."

Colin looked relieved. " It would only give the house a bad name," he ended lamely.

" And what do you intend to do with this thief ? " Mrs. Otway demanded. " I have nothing against the girl personally, but it is the principle that matters. Robbery should not be encouraged. Slackness is the cause of half the troubles nowadays. I'd give no mercy to thieves."

" Oh, mother, you can't expect me to have a kid of sixteen jailed, can you ? "

Mrs. Otway dried some tears with the corner of her handkerchief, for she was quite upset. " If you are going to harbour thieves in Duisk House, Colin, we may as well introduce them into the family," she moaned.

"Annie, we won't want you for a little. Where is the girl at present ? Very well, send her up."

"I don't want to see that girl," his mother interrupted quickly. "It's not your place to have anything more to say to her."

"Someone's got to see her," he said glumly. "Thank you, Annie."

They waited in a nervous silence after the cook had departed, and the young man, observing his mother's agitated condition, immediately regretted his resolve. Shortly there was a little tap at the door. "Come in," he called in what struck him at the time as an extra loud tone.

The door was opened, and a little thin girl entered the room, and there stopped. Her hair was reddish fair, of the kind that is dry and colourless from exposure to all kinds of weather, her skin was brick-coloured, her eyes very grey. Her features were both nervous and ferret-like, and at present were tear-begrutten with fear and shame. She was neat in cap and wrapper.

"Close the door, please," said the laird, "and come here."

Martha did as he bade her and stood before him, gazing at him with eyes of terror as though expecting immediate sentence, and Colin half turned his head from the light and thrust his twitching fingers into his pocket, feeling his heart throbbing the while.

"You have been stealing ? " he asked.

She said Yes, with a gasping outrush of breath, keeping her eyes fixed fearfully on his.

"You stole Miss Anson's turquoise brooch ? "

"Yes."

" You stole money from the other two servants, and a brooch from one of them ? "

" Yes."

" Have you stolen anything else ? "

" Yes," she whispered.

He glanced rapidly at his mother, and saw her triumphant nod. " What else ? " he demanded irritably.

" I stole the wee fox in the library," she said in an almost inaudible voice.

" The paper weight," he said blankly.

" Do you not know to address your master as ' sir ' when you speak to him ? " Mrs. Otway asked spitefully.

" Yes, sir," she said.

" Is that all you stole ? " Colin asked.

" Yes, sir."

" Did you realize when you stole——"

" Where is the silver fox ? " asked Mrs. Otway.

" I put it back again," said Martha, and commenced to cry.

" Do you realize the serious nature of your actions ? " Colin resumed. " You have been introduced here with a good reference from the young woman at the farm. You have shamed her. You have been the means of throwing suspicion on the other servants, you have introduced crime into this house. This is very serious. Do you realize the seriousness of what you have done ? "

" Yes, sir."

" Do you understand that a crime of this nature is punished with imprisonment ? "

Martha sobbed hopelessly.

" I think she might have sufficient respect for you as to answer your questions," Mrs. Otway interposed.

" Yes, sir," Martha answered shakily.

" You realize all that ? "

" Yes, sir." Martha's agitation suddenly became paroxysmal. " Oh, don't send me to jail," she cried pleadingly. " Oh, I'm not wanting to be sent to the jail. Oh, you'll not be sending me to the jail," and her voice wailed away on a note of bitterest anguish.

Colin regarded the forlorn figure with irresolution. " What was your reason for doing what you did ? " he asked.

" I don't know," Martha sobbed.

" You don't know ? " Mrs. Otway cried, scandalized. " Colin ! "

" You must have had a reason," Colin pursued, " and I think decency should compel you to tell us. No one steals without a reason."

" I—I was needing the money," the girl confessed, turning a piteous face to him, " . . . and I wanted the other things."

" Why ? " demanded Mrs. Otway pertinaciously.

" Because they were so pretty," Martha whispered, " and I wanted them."

" Well ! " said Mrs. Otway.

Colin contemplated Martha in silence. " You have been a very bad girl," he said at last, " and I hope this will be a lesson to you. I hope it will be a life-long lesson. Theft is a terrible crime. A girl of your age shouldn't know what theft means." He stopped, and Martha dazedly rubbed her knuckles against her eyes.

" Do you hear Mr. Campbell speaking to you ? " Mrs. Otway asked with enjoyment.

" Yes, sir."

" I have decided what I am going to do——" Colin began.

" Oh, please don't be sending me to the jail," Martha cried appealingly with a fresh gush of tears. " It will be in all the papers, and my mother . . ."

" No, no," said Colin hastily. " You won't be sent to jail. But let this be a warning to you. You are dismissed from Duisk. Do you understand ? "

" Yes, sir," said the miserable girl.

" And I cannot give you a reference."

Martha stood, with heaving bosom, making odd little gasps and choking noises. He looked at her with a feeling of compunction. " I am not giving you a reference," he repeated as though she was disputing with him. " I hope you will be more careful in future."

" Do you realize how kind Mr. Campbell is to you ? "

" Yes, mam."

" And that you are being given another chance in life ? "

" Yes, mam," said Martha faintly.

" Leave the room," said the laird. When Martha had gone he said : " Thank Heaven that's over." He was surprised to see that his mother was as much upset as himself, surprised when comparing her agitation with her interpolations.

" You acted very firmly, my boy," she remarked wearily, " although you should have pointed out the great advantages she was gaining by service in our family, and which she has lost through her own wickedness. I can't understand what Christina Mac-Lachlan was thinking about. That young girl resembles a little tinker. I feel sorry for her, but one must be firm."

He laughed suddenly, throwing his head back. " Perhaps Christina was giving her a chance at our expense, just as I'll have to look for a chance at someone else's expense. I'm glad I never thought of studying for the Bar."

The excitement caused by this diversion gave Mrs. Otway a subject for conversation all afternoon, and she was still talking about the fine opportunities the girl had thrown away of acquiring a good training in their household when the newspapers arrived. " I see," she remarked idly, " that someone else is going to risk his life on an Atlantic flight. That girl Smith will be regretting her folly very deeply by this time. It's most remarkable the way those war debts are always——" Mrs. Otway suddenly gave a little scream, and fainted.

IV

There had been general satisfaction over Colin's engagement to Miss Anson. Elissa's friendship with Hester was very sincere, and her delight consequently great. Mrs. Otway had been unfeignedly pleased that her son, despite disablement and crippled prospects, should have won so nice a girl.

" And where did he propose to you ? " she had inquired with irrepressible curiosity. " In the library ; what an odd place, really. And were you surprised, Hester dear ? "

" I can't remember. He just did it *all of a sudden*,"
Hester had explained simply.

Colin had been dazedly pleased. He had been
very fond of Hester for a considerable time, but
would not have ventured a proposal. Fortunately
for himself, he had spoken his inmost thoughts so
often and so unconsciously that she had felt thoroughly
justified in assisting him.

On the Saturday evening following the announcement Kirsty MacLachlan, with a woman's intense
interest in such matters, detailed the news to Neil.
" She is a very handsome young lady," she said
delightedly.

The word ' lady ' jarred Neil. " Was she speaking
to you ? "

" Yes, indeed ; and the maids at the Big House
think the world of her, she thanked them so much
for looking for the brooch that she has lost."

" She's not getting much of a catch."

" I'm sure if she likes him she'll not be caring.
And Mary MacAnsh tells me they're very fond of
each other."

" He'll be a man of thirty now. It is time he
was getting married."

" Yes, and you're thirty-two, Neil Campbell," she
cried, laughing. " But there are no signs of you
settling down, I'm thinking."

" Och, I've been thinking about it," he said casually.

" We'll all be subscribing for a wedding gift," she
remarked with pleasure, " and we'll have to think
of something nice for them."

Neil smiled cynically. " They will be hurrying
this marriage for fear someone buys Duisk, so that

they'll be sure of their present. And Miss Campbell—it's a wonder she can't get a man for herself,
and her present forbye."

" Miss Elissa could have been married long ago.
She told me so. Only she will need a husband with
plenty of money, as she deserves. She went off to
London on Thursday with Miss Anson, but I hear
they're both coming back very soon. Miss Elissa
is bound to make a fine match. They say one of
the family married a duke."

" They won't do that nowadays. But duke or
not, she'll have to get her present."

When they next met, Kirsty was in a state of
great excitement, due to the downfall of Martha
Smith. She felt directly responsible for the thefts.
She was torn between compassion for Martha and
responsibility to the Campbells—indeed, she had gone
to Mrs. Otway offering her regrets for her protégée's
ingratitude, and had received but slight exoneration
from that person.

" We had *so* depended on you to find us an honest
reliable girl," Mrs. Otway had said, with a smile.

Kirsty had returned to the farm conscious of
rebuff, and inwardly admitting that she deserved it.

" Martha is a little monkey," she remarked without resentment to her mother. " She is just a little
monkey, poor wee soul that she is. I might have
known better than to have got her into Duisk, and
I don't know what Mrs. Otway or the laird can be
thinking of me."

She viewed theft with honest horror, like all her
race, and the thought of Martha would have weighed
heavily on her for long enough had it not been dis-

pelled by the news of the sale of Duisk. Her mother
and she discussed the certain departure of the Campbells with a feeling of awe ; there was tragedy in the
knowledge that a family so long rooted in the district was about to leave it for ever, about to leave
the fine avenues they had planted, and the hills they
owned, the house they had built. The two women
had little time for rest in the farm duties they had
shouldered when the father died, but for a time it
was devoted to bated speech about the Campbells
of Duisk, their former greatness and their imminent
self-imposed banishment. Kirsty loved her native
district with a religious passion ; she could conceive
of no other existence so desirable as that on Lochaweside, and was consequently heartfelt sorry for
the laird, his mother, and his sister. They had
always been very amiable and pleasant to her, and
Colin and Elissa would often enter the farm-house
kitchen for a talk, as their dead uncle the colonel
had done. Certainly, she realized, they had not
been conversations based on a social equality, but
they had been friendly and agreeable. Kirsty felt
that she would be lonely once the Campbells had
departed. " I'm sure the house itself will be sorry
to see them go," she said.

" Donald MacKillop always said that the house
was haunted by one of the family who was a great
general, but he'll see none of his relations after this,"
the mother answered. " A maid at the Big House
thirty years ago swore she saw the ghost—a big
proud man in a grand uniform, walking down the
stairs."

" Well," said Kirsty, " and I'm not the one to

disbelieve it. I wonder what like the new laird will be."

" It's yon big thin gentleman who saw over the house the week before the Campbells came home," Mrs. MacLachlan answered. " A fine-looking gentleman, and they say his forbears were Glassary people. He's a Fletcher, I was told."

" There's Neil," said Kirsty, pleased. " My, he's got on a new pair of boots, for I can hear them squeaking. He's becoming a great swell, surely."

Neil came up the incline from the road, smiling broadly. " There's some sweeties for your mother," he said, handing her a box as she met him at the door.

" Oh, thanks very much, Neil. What nice boots ! But you know my mother never cares too much for sweet things."

" Och well," he said with finality. " You should have been in Ardrishaig to-day," he went on. " There was a big crowd off the *Columba*. A lot of the local folk are home for the holidays. You should have seen them. The buses for Tayvallich and Kilmartin were filled in no time, and there was a good crowd bound for Lochgair."

" It's wonderful," she said. " And you'll be ready for a cup of tea, Neil."

" I'll not say that I'm not," he answered, following her into the kitchen.

He talked with Mrs. MacLachlan while Kirsty set the table. It was the customary procedure. The mother regarded him with a peculiar liking, inasmuch as he had been the close comrade from boyhood to death of her beloved son. She saw in Neil Campbell a memento, a reminder of the dead Jochkie, the souvenir of a shade. Nor were Kirsty's feelings any less warm, although their course was diverted and reinforced by other thoughts. From one week's end to another she looked forward to the visit of the lodge-keeper's son.

"I wonder what will happen to your father, Neil," Mrs. MacLachlan said inquiringly. "Will the new laird be keeping him on, I wonder."

"If he doesn't I'll take care of my father and mother," he said tranquilly. "Although they will maybe not be too keen on going to Ardrishaig."

"I hope he'll be a good laird and not start raising the rent of the farm," Kirsty remarked.

"It would suit him better to start reducing it," said the young man. "It's high enough as it is."

"Well, we can't be blaming Mr. Fletcher for that. I hope he will be a good laird."

"He'll just be like all the rest," responded Neil. "He will start making fine promises, and before the year is out he will be like all the lairds in Duisk before him."

He spoke lightly, but something in his tone vaguely irritated Kirsty. She thought : he pretends to consider himself the equal of the Otway-Campbells, but he does not despise them at all ; he dislikes them, and makes himself their inferior by disliking them. And he doesn't realize that. Aloud she said : "Well, Neil, the Campbells at the Big House will be going away soon enough, so you will be quite pleased."

"If they had any decency they would have gone away during the week," he said quietly.

"And why ? And Miss Anson and Miss Elissa will be returning——"

"If Miss Campbell has a sense of shame she will never come near Duisk House again." He smiled with provoking enjoyment at their questioning looks. "Do you not get any of the papers here ?—any of the city papers ? "

"No, we do not, Neil, for there is never any news in them. We only get the *Oban Times* and the *Advertiser*."

"Well," he said, "read that," and threw a newspaper on the table before them.

v

In olden times the quickest way to Duisk from the Lowlands had been by Loch Lomond and through Glen Croe, round Lochfynehead to the county town, and thence by Glenaray to Loch Awe.

The steamship had changed that, the approach being made by sea from Glasgow to Ardrishaig, and then by a coach through the valley of Kilmartin. But with the coming of the motor-car the northern approach had again been adopted, and it was by the old way that Elissa and Hester Anson returned to the house of Duisk some weeks later.

They had motored from London. As the car swung through the arch at Inveraray and up towards the wide stretches of wind-swept glen, Miss Otway-Campbell's lips tightened. But she only remarked : "I've an appetite like a horse."

The evening sun was deep upon the hills as the car slipped past the Place of Kneeling. Cruachan's topmost peaks were glittering ; the islands dreamed upon the azure loch. They dropped down to Port Sonachan, and to the road beside the shore.

No others were on the road. There was a hush around that the car did not dispel. The white tails of rabbits bobbed convulsively among the bracken ; in the woods of Eredine there was a silence as of death. And all along the route they drove in sunshine, with the cool air of Loch Awe to fan their cheeks.

" I could live here for a lifetime, I think," said Hester.

" Well," said Elissa, " you'll be here for a few days at any rate."

She steered into the north avenue, along where the firs were giving heavy scent, and stopped the car on the terrace. Colin came out to greet them.

" How's mother ? " Elissa asked. " Oh, dear me, she shouldn't worry. I ?—oh, I'm all right, thanks." She walked into the house, leaving him with Miss Anson. " Well, mother," she said, and kissed Albertine affectionately. " You shouldn't worry."

Mrs. Otway commenced to weep, and her daughter turned an apprehensive glance backward. " Never mind, mother. I'm here in the flesh. You shouldn't have worried."

" I wanted—I wanted to go to London," the mother protested apologetically. " But Colin said I could never stand the journey. He was most solicitous. He said I was far too much upset."

" You'll stand the journey all right next week, mamma darling—you'll have to," was the calm response. " Colin would be fed up to the teeth with me, by his way of it." She smiled, scrutinizing her brother and future sister-in-law, who were mounting the steps. " Colin would be ashamed and disgusted, and all the rest of it. Never mind. I've some things here I want to pack before we go for good. What a pile of publicity!" She left her mother and ran lightly up the stairs, humming a tune.

The poignancy of parting with his property was alleviated to some extent with the laird by the presence of Miss Anson. In an uncomfortable world he found her friendly and sympathetic. For her sake, of all people, he regretted the loss of Duisk, but her very presence lightened his sorrow even while reviving it.

For a time there was a constraint on all of them which Elissa alone could break, and she did break it on the following day with characteristic abruptness.

"I suppose all the people in Argyllshire are gloating over this affair," she said, when they were all present after lunch.

Mrs. Otway murmured some weakly response. "Never mind, dear," Miss Anson said loyally, "Mrs. Otway and Colin understand, I'm sure."

"I'm out something for legal and medical fees," Elissa pursued regardlessly, "but, of course, I'll pay that from my whack of the purchase money. It's a nuisance, all the same . . . just when I was going to be in funds." Her glance swept over them with the swift appraisement of a hawk. "I know you're both dying to know. Aren't you, Colin?"

"Please yourself, Elissa."

"It was a dreadful affair—really dreadful, darling—such an ordeal," Mrs. Otway exclaimed distressfully. "Such an experience . . ."

"It was, mother."

"But we knew there was some terrible mistake. We knew that, of course, Elissa. And that's what we want to know, Elissa dear. I was so anxious to be with you, but Colin . . ."

"I know, mother."

"I daresay you felt best able to fight for yourself, Elissa."

"That's right, Colin."

"There wasn't much use in mother or myself barging into what was really your own private affair, was there?"

"That's right, Colin."

"And, in any case, I felt that it was no concern of mine, although the newspapers always took care to mention that you were my sister."

"Didn't they just, Colin!"

Hester interposed, distressed. "Elissa, I will explain the whole business——"

"You weren't there."

"I was in the court, Elissa. I'll explain the whole thing to your mother and Colin . . . later."

"Colin wants to know now," replied Elissa with a smile. "Plenty of clan spirit, eh! He wants the full details without the cost of travel. Did you not read the papers, Colin?"

"I read them all," he answered bleakly.

"One Sunday paper had a photograph of Dusk. It was an old photograph, showing us all at the door . . . how they got hold of it goodness knows."

Mrs. Otway began to cry.

"Mrs. Otway, you must go to your room," Hester declared, seeming to be perilously near tears herself.

"No—no," said the mother weakly.

" Mother wants to hear," Elissa exclaimed. " Colin wants to hear also, in spite of all the newspapers."

" You're not well enough," Hester protested. " You're excited, Elissa."

" Of course I'm not well . . . I've enough doctors' certificates to paper the room." Elissa's glance flashed from one to the other, returning always to her brother. " I thought you'd have been man enough to back me when I was facing the music, anyway," she burst out suddenly. " You could have come to London, at the least, Colin."

" To be interviewed ? "

" Oh, you're a coward," his sister cried angrily. " Mother, I'm sorry about this . . . I'm beastly sorry." Mrs. Otway, down whose cheeks the tears were rolling rapidly, made a gesture of maternal love, and the girl on an impulse kissed her. " I couldn't help it, mother. I couldn't. It was all done before I knew what I was doing. And then a horrible man tapped me on the arm . . . I was asked to go to the manager's room, mother . . . I'd to open my bag and produce the beastly thing . . . I didn't mean to take it, mother ; I didn't. It was agony, mother. Oh, it was such a humiliation," she exclaimed with a sob. " And they'd take no excuses, no apologies. I said it was a mistake, that I meant to pay for the beastly thing. They wouldn't listen —said they'd had far too many cases like it before. Oh, mother ! And then they called the police— imagine, they arrested me ! " Elissa laid her head on her mother's bosom and the two sobbed together hopelessly. Colin sat white and silent, with his gaze on the floor, and Hester stared from one to

another with an anguished glance. " Imagine,
mother !—the police. They arrested me, and I'd to
tell them who I was, and where I lived, and . . .
oh, it was too dreadful. And then I was afraid to
write at first ; I wanted to write, and I was afraid
to write until I saw that the whole business was
to be made public. And Colin never came. He's
a brute, mother. He's so unforgiving. He's not a
man at all, or he would have imagined what I was
suffering. What's family pride compared to family
decency. And the agony of the whole business ! . . .
And the people staring like a lot of gloating animals.
. . . And I was so worried all the time because
I knew what you were suffering. And Hester was
an angel. And then Doctor Langmaid and Doctor
Surenne questioned me and knew I hadn't really
stolen, hadn't really intended to steal—they knew
it was a temporary . . . that I wasn't really a thief.
And everyone thinks I'm a thief, mother, and all
the time I'm not. It was horrible—and the publicity—and the photographs. And Colin has been such
a callous beast . . . not even a post-card." Elissa's
voice was rising higher ; she seemed to be on the
verge of hysteria, her breath was coming in gasping sobs and she clung tightly to her mother. " Oh,
it was terrible . . . and then they proved that as
I had means and was educated I couldn't possibly
be a thief, because I could only have stolen the
beastly thing if I hadn't had money to pay for it,
and the doctors explained that I had Neurasthenic
Kleptomania and that I wasn't a thief at all. And
I was acquitted. Oh, mother darling, the shame of
it ! . . . and the papers all full of my name, and

yours, and Colin's, and Duisk. And Hester has been such a pet, and such a decent pal, and not ashamed to let people know she was my friend. And Colin has been *such* a cad. And here am I with Neurasthenic Kleptomania . . . perhaps for life."

Colin alone had dry eyes, but his were hot, and there was a lump in his throat as he mumbled that he didn't imagine it had been as bad as that. " I wish I'd gone to you," he said shamefacedly.

" Oh, I forgive you, Colin," Elissa sobbed in fresh abandonment.

" Poor, poor Elissa," Mrs. Otway moaned, while Hester tried desperately to comfort both mother and daughter, with an arm around the neck of each. " Poor, poor Elissa," Mrs. Otway continued to repeat. " My poor dear darling. Oh, my poor child, whatever made you take that horrid watch ? "

" Because it was so pretty," Elissa answered in a voice of anguish. " And I wanted it."

Albertine and her daughter had both reached such a condition of nerves that their retirement was a matter of urgency, and the laird and his fiancée were left gloomily alone. Colin, conscience-stricken by the late scene, poured forth his regrets, and Hester, fresh from consoling the mother and the daughter, now devoted her energies to comforting the son.

" I was angry," he confessed remorsefully. " It was such a blow to the family pride. I wish she hadn't tried to pinch it until we had left Duisk."

" It will soon blow over," she answered philosophically. " In any case, these things are done without thinking. They're done on the spur of the moment, and aren't really crimes."

" I don't know," he said glumly. " If she'd wanted
to steal she should have stolen on a big scale, and
she'd have got off with it. If we came into Duisk
by theft, as we're accused of doing, it would be better
if we cleared out of it with something better than
the theft of a gold wristlet watch."

VI

Already some of the household effects had been
sent south ; others would follow in the wake of the
family. The remainder were to be sold.

Of late, Colin had frequently walked over his
ground, noting the familiar landmarks with quiet
intensity, and in this morning of leavetaking he
went through all the spacious airy rooms with a
feeling of emptiness, of being lost. From the walls
the heavy parchment features of Sir Scipio Campbell stared with averted eyes, and the absorbed gaze
of Cydalise Cœur-de-roi seemed regardless of both
husband and inheritor. They were both to be sold
for what they might fetch ; as Victoria had said,
their originals had chosen a painter of no celebrity,
and they were valueless.

In these last hours the old house thrust its personality upon them ; they were awed by the sense
of imminent loss. Mrs. Otway's nose and eyes were
red, and her daughter, whose spirits had lately taken
an upward flight, was again subdued, while Hester
was preoccupied by thought of the fine house that
she might have ruled and that would never now
be hers.

She walked with Colin in the garden, trying to
comfort him, and thinking with surprise how he at

the age of nineteen had shown so much reckless courage in war and ten years later was so irresolute in the struggle to maintain his old home. He was so nice, she thought, and yet so nerveless. She remembered his reiterated explanations about the rent of Duisk falling short of their necessities, and wondered how many of the Otway-Campbell necessities were really necessities. She could not reconcile their odd frantic economies with their possession of three motor cars.

"When we are married, dear," she said, " I'm going to make a lot of splendid economies for you."

" I don't know where you could begin," he said doubtfully.

"Wait and see, Colin, and you'll get wonderful surprises," she promised him.

" You'll just do whatever you please, Hester. You know how much I like you, Hester."

" I haven't the faintest idea," she confessed.

They left the garden and strolled to the bridge that spanned the burn. For a time they gazed into the brown rush of water, without speaking. The sound of it was pleasant in their ears, and it was mingled with the song of birds. The sun shone brightly, and they could see the distorted reflections of their faces in the water. Hester laughed delightedly. " I'd never marry a man with a face like that," she cried, but his smile was very wry.

They returned again by the garden, a place of silence with its outer cincture of tall and stately trees. Elissa met them there. The moment for leaving Duisk had come.

Annie and Mary, who were not being retained,

stood in the hall with tearful eyes. The laird bade
them good-bye—he had already given them refer-
ences and parting gifts—and hurried out to the front.
Barrill Castle, long ago Campbell-less, was smiling
across the loch, a medley of red stone and green ivy.
Colin looked up at his house, to the achievement of
arms on the pediment. He was surprised, feeling
that he had hardly noticed it before. The carving
was clear cut and elaborate. His glance passed along
the balustrade, over the symmetrical fenestration.
" I am *so* sorry," he could hear his mother saying
complainingly ; " *so* sorry to lose you both."

" I hope you will have many happy days, Mrs.
Otway, and come back to Lochaweside again."

" Oh, thank you, Annie, thank you. But . . ."
Mrs. Otway commenced the descent of the steps,
supported by Mary, who was gladly performing this
last duty. " I am *so* sorry," she repeated vaguely.
" *So* sorry . . ."

They were all down beside the car. Mrs. Otway
was assisted in. Colin quelled a passionate wish to
run away from them all. His heart was pumping
violently.

" The big box—is it away, Annie ? " he asked
irrelevantly, feeling that he had to say something.
" The one to go by boat. Oh, that's good. Who
called for it ? " he asked indifferently. " Was it
Neil Campbell ? "

" It was his cousin Archy Leitch from Ardrishaig."

" Oh, that's good." He looked at them all helplessly. " Well," he said, " I suppose we'll have to
be going."

" We're all ready," said Elissa. " Jump in, Colin."

" Did you say good-bye to Annie and Mary, Sidney ? "

" Yes, sir," said the chauffeur.

" You have everything, then ? " he asked the ladies, stepping in beside them.

" Everything except Duisk," Elissa replied, and her brother darted an angry look at her.

" I hope you will be back soon again, Mr. Campbell," said Annie almost inaudibly, " and yourself, too, Miss Elissa."

" Thank you, Annie," said Elissa. " You're a brick."

" Good-bye, Annie ; good-bye, Mary," Mrs. Otway called weakly as the car began slowly to move, and fluttered a hand in response to the farewell obeisances of the maids.

Hester had remained silent and serious.

" We will never be back to Duisk," Mrs. Otway said wailingly. She placed a sympathetic hand over the only hand of her son.

" That's called Sir Scipio's Tree," he said to Hester, nodding at a beech upon the lawn. " I don't think I told you, did I ? "

" No," she said, looking at it.

" It was old Donald Campbell told me. He has all the traditions. The general used to sit under——" he stopped, staring with an intent and hungry gaze at the old house, standing so serene and proud amid its lawns and trees. He gazed at it with tragic eyes till it was hid from view ; he saw all that he had inherited swept from his grasp, exchanged for evanescent money.

At the lodge they stopped. Donald and Margaret

shook their hands, full of sorrow and concern. "You will come back," Donald kept repeating. "You will not be able to stay away from Duisk." The car moved on. The old man stood by the pillar, nodding his head as long as it was in sight, and then slowly closed the gates and entered his house again.

"Here they come!" Neil Campbell said, as he stood with Kirsty in the shadow of the farm-house doorway.

"Poor souls," said the young woman commiseratingly. "Mr. Campbell will be lost without his estate."

"He will have been paid a good price for it. And the first of them paid nothing for it."

"I was heart sorry for Miss Elissa when she called yesterday to say good-bye. Poor soul."

"Did she show her face here!" he exclaimed incredulously. "Is she not brazen, and her an unconvicted thief!"

"Oh, Neil——"

He watched the car pass by the shore. "There they go!" he said satirically. "And they'll be thinking they'll be missed. They've no cause for complaint. They've had a good run for their money."

Kirsty stepped eagerly out to gain a better view of the receding car. "Poor souls," she repeated involuntarily. "And Mr. Campbell and Miss Anson going to be married."

"And they never got their present!"

"I'm sure," she replied indignantly, "that it matters very little whether a married couple get presents or not, so long as they are happy."

" I think so, too, Kirsty," he said.

She looked at him sharply.

" Marriage is in the air, I'm thinking," he added soberly. " I was thinking, Kirsty, that maybe you and I could get married too. We know each other very well."

She did not reply, looking to Loch Awe instead, with a smile on her lips.

" Would you like to think it over, maybe," he said awkwardly.

" No, Neil, and indeed I would not," she said, turning suddenly to him, and his heart was gladdened by the manner of her tone.

The car sped on. It was making north, by way of Sonachan to Inveraray, the route that Colin Buie had chosen when he journeyed first to Duisk. At first the travellers were silent. Mrs. Otway began to doze, and Elissa lit a cigarette. Colin and Hester were sitting side by side.

" We should be in Glasgow in time for dinner," Miss Otway-Campbell observed suddenly.

The remark awoke her mother. " I do wish you wouldn't smoke in the car," she commented complainingly. " The smoke flies about so."

" I didn't think it would bother you, with the car open," Elissa replied. " It's different with a closed car, mamma."

" It is when the car is open that the breeze chases the smoke about," her mother retorted peevishly.

" I'm very sorry. I didn't——"

" I know, darling," Mrs. Otway said decidedly. " But the smoke is never nearly so troublesome when the car is closed. You know, Elissa——"

Hester whispered in Colin's ear: "You'll help me when we reach home; won't you, Colin?"

He turned a dejected face to hers. "Help you —with what?" he asked curiously.

"Will we not be looking for a house, Colin?" she whispered. "A new one—one for ourselves."

He studied the dark-haired smiling girl with re-newed gratitude, and with sudden insight. The glories of inheritance seemed suddenly lessened compared with the boon of individual happiness.

"Will we not?" she repeated sweetly.

Mrs. Otway and Elissa had discontinued their argument. He could not answer, but a new tranquillity descended upon him. He thought of all that he had lost, and sighed; and smiled at knowing what he had gained.

The car sped on, bearing them far from that magnificent tangle of lochs and mountains, away from the traditions they had not comprehended, the responsibilities they had neglected, the privileges they had lost; away from Duisk.

O PEOPLE!

"A fine book. There are thumbnail sketches of contemporary Scots, thinly disguised, that will make the originals squirm; there is lovely writing; and there is effective satire. An unusual, sincere book."—*Evening Standard.*

"It has humour, a fine sense of humanity, and a real originality. Laughter and sentiment go hand and hand in these pages."—*The Times.*

"Its spiritual qualities set it entirely apart."—*Aberdeen Press.*

7s. 6d. net

LUCY FLOCKHART

"Displays an energy in description and characterisation that undoubtedly commands attention."—*Morning Post.*

"Scottish art has received a notable recruit in Mr. Craig. Few first novels have the passion and colour of 'Lucy Flockhart.'"—*Edinburgh Evening News.*

"A remarkable work, full of promise and most arresting. The character-drawing is excellent."—*Irish Times.*

7s. 6d. net

Printed in the United Kingdom by
Lightning Source UK Ltd., Milton Keynes
138044UK00001B/4/P